Christmas 2005. New Labour's honeymoon is over but the London bombings have provided an excuse for meddling in the affairs of the general public. While political correctness is gaining momentum the country has lost control of its borders and is reeling under the influx of foreigners from the EU and beyond. Criminals from across the world are finding easy pickings while the police spend most of their time filling in forms. The prisons are overflowing and there are more guns on the street than ever, but now it's the police that are carrying most of them. While the country implodes the government concerns itself with Respect Agendas, the fast-tracking of ethnic-minority candidates, ASBOs and PCSOs, as well as banning smoking in public places, building super casinos, spying on household rubbish and whether, in this land of the blind, the one-eyed man will be king sooner rather than later…

Crime rates are rising and people are still getting hurt.

A LITTLE BIT OF PREVIOUS

a novel by

I K WATSON

Also by I K Watson

Fiction:
Manor
Wolves aren't White
Cops and other Robbers
London Town

Non-fiction:
Quality is Excellence

First published in 2011 by MP Publishing Limited
6 Petaluma Blvd. North, Suite B6, Petaluma, CA 94952
and
12 Strathallan Crescent, Douglas, Isle of Man IM2 4NR

Watson, I. K., 1947-
A little bit of previous : a novel / by I.K. Watson.
p. cm.
ISBN-13: 978-1-84982-114-8
ISBN-10: 1-84982-114-3

1. Police--England--London--Fiction. 2. Serial
murderers--England--London--Fiction. 3. Criminals--
England--London--Fiction. 4. England--Fiction.
5. Detective and mystery stories, English. I. Title.

PR6073.A8626L58 2011   823'.914
                              QBI11-600110

A CIP catalogue record for this book is also available from the British Library

ISBN: 978-1-84982-114-8

web site: www.ik-watson.com

Artwork and website designed by
Hibernian Integrated Business Solutions
www.hibernian.co.im
Contact: mike@hibernian.co.im

Book & jacket design by Maria Smith

For Hazel and hers
and Steven and his
and for my parents
who will never read it.

A LITTLE BIT OF PREVIOUS

a novel by

I K WATSON

An explosion rattled the windows. It was followed immediately by the sound of glass smashing and a car leaving tread on tarmac.

Rick Cole said, "What the…?" then he heard a voice from the past. He pressed the phone closer to his ear.

"I need a favour. I seem to remember you owe me one."

Cole answered, "Now's not a good time. Did you hear it?"

"Hear what?"

"Sounded like a bomb, in the High Road."

Cole's door was open. In the main office every phone was ringing. In the corridor coppers were on the move, perked up like sniffer-dogs on heat. Even for old-timers alarm bells and distant sirens were shots of adrenalin.

"How the fuck would I hear it? They could nuke your part of town and I wouldn't hear it from here. Too many council estates between us. Anyway, good times are things of the past. So give me a time?"

Cole paused, then, "Midnight."

"Right. Same place. You remember the place?"

Cole nodded into the phone and hung up. He remembered the place. Sooner or later it was always going to pull him back. There was nothing more certain. Unless you counted booze on a copper's breath. He moved into the main office to join the confusion.

Chapter 1

The first guest to arrive for the party left the train at King's Cross and picked up a minicab at the back of the station. The black cabs at the front were for people who didn't know the difference. He hadn't been to London for over a year but some things never changed. Getting ripped off was one of them.

"Falcon Street. It's off Sheerham High Road."

"Got it, Boss, but there might be a delay. There's been a bomb. It was on the news."

The passenger grunted indifference and climbed in.

The driver was black as night, packing designer gear and gold trinkets. His patch was Shaftsbury, his punters the tourists. But most of them were tucked up in restaurant or theatre seats by now; between eight and ten were the dead hours. That's when he hit the stations. King's Cross was favourite because it carried the northerners, from Newcastle and beyond. And northerners were easy pickings. They carried a heavy reputation for being tight so they felt obliged to make amends. The Scots were different. They enjoyed the stigma so much it made them even tighter.

"What do you want, Boss? Give me the word. You want to enjoy the night, right?"

London, like the rest of the country, was floating in dope.

The passenger spoke. "And I was going to find a hot dog stand. Silly me."

The cabbie recognized an accent. Not London, but not far off. Reading, maybe. There were a lot of dodgy bastards there. His surprise registered in the mirror.

The passenger saw it and smiled. It was a tricky, dangerous smile, the sort of smile you saw just before something nasty and sharp and reflecting your image in silver, flashed toward you.

A little less certain the cabbie said, "It's the gear, Boss, and the price is right. If you want your shit mashed then you go down to Brixton or up to Stevenage."

They motored north and hit the Great Cambridge. In the old days highwaymen had loved this road. They still did but now they called themselves something different and in front their lights were flashing. Traffic police were throwing their weight about. They were always making their random checks on cabbies, easy targets to enhance their arrest statistics. The weapon of mass destruction, Islam, had given them fresh impetus and although the traffic police were not necessarily armed it didn't stop them enjoying the increased sense of potency.

"Charlie…"

The cabbie licked thick lips. They came all the way from St Lucia.

"Hey, I'm your man. We call the top gear Kate. Best price. I can drop it off."

"Yeah, course you can."

Another frightening look poured out of the mirror. The driver hesitated. "Your call, Boss. Here's my card, my number. Just ask for Wes, or Father Christmas for short."

The passenger read the card out loud. "Benny's Mini Cabs."

"Twenty-four hour service at your disposal. Deliveries free of charge. Anything else you want, company, just give us the nod. You name it, you got it. Any denomination, any age. Our aim's to please."

"I get my own company."

"Figured you would, Boss. That much is crystal."

"I'll bell you."

"Right on."

They turned into the High Road. The Carrington theatre loomed before them. Yellow light creamed the Victorian building and made the red brick glow. A line of punters waited at the box office while a bunch of East-European beggars and the odd blown-out Jesus freak annoyed them and the traffic roared past. The passenger turned in his seat. A massive cut-out of a scantily clad Anthea Palmer had caught his eye. She wore black underwear, fishnet stockings and lethal high heels. It was an image almost guaranteed to cause a traffic pile-up. The driver noticed his interest. "You want tickets, Boss? I can get you tickets. Best seats in the house. If you want to meet with Anthea, I'll have to work on that one." He chuckled.

The passenger flashed his straight teeth, sharing the joke.

The driver glanced again in his rear-view. His passenger was in his early thirties and blond hair in a unisex spiky style scrubbed him clean, smoothed out his face, but it was his smile that did the trick. A wolfish smile with a cheeky glint, lighting up the soulless pale-grey eyes.

It sent a shiver of night down the driver's spine.

The passenger left the cab and waited until it had disappeared before carrying his bag to a blue wrought-iron gate that swung silently open to a four-storey terraced house that had been built in the grey fifties. In the nineties it had been converted by Pakistani property developers into four self-contained flats. Six flights of stairs took him to the third floor. There was no lift. It belonged to a friend of a friend who used it only sparingly and let it out for an outrageous fee. It was close enough to the centre to be convenient yet far enough away to remain discreet. For those who used it discretion was the thing.

He'd seen the invitation on a website.

> You a creature of the night?
> Wanna twin?
> Wanna come?
> We're skippering over at Sheerham Dec 10/23.
> And you're all invited.
> Wanna play?
> Andrew Grant's new musical, Bikini Line,
> featuring former weather girl, Anthea Palmer, is to
> get an extended run at the revamped Carrington
> Theatre before moving to the West End...

7

He smiled at the memory. So there it was. A theatrical production. But the audience sounded right up his street. And what about Anthea? Since leaving the weather show she was making a name for herself. Barely a day went by without her photograph appearing in one of the tabloids. And on the front cover of *Loaded* her black plastic micro dress had only half concealed her nipples and in the interview inside she'd confided to the reporter and the thousands of readers, that during the shoot she'd worn no underwear. His kind of girl.

He unpacked leisurely, as though enjoying the routine of placing his gear neatly into the various drawers and cupboards. It was all about anticipation, working the fantasy, letting that fluttering sensation spread until it became—almost—unbearable. He took a photograph from his case, the final item. It was in a silver frame, in colour, a photograph of a woman in her early twenties. Her clothes and hairstyle were out of the seventies. He placed it carefully on the bedside table.

In the shower he used a pumice-stone then shaved his legs and underarms. He used Givenchy's Amarige behind his ears, inside his elbows, behind his knees and on his wrists. The perfume of indulgence. Back in the bedroom he stood before a full-length mirror. He'd worked hard to keep the youthful unblemished shape. He moved to the dresser and another mirror. The unfamiliar shag on the stool felt better than good. With an experienced hand he applied his make-up and slowly his face changed. Beneath the blond hair it became soft and oddly beautiful. Blond became blonde.

Before dressing he cut twin lines of dust on the dresser's polished top and used a custom-built straw. He was charlied in seconds, getting off on his own dangerous eyes as the euphoria took hold. The city was waiting and he was the celeb, up there with Anthea Palmer, on stage, a catwalk queen. A high-heeled bitch.

He watched himself move to the bed, swinging his hips like a tom with fifties in her eye. He'd pass go, no problem. Better than Anthea Palmer. He pulled on the knickers. The lace stretched, eighty-six percent nylon, the colour of his lipstick. It felt like a slight caress against his dick, a touch of butterfly wings. He put on the matching lace bra, ninety-eight percent nylon, padded, A cup, 34, and changed the plain gold studs in his ears for a couple of danglers with glittering blue stones.

He checked the full-length again. His legs were slim and as smooth as a woman's after waxing. He turned for his dress, a short shift in shantung fabric, dry-clean only, burgundy, any year's colour. His penis bulged slightly, but no more than a skinny girl's muff.

He slipped into black satin sandals, size 7, and in the three-inch heels he looked better still. His painted toenails, the colour of his dress and lipstick, poked through.

The first guest had arrived and was ready for the party. He slid into a black Paul Smith jacket that was almost as old as him but looked like new for he kept it for special occasions, and picked up his Elle handbag, reached the door and paused. In his feel-good mode he'd forgotten his accessories. He went back to the drawer of the dresser and selected a blade that was as sharp as a Gillette razor. But it wasn't a safety.

Chapter 2

Mr Lawrence had about him the peace of the passing of unhurried years, a contentment in the knowledge that today would be like yesterday and yesterday had been survived.

He had always been a quiet man. He didn't need long stretches of solitude to direct his attention inward for that ability came quite naturally. He didn't need the absence of other people either, for he was adept at mental absenteeism. He was in need of absolutely nothing save for the odd customer in his shop.

Mr Lawrence owned the Gallery, a shop in the High Road.

The explosion that rattled the police station windows was distant but unmistakable and was followed by the sounds of sirens and raised voices coming in from the road outside. He thought of terrorists, the Arabs and the Irish, but barely paused in his work, just poured a little more white spirit and rubbed a picture-frame a little harder. He did like anarchists, no matter where they came from, particularly the majority who showed their mental health problems up front. In a way, he wished he were a part of the revolution. But revolutions were for young men without sense and women without bras and he had spent his younger days in another place where ordinary folk, anarchists included, would not dare to follow.

The Gallery with its strange side-wall finished quickly with shades of grey pebble-dash and with its small flat above hadn't always been an end of terrace. Before the shadowy town planners had decided a new road was necessary to link the High Road to the growing Richmond Park council estate, Mrs Meacham's small shop that sold wool and lace and dress-making patterns had been on the end of the row. It all seemed so long ago that now he could barely summon the old days or the old girl. Even so, he might have been her last customer, he thought, remembering the lace antimacassars he'd purchased from her closing down sale.

During the afternoon he would watch gangs of youths walk past his shop swinging their high-strength bottles, followed a few moments later by tottering slappers as they tracked the spunk-scented trail of testosterone.

As the day wore on the gangs became louder and more abusive and shoppers moved out of their way, shop-keepers took in their pavement displays and a few more cowardly or wise, pulled down their steel shutters. And while the trouble brewed—and there was always trouble—the police were not about. They were too busy form-filling and using their speed-guns on speeding motorists and their CS spray on pensioners; easy targets to enhance the crime figures for the government to manipulate.

And in the road the brewing went on until, at one end or the other, a small argument would start and that would do it. Nothing much. It was, after all, only an excuse.

And then the darkness fell.

And a cosy routine fell with it.

And with his shop bolted and as secure as it could be in this part of town, he made his slow way to The British.

Out of the inky night the illuminations threw a jaundiced glow of Christmas message. Half the world was sick, apart from the Chinese who were always that colour.

Along the High Road the bare trees crackled beneath the rushing clouds and the last withering leaves scampered, a mad palette of neon stained the wet surfaces and the early evening pavements thronged.

Oh, how he hated Christmas with its false friendships and packed pavements and its queues and its once-a-year drinkers blocking the bars. He sighed heavily and under the weight of the festive season he shuffled on his way.

The British were about old things. Old wood in particular. In The British the only brick was about two huge fireplaces that, winter or summer, were piled with smouldering logs that spat at you as you passed. The seating was in narrow alcoves opposite the long bar, some said the longest bar in Britain. It reminded him of an old British Rail platform where the trains smoked and doors slammed and a blue-uniformed guard blew his whistle.

But there was a difference in The British, on the platform, for here the passengers were going nowhere.

The British was staffed by Roger, the owner, who had once rowed in a boat race, perhaps the *boat race*, a no-nonsense stocky owner in his late thirties who was always losing weight but never seemed to lose it, and half a dozen young serving staff wearing tight black pub skirts. Roger kept the older women in the back, nuking the pies and cutting the sandwiches.

Roger's wife was upstairs looking after their baby.

Mr Lawrence had been surprised to find that Roger had a wife, never mind that she had been pregnant all these months.

They had called her Erin.

An Irish name.

And she was beautiful. He had seen her moving pictures on Roger's mobile. Technology was quite wonderful. In looks she took after his wife which was a good thing.

Roger was the man that Japan and Germany dreamt about. He had to have the latest in TVs and DVDs and sound systems. And he could think of nothing finer than trawling the HMV shops for the 3-for-£20 DVDs. And sooner or later he was going to hang a giant half-inch thick plasma on to The British wall. It would show Sky Sports and Sky News and a Sky slant on the world.

In the meantime, before Roger put up the screen and perhaps while they waited for it, the row of men at the bar missed nothing while they pretended not to watch. They watched the girls bend to the lower shelves, or bend forward toward the sinks beneath the bar. They held their breaths while buttons pulled and hems rose. They appreciated the smiles and empty promises. This was drinking land. The ticket to nowhere gave them the girls to look at while they were getting there; service with a cold smile.

He liked The British, the comfort, the smell of the burning logs, the smell of anonymity. People lied, he knew they did, but it didn't matter because they didn't matter. It was an indifferent place, there was no danger of being found out because no one cared. Everyone knew the stories that beer told.

Occasionally the stories were interrupted by the sounds of a fire-engine or the screech of burning rubber, a police siren, smashing glass, the clatter of footsteps and shouts from the street, but those breaks were short-lived. Reality was only a short pause for the pub's heavy doors shut it out. That's why they came, the same familiar booze-smacked faces, day after day, to live in pickled suspension, free, utterly free from interference.

Albert was there, a tall big-nosed man, his body hidden by a navy-blue coat. The jeweller, incognito, except that everyone knew him and what he was. He was fifty and probably dangerous. He wasn't interested in the girls. The only thing that interested Albert was measured in carats.

"Good evening, Albert."

"Good evening to you, Mr Lawrence," he said and his black eyes shone brighter than two of his precious stones. "Did you hear the bang? Quite a bang, it was."

The colonel was there. Most of him was always there. The bits of him that were not were in the sands of El Alamein. A short, squat man with stiff shoulders, at attention even while at ease.

"Good evening, Colonel."

"Good evening," he muttered absently over his gin and tonic with a slice of lemon. No lime for the juniper in Roger's boozer. The colonel's mind was on other things. "The EU could be a problem. The krauts and the frogs could be a problem." He shook his preoccupied head. His thin rheumatoid fingers gripped the glass and carried it to his thin lips. The old eyes that had once looked out over the wavering desert and had seen the sun glint on Rommel's half-tracks and Panzers, shifted from Mr Lawrence to Roger. At length he said, "They blew up the allotments, you know?"

"The allotments? The French? The Germans?"

"No, not the frogs or the krauts. A shed on the allotments. Probably the Greens. Somebody doesn't like their greens."

Rasher was there. A fly-by-night sort, Rasher, granted the handle because his father was from Denmark. He was thick-bodied and blue-eyed and covered in gold: earrings, chains, medallions, rings, watch, nameplate. His mother had been a fortune-teller from Hackney who somehow, only God knows how, got mixed up with a cold wood-cutting Scandinavian. His clothes were beautifully cut and his shoes were hand-stitched. He wore waistcoats and red braces. He gripped the bar, hands either side of a glass of strong ale. He spent his day in the same position, until closing when his minders helped him out. Only his grip tightened as the day wore on. He had been there for nine months, ever since his pregnant wife had left him. There were photographs of her to remind him, in the bus shelters and in shop windows. Missing, they said. Have you seen this woman, they asked. People who knew Rasher wondered whether his mother had predicted his bad fortune.

"Good evening, Rasher."

Rasher nodded thoughtfully. Perhaps it was a good evening, perhaps it was.

There was a safety in The British reminiscent of the bomb shelters during the war and in there were the same weary expressions, pale in the gloom, in the manufactured wattage. Yellow faces in the yellow light bouncing off the nicotine yellow ceiling. And not a Chinese in sight. Chinese didn't use the boozers; too many old soldiers in the boozers who would mistake them for Japanese.

Albert frowned as a younger, much shorter man—more of a boy, really—told him, "Got out Wednesday, didn't I?"

"On Wednesday you got out. Strange. That you expect me to know. How would I know? From Adam, I don't know you, so how should I know when you got out?"

Puzzlement crossed the youngster's pale brow and narrowed his blue-grey eyes and he uttered, "Come again?"

"Come again? Come where, again?"

"What are you talking about?"

"A question you asked me. How would I know that you got out on Wednesday? I didn't know that you'd been in." Albert looked down at the younger man. He bent forward, as tall men often do.

"Just told you, didn't I?"

"Did you? Did you?" Albert nodded and drank some beer then said, "So, you went away for eighteen months and on Wednesday you came back. Miss you, I didn't. Like I said, I didn't even know you'd gone. Did you miss him, Colonel?"

The colonel offered a critical glance and said disapprovingly, "A.W.L., eh? Don't approve. Jankers, my lad, for you."

Albert sighed. "AWOL, I think it is. There you are, an old soldier even, mistakes can make. Rasher, what do you think? Rasher?"

Rasher didn't move.

"Well, Rasher?"

From the corner of Rasher's mouth came, "Don'tgiveafuck!" And that was true. There was only one thing that Rasher cared about and she was so distant now that in the dark he forgot what she looked like. Albert nodded slyly and his gaze fell on Mr Lawrence. He thought better of asking his opinion and turned back to the young man who, standing on one leg with the other wrapped around his calf, was waiting patiently.

"So, on Wednesday you got out. For what did you go in?"

"Stitched up, wasn't I?"

"Were you? How did I know that?"

"Filth put a bag of tools in my hand and threw me in a car. A police car. They punched my head in so that I didn't hit my head on the…the door, the door, like…?"

"Frame?"

"Yeah, that's good, the door frame. Is that what it's called on a car?"

Albert pulled up his eyebrows and for a moment they hid the deep lines on his forehead.

"Took me down to the nick and put the boot in. Kept booting till I signed up for twelve months. Well, eighteen months actually. Got six off for good behaviour."

"And now?"

"Straight, innI? Learned my lesson. Mustn't accept gifts from the filth." With a huge hand Albert patted the young man's back.

"That's good. Good, that is," he said. "Two lives we should live, one for rehearsal. Then sorry we wouldn't keep saying. Still, you are young enough to start again but, unfortunately, not old enough to learn by your mistakes. Some people never learn, no matter how old they get." He glanced across at Mr Lawrence.

Roger noticed that in his profundity Albert had stopped sounding Jewish.

Albert went on, "Where are you living now?"

"That's the problem, innit?" The young man's face dropped. "Squattin' down Avenue Road, know it?"

Albert blew out his cheeks. His whiskers separated, stood out as though they'd been shot with static and, only slowly gathered together again. "Avenue Road, Ticker Harrison runs." The Jew had returned. "Squatting on his manor is not healthy. No sir, not to be recommended. Ticker Harrison is a dangerous man. More than that, even, he's a fucking dangerous man."

Roger interrupted, "I told you I don't want any fucking in this boozer. I've got a wife and daughter upstairs. Blair's bringing in a fucking law to outlaw bad language along with smoking. He's going to put me out of business but does he care? The only thing he cares about is Bush, and I'm not talking about Cherie's bush either. I'm not surprised the bastard's turning Catholic. For what he's done to this country he'll need to spend the rest of his life in the confessional box."

Albert shook his head and sent dandruff flying. He looked at the youngster out of calculating eyes and said, "I was saying, Ticker Harrison is a dangerous man."

"That's it, innit? The kids in there, makes me feel old, half of them out of their heads. Sniffin', snortin'. At their age. I ask you? In trouble, innI?"

16

"Problems. I know just what you mean. Children and wives you need, ethnic parentage, an asylum seeker you need to be or, you need to have capital with which to bribe the housing authorities. Then all right you'd be. I fear it's Cardboard City for you, my son. Written all over you, it is. On your face is the address. Capital letters. Cardboard City." Albert's huge hand gripped the young man's shoulder before he went on, "Now, if by chance you should happen on a few trinkets, things that sparkle in the night, then into instant readies I could turn them. Then Cardboard City would remain a distant place. Now, to welcome you back, a drink I will buy you." He caught the cold eye of a girl in a tight black skirt. "Miss," he said firmly. "Put a half a pint into this young man's pint pot."

The youngster watched the girl bend to pull his drink and fixed his gaze on the curve of her cleavage. He'd been inside too long, forgotten the subtleties of light and shade, of big and bigger.

Albert said, "Strapped across that, you would like to get, I bet."

The young man nodded enthusiastically. "Yes, I would."

"Find the trinkets, my son. Girls like that, barmaids in particular, like men with bulging pockets."

At pub closing time the local restaurants filled up quickly. Chinese and Indian were three doors apart and midway between The British and the Gallery. Squeezed between the Hong Kong House and the Spice of India were a launderette, a DVD rental shop and a pet shop.

The Indian glowed red through white net and the air outside was filled with the farts the diners left behind. Candles on the window tables were shimmering beacons in a red mist.

The Chinese was brighter. Perhaps it had less to hide, thought Mr Lawrence, but then he remembered the salt used in the cooking and the dark alley, a narrow gap between the restaurant and the shop next door.

Dangerous places, alleys, where cats screamed and the air was soaked in piss.

Mr Lawrence had set his mind on Madras but a bunch of youths blocked the pavement so he ducked into the Chinese.

He was settled with 7, 14 and 21, when the young man entered. Albert or the colonel must have mentioned where Mr Lawrence dined. The young man who had just got out had come in to make a beeline for his table. On his face was a look of surprise, the coincidence of meeting him again, and the softer look of friendship.

Chapter 3

Out of the darkness a copper's cheap lighter flared and in an icy wind sparks shot away.

The JPS felt heavy in Rick Cole's chest. He breathed white into the night and coughed a smoker's cough.

River water slapped impatiently against concrete and in the distance flames leapt from steel drums and threw a pale glow on the lonely figures surrounding them.

A villain's voice came out of the darkness. "A bit Pearl Harbour, boy. A nip in the air. Thank Gawd for global warming otherwise it might be really chilly."

"Forget the Nips. I'll lay odds there's a bunch of skags clocking us."

"Those cunts wouldn't recognize themselves in the mirror."

The wind gusted again and more angry flames burst from the drums. In a few days the missions would open and for a week at least, for the shadows, there'd be a mattress and a guaranteed dawn.

The cold smacked the DI's face.

Seriousness crept into the villain's tone, "The city's a dangerous place, always has been, but not for us, never was. Think about it. We're the dangerous fuckers around here and people know it."

Cole grunted indifference.

"It's been a long time. So what's happening?"

A pause, then Cole relented, "Shovelling the same shit. A city full of yobs and villains and now you can add the fucking terrorists. We always had the micks but this is different. These fuckers don't mind killing themselves to make a point. The average man is in more danger now than he was during the war."

"There's a few dirty fuckers I know who wouldn't mind topping themselves if they thought they could shag a hundred and fifty virgins on the other side."

"Ton and a half?"

"Inflation. Why should heaven be any fucking different?" Another pause sharpened the darkness, a chuckle, then, "So, it was on the news. The bomb. Who'd want to bomb a deserted shed?"

"Maybe it was being kept there. Who knows?"

"The arse in the air brigade? Bastards get everywhere. That's the trouble with this country, Rick. I don't even understand some of the cunts on the BBC News nowadays, never mind the weather. Every fucking arse is a potential launch pad, right?"

"Bomb Squad say not. This was amateur."

"Another Nazi nail bomber, then. Maybe it was a test. Everyone's got to start somewhere."

He was referring to the London bombing campaign against Asians, blacks and gays. The Admiral Duncan pub explosion, as well as Brixton and Brick Lane, had used up a lot of man-hours. The older coppers wouldn't forget David Copeland in a hurry. The younger ones had probably never heard of him.

The villain rubbed his hands together. "So, your people killed any more innocent Brazilians lately? I thought dumdums were illegal?"

He was referring this time to Jean Charles de Menezes.

"They were hollow point, not soft-headed. In any case, they're only illegal in war, against the enemy. You can still use them against civvies."

"Yeah, well, that makes a lot of fucking sense, I'm sure. They must have taken his fucking head off. I heard there were eleven shots but only eight hits. How could they miss three times from two feet? Even my guys would manage to hit something from two feet away, especially if it was pinned to the fucking floor!"

Cole wasn't drawn. He said, "So what do you want?"

"You ain't changed, Rick. You got no sense of small talk or self-preservation. People like you, people who don't give a fuck, are the scariest people on earth. Go ask the psychiatrists, they should know. Even I'm scared of you, and I'm the fucking crown jewels around here. One day I'll find out what turned you against yourself."

"You'll never come close."

"Guarantee there was a woman involved."

"Let's get on with it."

"This is important, Rick. It upsets me to ask you for help."

"Course it does."

"Helen's done a runner."

It didn't show or, rather, it wasn't heard, but Cole was surprised. He managed, "Go to relate."

"This isn't funny. I can't have people taking the piss, understand? It's hard enough running a business as it is. You people are not doing your jobs. I've got hassle with the youngsters who believe in free enterprise, the Maltesers are playing up again—God knows why with that shithouse of a fucking place they come from—and every black bastard in town is packing enough hardware to start world war three. And now the fucking Albanians are trying it on. They're into everything going and they're organized. You've got to blame Blair for letting all these fuckers in. Talk about the blind leading the fucking blind. Asylum seekers. These fuckers are controlling half of London's dope and they've only been in the country two minutes. Even the Chinese are getting pissed off. And they're hurting me too. Passing off their toms as Spanish and Italians. They need the fucking trade description act thrown at them. Pay up front for a Latin quarter and find you've got two fingers up a Balkan arse, it ain't funny. It's like going to a Gordon Ramsey and being dished up condemned meat. Well out of order. It's not right. There's no fucking respect anymore. She's been gone a week."

He slipped it in, out of the blue, and tightened Cole's features.

"A week?"

"She's never left before. I put the word out, my own people, but they couldn't find a fucking nigger on the North Pole. Kicking the shit out of someone they can do, but using their bonces... They ain't so hot on

21

subtlety, you know? Like fucking Barclays. Big doesn't appeal if it's out of the bedroom. The cunts think pie and mash comes with an alcoholic beverage. What can I do? All the good guys have gone soft in middle age or they're banged up. They talk about the old days, but the old days were never that tasty, we know that. Those old bastards wouldn't make second division today. Not with the fuckers I've got to deal with. These bastards today have got no style at all, Rick. You think you've cut a deal, they'll go to the shithouse, come back looking like they've stuck their hooters in a tray full of baking powder and start blasting away. How can you do business like that? We need to build another iron curtain just to keep these fuckers out and that includes the cunt who bought my football team."

"I didn't know you were a Chelsea fan."

"It's not something you spread around, Rick. Who admits to a sack-and-crack job?"

"Maybe you should put a card in the Jobcentre window."

"This is important and you're taking the piss. I can't afford a scene; not when I've got every fucker in town trying to muscle in. This has come at a bad time for me. At the moment I'm talking, being very reasonable, but these fucked-up foreigners aren't reasonable people. As for the youngsters, what the fuck do they teach them nowadays? A month out of school and they think they can run a deal on my manor. This country has gone to the fucking dogs, Rick. Fuck New Labour and all their fucking promises. These little fucks are actually squatting in some of my properties while they deal and half the fuckers are on benefits. Can you believe that? That's a fucking liberty."

"You're right."

"Listen, Christmas is coming. I want my family back for Christmas. I want us singing around a fucking tree. A real fucking tree. Not one of these fucked-up plastic ones. Once in fucking David City. Right? I'm willing to forgive her. Whatever she's done."

"Benevolent, you?"

"I'm serious. I've thought about it. We all make mistakes. This is the season of goodwill. Look at me. If it wasn't dark you'd see the sincerity. I'm in love with her. Always was. Can't help it. Want to, but can't."

"And?"

"I told you, I'm a reasonable man. I read about these other missing women; see the posters all over the shop. Got me thinking, worrying. Know what I mean? Maybe she didn't do a runner. Maybe there is more to it. Maybe that's why she didn't take her things with her."

A ship's horn carried through space. A plane heading for Heathrow shone brighter than Venus. The darkness deepened; even the fires seemed farther away.

"She didn't take her things?"

"Not so you'd notice, but she's got so many clothes and drawers stuffed with crap, how am I to know?"

"What about cash?"

"Cash I do know."

Cole sensed the shake of his head.

"You know Helen. She never wore a damned thing for more than an hour."

"I remember."

It was true. Cole knew Helen. She had looks that would pull you over from a hundred yards in a room full of beautiful people. But behind the feminine bit she was as cold as a Russian handshake. Even in those days she had Ticker Harrison wrapped around her little finger, even if he didn't know it. Yes, Cole knew Helen. More than Ticker would ever know.

"On the boat she monopolized you. Remember? We still got photos of the three of us on deck. What the fuck was that place called?"

Cole remembered well and either the cold or the thought that Ticker had held on to the photographs made him shiver. He remembered a white bikini and the top coming off and, later, after Ticker had gone ashore, the bottom coming off too. At length he said, "Greece. And it was a long time ago."

"It doesn't seem that long."

"In this weather, right now, it does."

"Will you help me out?"

After a pause Cole said, "It doesn't sound right. You're not levelling with me."

A sigh came from the darkness. The river slapped some more, then, "We had an argument. I was never so hot with words, the old fucking... GCE, eleven plus, you know that."

"What was the argument about?"

"Fuck knows." Another pause then, in a lowered more rueful tone: "Listen, she's been on to me for months about having a kid. Like a fucking jumping record, know what I mean? I hate fucking kids. She'll have me on the park next, kicking a fucking ball. Anyway, she leaves off the pill. Informs me that she's missed two months. Eight fucking weeks, right? I can fucking count. I try to be reasonable. Like I said, I'm a reasonable man. We'll get shot of it, I say, terminated. Arnold fucking Schwarzenegger. No problem. But that ain't what she's got in mind. No way. She wants to look like a fucking telephone box for nine months, then lose her figure for the rest of her life. Run around with tits stretched from here to Southend and piles dragging on the back of her knees. You know me, I'm fucking reasonable, but I don't need this shit. She don't realize she's on my arm, she's got to look the part. For fuck's sake, she's Mrs Ticker Fucking Harrison. You marry into royalty, boy, you got to take some responsibility. Right? If you don't you get problems. You get your toes sucked and your tits all over Fleet Street or some arsehole creeping butler telling everyone your favourite position. I'm the bollocks around here. It was my dick that fucking moaning tart was sitting on when her picture was painted. There was nothing enigmatic about that expression, boy, that was fucking ecstasy."

"That sounds pretty reasonable to me."

"Well, anyway, I lost it for a moment. Slapped her. Aimed for the air, just to make a point, but got it wrong. She went out like a fucking light. I get our own GP out. Cost don't come into it. She gets the special treatment but does it make a difference? Does she care? Not a bit. When I come home two hours later she's gone. Faster than a Jewish foreskin."

"You left her with the doctor?"

"No. He'd gone by then. Left her having a lie-down. Just popped out; a bit of business. Even cut that short to get back to her and that cost me fucking money. That's love for you."

"But nothing went with her?"

"That's what I said. Can you help me out? I want to know about these other missing women. It's stupid, I know, and she'll turn up having taught me a right old lesson, but I can't help worrying. I got to point my people in the right direction."

After a long silence Cole said, "I'll poke around but they're dealing with it over at Hinckley. They won't like interference. You understand I can't make it official unless you do."

"Me, go to the kozzers? Do you want me to lose all credibility?"

"She's a missing person; you should report it."

Ticker Harrison drew a long breath and said quietly, so the night wouldn't hear, "You do it for me. Put the word out. Let's do it on the quiet. Get someone to call over, discreetly. Make out it's a speeding ticket or something. If you can find her tell her I love her, that I love kids. I've changed my fucking mind. There's nothing I'd like more than kick a fucking ball on the park, diving into dog shit, that sort of thing. Tell her any fucking thing she wants to hear. I'm relying on you, Rick."

"Let's find her first, worry about the rest later."

"That's all I'm asking. She'll trust you. After all, you're a fucking kozzer. And I know she liked you. She's often mentioned the boat and what a great time we had. She's often asked about you. Unfortunately these girls don't grasp the reality. You and me. Know what I mean? That we can't have Sunday dinner together."

The gangster, Ticker Harrison, was even more concerned than he made out. He wouldn't have involved Cole unless he was really worried. He'd read about the missing women. It was hard to miss them. They'd been all over the papers these last few months. There were photographs of them in shop windows and stuck to bus shelters. Have you seen this person, they asked. They meant the police hadn't got a clue.

The Helen Harrison that Cole remembered might well have run away, but not for a slap in the mouth, and even then she would have taken with her everything she could have carried. Helen was thirty-six

25

and she'd been around. For a slap in the mouth she'd have just gone out the next day and spent five grand on his credit card.

They parted, strangers again, as far apart as men could be but in the same business, on the same ladder. Lie some ladders on the ground it's difficult to tell top from bottom.

But the villain had got it right. Cole had turned against himself and there had been a woman involved. The memory of it was bitter; it ground his edge, sharpened his indifference, increased the force he used when digging low-life in the kidneys.

Chapter 4

Sunday morning started early.

Just a few minutes after the bells chimed six and still an hour before the break of a cold dawn, another explosion shook the capital and could be heard as far away as Calais. But this wasn't another garden shed. The oil storage terminal at Buncefield in Hertfordshire went up in the UK's biggest peacetime fire and a plume of black smoke began to fill the north-western sky. Although the authorities were shaken from their beds to begin an emergency evacuation of the surrounding area, it was quickly established that the cause of the blaze was down to the failure of a number of safety features and not more terrorist activity.

In Sheerham, under the darkening smoke-filled sky, life went on. And death.

Outside his window a heavily pregnant woman paused to search in her handbag and in his shop doorway a man sheltered from a sharp December wind to light a cigarette.

The Gallery was split into two large rooms. It had grown out of an antique business when customers had wised up and wouldn't pay the prices. Now both rooms were turned over to original works. In the front room one wall was taken by a collection of wildlife paintings from reasonably well-known artists and across from that, beyond a small collection of life studies and erotica were works by Reynolds and Allison whose real names were probably Chan or Chang who worked out of factories in Hong Kong or Thailand. In the alcoves, beneath original brick arches and illuminated by soft light, were the remnants of the old business, an odd chair, cast-bronze ballerinas and, suspended in isolation, a blackened 1830 chestnut cooking pan. Behind the shop was a studio where he spent most of his time. It was the place he unpacked the crates and stretched and framed the canvases and where, when he was not busy, he took on commissioned work. People liked to own paintings of their homes and front gardens.

Above the shop and the studio was the flat where he lived.

Mrs Puzey cleaned the shop and the flat above; she was barred from the studio. Mrs Puzey and her tribe of five children. She was a Caribbean lady of huge proportions, quite frightening, really. She and her children made a living cleaning five or six shops in the High Road. Her husband was a jazz musician who had disappeared along with his sax about five or six years ago. They arrived daily brandishing Hoovers and feather-dusters and black bin-liners. They arrived in a fit of laughter and chatter and for an hour there was bustle and chaos and when they had gone the silence was wonderful and the place was clean. Mrs Puzey's eldest daughter, Laura, supplemented her income with a little night work. She worked out of the endless bar of The British. Her clientele was small, restricted to married men who remained faithful to her. Mrs Puzey and her tribe didn't clean on Sundays. On Sundays they went to the Pentecostal church. They marched past the shop in their Sunday clothes with Mrs Puzey in front and the children behind in descending order of height. On Sunday they prayed.

On Saturday night, against his better judgement and because he needed some Christmas help, Mr Lawrence said, "You can stay until next weekend, no longer, and only if you make yourself useful in the shop."

Good deeds bring bad fortune—an old Chinese proverb. He should have remembered.

He woke up suddenly and knew he'd been snoring. There was a handful of froth on his chin.

You could touch the Sunday dawn. You could walk through the grey light and feel its weight on your shoulders.

The aftermath of the Saturday night war, the takeaway cartons and broken beer bottles, littered the road. Puddles of vomit and urine were stirred by the weak vitamins of the winter sun to burst with an occasional bubble of British gas.

One of his two bottles of milk had been stolen by a considerate thief or the milkman had short delivered again.

Mrs Puzey waddled along in her Sunday blue suit and her Sunday hat. Her children followed; ducklings following their mother to the water: in this case, blessed holy water. She saw him and hurried past without acknowledgement. Only Laura, third in line, gave a half-smile of recognition. Laura, the black vixen of The British.

He closed his door again and threw the bolts and was at the counter when the thumping began. Through the glass, beyond the security bars, open-mouthed and puzzled at his inability to gain entry, the young man peered in. His features were flattened grotesquely against the glass.

Mr Lawrence groaned. Oh God, it hadn't been a dream. He really had invited him to stay.

He threw back the bolts again and opened the door to the young man's wide grin. The young man waited until the old bell finished and then quickly moved forward as though afraid that Mr Lawrence might change his mind. His leading foot skidded in a puddle, the plastic bag he carried was projected forward and ended up in Mr Lawrence's arms and the young man, Paul, Paul Knight, ended up sitting in the wet.

"Stone the crows, Mr Lawrence," he said as his finger hovered just below his nose. "Some dirty bastard's pissed in your doorway!" He paused, then: "There's a fire out there. The sky's turning black. You can smell the smoke. It might be the end of the world!"

"Hey! Like it! What's it do?" Paul reached up to a steel hook and chain that extended from a ceiling runway.

"It carries the crates from the back of the shop. At one time we carried a range of sculptures, some by Henry Moore..."

"I know. I know. Don't tell me! He was the geezer who had his head...You know, by the king? Religion, innit?"

29

"I think that might have been Thomas More who wrote *Utopia*."

Paul stuck out a wagging finger. "*Utopia*, yeah, that's the geezer. These old sculptures then, they were pretty old, eh?"

Mr Lawrence raised a blown eyebrow. "Yes, I suppose so. Anyway, they weighed a ton, hence the block and tackle."

"Nice word, that, Mr Lawrence. Tackle. I like that."

Mr Lawrence felt the plastic bag. "Is this all you've got?"

"Left some at the squat. I'll bring it round."

"What about clothes?"

"Still got to go shopping, see? In the squat there's no point in having anything. You have to sleep with your shoes on in there."

"My goodness, it sounds like a dreadful place."

"Yeah, that's it."

Mr Lawrence led the way. Paul followed, unsticking his jeans as he went.

"Like the Tate, innit?" He paused to admire one of the cast bronze ballerinas and stooped slightly to check out her underwear. He showed no sign of disappointment as he followed Mr Lawrence to the stairs.

"I'm a bit surprised, with respect of course, that you are acquainted with the Tate Gallery."

Paul threw him an off-the-shoulder look and a smile made his lips flutter. "It is a bit surprising, I suppose. But me and the Tate, mate…"

"Through there is my studio."

Paul followed the line of the older man's finger to the closed door at the bottom of the stairs.

"It's out of bounds. No entry. Strictly no entry!"

"No sweat. Perfectly understood. Don't come to you with the best of references. I know that. We've got to learn to trust one another. Right?"

On the stairs Mr Lawrence paused to consider the statement and Paul stumbled against him.

"Trust, that's the main thing." He stood on the stairs carrying his Robot City plastic bag. "Don't nick nothing from no one who does you a turn. Ain't that it?"

Mr Lawrence narrowed his eyes. Too many negatives, too many for a Sunday morning, anyway. He went onward and led the youngster through the flat.

In the sitting room Paul stood rooted, shocked.

"There's no streamers, Mr Lawrence, and no Christmas cards!"

"I didn't get any cards this year. A couple came addressed to the shop but they weren't personal, simply prints of old favourites and nothing to do with Christmas or the birth of Christ. One had little girls in tutus and the other was a scene of the Thames before the London Eye. It might even have been before the fire of London."

"There's no glittering balls and no fairy on top of your Christmas tree. Oh, Mr Lawrence, you haven't even got a tree!"

"No, no tree and no…fairy."

"But everyone has a tree. It isn't Christmas without a tree."

"I like to paint trees, but not in the parlour, and certainly not coniferous trees. The dreaded fir has become a dividing line between council-house back gardens. They are not real trees. They don't shut down in autumn like real trees. There is no decay and death, nothing to stimulate the artist."

Paul gave him an exaggerated frown, as children do, and said, "We even had a Christmas tree in the…"

"Prison?"

"That's it. But there were no pressies under it." He explored further, then, "There's no TV?"

"You're right. No TV."

"In for repair, is it?"

"No."

"How can you live without a TV?"

"I manage."

"Grief!" The thought shook Paul's head. "Still, it's a big place, I'll give you that. You could put up four people here, without bother."

Mr Lawrence put in quickly, "It's a small flat, suitable for one."

"Absolutely," Paul agreed and offered a winning smile. "One and a lodger."

They moved into the smaller of two bedrooms.

"This is it," Mr Lawrence said as Paul bounced on the bed. "There's a walk-in wardrobe here where you can hide, if you like. The airing cupboard is outside your door. Blankets, pillows and sheets in there."

"Brilliant. This is the first time I've had a room to myself in months. Not since I did a month in solitary." He continued to bounce.

"Solitary?"

"I put some bleach in the screw's coffee. He wasn't a happy screw after that."

"Goodness me. What happened to him?"

"Well, screw became screwed. He went to see the doctor, Mr Lawrence, with a bit of a tummy upset."

Paul noticed the older man's concern. He stopped bouncing and said, "I won't be no trouble. Honest. I'll make myself useful, you'll see. Anything you want doing...electrics, cooking, you name it. I'm the man. I'll be out most evenings. Chess, go to the chess club, see?"

Mr Lawrence backed out.

"Just one thing," Paul continued. "I'm back late. How about a key?"

"Yes. If it's late you'll need a key."

"It is late. Wouldn't want to disturb you."

"No noise."

"No noise," he agreed. "Quiet as a...lamb, innit? Baby, sleeping baby! You won't even know I'm here."

Mr Lawrence closed the door and reached the kitchen when the sounds of Madonna's Like a Virgin rattled the dishes. The noise came from one of the two items held in the Robot City plastic carrier bag. The other item was a toothbrush.

Mr Lawrence hated Sundays.

Chapter 5

DS Sam Butler thought that Cole was a workaholic, perhaps an alcoholic too. A man full of bitter memories of a wife who'd gone off with another man. The thought was painful. He'd gone through a similar state of affairs but his wife hadn't gone off. Instead she had presented him with a daughter. His, so she said, and he believed her or, rather, wanted to. It seemed a long time ago but it never went away, not completely, and you could never forgive, not entirely, but if you cared enough, then you could live with it. It was more of a strength than a weakness.

Butler was part of Inspector Jack Wooderson's team at Hinckley nick, transferred from Sheerham when sleepless nights had arrived with his daughter. Every minute in bed counted and Hinckley was five minutes closer to home. Lately he'd seen little of Cole and it came as a surprise when the DI asked him to call into HQ, off the record. They'd worked together in the past but they'd never been close. No one ever got close to Rick Cole.

The office brought back memories, serious incidents. A copper's mind was notched with memories of results, good and bad. Putting them aside was the difficult bit. It was too easy to lie there and get off on them again. You could never get away from the job. It followed you around like a shadow and it threw a shadow over everything else too.

Butler said, "Heard about the bomb."

Cole tried a smile. "You're lucky. It rattled our windows. Marsh has taken it very personally."

Marsh was the chief superintendent who took everything personally.

The DS grinned. "A garden shed?"

"On the allotments."

"Strange."

"Schoolboys. A chemistry set for Christmas or, more likely, leftover fireworks; broke them open and put all the powder together in a bog roll or, in this case, some steel tubing. We've all been there."

"Still…"

"Barry Scot's looking after it. He'll be pleased to see you."

Butler nodded and said, "I thought there was another one yesterday. Another seven-seven."

"Didn't we all. Half the plods are still over at Buncefield. It doesn't help when you close the M1."

"Shame it can't be permanent."

"I know what you mean." Cole paused. The informalities were over. "Are you getting anywhere with these missing women?"

Butler's hesitation went on too long. Between the detectives there were boundaries you didn't cross. Guarding your own investigations became a way of life.

"Jesus, Sam. We know each other better than this."

Butler relaxed. His shoulders fell. He threw Cole a careless wave. "You're right. I don't know what the hell's the matter with me lately. Put it down to lack of sleep."

Without saying so they both knew the problem. Left behind at Hinckley Inspector Jack Wooderson had turned resentment into an art form.

Butler concentrated on the subject. "Frankly, we've got zilch. You know Jack. He gets one idea in his head and we're despatched to all parts of the country. I was in Worthing. Have you ever been to Worthing in the winter?"

Cole shook his head. "Not even the summer."

"It's not a place I'd recommend."

"So what's in Worthing?"

"They've got ten missing women. Teenagers, mostly black, all vanished in the last eighteen months. It sounds like the skin trade. They're convinced they'll surface in northern Italy. Most of them come from Nigeria, Liberia and every other messed up African country. Interpol, the Refugee Council and Immigration are all involved. It's not for us. I could have told him the MO was different without the pleasure of seeing the place."

"Have you got anything at all?"

Butler shrugged weakly. "I've had my fill of MPS if that's what you mean." He was referring to the Territorial Policing Headquarters where Operation Compass—the MPS Central Missing Persons Unit—was set up to coordinate the investigations of missing people across London.

He continued, "We haven't found a single connection. Credit cards not maxed, no apparent debts, no life insurance worth mentioning, no affairs as far as we can tell, no suspicion of crime. It's over a year since the first disappeared—no rhyme, no reason. You saw the reports—over two hundred witness statements, over two hundred local properties searched, fifty plods and forensics combing over a mile around each of their addresses and retracing last known… nothing. We've plastered the town with flyers and posters, we've hit the local and national papers. They've just been swallowed up. It's already been scaled down and unless something breaks very soon they'll move into cold storage. Jack doesn't exactly live the ACPO values."

"Hate to say it but he's got a point. Has Margaret had a look?"

Margaret Domey was the resident psychologist based at Sheerham but her remit covered the substations.

"For a connection, you mean?" Butler shook his head again but this time resignation was mixed with curiosity. "You haven't heard?"

Cole frowned.

"Margaret's at home with her head down the pan. Morning sickness."

That he hadn't heard shouldn't have surprised Cole. He kept out of her way. He said, "I didn't know."

Butler grinned. Not many people would miss the psychologist. Not unless she'd changed a lot since his transfer. Margaret Domey didn't use ice in her drinks. She just breathed on them.

Cole said, "It must be catching."

35

"What's that, Guv?"

"It's the second pregnancy I've heard about in as many days. The first belonged to Mrs Ticker Harrison."

Butler's features firmed up.

"And unless there's been a change of circumstances you can add her name to your list of missing women."

"Helen Harrison is missing?"

Cole nodded.

"Did Ticker report it? Christ, I'd like to have been a fly on the wall."

"It's all unofficial, you understand?"

Butler pulled an unkind face. Most of the kozzers would have given a month's pay to nick Ticker Harrison.

"It might be worth checking out with a quiet visit. Probably a waste of time but it might throw up a connection."

Butler nodded thoughtfully.

"It was a whisper, nothing more."

"Right."

He got up to leave.

"You don't need an invitation to call in, Sam."

The DS hesitated. "Right," he said again, softly this time, remembering the old days, then he headed for the door.

Once out of there, curiously, he felt relieved.

C13 Anti-Terrorist Branch were full of themselves, a bit like the Flying Squad of the sixties. Since the IRA had calmed down they had been kept under wraps but with the weapons of mass destruction on the agenda they were back, enjoying the attention.

Once it was discovered that terrorists were not involved in the explosion they quickly lost interest and moved back to their shadowy world. They left their prelim report and an officer to explain it, and left forensics to get on with it.

In the briefing room they had covered the fire at Buncefield and a vicious knife attack on a young woman and had moved to their own explosion. Superintendent Billingham in his crisp uniform sat tight-lipped, square-shouldered and cross-armed as he watched Inspector John Knight go through the motions. The uniforms seemed strangely restless. The obligatory plain-clothes observer sat to one side of the crowded room, detached, bored by the drawn-out custom. On the CID side DS Barry Scot and DC Martin James were handling the case but the DS was too wily to get caught up in the briefing. He was out interviewing schoolboys he knew had a penchant for fireworks. Back in November he'd interviewed the same lads for stuffing Roman candles through the letterboxes of some pensioners who'd stopped them playing football on the road outside their homes. For DS Barry Scot those kids were favourite for the shed but his hunch meant that Martin James had pulled the briefing.

The inspector's address was winding down. "All chemists, garden centres and shops that might stock garden chemicals or children's chemistry sets to be visited today." He glanced at Sergeant Mike Wilson. "Sergeant Wilson will be coordinating this exercise. Do not sit on any information. The trail is still warm, the crater is still smoking. I want this sorted before some children turn up at the hospital minus their arms." He turned to the DC. "Anything to add, Martin?"

DC Martin James cleared his throat and tried to ignore the superintendent's glare. The super hated all things plain-clothed. It wasn't jealousy, exactly. Billingham had promotional ambitions and was wise enough to know that chief coppers thought that real policemen were those in uniform.

"Apart from the fuse I think you've covered it, Sir."

"Ah yes, the fuse. The fuse was made out of steel tubing so add ironmongers and builders' merchants to your list. Sergeant Wilson will supply the details."

The briefing was over. Chairs scraped back, heavy feet smacked the floor, the plods were on the move. Before long the uniforms would be on the street where they belonged and the mobiles would be pulling out and the world—or at least the streets in their part of the city—would be a safer place. Superintendent Billingham watched it happen. He was immensely proud of his well-oiled blue machine.

Martin James fought his way through the uniforms to the coffee machine. Sam Butler was making doubly sure he'd left no change in the slot.

"Hello Sam. How's the baby?"

"Noisy."

"You slumming it?"

Butler grinned. "Just passing through." He stood aside for James and said, "How'd it go?"

"Same old shit."

"Things don't change then?"

"Would it make a difference if the super was on speaking terms with Baxter?"

Detective Superintendent Baxter was Billingham's CID counterpart, an altogether different character. Not friendly, never that, but less severe.

"No," Butler said with some certainty. "Not a bit. Billingham is a natural bastard. Baxter has to work at it."

Chapter 6

"Anian, you're with me," DS Sam Butler said. He'd been back at Hinckley just long enough to catch up with his e-mails and drink a machine coffee.

DC Anian Stanford jumped at the chance to get away from the telephone and asked eagerly, "Where to?"

She had spent the last hour double-checking with Centrepoint, Crisis, Reunite, Shelter, British Red Cross and the London Refuge, all likely starting points in the search for a missing person. MPS were supposed to update the police national computer with information from these places along with cross-referring to all unidentified bodies found in the UK, but you'd get more joy from the Big Issue or the Black Sisters. The place was filled with officers taken from the front line or winding down to their pensions. To the kozzers on the street it had become a joke. It was almost as funny as Tintagel House on the South Bank where bad cops faced their day of judgement.

Anian had a restless face with bright dark-brown eyes that were not particularly friendly. They held a hint of petulance and maybe a question. Anian worked out, hit the pavements in tracksuit and Reeboks and burned everything off, including the good bits.

Anian Stanford was a DC based at Hinckley. That she was female and the colour of antique pine were stumbling blocks in the way of promotion. She was the only Asian woman in the division. It was something the top coppers were trying to put right but only because they'd been ordered to for political reasons.

"Where to?" she repeated as she pulled her jacket from the back of her chair.

Two PCs looked up from the paperwork they were completing in triplicate, their dull eyes reflecting the monotony, boring through her clothes more out of instinct than interest.

"Ticker Harrison," Butler said. "Heard of him?" He was joking, of course.

She found an arm and struggled with the tight fit. "Sheerham's most respected resident? Who hasn't?"

Butler picked up some MP forms and stuffed them in his pocket.

"What's happened?"

"His missus has done a bunk."

"And we go to him?"

"Only cos it suits us, girl. No other reason at all. We're looking for a link."

She nodded thoughtfully but not at all convinced and followed the DS to the door.

The two PCs watched her go then shared an indifferent glance.

Ticker Harrison lived just off the Ridgeway in North Sheerham, a few hundred yards on from the Adam and Eve boozer.

They left Butler's car at the gate and made their way along a gravel drive curling through rhododendrons and camellias to a double garage where a silver Corvette Stingray coupe lined up next to a black ash Mercedes convertible. Their mint condition had Butler stooping for a peep at the interiors. He was still flicking tears of envy as they reached the door of a continental-style villa, more in tune with the Costas than north Sheerham. He used the bell and Anian whispered, "Who said crime doesn't pay? We're in the wrong business."

"Would you run away from this?"

"That depends."

"On what?"

"Who was living with me. Not even Buckingham Palace would keep me with Ticker Harrison."

"Charlie?"

"At a push I'd sooner have Charles than Ticker, but only if I didn't have to meet the relatives."

"What about the trees? You'd have to talk to the trees."

Butler's easy smile vanished as the door opened.

Ticker Harrison was five-eight and built for the scrum; no neck but shoulders a loosehead prop would have been proud of. His grey hair was crew cut short and sideburns swept below the line of his ears. He had the dark skin of travellers, eyes that were greyish and humorous. He was dressed in grey trousers, white cotton shirt that was unbuttoned down to show his tanned pectorals, a silky blue waistcoat and brown slip-ons. He took one look at Butler and without giving him chance to flash his card said, "Come on in."

Butler closed the door behind Anian Stanford then followed the two of them across a wide oak-panelled reception into a sitting room. The furnishings in one small corner could have bought Butler's place. Harrison turned to face them. His eyes lingered too critically on Anian. They'd stopped at the skin. He didn't notice her clothes, black jacket and straight blue skirt over black tights, or how tall she was, five-eleven in flat shoes. Instead he looked at Butler with a question in his eyes.

"DC Stanford," Butler said. "Watch the lips so you get it in one. Detective Constable Stanford. I'm Detective Sergeant Butler from Hinckley nick."

Harrison shot the woman another glance and shrugged. He said, "Drink?"

Butler said, "Why not? Scotch will do nicely. No ice, thank you."

"You're supposed to say no thanks I'm on duty."

"Bollocks to that. You've been watching too much Bill."

"What about the Indians? Are they allowed alcohol?"

Anian said, "We are. But not if you're buying. And for your information, the gypsies are related to Hindi. They came from India."

Harrison didn't hesitate and threw her a grin that flashed white teeth, "You calling me a pikey? That's well out of order." He looked at Butler. "You going to let her get away with that? Racial prejudice in the police force? That's diabolical."

Butler threw up his hands. "I'm saying nothing, Sir. And I wouldn't go down that road with DC Stanford if I were you."

Harrison nodded and said, "I see what you mean." Whisky hit a glass and left splashes on the black-lacquered surface of the cellaret. There was an ivory inlay of Chinese figures. "Now look what you've made me do. You women are all the same, causing us all kinds of grief." The traveller in his blood was irresistible. Little wonder they were market traders. His smile was disconcerting and as crafty as a spin doctor's on a Brighton stage. His wife had disappeared but it didn't get in the way of humour. Priorities. All that. Some things couldn't be helped.

Sam Butler said sharply, "Right, let's get on with it." He accepted his drink, a tumbler full to the brim, and spread the forms on a polished glass coffee-table, easing himself into a cream leather armchair as he did so. The studded leather was as cracked as an old woman's face. He tapped the leather and said, "Trouble with this colour, it shows up the dirt."

"You should know," the villain said. "You don't earn in a year what this fucking thing cost. Not that the cost means nothing. It's all relative, right? Who gives a fuck apart from the fuckers who haven't got it? I could feed half of India with the bread I paid for this, but who gives a fuck about half of India?"

He latched on to Anian again and stayed there for a moment, then added, "Or Pakistan."

Butler smiled. "You're probably right, about the wages. But it still shows up the dirt, and there's a lot of it around here. Right?"

Harrison nodded slowly, weighing up the DS, then he turned back to Anian. "You sure I can't tempt you, coke or tea? I do a great line in tea—Assam, Earl Grey, Lapsang Souchong, camomile, even Indian."

She flashed him an odd look that Butler couldn't work out. It might have been perplexity, but he wasn't sure.

Harrison shrugged and offered a little smile of resignation then sat on the sofa to face the DS over the coffee table. He leant forward, his massive hands cupping his glass.

"OK, person who logged the report," Butler said with his pen poised. He was finding it difficult to accept that Harrison was top of Sheerham's hit-list and one of the most dangerous villains in the capital.

Yet he knew it was true. Harrison had been behind some of the nastiest headlines in the last twenty years and that the coppers hadn't been able to nail him was down to fear. It would take a brave man or a man with a death wish to grass on Ticker Harrison.

"That's me." He pulled a face at DC Stanford.

She tightened her lips, trying not to smile.

Butler dragged them back. "Harrison, fine. Ticker?"

"Edward. But don't spread it around. I don't want people mixing me up with that geezer who married Sophie."

"I can see your point. Easy mistake to make."

Anian was having trouble. Her eyes betrayed her.

Butler went on, "Relationship husband. Full name of missing person?"

"Helen Anne Harrison."

"Is that with an E?"

"Two Es."

"Anne?"

"Oh, yeah, with an E."

The DC had to turn away but her silent laugh still shook her shoulders.

Butler ignored her and proceeded with the rest: DOB, age, place of birth, height, weight, physical peculiarities.

Harrison said, "What the fuck do you mean? She's perfect."

"Freckles, tattoos, scarring from an operation or an injury, maybe?"

"Oh. No, no freckles. Maybe one or two on her shoulders, after the sun."

"False teeth?"

"Are you taking the piss?"

"No, but I am enjoying it. Birthmarks?"

"One, not that you'll ever see it."

"Well, you know? Just for the record."

"A little thing on the side of her fanny, shaped like a pear."

"Is that an American fanny or a British fanny?"

"What?"

"Front or back, boot or bonnet?"

Anian turned back to them. She seemed a little more composed but her eyes still sparkled and Butler knew it wouldn't take much to start her off again. What annoyed him most was that she was laughing with Ticker Harrison and not at him. She smiled sweetly.

"Front for fuck's sake."

"English then. Top of her leg?"

"No, no, next to the old BBC."

"Shepherd's Bush, then. You wouldn't have a photograph of it, would you, Sir?"

Harrison's eyes turned to slits.

"No, right. What side would the birthmark be on? Right or left?"

"As I'm looking at it, right."

"That would be her left?"

"Right."

"How big?"

Harrison made a hole with his finger. "The size of a pea, maybe, the colour of..." he nodded toward the DC.

"DC Stanford?"

"Right."

"Nescafe, then, with cream."

"You know Cole, don't you?"

"DI Cole?"

"He taught you how to take the Irish?"

"No, Sir. I'm self-taught."

"Well, Sergeant..."

"Butler. Detective Sergeant Butler."

"Well, Detective Sergeant Butler, do yourself a favour and teach yourself something else. Things have a way of coming round. One day you're going to need a favour and somebody's going to take the piss out of you..."

"Right," Butler said. "Let's carry on."

They went through the rest, friends or relatives, places she might have frequented, health or medical conditions and so on.

Butler said, "Does she have a driving licence?"

"Yeah, she's got a licence."

"Does she have her own car?"

"You kidding? The way she drives there's no way she's driving mine."

"She took it with her?"

"Well, of course she did. She'd drive to the fucking bathroom if that was possible."

From the side of the room Anian said, "Is this Helen?" She stood gazing at a framed painting of a naked woman. An oil, subdued, heavy paint where the light shone through, lots of knife.

Ticker Harrison said, "That's Helen. Now tell me, if you can, that she ain't perfect?"

Butler's interest picked up. Maybe it was the woman's lack of inhibition; there wasn't much left to the imagination. He was surprised he hadn't noticed it before. It was a pose guaranteed to draw the eye. He asked, "When was this painted, Sir?"

"Finished about a month ago. No more than that. Paint's hardly dry. What do you think?"

Butler turned back to Harrison and said, "You're right, you do have a very beautiful wife and your description of the birthmark was spot on. If you can give us a recent photograph and a car registration, we'll go and try to find her."

On their patch three women were officially missing; Helen Harrison would make it four.

Where adults were concerned the police faced a dilemma when dealing with a missing person case. ACPO's national guidance and the new policy and procedure from Operation Compass was designed to increase the investigative standards, but apart from logging and having closer contact with the other agencies and reports going to the MPS senior management team there was little else the police could do. Unless there was a suspicion of crime they weren't about to get the search teams out complete with dogs and helicopter. There was nothing illegal about running away. And most of those reported missing returned home within a week. In the majority of cases a domestic was involved, the missing person had moved in with someone else; sometimes they'd simply had enough and moved back in with the parents. Adultery was always first choice. Abuse, debt, illness, quarrels, depression, senility, alcohol misuse, other drugs, these were the main reasons for someone taking a hike. But adultery came first. Old Freud had got it right. A healthy stalk, tall or short, fat or thin, was essential to the hearty bush. Abduction was way down, the least likely scenario.

NMPH, the National Missing Persons Helpline, took over eighty thousand calls a year and they held fourteen thousand open files.

Just occasionally the police showed more than a passing interest. In such cases it was standard procedure to search the home address and obtain a DNA sample from something personal like a toothbrush, to go into their financial details and get their bank account and credit card details, to get details of their GP and dentist and then to get consent for publicity. Then it was a case of checking with family and friends to build a picture. You didn't have to dig deep to find out if all was well. Even a PC could do it and that was saying something. What the missing person took with them was the first indication, it meant the difference between something planned and something else and, if it was planned, then the police weren't interested. Moving out, whether you told someone or not, didn't constitute a crime. And that a husband knew little about his wife's emotional state was nothing new.

As though reading Sam Butler's mind Inspector Jack Wooderson said, "Is there any crime you might read into this?"

"Apart from Imelda Cooke, no Guv."

"I've looked at it; we've spent a lot of man-hours, more than the books can afford."

"She had kids."

Wooderson nodded thoughtfully. It was not a good sign when women went missing without taking their children. But it did happen. And just lately it was happening more and more. Responsibility was something of the past.

"Anything else?"

"No."

"Then put it to bed. We've exhausted every line on this and there's nothing else to do. Unless you can come up with something new then let's not waste any more time."

It grieved Butler to know that his inspector was absolutely right. And yet he had a feeling about this one—the sixth sense that was the mark of a good kozzer.

An experienced copper's intuition was often more important than the evidence, or lack of it. Here, there was nothing concrete, not even a crime, yet Butler's gut tightened. It was the feeling you had the morning after the night before that you couldn't remember. A sickening feeling, just before you slept again, that somehow you'd messed up. Here, save for Helen Harrison, and who could blame her for leaving Ticker, the other women didn't fit the pattern to take a walk. And yet, at the back of his mind, was the knowledge of how little he'd known about his own wife when she'd had her affair.

It had gone on for months. Things had drifted, become commonplace, and it wasn't until the final few weeks that he suspected there was something wrong. He was a copper, damn it, and even he hadn't realized what was going on under his own roof, in his own bed. It had just been a gut feeling that had led him home. Intuition. The copper's best friend. And there they were, the after-blast of coition burning their faces. Until they saw him. Then the glow faded quickly. But had he not found them then he was certain that one day he would have gone home to an empty house. Just like Ticker Harrison. Just like Rick Cole.

As far as Helen Harrison was concerned Butler guessed that she was seeing another man. Putting distance between herself and her husband was all that she could do. There could never be an amicable arrangement with a man like Ticker, and for his wife, unto death would be exactly that.

DC Anian Stanford turned on the light and the flickering strip made him blink, made him realize how much time had been lost while the early afternoon gloom had closed in. He acknowledged her with a quick smile then tuned into the report again, hoping to find that illusive connection, wondering whether he should break the unwritten rule. Taking a chance wasn't like him at all. Reluctantly, he lifted the telephone and after a few moments said, "Guv, it's Sam."

"How did you get on with Ticker?"

Butler double-checked that Wooderson's door was closed then in a lowered voice said, "Listen, can we meet up tonight? Better still, come to dinner."

"This isn't like you, Sam. You seem worried?"

That was a joke although Butler didn't get it. The DS wasn't happy unless he had something to worry about.

"I saw Ticker, filed the report."

"Good."

"Come to dinner. Janet would love to see you again."

"Does she know I'm coming?" A long silence answered the question. Eventually Cole asked, "What time?"

"Make it eight."

Butler sat with the phone tapping against his chin before he nodded purposefully and said to Anian, "You're coming to dinner tonight, eight o'clock. It's business."

"Overtime, Sarge?"

"Don't take the piss, Anian, there's a good girl."

Chapter 7

Rick Cole showered and changed and downed a large Teacher's before driving out towards the Butler's place. To get there he had to drive across town.

Cole knew the city. A lifetime ago he had plodded there, to begin with under the guidance of a parent constable. Now they were called street duty PCs. A dozen years later he was wearing plain clothes at the Yard but those days were so distant that he sometimes wondered if they'd really happened. For one reason or another everything had come unstuck and he had ended up at Sheerham. It could have been worse. He was acting up and had an office to himself and that in itself was a luxury for a DI. It wouldn't last indefinitely and the grapevine buzzed with rumours of a fresh-faced DCI coming over from the Yard.

Driving through town most people would use the main road that passed through the south on its way to the city, and they'd find it one of those places that didn't register. Perhaps unconsciously, they'd closed their eyes. The south was where most of the blacks lived, congested, noisy, filled with litter. It was a place to leave behind.

The MP was black, Gilly Brown, a leftie whose heart was in the West Indies. He controlled the council, or at least his siblings who made up the majority, and on his behalf they spent more council tax on dyke coffee mornings than libraries, more on banning the black from blackhead than bus passes for the elderly. But he was laughing at the system. His pockets were comfortably lined. One day he would be back off to the Caribbean with his massive family and all the cash he had creamed and the country would rise out of the sea by an inch. Gilly Brown was living proof that enough split votes would let in the wackos. He'd swear allegiance to the Queen and country, Princess Anne too. He'd swear to anything that moved so long as it added to his bank balance.

Tower blocks littered the skyline, council estates were run down. Finer roads ran through the north of the town where properties had their own drives and bordered a well-maintained parkland. Most of the Jews—the spill over from Hampstead Garden and Golders Green— lived there along with the Maltese gangsters and Gilly Brown. And Ticker Harrison.

The Sheerham High Road ran through the centre of town. It was the main shopping precinct which was dominated by the Carrington Theatre, a huge red-brick building that once, long ago, attracted the stars. Narrow side-streets criss-crossed the High Road but the shops on these petered out quickly to the odd Asian grocery that sold everything day and night and Christmas Day. Then it was row upon row of terraced housing. The front gardens were about a yard wide and out back was enough room to keep the lawnmower. Most of these buildings were in poor shape, windows were cracked or boarded and doors were blistered. It was a place covered in graffiti and litter. It was the place that produced most of the criminals and the highest unemployment figures.

As the night fell and the neon took over, the pensioners barricaded themselves indoors and the youngsters came out to play. It happened in every town and city across the country yet here it was concentrated, the overspill from the city, and the energy was frightening. The bars and clubs were packed with young drinkers slamming down their high-powered bottles.

This was Sheerham.

Cole's patch.

While he waited at the crossroads before the Carrington Theatre he noticed that something from the past was stirring. Lottery money and local taxes had revamped the Class A building and given it an exotic quality. The red brick glowed and threw out a ray of comfort over the

Romanian beggars as they pushed their smack-faced kids at the box-office queue. There was a woman on the billboard, eight-feet high, in skimpy black underwear and high heels.

Rick Cole took a second glance at the cardboard blonde, Anthea Palmer, ex-weather girl, and while traffic lights held him back he decided that the smile on her face was as false as the promise of the theatre's new dawn.

Janet Butler was forty and a rinsed blonde. She might have walked in from the sixties. She had settled comfortably into motherhood, surprising most who knew her, including her husband. She'd met Cole on a dozen or so occasions, mostly police functions when Cole used to go to them. Her eyes, like only an older woman's could, promised everything and nothing at all. She flirted and he let her. It was all very cosy, like an afternoon tea dance without the afters. Safe and easy and none of it serious. At the door she gave him a decorous little hug and her perfume touched a memory.

"Rick, it's been a long, long time."

She was warm and familiar. It took him a moment to adjust. To remember that beneath it all she was as cold as the rest of them. That once upon a time she'd had an affair and left her husband devastated.

"Too long, Janet. You're looking good."

"Better than good. Take another look."

She gave him a little twirl.

"Agreed. How's the baby."

"The baby's name is Lucy and she's good too. If you're very, very quiet you can take a peep into her bedroom. That'll be a treat for you. Come on in." She fumbled for his hand, more of a caress really and, rubbing his hand all the way, led him into the dining room.

Cole heard voices before the door was opened so finding another guest was hardly a surprise. Discovering that it was DC Anian Stanford definitely was.

She stood by a midi sound system, glass in hand, while Butler knelt searching through a pile of discs. In place of her working clothes were black jeans, brown vest and sneakers that left a strip of olive instep. There was nothing under the vest. Her nipples stuck out like a couple of filter-tips that looked good enough to smoke. Her hair was down, black as tar and elbow length. He noticed for the first time how tall and skinny she was.

Janet spread her hand and said matter-of-factly, "You know Anian?"

Cole nodded briefly. Anian returned his acknowledgement with a quick nervous smile.

Butler found his CD and waved the disc toward his guest. "Guv."

"Sam."

The DS struggled to his feet. "Drink?"

"Good idea."

Leaving Anian to load the music, they moved to the drinks cabinet, out of earshot, and while he poured, Butler said, "Anian's working the case with me."

"Right."

"You don't mind?"

"You should have mentioned it, that's all."

Butler tut-tutted the idea. "Didn't seem important."

"She's not my type."

Butler fell in. "Colour? You?"

"Figure. She hasn't got one."

"Nor have the fashion models. It's the fashion."

"I'm an old-fashioned guy."

Butler smiled and raised his glass. "To old times, Guv."

Cole nodded. "I'll go with that." He emptied half his glass. Butler held on to the bottle, waiting, then topped up as Red Red Wine filled the room.

"I want her to be in on this. She's done most of the legwork."

"Talking shop. Janet will love you."

"I've primed her. We'll get shot of it while she's serving up. That all right with you?"

Cole shrugged and wondered whether he'd made a mistake. He was already feeling the limb that he knew Butler was going to put him on.

The women were on the sofa, drinking Jacob's Creek and jabbering like women do. Their conversation ended abruptly as the men approached.

"I've been telling her all about you, Rick. Everything. She's been at Hinckley... How long?"

"Almost a year."

"And you've barely said hello. That's disgraceful. It really, really is."

"Sweetheart," Butler put in. "It's not like that."

"Yes it is. It's exactly like that. Give a man rank and you create a monster." She turned to Anian. "The days have gone when men were men and women were proud of them. Agreed?"

Anian's laugh was forced and apprehensive.

Cole caught Janet's exaggerated look of indignation and laughed out loud.

Janet moved into the kitchen. Butler topped the glasses again before he turned to Cole.

"So how was Ticker?"

Butler shrugged weakly. "Anian held her own."

Cole glanced at the girl and murmured, "I expect she did."

Butler put in quickly, "Jack's not interested, told me to put it to bed."

"So what's the problem?"

"The problem, Guv, is that three of the four women are pregnant. What are the odds on that happening? It'd make the lottery look good. On our patch we've got four missing women, forget the kids, the runaways. Just concentrate on adult females. We've got four."

"And three are pregnant?"

"Right," Butler said earnestly. "And statistically, pregnant women—those with a partner—don't take off. Single, yes. They run from parents or the perceived shame. And the forties and fifties, they take off after the kids have left, looking for the last-chance saloon, looking for something better or someone better, or maybe they're wanting space again, I don't know. But not when they're pregnant. Not unless the father lives someplace else."

"How pregnant?"

"At the time of them going missing they ranged from a few weeks to four months. Helen Harrison only just found out. You know that."

"And do they play around?"

Anian raised her eyebrows and shook her head.

"It's a fair question," Cole said sharply. "You're a copper, not a social worker. Coppers can't afford the luxury of being politically correct or non-judgemental. A spade is a spade and around here, like everywhere else, married women do fuck around."

She didn't like it but she nodded.

Butler didn't like it either for it touched an open wound. He sighed and said, "You tell me about Helen. But the others, who knows? How the hell do you tell? My guess would be that they don't, play around that is, but what do I know?"

Cole smiled at the detective sergeant's wry humour. Self-deprecation suited the worry lines on his face.

"Does Jack know about the pregnancies?"

Butler shook his head. "Until we knew about Helen it was only two out of three and it didn't even register. Two's a coincidence but three's a wake-up call."

Cole said, "So, talk to me. What do you want?"

Anian sat listening intently, steadying her glass on the arm of the sofa, her fierce eyes more on the DI than the DS.

Butler spread his hands. "I'm in a fix. I've got a gut feeling about it, Guv."

Cole nodded. The ghosts of other missing persons, Suzy Lamplugh and the rest, came back to haunt him. Cole remembered the young woman who'd vanished after going to meet the mysterious Mr Kipper. Even though her body had never been found she'd been declared dead in 1994. "Get on to the index and spread out. Go back a few years and find some common ground, anything. There might be some cold files knocking around. If you come up with something then stick it under Jack's nose. If he's not interested then come back to me. But it won't come to that. If you find something then he'll be interested. But you should have mentioned the pregnancy connection. It seems pretty relevant, particularly in view of your earlier comments. You've been looking for a connection and you've got one."

Anian said abruptly, "So what are we looking for? Prenatal clinics?

Marie Stopes? There's an awful lot of places around here where you can turn up with five-hundred quid and an overnight bag and get in line with the girls from Dublin?"

The DI glanced at Butler. "I think that might be jumping the gun. But it might be worth having another look at the odd one out. Clutching at straws, but that's what we do best. If you can eliminate her then all your girls are pregnant. I'm still not sure it will get you anywhere. Jack does have a point. To be honest, pregnancies or not, I'm leaning towards him on this. You're not looking for a villain here, you're looking for a crime. At the moment you haven't got one and we've got plenty of others to concentrate on. It can't go on indefinitely."

"Christ, Rick, it was you who asked me to see Ticker!"

"You're right, and it has added weight to your pregnancy theory, but you need more, or you can leave it to MPS."

Butler's nod was resigned.

From the kitchen Janet called, "I'm coming through."

Cole threw Butler an appraising look. "Come back to me with something solid, concentrate on Helen Harrison. Her trail is fresh. Don't waste time. If Jack decides to call it quits I won't be in a position to argue. You'll have to find me something to use." He nodded and repeated, "Helen Harrison. Get to know her better than Ticker does. He's obviously missed something that's right under his nose."

Butler topped Cole's glass again and watched as his old colleague made small work of it. They sat at the table where Janet was pouring Australian white. Anian sat opposite Cole and he stole a glance. Her nipples still poked through. They hadn't changed. He had. The scotch was doing the trick and lifting away the curse of Orpheus.

His phone went.

Janet looked horrified and said, "Shit!"

Butler pulled a face.

Anian looked at Cole over her wine glass and smiled sweetly. She knew something; maybe she'd caught his earlier glance.

Cole checked the number and said to Janet, "Sorry." He stole a single green olive then moved out of earshot to make his call.

As Cole climbed into his midnight-blue copper's car and Janet threw him a tentative wave from the door, he wasn't altogether unhappy that dinner had been cut short. Take shoptalk away from Sam Butler and there wasn't much left, not lately. The girl might have been interesting but now he would never know. Cole wasn't a social animal anymore, if ever he had been; that side of him had been kicked to touch by a woman and an unforgiving job. Tonight had been the exception. The booze had softened him up; that, and something faintly exotic. The phone had saved him and opened up the gates to the underworld.

He stepped on the pedal. He was on his way to a scene of crime and a major incident. Ahead of him a battlefield lay waiting and, with it, shattered lives and broken bodies. The thought spurred him on and lifted his mood. He loved it, the idea of another fight where the rules could once again be set aside. He caught his dimly lit reflection in the rear-view and something blue-eyed and colder than the December night looked back.

Chapter 8

CB1 was Charlie Bravo One, an Astra hatchback panda, driven by PC 7231 Wendy Booth. The car was three years old but looked older. Wendy Booth was twenty-nine but felt older. She had been on the job for ten years and on driving duties, which was her choice, for the last five. She was on the late shift, which she preferred, for it was the shift most likely to involve both ends of society: the brain-dead yobs who thought they controlled the streets and the pinstriped suits who staggered to their cars from the wine bars who probably did.

At 2115 she was parked up in a lay-by smoking one of her twenty-a- day Silk Cuts that occasionally ran to thirty, listening to the excited voices on the radio and waiting for the shout to come her way. It came at 2123 and five minutes later she picked up the skipper, Sergeant Mike Wilson. He was tall, slim and forty-two. All boots, bollocks and baggy uniform, was how Wendy described him to her friends. His face was friendly, big nose, soft eyes, easy smile and tufts of ginger whiskers that he'd missed in the shaving mirror. In the old days, before the lunatic fringe had gone PC crazy, he would have made a perfect plod. Everyone loved him and he had a big boot for the local troublemakers. Unfortunately his day was done and, sooner or later, one of the freeloaders from Westminster or, more likely, Brussels, would have him out of the job.

At 2131 she was moving along the High Road to the Square and the leisure centre. She saw the flashing cars and vans, the streamers of fluttering police tape and the army of plods spreading out from the

SOC. The ambulance had already left. As they passed she saw the white boiler-suited SOCOs beginning their fingertip search.

Another woman had been attacked, the second in two days and, by all accounts, it was the same MO. A bad one.

A psycho had used a knife, one of the personality disorders that the experts on the various committees decided were no longer a danger to the public. Care in the community. Keep taking the pills, my son, and off you go. Unfortunately it wasn't the guardians of public safety who were in the firing line. Tucked away in their comfort zones of index-related and reserved car parking they weren't the people getting maimed and killed. If there was one thing that upset the police more than anything it was the need to collar the same bastard twice.

They drove into the Square where the red lights from the dirty bookshops and sex shops with their DVD booths still flickered. Gangs of teenagers spilled into the road and the drunks zigzagged across the pavements.

Sergeant Mike Wilson said soberly, "Where do these people come from?"

"I don't know where they come from, Skip, but for most of them this is the end of the line."

He grunted.

"What exactly are we doing here, Skip?"

"We're showing a police presence. It's good for the troops on the ground and the front pages in the morning. And of course, we can keep our eyes open for weirdos. Not the weirdo, mind you, he'll be long gone, but any weirdo will do."

"They're all weirdos. Show me someone normal around here."

"She'll do for a start. Pull over."

Wendy slid the car to stop beside a forty-something woman. She wore a black miniskirt, black high-heeled pointed boots, black patterned hosiery and black lipstick that, as she smiled, cut her face in half.

"'Ello Mikey, don't 'ave to ask what you're doin' daaahn 'ere, do I? You arfta anuver discount, are you?" She leant down toward his open window and rested a thin white arm on the door. Light from the sex shop behind her gathered in the fair hairs on her forearm.

"Now, now, Elizabeth, don't give me Mikey or even the micky. There's people here who might not understand your sense of humour and go off telling others that I'm a customer."

"Oooh, Mikey, are you insinuatin' that I'm a strumpet? Everyone knows that men with a todger as big as yours gets it for free." She leant closer so that her white blouse sagged and showed him her dark nipples. She looked across at the grinning PC. "'Ello, Wendy darlin', you all right? You're not getting sexually 'arassed by this man are you?"

"I'm all right, Lizzy. I can hold my own."

"Yes, darlin', I've 'eard you can. Better than most, I 'eard. Well, darlin', even so, if he asks you to take it up the arse make sure you get a decent dinner out of it. None of this Big Mac Pizza 'Ouse shit."

"I'll keep that in mind."

Mike Wilson tapped his nose. "You heard about the business back there?"

"Who 'asn't, darlin'? It's all over the Square. All the plods knockin' about is messing with the trade. We're thinkin' of reportin' you to the Department of Trade and Industry."

"Didn't see anything, hear anything?"

"Not a thing, darlin'. First we knew about it was the ambulance."

"What about last night?"

"That was just a one-off at the time so it didn't cause a stir. One-offs is 'appenin' all the time, you know that. Disgruntled punters or pissed-off managers who think you're 'oldin' back. But these girls are civvies. They wouldn't know a trick from a treat."

"Be a good girl and ask around."

"For you Mikey, anythin'. If there's so much as a whisper I'll be in touch."

"Appreciate it."

She gave him an intimate little smile while her eyes brimmed with melancholy. She blinked and looked across at Wendy again. "You take good care of 'im, Wendy darlin'. 'E's one in a million." With that she stood upright and faded into a crowd that had gathered outside the sex-shop window.

PC Wendy Booth slid the car back into traffic. Lizzy's final look had opened a tap of emotion and she swallowed hard before finding her voice. "First time I've heard a pimp called a manager." She threw him a sideways glance. "One in a million, eh?"

"These girls are very astute. You could learn a few things, Wendy Booth."

"If ever I want evening classes, Skip, I'll know where to come."

"Don't you fancy me, then, PC Booth?"

"I do, I do, and I'm having to hold myself back from jumping all over you, but I'm great mates with your wife and I love your three kids to bits so I'll just have to live with it."

Sergeant Mike Wilson nodded and said, "Right. So you're a lesbian then, are you?"

Chapter 9

Eleven years ago Donna Fitzgerald had joined the force as a seventeen-year-old cadet. It had been her ambition for as long as she could remember and she had never considered an alternative career. She had passed the interviews, the physical and psychometric tests and joined the force in August, she remembered, the month that produced the worst crime figures. She was also reasonably happy to be one of the few officers at Sheerham schooled in the bedside manner; hers was the sympathetic ear for the victims of rape and domestic violence and other serious sexual assaults. She could have been part of a Sapphire Unit and might even have been a substantive DC by now but that she was still in uniform was her own choice. She had learned long ago that CID was not for her. She had, nevertheless, accepted the role of chaperon and learned the gentle touch technique.

Behind it lay the urgent requirement for information, the gentle prod, encouragement, we're all girls together and all men are bastards, and so on. You made notes afterwards, once you'd milked them and sent them off to Victim Support. It was a job and you'd heard it all before. You were a copper. The freezing process began on day one.

Donna Fitzgerald was on the wind-down of her shift when the duty sergeant caught her. She was adjusting her heavy belt kit—extendable metal asp, quick-cuffs, CS spray, torch and radio—non-digital for Sheerham didn't run to the upgraded 390Mhz and the Tetra network—and was making her slow way to the locker room when she caught sight of his scrawny features, recognized the look in his sly eyes and felt a sinking sensation in her stomach. The prospect of a DVD and a few vods after a Chinese diminished as his footsteps on the corridor floor grew louder.

"Got one that's right up your street, Donna."

She pulled a face. "Skipper, I'm on my way home."

He smiled gleefully, enjoying himself. "You mean you were, lass. We're stretched. Another woman has been attacked. It sounds like the same guy."

She'd already heard. The news had been all over the radio. Twenty-four hours earlier a woman named Carol Sapolsky had been knifed in what appeared to be a seemingly random attack. The police were still looking for a motive and some return from a hastily arranged appeal for information from the public.

She brushed some creases from the leg of her uniform and noticed the front of her body armour was streaked with cigarette ash. She fiddled with her regulation clip-on tie and tried to swallow from a dry mouth.

The sergeant read her thoughts. "Get rid of all that armour and grab yourself a cup of refreshing tea which you can drink on the way. Don't want you frightening her to death, do we? Not before you get some details. Get down to the North Mid as quickly as possible and get me something before they start. Make sure you don't catch MRSA or something."

Once the medical examination began the police would have to wait. In the case of assault by a stranger the trail went cold quickly. It was called the golden hour. An hour could make all the difference.

Donna hitched her belt and threw him a tight-lipped look that pleased him no end. He watched her arse all the way out until a door swung shut and cut the view.

Breakfast was being served to plods in the canteen when the incident room filled up with plain clothes. There were two faces that Cole didn't recognize. They'd had to pull in detectives from other districts. The new case was stretching them and they still had the bomb to deal with. That was beside the usual crimes that had come in overnight and they never stopped—burglaries, muggings, car thefts, GBHs and drug-related offences, not to mention the petty crime and the increased number of racial attacks. Not that the racial element was ever recorded. If you could mark them down as anything other than racist then the directive from the HO was to do so. The public were to be kept in the dark. They didn't want the anxiety caused by the foreign face gaining momentum and turning into an Enoch river. But people were still getting hurt. And every incident took up man-hours. More than they had. Half the burglaries, particularly on the estate, weren't even visited.

There were eight people in the room, all but two plain-clothed.

The incident room was makeshift, an old changing room. All the junk had been cleared and the steel lockers were restricting the corridor outside. In their place were monitors, telephones, desks, and portable screens covered with photographs and maps of the SOCs.

When Detective Superintendent Baxter walked in the chatter stopped. He was an overweight man in dark suit and tie. Spectacles enlarged his brown eyes.

"OK, everyone, thanks for getting here so quickly. It's appreciated. I know it's Christmas and sixteen-hour days are not an attractive proposition, but think of the overtime. For those of you who don't know, I'm the super. My name's Tony Baxter." He sounded fine but self-assurance and the keen attention he received from the locals, left his credentials in little doubt. He went on, "This is DI Rick Cole. He'll be SIO on this. Chas Walker is exhibits officer. Peter Wood has come from the Yard to help out. David Carter is from Tottenham. Get this sorted quickly and you can all go home. I'm transferring PC Donna Fitzgerald for the duration. She's going to be chaperon. She's got the hard bit, the victims."

Chas Walker asked, "So where's Donna now?" He was uneasy. She'd have a direct line to Billingham, spilling their trade secrets.

Baxter understood DC Walker's concern. Uniform and plain clothes didn't mix. Usually it was no more than healthy competition but the ex-commissioner's policies had fuelled the friction and blown it out of proportion. CID, particularly in the MET, was fighting for survival.

Baxter answered, "She's at the hospital. She's been there most of the night while you lot were getting your beauty sleep. Now, you've all heard what happened to the latest. Elizabeth Rayner, twenty-eight, single, by all accounts a nice professional woman, on her way home from her health club... DI Cole will brief you. I want progress reports every day at nine and six. And I mean progress." He turned to Cole. "I'll leave it to you."

The others recognized an intimacy between them, something more than the job.

Once the door had shut Cole said, "Right, let's get on with it. Chas has got his work cut out. Peter you look after the indexes. David, take care of the usual faces and the door-to-door. I want to know about Elizabeth Rayner and the first victim, Carol Sapolsky. I want some common ground. So, boyfriends, ex-boyfriends, workmates, clubs, the business. The uniforms have made a start but now we want it done properly. So far fingertips have produced zilch but they're still looking at the drains and bins. Priorities? CCTV footage from the streets, boozers, shops and garages. And let's have a go at the KCs. They're not going to come forward without a nudge but if we can find them then they will be very helpful. For those of you who don't know the Square is our local area of disrepute and it goes without saying that the girls are going to be really pissed off seeing us, the KCs even more, and that will work in our favour. They'll want to help in order to get rid of us. Concentrate on the local hit list. I want every one of them TIED without exception."

TIED is traced, interviewed and eliminated. KCs are kerb-crawlers.

"We've already taken seventy calls regarding Miss Sapolsky and these have produced a dozen possibilities. Let's have every one of them followed up today. Check with Catchem and Guys, see if anyone has a predilection for Stanley knives and women's breasts. Chas, sort out a desk for Donna. All of you please note that she is part of this team for the duration. I don't want to hear any plod jokes. Questions?"

"What about sexist jokes, Guv?" Chas Walker asked and the secondments shared an anxious moment.

"Sexist jokes I can live with," Cole said and heard a collective sigh of relief.

Cole found Detective Superintendent Baxter in his office, coffee in hand, open BacoFoil on his desk revealing what was left of six rounds of ham and tomato sandwiches. A knife had left a lane of English mustard across one half of the rounds. The other half was only one step deep. Baxter brushed a crumb from his lips, almost embarrassed, and made a half-hearted attempt to wrap the sandwiches. After a moment he pushed them aside, placed his coffee carefully on the desk and said, "Sod it, Rick. Early lunch."

Cole glanced at his watch. It wasn't yet ten.

Baxter adjusted his spectacles and frowned. "I'm not happy with this. A serial slasher?"

"We're still one light for a serial and the MO might throw something up. They could be unrelated."

Baxter made a dismissive noise. "Not much chance of that."

"I know it's early days but I was thinking about a profile."

"A bottle-fed psycho. What else do you want to know? What else will we learn? A history of violence, a strong connection with the area, a loner who finds relationships difficult?" Baxter touched the glass of his spectacles then took them off and began to polish. Without them he looked hollow-eyed and older.

"I was thinking of Geoff Maynard."

"No," Baxter said too quickly. He replaced his spectacles. "Not yet. The last thing I want is a psychologist muddying the water. We've got rid of one or, at least, *nausea gravidarum* has. We don't want another. Let's see what we've got at the end of the day."

It was well known that Baxter did not have much time for psychologists, even one as eminent as Geoff Maynard. Until its disbandment he had been in charge of HOPE, the Home Office Psychological Experimental Unit at Green Park. As far as Baxter was concerned they were detrimental to an investigation. They narrowed the field, called it tunnel vision, and bits of evidence outside that narrow track were lost. Profiling, the concept of the nineties, had gone the way of the magnifying glass. Paul Britton and the judge who kicked Colin Stagg out of court had seen to that. What was more, much of the work was being duplicated at Catchem and the National Crime Faculty at

Bramshill.

After a moment's reflection Baxter said, "But I suppose it wouldn't hurt to find out where he is and what he's up to."

Baxter didn't catch the look of mild satisfaction that softened the DI's eyes.

The fire at Buncefield had been more or less extinguished and the sky was clearing but the smell of smoke hung on like a rerun of bonfire night.

Donna Fitzgerald arrived in civvies: short black skirt, black jacket over white shirt, all of it fitting rather snugly. In the corridor a couple of plods paused to watch her until she turned into the IR then they shared a nod and a knowing smile and a lot of wishful thinking.

Cole sat on the edge of Chas Walker's desk, arms crossed. They watched her approach and Walker's eyes lingered too long on various places between neck and hemline. She cleared her throat, loudly, and pulled his attention northward. Her glare held an icy threat. Robert Peary would have been proud of her.

Cole enjoyed her response. He asked, "What's happening?"

"Surgery is finished but she's still under. I'll get back later. Her mother's arrived."

"Did we get anything?"

"Guv, she's too traumatised to give a coherent account, but she did recognize his aftershave. Unfortunately she couldn't put a name to it. Expensive, though, forty quid a shot. It'll come to her."

Walker said, "He's not short of a few bob then. I make do with Lynx."

"It notices."

Cole said, "Injuries?"

"One breast was all but severed. They've had to remove it. Fifty stitches to the abdomen and severe internal injuries. I didn't have much time. He came at her from behind. It was dark. All she saw was his arm. He was wearing a dark jacket, possibly black. He had his arm around her neck and slammed her into a wall. She thinks she lost consciousness."

"Whatever else you can get will be useful. You know the form. Does she smoke?"

"Not in hospital. Why?"

"If she doesn't she'll be able to tell you if he does. Even forty quid aftershave can't hide it."

She glanced at Walker. "Nor can Africa." She looked back at Cole. "Right, Guv. How long do I stay with her?"

"As long as it takes. It's down to you to get us something useful. Did you get to see Carol Sapolsky?"

"Briefly. Nothing more to add. Came at her from behind. She didn't get a look."

"Try her again, Donna. It's a long shot but if there's a connection between the two women…"

Donna nodded. She hadn't worked with Cole before but she'd heard about him. He came with danger signs. Her sashay from the room was even more decided and Chas Walker found it difficult not to follow. Once she'd gone he shook away her image and said, "Not much."

Cole nodded, "Depends what you're referring to."

"Experience, Guv. She's a uniform. Maybe a more experienced…"

"Forget it. Don't even go there."

Walker was a copper who went through the motions but he would never climb the ranks. Sooner or later he would move over to security which would suit him better. He'd arrived from the army with a squaddie's attitude and six years on the job hadn't made a difference.

Cole headed for the coffee machine. He found Donna standing next to it, head slightly bowed, shoulders stooped, her coffee making waves.

"You all right?"

"I'm all right. I was up late."

"Of course you were."

"And the couple of hours I managed weren't good. Just little things. Some bastard holding me around the neck while he…"

Cole stopped her there. "Right."

"It just got a bit too close. Elizabeth Rayner had everything going for her; looks, job, everything. In thirty seconds, wrong time, wrong place, she's destroyed."

Empathy was beyond Cole. He was a copper. He put a coin in the slot and pressed 13, with and with. The machine groaned and dropped a plastic cup.

Donna said, "Say something, like do you need counselling, or something."

Cole picked up his coffee and raised it towards her. "You're very beautiful, you know that?"

Her face broke into a smile. She said, "Not at the moment, but catch me at the right time…"

Cole smiled back.

"What?" she asked.

"You married?"

She flashed him a ring. A tiny diamond glittered. "Engaged," she said.

"Pity."

The signs were right.

She said, "Yeah."

Cole was updating Detective Superintendent Baxter when DS Peter Ward knocked on the door.

"Boss, a result. One of the instructors at the fitness club has come up with a name. Apparently he's been hanging around for some time, using the coffee shop. Elizabeth Rayner complained about the way he was staring at people and they threw him out. He shouted that he'd get her. Quite a few people heard."

Baxter was on his feet.

They followed Ward to the IR where the team gathered around Carter on the screen. Donna Fitzgerald saw their approach and, remembering her earlier banter with Cole, smiled a quick acknowledgement.

The screen moved upward. Carter said, "Rodney Grant, forty-six. A string of previous. Look at this! GBH, burglary. Bailed. Any takers that he's done a runner?" He hadn't noticed the super. As he made eye contact he muttered, "Right, sorry."

Defusing it, Cole said, "What else?"

"Here we go. Indecent assault and cruelty, two USIs and a sod on an eleven-year-old boy, did three. Got out last year."

USI is unlawful sexual intercourse.

68

Chas Walker muttered, "He doesn't care, does he?"

Cole said impatiently, "Come on, David. Let's have an address?"

"Bail address, Guv. Girlfriend."

Cole nodded thoughtfully.

Walker put in, "Shall I get firearms in, Sir?" The GBH count made the difference.

Baxter spoke quietly, mostly to Cole. "I don't think we need any more Brazilians shot full of holes, do you? They'll just muddy the pitch, as they do. Let's go for surprise. Mess up some paintwork. HET will suffice."

Most coppers treated the firearms support units with a little circumspection.

HET is the heavyweight House Entry Team. They came complete with helmets and shields, secured the house then handed over to the incident team. They were everyone's friends because they took the shotgun in the face.

Cole agreed and glanced at his watch. "Right. Four AM. Everybody here at three-thirty. No excuses." He turned to the super. "Anything to add, Sir?"

Baxter shook his head and smiled briefly. "Let's make this work. Then we can concentrate on Christmas shopping."

The murmur of laughter and anticipation filled the IR but it was edged with disquiet. It was all too effortless. They hadn't worked for it. It was just a feeling, but it was nagging.

There's a road or street in every district known to Social Services and FPU. It's a place where perhaps people with learning difficulties are housed, where the more vulnerable members of society live, a place where children are more likely to be left unprotected. It's also the place where Schedule One offenders take lodgings, among the easy pickings. In Sheerham, that road was Shephall Way.

Police cars making their way along Shephall Way crunched on the glittering surface. Uniforms led the way to the front and rear of number six. They had their batons out and they wanted to use them. The front of the terraced row was well lit by street lamps.

The officers moved in, crouching low beneath garden walls and hedges. The steel ram, the key, was used and, with two thrusts the front door was smashed aside. Then silence was irrelevant. Commands were shouted, lights were thrown on, heavy boots thumped on the stairs and officers crowded into every room. They found two children in the small bedroom, the adults in the rear. Rodney Grant was allowed to dress while his girlfriend screamed abuse. Cuffed and flanked by two eager PCs he was marched to the nearest police car. Lights in neighbouring houses were switched on. More curious neighbours watched from their front gardens.

In the car in front the buzz increased the volume. The bust was great and the anticlimax of the paperwork hadn't yet kicked in.

Chas Walker told Peter Ward and anyone else who was listening, "That tart had so many rings on her face you could've hung a fucking curtain on it." He was referring to Rodney Grant's girlfriend.

In the back seat Donna Fitzgerald remained tight-lipped. At the beginning of the day, just like at the end of it, all men were bastards. Right?

Rodney Grant was scrawny, tattooed, no more than nine stone and no taller than five-seven. And the closest he'd come to forty-quid aftershave was in his girlfriend's catalogue. He reeked of stale beer, tobacco and tooth decay.

Cole's eyes were sleepless. By the time he arrived at interview room 3 he was already shaking his head in the knowledge that they had the wrong man.

He toyed with the notion of giving the interview to Fitzgerald and Carter. It was always a good idea to keep the big guns until later. Watch it through the screen, perhaps. See what the body language told you, the nervous scratch on the nose, the unconscious hiding of the lips, the sweat, that sort of thing. But he needed to move this one forward without wasting time. He wanted Grant TIED so they could concentrate on the real thing.

A uniform stood aside as Cole entered. Donna Fitzgerald sat before Rodney Grant. Grant was smoking, elbows on the table, faded tattoo of a snake wrapped around a knife on his left forearm, not at all fazed. He was a regular and police interviews were no big deal. He was almost bored by the proceedings.

Cole took in the sunken features, the sharp eyes and the lines of corruption that etched his face. He sat opposite.

Grant blew him some smoke and said calmly, "Can we get on with this? I'm tired. I was up early."

"This is a no-smoking area so put that fucking thing out."

Grant's eyes widened. He looked for an ashtray then ground the butt beneath his heel.

He said, "Happy?"

Cole said, "No, I'm not. And most of it's down to little toerags like you."

PC Fizgerald reached to the recorder.

Cole said, "You don't want a brief?"

"No need."

"What do you do for a living, Rodney?"

"This and that. At the moment I'm caretaker at the Carrington. Get you some tickets if you like. You'd get to see Anthea take her clothes off."

"Day before yesterday, around eight in the evening?"

"I was out."

Cole waited. His eyes grew colder.

"Walking, you know? Contemplating the state of the nation, that sort of thing."

"That's good."

Donna watched Cole with more interest than was healthy, but she couldn't help herself. She was in free fall, helpless, caught up in some chemical reaction that was beyond logic.

Cole continued, "I want you to think carefully about your next answer."

Grant looked into Cole's eyes and recognized something he didn't like at all. He shifted in his seat. The lines on his face looked painful. His lips twisted and he rubbed the snake tattoo so that it appeared to slither around the dagger.

"Right," Grant said suddenly. "I've thought. Call it community spirit."

Cole nodded, "That's good. I do like it when the public cooperate."

"What then?"

"Simple. Let's run thought it, shall we? Why were you in the fitness club and why did the instructor find it necessary to ask you to leave?"

Grant pulled a face. "I suppose you know already."

"Maybe, but just for the record."

"By the pool, right? Clocking the latest fashions."

"On the kids?"

"Right, see? I'm into fashion."

Donna frowned. Cole's voice pulled her attention.

"And what about the woman who complained?"

"What about her?"

"You threatened her?"

"Just an idle threat. It wasn't meant. She caused me grief, that's it."

"Now tell me about the evening?"

"Well, what time, eight wasn't it?"

"That'll do to start."

"Yeah, a bit later maybe. Got to do it, haven't you? Pulled in the square."

"Rented?"

Grant made eye contact with Donna, enjoying the moment.

"That's what I mean. He took the money."

"Where did it happen?"

"Supermarket. Car park."

"Did you get his name?"

"I call him Jason, but you can call him anything you like. He lets you choose."

"He's a regular?"

"He's been around."

"A local boy?"

"Maybe. Who knows? No accent on him that I picked up."

"You could pick him out?"

"I could do that."

"You know him well?"

"No, only bits of him, you know?"

"I know."

"What are you? A social worker? What do you care? He's got a

72

menu. Bareback costs an extra score!"

"Have you seen anyone else hanging around the club, a stranger, anything unusual?"

The lips contorted, made the nostrils flare, showed off strands of black hair that would hold the bead of snot. Eventually he shook his head. "I go to the Square to see the kids, don't I? That's all I'm clocking. Jason would know. He knows everything that's going on. Every new face is business, right?"

"That's a pity. It means you're going to have to find this rent boy for me. Let's call him Jason. If you can find him, and if he confirms your story, then you can go home."

"Fair enough. I can do that. He's always there, on the Square. Good as gold."

"Is now a good time?"

Grant shook his head and spread his hands. "It's got to be later, maybe seven."

"In that case you can catch up on your sleep. There's a room downstairs that's very quiet and no one will disturb you."

Donna Fitzgerald had her eyes on Cole anyway, so they didn't need to move. She said, "I'll wake him, Guv." As she spoke she fingered her engagement ring, pulled it up and down her finger and, for just a moment, almost off. Her prior arrangements for the evening to make up for the one she missed—sweet and sour and the rest—never crossed her mind.

Free fall. They call it. And the rip-cord was slippery.

In the corridor she said, "Why didn't you mention Carol Sapolsky. Why not tie up Grant's alibi once and for all?"

"He's not our man. This kid, Jason or whatever he's called, is probably our best bet. We need to find him. Not for Grant. For the other faces he can give us."

"Guv, the sarge knows all the toms by name. It's his patch and he keeps both eyes on what goes on."

"Mike will be out there doing his bit and so will every other copper. But that doesn't mean we can't help. Let's find this kid. You'd be surprised just how much kids notice that adults don't."

Donna struggled, not at all convinced.

Cole reported back to Chief Superintendent Baxter. The super sighed and said reluctantly, "Your earlier thoughts, Rick. Perhaps you better get in touch with your old mate. We've got a psychopath knocking on our door. We need someone to open it."

Cole nodded.

"And you better find out if Margaret Domey's feeling any better. In for a penny, I suppose. If we're going to have these people under our feet she might as well be a part of it. She might learn something."

"It won't be modesty, not from Geoff Maynard."

Baxter groaned and tucked in to a sandwich. Thick smoked ham from Yorkshire with English mustard and real Anchor butter on freshly baked crusty bread—none of your supermarket shit. And on the side, a manly slab of Lincolnshire pork pie. Forget the job, the super was in heaven. His wife knew how to keep a man happy.

So in the happy hour, when doubles were the price of one and pints were pegged at a pound, the coppers hit the High Road and the streets behind where single lights blinked red and where boys and girls from eight to eighty were trading. It was a growth industry; from about four to eight, if you were counting in inches, more if you were black and slightly less in cold weather. Or so they said.

Chas Walker had pulled the short straw and he drove and Rodney Grant checked out the faces and in the back Donna Fitzgerald wondered what the DI would feel like inside her. The thought was exciting, disorientating and heightened by lack of sleep. She wondered whether he was still working. He'd still been in the office when they left and she'd caught a fleeting—speculative—glance. In what was it? Three days? The kozzer in his dark suit had turned her world on its head. She was a teenager again, straight out of fourth form, full of uncertainty, looking forward to bed so she could think slow thoughts of him and nothing else.

This Sheerham is a crazy old place, where people lie in bed alone listening to the person beside them, where heaven wears suspenders and a come-on smile and is suspended twelve feet off the ground. Anthea Palmer, ex-weather girl, lit up in soft neon, looked out across the town. Her stockings glistened and the gap between her thighs sent shivers down the backs of the passers-by. These admen knew a trick or two.

And a queue formed at the box office.

That night, Jason, for want of his real name, took the night off, and they didn't find him.

Chapter 10

The song from the show went: "Oh, Mr Lawrence, I really missed you…"

And incredibly, given the old-fashioned lyrics, it was climbing the Christmas charts.

But Mr Lawrence wasn't aware of it. Mr Lawrence agreed with the colonel: pop music was for drug-takers and men with rings in their ears.

Mr Lawrence was not fashion conscious. He considered the vagaries of fashion were such that if you wore something long enough then, sooner or later, it would become the height of fashion again. He agreed with the colonel that the fashion houses were in league with the Germans to bring back, sooner or later, the Nazi uniform. He was, however, rather taken with the latest fashion, the miniskirt that was shorter than ever and, in particular, the naked navel—the young firm flat navel, the slightly swollen navel, even the coloured navel and the navel that glinted in gold.

It was mid-afternoon on a depressing December day and the shadows were sucking at the light and leaving the rest dirty. The trees, those that grew from the pavements, were bare, and the colour, both on the ground and above it, was grey. Three couples were in his shop, taking their time to stand before the paintings, whispering. Art galleries were like that: people whispered. There was the spell of the library about them. People forgot that they were shops.

He was discussing frames with a middle-aged couple when the brass bell on the heavy door announced the arrival of a young woman and he saw her for the first time. She breezed in with a blow of winter and Mr Lawrence filled his chest and smiled a secret smile. She was tall and slim, her face partly masked by large spectacles that fractionally enlarged her eyes, dark eyes that fixed on him like the eyes of a big cat eyeing potential prey. While he finished with the couple she flitted from piece to polished piece and from canvas to glinting canvas like a shop-lifter, pretending to examine, more intent on who was watching her. For a few moments she stood gazing up at an old chestnut cooking pot that hung from the painted brick wall and then a large painting of a brick wall itself caught her eye and she moved to that.

The middle-aged couple finally chose a frame for their painting of ducks flying from a green pond and once they had gone the woman moved to the counter.

A thick woollen ruff on her sweater held her jaw high and tramlines of green wool ran over her slight breasts and hugged her waist. Pleats fanned out from her cream-coloured skirt and reached below her knees. It was clingy and tantalizing and yet oddly demure and old-fashioned. Beneath it her calves were on the slim side and she wore white sneakers. Her mouth was wide and thin, the top lip slightly askew, slightly down-turned. Her face was firm, her nose prettily upturned, her cheekbones prominent and her jaw-line solid. Black hair trailed down to the small of her back.

She moved easily, gracefully, accustomed to the flat heels, her long thighs moving against the cream. She was five ten or eleven but looked even taller in her slender frame. There was something youthful about her, her features, her movement, her fitness, which made her seem even younger than she was, which Mr Lawrence put at around the late twenties, and there was a sign of perplexity in her bright eyes, as though this moment was perfect but the next uncertain.

On her long finger were two rings, an engagement and a wedding, and as she placed her slim, almost bony hand, on the polished counter, he noticed that they were slightly worn, fifteen or twenty years old.

Mr Lawrence gave them a long look and shrugged before looking up to meet her.

Her fixed gaze softened to a perfunctory yet nervous smile and in a voice that was full of London she said, "Mr Lawrence? Can you help me?"

Of course he could.

"Photographs lie," he told her.

As he made his way to The British, hugging the pavement beneath the slate-grey sky and the grey slate roofs and the stacks of clay chimney pots lined up and reminding him of an advancing guard of the 15th Hussars, he reflected on the encounter.

Photographs lie; the shadows give a false impression. They find form where there is none and nothing of subtle form. And what is more, they will never probe beneath the surface for hidden expression, they will never explore a sensation or the temper of either the artist or his subject. There is no art in a reflection. If there were then a mirror with its reflection would be a work of art. The art lies entirely in the passion behind the image, the discovery of the truth, or the lie.

She frowned, puzzled, and threw him a look that indicated his sentiments were wasted.

But he continued.

A camera will give you the moment, something that might bring back the memory, if you like, but nothing more. And what is more, it will not give you the truth of the moment, or the lie, and it won't live and breathe and excite you. And what is even more, ultimately it will leave you cold, wanting more.

They'd already discussed the fee and it didn't seem to bother her. She'd offered a deposit that wasn't necessary.

"I understand you take on commissioned work," she had begun.

"Sometimes I do. Sometimes, when I am not busy."

"Well, are you busy now? My friend Helen…"

"Mrs Harrison."

"Mrs Helen Harrison," she agreed. "Showed me the painting you did for her. My husband liked it, rather. I thought, perhaps, it would make a nice Christmas present."

"Ah, Christmas, yes, it's coming. But my dear, the oil wouldn't dry in time. We'd be pushed to get all the sittings in."

She seemed downhearted.

He scratched his chin and said, "On the other hand, perhaps…"

"Oh, could you?"

"The portrait of Mrs Harrison turned out rather well. I was rather pleased with it."

"Well then, will you fit me in?"

"I will have to check my diaries."

"You have more than one?"

"Dear girl, you might not know this but there is an increasing demand for original work. People are fed up with vacant prints and copies. Framed in expensive frames it is only the frame you pay for."

Another couple in the shop looked across as he turned up the volume. The thought of prints had always raised his voice.

They discussed sittings and arranged the first. He wrote it carefully in one of his diaries.

"What shall I wear?"

"Wear? Clothes?" Now Mr Lawrence looked downhearted.

"Oh, you didn't think…? Not like Helen, for goodness sake?"

She blushed. He hadn't seen an Indian blush before and it tickled him.

He said sombrely, "I see. Or rather, I shall not see."

Her eyes narrowed.

"Low heels," he said.

She walked from the shop. The pleats of her cream-coloured skirt swayed gently with each certain step. The old-fashioned bell rang out her exit and a block of chilled December air came in to fill the space.

On the cold road to The British a Jehovah's Witness or some other such nonsense stopped him in his tracks, a spotty teenager in a cheap suit. His bright smile and wondrous eyes offered to share the secret of life. "Can I show you the way to true happiness, Sir?" An American or Canadian accent came at him from between flashing white teeth.

"Don't be absurd." Mr Lawrence made to push by.

But the boy from the New World persisted and his teeth flashed again. "Have you ever thought about our Lord Jesus, Sir?"

As Mr Lawrence groaned, lost for real words, the youngster saw something in his eyes that unsettled him and he at once stood aside.

"Have a nice day, Sir," he said then moved away, quickly.

On the road to The British Mr Lawrence thought of the girl again. She wouldn't go away; she'd become an imprint and stamped herself over all else.

"You said your husband liked it, rather. Is that rather than you?"

Her eyes had narrowed fractionally; each held the glossy mahogany-coloured reflection of her prey. Her lips parted in a sudden smile and revealed a line of straight white teeth. These people from the subcontinent and Africa have such wonderful teeth, thought Mr Lawrence, as he tightened his lips. People from the USA had wonderful teeth too, but they paid for theirs. Theirs had been…manufactured.

She had said, "Yes, I liked it too. You caught her expression just right."

"Which expression was that?"

"The one on her face."

"Of course."

When she walked from the shop the cream pleats of her skirt swayed gently with each step. The cloth, tight on her boyish behind, clung to her every move. The old brass bell rang out her exit and the cold air rushed in and he shivered even though in his chest there was something beginning to beat again.

He made a decision. It would be Madras tonight, after the pub. The girl had left him with the curious flavour of India.

Much later, when he ordered, he was still thinking about her. "Chicken Madras with Sudan One, Para red, Orange Two, Rhodamine B and red chalk dust."

"Ahhh! You are speaking of illegal additives, isn't it? That is a very fine English joke, Sir." The waiter leant forward and in a conspiratorial tone added, "You will be noticing that I am serving the salt in these very small dishes. That is because somebody has stolen all my salt-cellars, isn't it?"

Once a week he closed the shop at noon. His usual custom was to have lunch at The British then go off to spend his hard-earned, Brown-taxed pound, but the woman was due for her first session and that meant everything was going to be hurried. Still, it meant a change to the routine: shop first and then lunch.

The way women change your life. A little flash of the eyes, a beguiling smile, a hint of coyness... The colonel was right. They should come with a health warning.

Beyond The British, perhaps a hundred yards or so, was Robot City, a supermarket owned by one of the country's richest families but it didn't sell much kosher food. Maybe they didn't shop in their own shops. Maybe they knew something. In Robot City, with its forty tills and plastic merit cards that kept a note of what you ate and how many times you defecated—assuming that you used the average seven point four squares of Andrex a time—the robots shopped. They shopped for buy-one-and-get-one-free and nutritionally balanced diets containing all the additives and chemicals that were absolutely safe for human consumption.

As he paused by the fish counter he wondered whether the fish farmed around Sellafield tasted any different, perhaps hotter, and whether one day they might leap from the Irish Sea as a ready-cooked meal.

Most of the chippies had been taken over by the Chinese and maybe that was the reason the fish and chips never tasted as good as they did in the old days. Even so, it was beginning to make sense. There was, after all, a lot of salt used on the chips.

In the vast superstore he checked out the new Colline collection of cropped trousers which were ideal for the beginning of pregnancy but could also be worn right through to the ninth month. They were made of poplin, which would gently expand to fit the shape of the eighth-month figure. They even had one-piece swimsuits for expectant mums that came with lined gussets. They had maternity nighties and bras with efficient support and briefs made of supple elastic. They even had creams and lotions to eliminate stretch-marks. It was marvellous what was on offer nowadays.

But it was a pity about the fish and chips.

Sid the Nerve, Nervous Sid, was in The British. He watched Mr Lawrence walk in and then said miserably, "It's funny how life turns out."

Mr Lawrence regarded him for a moment and said, "Yes, you're right." He deposited his heavy goods in an alcove and sighed relief and rubbed his hands together in an attempt to regain some circulation, although, it might also have been in anticipation for it was lunch-time. A pub lunch-time. Real gravy and cholesterol you could taste and pellets of sweet corn and molested tomatoes with everything. Pub cooking cooked by fat housewives with aprons tied around their bristly armpits was the cornerstone of Darwinian theory. They'd been growing families on it since life began without a bottle of Filippo Berio in sight—tit first and then lard the old-fashioned way.

He asked the girl behind the bar, "Tell me, my dear, do you peel the carrots?"

She rested her chin on her hands that were spread on the bar and looked up out of doleful eyes. Behind her the reflection of her tanned thighs and trim behind slid around the curve of a thousand bottles. A magnificent sight and a stirring thought to go with the pub food. Life would have to go some to get better than this. Her lips toyed with a dead smile and she said, "Not personally, Sir. I serve the drinks as you can see, but we always wash and peel all our fruit and veg. Why do you ask?"

"There are more chemicals in the skin of a supermarket carrot than they've got on the shelves in Boots."

She nodded her fascination and said, "How interesting."

In the background Roger crossed his arms, braced his legs and beamed her a smile that she must have felt on the back of her head.

Mr Lawrence said, "I'll have the beef curry please, with rice. No chips."

"That's an excellent choice, Sir. Would you like a drink with your order?"

"Yes, I think so. Would the water that comes with my Scotch be mineral water or…?"

Her eyes grew. He had never seen such honesty in a pair of fluttering eyes. "Our mineral water comes all the way from Scotland, Sir, from a place called Dounreay…"

Albert and the colonel nodded to acknowledge him. They didn't smile. Rasher flicked him a sideways flick of the eyes. He didn't smile or nod. He tilted. His two minders rushed to stand him upright again.

Nervous Sid oozed up to him. Short and thin he melted on to a bar stool while Mr Lawrence waited for his drink. He was West Indian and wracked by shakes. Perhaps Parkinson's shakes. He shook a ring under Mr Lawrence's nose. A valuable ring, he told him, which he could have for twenty pounds. Five pounds was his last offer. Five pounds and the knowledge that Albert wouldn't get it.

The last bit was tempting.

Albert's eyes sparkled mischievously. "How are you getting on with young Paul?"

Mr Lawrence said, "It's cold enough to snow out there."

Albert put his nose in the air and returned his attention to the colonel.

Mr Lawrence could have told him that he hadn't seen much of Paul, that the lad had gone out at six last night and hadn't returned until the early hours. But his room had been transformed. He'd been shopping. God knows how he got his money or, come to that, the shops to open at that time of night. His wardrobe was filled with a selection of jackets and jeans and slip-on shoes, all with designer labels. He'd got himself a TV, DVD recorder and converter box. He'd spent the whole of the morning rigging a dish and running cable. He was stocking an awful lot of gear for such a short stay. Seeing that he was something of a handyman Mr Lawrence asked him to run a cable to the shop window.

"A warm Christmassy light on the display of bronze ballerinas might look nice."

"No problem, Mr Lawrence. Leave it to me. I'm the man, see?"

He'd gone out again just before Mr Lawrence left for the supermarket and Mr Lawrence took a peep into his room. It wasn't nosiness or anything like that for the door had been left open. There was a cardboard box full of baby things, Pampers and Huggies with their price tags still attached, Milton, rattles, counting blocks, teddy bears and baby-growers. And a whole bunch of baby-wipes.

But the lad was proving quite useful. Mr Lawrence could have told Albert all that.

"Noticed the police were out in force last night, raiding the flats," Albert commented.

The colonel asked, "What were they looking for?"

"Missing women."

"Oh," Mr Lawrence said, absently. "Did they find any?"

"Plenty of women," Albert sniffed. "But none of them missing."

"All this business," Nervous Sid said. "Missing women, and the two that were attacked, just around the corner, man, it's turning brother against brother. We should all learn to kiss and cuddle like they do on the football pitches. All this trouble is no good, bad for the digestion. You can feel the tension out there. It's not good."

"I know," Albert said. "I can feel it too, out there. Or it might even be in here."

The colonel said, "As long as it's only the women, it could be worse."

Roger said, "Well, I hope you keep all your kissing and cuddling outside. I won't have it in here."

Sid the Nerve shook his head despondently and moved off shaking his ring.

Once he'd gone Roger said, "I'm thinking of banning the blacks..."

Albert shook his head. "Not possible with the race relations. You'd end up in court."

Roger continued, "...along with the Jews."

Albert turned to Mr Lawrence. "So, snow? I feel the chill, too."

At the shop Paul was helpful. He helped him unpack the shopping.

"Walnuts, Mr Lawrence, and shoe polish. You've already got shoe polish under the sink."

"You can never have too much shoe polish."

"You've bought lots of walnuts."

"Walnuts are the thing, Paul. They lower the cholesterol."

"Well, I didn't know that."

"And you've always got to put one in the sock you hang up on Christmas night."

"Oh, Mr Lawrence, does that mean I'm staying for Christmas?"

"Now, now, Paul, I didn't say that, did I?"

Downstairs Paul proved even more helpful. "I'll keep the shop open," he said.

"There's no need, really."

"No problem, really. It's getting close to Christmas. You never know. In any case, now we've put the walnuts away, I'm doing nothing else."

"As you like," Mr Lawrence said, secretly pleased.

"One thing, Mr Lawrence?"

"What's that, Paul?"

"Last night, late, I heard babies crying. It was coming through the walls."

"That will be the cats. I've heard them myself. When they cry they sound just like babies."

"Oh, that's all right then."

The woman from India or Pakistan or Luton, arrived at three-thirty five, five minutes late.

Mr Lawrence believed that punctuality marked the man—and the woman.

"What about the specs? I think I'll take them off."

"As you like," he said, still smarting.

"I'm long-sighted. They're bifocals. People wouldn't recognize me without them. What do you think?"

"I think I'd recognize you without them. But perhaps I don't know you well enough not to recognize you."

Her glance was quick and questioning.

"Off for now," he added, softening a little. It was difficult to maintain severity before such an engaging face. "We can always change our minds later."

Carefully she removed her spectacles, folded them and slipped them away. In the rich brown of her eyes was a challenge. Taking off the spectacles had removed the innocence. The bridge of her nose was slightly marked, as though she wasn't used to wearing them.

The thick green drapes behind her were going to lend their value to her skin tone. Her brown dress was loose; the pleats and folds presented a pleasing contrast.

She spoke from the side of her mouth. There was no need to keep still. When discomfort had set in maybe he would tell her.

"Have you painted for long?"

"Since before you were born."

"You used to teach?"

"Ah! Mrs Harrison told you that."

"Yes."

"It was a long time ago."

"You taught art?"

"Among other things."

"What other things?"

"Biology."

"I didn't know that."

"Why should you?"

"Why did you stop?"

"To concentrate on art. I still take small classes here. I find it more satisfying. And of course, working for myself, and shutting up whenever I feel like it, the holidays compare, although the teachers do edge it."

"You take classes in here?"

"There's room for five or six, eight at a push."

"Is there a particular age group?"

"Yes, indeed. We don't cater for children. They find it difficult to concentrate."

"It sounds interesting."

"Yes, it does."

"How much do your lessons cost?"

"There is no charge. It's more of a club. The members buy their materials from me but there's no obligation. They get them at cost in any case. The club charges a small annual subscription but you'd have to ask the treasurer about that. I am not a member. The subscription goes toward outings and transport. This summer, for instance, they spent a day in Essex discovering Constable, that sort of thing. Some of their work hangs in the gallery. It's not very good, really, but I show willing."

"When we are through you'll have to show me."

"Yes, I'll have to."

"You used to teach in school?"

"Yes."

"Why did you give up teaching?"

"I told you, to spend more time painting. And I discovered that I didn't like children. Do you have children?"

"No. I have a Labrador."

"Do you work?"

"In personnel or, rather, HR. BOC."

"I know it. In Wembley. How long have you been there?"

"Since school. Over ten years now."

"And have you been married long?"

"Three years."

"Is your husband in the same line of business?"

"No. He's in marketing. In the city."

"Do you have hobbies?"

"I play badminton."

"That's good. It's good to have a sport."

"Do you have a sport?"

"No."

"My husband's a runner. Weekends. Sometimes, I go to watch him run. Cheer him on."

"I bet he likes that. I don't know any runners. I've been out, painting, and they've run past. But they never stopped. Do you live far from here?"

"The Ridgeway."

"Of course, near Mrs Harrison."

"Well, Mrs Harrison isn't there at the moment. She's gone off somewhere. Mr Harrison is quite worried."

"My goodness, I bet he is. I hope she's not another missing woman. We've got enough of those. Hope we don't see her picture up in the bus shelters."

"How long have you lived here? Do you live here?"

"I moved here in the mid-eighties. There's a small flat upstairs, enough room for one."

"You're on your own, then?"

"I suppose I am. Apart from the lodger."

"You have a lodger?"

"Yes."

"It's good to have company."

"You think so?"

"Don't you?"

"I've been on my own so long it takes some getting used to."

"You never married?"

"No. No one would have me."

"I don't believe that."

"Every time I got close to a woman she disappeared."

"It's not a joke, Mr Lawrence."

"I wasn't joking."

"It's frightening."

"It's never frightened me. I suppose it should. But it doesn't."

A wide belt pinched her dress at the waist. She had an awkward hip that gave him trouble. There was a sharpness that needed smoothing. Part of the problem lay in her deportment. Her weight was on her heels, her shoulders dragged slightly forward to compensate. The main cause was a flat masculine behind. It wasn't in the picture but it took away the natural curve to the hip.

There were a couple of other areas where he could help out too. It depended how charitable he felt when it came to the detail. It depended on the mood and how ugly it was on the day.

Off the studio was a small kitchen with a sink and tea-making equipment. But he didn't make tea. He opened a bottle of red wine. While he fought with the cork the voice of his new assistant carried in from the shop. Moments earlier the doorbell had struck.

"Hang on! Hang on! Here it is: Reclining Nude on Red Settee with One Arm. Done by a geezer named Reynolds. What I can tell you about him, mate, is that he spent his life doing copies of Goya's... You know? Innit? This tart wasn't just any old tart. They were close. I mean very close. He must have changed his mind about her arm."

Red wine splashed into glasses. Mr Lawrence shook a wondrous head.

He carried two glasses into the studio and found her leafing through a pile of unframed canvasses on the worktop, part of the last batch from the Far East. She was thoughtful, tight-lipped, critical. She had resisted the temptation to examine the new canvas on the easel and that amused him. The idea that unfinished work should not be seen is only valid when the technique is wanting. Second-raters in life needed secret time to botch.

He handed her a glass. "It's Merlot-Malbec, one of my favourites."

"Did Helen drink wine?"

"Mrs Harrison? Always, before a session got too involved. It unfastened her inhibitions—not that she had many—and it added a delightful tinge to her cheeks. And for me it freed up my knife... My brush strokes. Red wine, my dear, is a necessary part of the procedure." He glanced at the paintings she'd been studying. "What do you think?"

She pulled a face.

"One or two are all right... They seem so similar. I'm not very keen on landscapes."

"They are factory paintings."

"You didn't paint them?"

"Good grief, woman!"

"I've hit a nerve."

"More than one."

Later, carrying a glass of red wine, Mr Lawrence paused by his lodger's door. Paul was talking to himself. The incoherence of it all left Mr Lawrence exasperated with a despairing view of the future. The situation was quite hopeless. The schools were churning out halfwits with fists full of worthless certificates. The teachers themselves could barely speak the Queen's English. He moved to his grimy window and peered out. He needed to have a word with his window-cleaner. His standards had fallen along with those of the schools, along with those of the whole of the country, a downward spiral, the result of old age. The magnificent past had become nothing more than a few dusty words in a second-hand history book that the teachers never opened.

Santa Claus was in the street on his mechanical sleigh, collecting for the Martin's Home for Gifted Children and Asylum Seekers Anonymous. The sounds of a scratched recording squeaked out "Have Yourself a Merry Little Christmas." In the shop windows and stuck to bus shelters were posters of runaway children and missing women and donkeys being hanged and a jazz group that was gigging that night at The British.

Chapter 11

There was a flagstone floor around the bar in The British where, if you were lucky, you would stub a toe. The stone gave way to red Kidderminster carpet, or that cheap alternative popular in two-star hotels and, with nothing better to do, time could be spent in joining the dots left by careless cigarettes.

Once a week, at the far end of the boozer's endless bar where the carpet gave in to a wooden-floored dancing area where the youngsters congregated, a band provided live music. Tonight it was a band called Jodie Foster's Boyfriends. For the regulars, it was a stressful time. It reminded some of the older customers of an air raid. Nervous Sid's foot would begin to tap and Luscious Laura, Mrs Puzey's gorgeous daughter, would begin to dance, usually by herself. She was probably following her absent father into the music business. She would clutch a bottle of Mexican Corona Extra with its slice of lemon—no lime in Roger's boozer. At such times her laugh was feverish; no noise, just lips drawn back over sparkling Afro-Caribbean teeth while the black bits of her eyes spread over the colour.

"The additives in the orange squash, it is," Albert said, unaware of Charlie lined up in the Ladies', his voice almost lost in the din.

"Never had that trouble in North Africa," the colonel shouted. The boyfriends, all girls, were really going for it. "Jungle juice. Pure dried oranges. They didn't use chemical warfare on them then, just DDT. Monty ran the Eighth Army on DDT."

"The orange squash cut out," Albert confirmed. "The additives, youngsters can't take. E-numbers, they are. E for extinction and exit. The very least you can expect from E-numbers is hyper something. And good that's not. The Eskimos think of. They are hyper something but with a capital H. They get their E-numbers from the fish. And the fish get them from the North Sea oil platforms. It's from the bottles of orange squash that the oil workers throw over the side. Tonic water feed them instead."

"And that," the colonel cut in excitedly. "Will keep the malaria away. It's difficult bringing up kids. In today's world even more. We didn't have drugs in our day. Apart from Woodbines. In our day the nation produced first class soldiers. They didn't go around moaning about cocktails of drugs. They got on with it. Dug in. Took what the krauts threw at them. No Common Market in those days. Nothing at all common about the krauts. They were good soldiers, let down only by a predilection for fornicating with their own mothers and eating children. We brewed up. Lived on bully beef. How old did you say Paul was?"

Mr Lawrence replied, "I didn't. He's about twenty-five but acts a lot younger, as a lot of people do."

"Difficult age," Albert said reflectively. "When I was that age it was difficult. Wanking took up most of my time."

The colonel agreed. "In the army we used to stop the wanking with jungle juice and a standing order. And there was a chemical that they added to your tea, but I forget the name." He nodded in agreement with himself.

"A sex destroyer," Roger suggested.

"Exactly," the colonel said.

"They should have tried married life, mate. Better than any chemical known to man."

The colonel's nod was despondent. "The thing is," he said. "Age is the enemy. It's not like the krauts. You can't beat it. You can't run at it with a bayonet and shout 'Have that you child-molesting jerry bastard!' It creeps up on you, more like a Nip or the taxes in a Brown budget, and you don't see it coming."

A stranger standing between the colonel and Rasher cut in: "With regard to Paul, it sounds a bit like schizophrenia or something similar."

Albert asked, "What about the something similar?"

"Yes, you're right. I didn't mean similar. I mean he sounds like a raving schizo."

They were all ears. Even Rasher managed a series of blinks. The stranger, well turned out in a suit and dark coat, had a bedside manner about him and an acceptable accent from the home counties. He was probably a doctor or a double-glazing salesman.

The colonel cut in, "Don't know about your schizophrenia but it seems to me that half the country is off with stress, the twenty-first century cop out. What's wrong with a good old-fashioned backache or even ME?"

"Ah, indeed," the stranger said. "Myalgic encephalomyelitis, also known as CFS, chronic fatigue syndrome. Caused quite a stir a few years back with half the establishment denying its existence, much like schizophrenia some years before. Mind you, even now, much of the establishment along with many old soldiers still believe it's a malingerer's charter."

They looked at the colonel who nodded his agreement. "Just like stress, then," he said. "Just like the vaccines and the Gulf War syndrome. We never complained about DDT in the porridge. So long as they kept it away from the old undercarriage we were happy."

"Mosquitoes?" Albert asked.

"In the desert? No. It kept away the flies. The real soldiers, the professionals, didn't mind the flies. You could always find an Arab by following the flies. And if you could find the Arab you could find the kraut. The krauts liked to fuck the Arabs. Little bits of information like that won us the war."

The stranger shook a bewildered head and went on, "The popular press and Hollywood, Hitchcock in particular, created the misnomer of the multiple personality but that has more to do with dissociative identity disorder than schizophrenia. The split personality is very unlikely, largely unfounded. Schizophrenia was originally called dementia praecox—mental deterioration in the early life—praecox. Usually a sensitive, retiring child who starts to develop peculiar behaviour in his early twenties, hallucinations, delusions, general withdrawal from society. When it occurs in later life it generally takes the form of a persecution complex—paranoia." The stranger swept back his greying hair. It was the narrow sideburns that worried the regulars. Beware of men with narrow sideburns and those who don't look you in the eye. The regulars were, however, all ears.

"A steady mental deterioration," Albert said gravely. "Cured can it be…cured?"

"Doubtful. In some cases drugs can help. Then there's electric shocks and cold water treatment. Then there's leucotomy. Crucifixion, as a last resort, cures it once and for all. But that has nasty side effects—religious wars and stuff like that."

"But the voice…?"

"Yes, there is generally a voice."

"And violence?"

"Sudden violent outbursts, certainly. Can't have a half-decent mental disorder without violence."

Roger, the manager, something of a movie buff, said, "When Alfred Hitchcock released his *Psycho* back in fifty-nine, the critics thought it was a joke on them. That at the end of the first reel he killed off his leading lady. That wasn't the done thing. Their cosy world was shattered."

"Shattered I was too, when that scene I saw," Albert said.

"It's a good thing to shatter the critics," the colonel said. "They're as useless as an Eyetie soldier. Having said that, Hitchcock was one of my favourite directors. I also liked David Lean and Robert Young."

"Robert Young?"

"He did that tele thing, *GBH*."

"Television doesn't count," Roger said. "It never did. Not when you're talking movies. Not even if their movies are better. My favourite film is *Paths of Glory*, a Kubrick movie. Every time I see that last scene where the German bird sings, I cry."

"You cry?"

"At the movies, I do. In real life, that's different, I don't."

While he had listened to Roger the colonel nodded and his eyes dulled as he recalled another day. He said, "When my wife was alive I had about two thousand films to watch—videos in those days. But by the time she had watched her soaps and all the other crap that was on I was too tired to start a film. I thought about installing a television in the other room but then I'd never have seen her. An odd consideration, but once she died, I couldn't be bothered watching the films. Came here instead."

Roger said impatiently, "Get back to the point. What's your favourite film?"

"OK then," the colonel said. "I liked *Ice Cold in Alex* with John Mills."

Albert was sheepish. Finally he admitted, "All right, all right. *Fun in Acapulco*."

Everyone took a step back from Albert and waited for clarification. Albert sucked on his thin lips and, although there was nothing remotely Gallic about him, shrugged a Gallic shrug, playing for time and all the time wondering if he'd made a terrible mistake.

"Well," he said nervously, "He was a nice lad."

Unfortunately this explanation, when all was said and done, made things much worse. Roger wandered away to the other end of his long bar, the colonel bristled from indignation and Mr Lawrence wondered who the nice lad was but one thing was certain, Albert was left quite alone.

He was out when Mr Lawrence got in. The following morning he was running in the electric cable. The electricity distribution box in the stair recess was open and a coil of black cable snaked out towards the shop. It was a worrying sight and Mr Lawrence was rightly worried. He reached the door when an almighty crash had him ducking for cover and for a moment he wondered if one of the colonel's krauts had followed him home and lobbed a hand-grenade. The shop lights went out without a flicker and Paul yelped and a bronze ballerina in the shop window pirouetted off her stand.

"It's arced!" Paul screamed. "It's arced!" He vaulted from the recess and crashed into the wall opposite and, as he slid slowly southward, smiled sweetly at Mr Lawrence.

Mr Lawrence thought back to the conversation in The British and wondered whether the double-glazing salesman's electric shock treatment might help.

Nervous Sid was in The British, Sid the Nerve, playing the devil's drum on the bottom rung of his bar stool. He worried that the DSS or whatever they were called nowadays had cancelled his weekly benefit. How would they like to be black with a little receiving form? It was all right for them with their index-related pay, but what about him? They treated illegal immigrants better than they treated him.

Nervous Sid turned to children; they were on his mind. The ASBOs were a complete waste of time and money; they had become a badge of honour. The kids actually felt out of it if they didn't own one. Nervous Sid agreed with the colonel. The answer to their worrying ways was a sharp stab in the arse with a bayonet and then three years in a detention centre fed on nothing but green veg, sprouts if possible. No orange squash or trips out to holiday centres.

Children—they seemed wiser, more mature, less child-like. The boys were ill-natured, rude little gits and the girls had contemptuous, knowing eyes. Even twelve-year-olds knew what made the world go around. They looked as though they were waiting to get a little bigger so they could pay you back. A frightening thought, the thought of growing old and defenceless, and the only thing to do, he supposed, was to get them first, before they grew up. Devastating, really. It was all these fucking chemicals in the crops. All these E-numbers the colonel and Albert kept going on about. They were modifying the kids and not in a good way. Sod these GM crops. Sid the Nerve would take more notice in future. He made a mental note that if ever his luck changed and his number came in, he wouldn't buy a motor car from those bastards.

He went on to explain that when he threw stones at a group of them who were climbing on his garage roof they threw them back again. And they were better shots. He lifted the plaster on his cheek to show Mr Lawrence the damage. They were aiming at his eye, he said, because he was black. They were still on his garage roof. He'd made a speedy retreat. The long way round. Sod that for a living.

Then he said, "Is that Paul still with you?"

"Yes, I suppose that Paul is. Although, technically, he's in hospital at the moment."

"Kids?"

"No. Electricity."

"Oh." He sipped his shaking pint, spilling a little down his chin. His foot-tapping quickened in tempo.

Mr Lawrence prompted, "Why do you ask?"

Nervous Sid's attention returned from parts of the barmaid.

"Someone was asking about him. A very dodgy looking character. Fact is, dodgy isn't the word. Not really. Not at all. Dangerous is probably closer. Fucking dangerous closer still. A big bad bastard."

"My goodness. What did he want?"

"He said he wanted Paul."

"Did he say what for?"

"No, he didn't say and I didn't ask. You don't prolong the conversation with people like that. I wanted out. Like…out. As soon as poss. Registered mail. Know what I mean?"

"Did you tell him he was staying with me?"

"Of course not. What do you take me for?" Sid the Nerve shook out the words, saddened by the suggestion.

On his way to the door Mr Lawrence passed Albert and the colonel and Rasher who stood studying the tearaway nuts between the bottles.

"Mr Lawrence, a moment of your time," Albert muttered. "For young Paul someone's been looking. An unsuitable type. With more care you should choose his friends."

"Did you tell this character that Paul was staying with me?"

Albert's eyes glinted and his half-hidden lips widened. "Of course."

"That's kind of you, Albert."

Mr Lawrence left The British early to visit Paul at the hospital. He didn't mind making the odd sacrifice. He picked up a brown paper bag of grapes from a Pakistani shop that opened all night, every night, even Christmas night. He had Christmas lights in his window next to a photograph of Mecca.

Green seedless grapes, brown-bagged, cheaper than Tesco and guaranteed by the foreign gentleman not to contain the fungicide Vinclozolin.

Isn't it?

The Salvation Army were playing near the hospital entrance, belting out Jerusalem, and a few patients who could walk or manoeuvre their wheelchairs had gathered to listen. Sensing danger, Mr Lawrence hurried past the uniformed women who were brandishing their collection boxes and *War Cries*.

Paul sat up straight in his bed, a lonely figure, his gaze haunted, focussed on the hills that his feet and knotted knees made on the blanket. Under the wash of the bright strip he looked pale. Patients in the other beds were involved with their visitors. Paul was in another place. Not in this world.

"How are you?"

His eyes came back slowly. They slid towards Mr Lawrence. Nothing else on his body moved. It took a few moments for recognition and then he smiled and turned and caught up with his eyes.

"Mr Lawrence."

"How are you?"

"Mr Lawrence?"

"You're looking better."

"Mr Lawrence, what are you doing here?"

"I brought you some grapes. I should have posted them."

"You shouldn't have."

"You're right. The postman might have squashed them."

"You shouldn't have bothered coming."

"You're right again. How are you?"

"I'm fine. Just fine. They're keeping me in overnight. I'll be out tomorrow. It's the heart, irregular or something. The shock, I expect."

"I expect it was."

"Funny that. They use electric shocks to start a stopped heart and they use a pacemaker to keep a heart ticking over yet electricity sent mine the other way. Funny."

"Yes, I see what you mean. But changing the subject for just a moment, someone's been asking about you."

He frowned.

"A big chap. A big…chap."

Paul sighed and shook his head. "You didn't tell him I was staying with you?"

"No. No I didn't and nor did Sid."

He relaxed.

"Albert did."

He grimaced. "Everything's going wrong," he said. "Stuck in here innI? Haven't got time to find a place. Christmas's coming, you want me out by the weekend and now that bastard's looking for me."

"Who is that bastard exactly?"

"Someone I lived with."

"My goodness, come again, exactly what does that mean?"

"Inside, Mr Lawrence. Prison overcrowding, innit? You don't get a cell to yourself. Not unless you write books or something. I knew him inside, see. Shared a cell."

"And now he's outside. Is he dangerous?"

Paul shrugged white bony shoulders.

"Why is he looking for you?"

Paul looked up appealingly and said meekly, "He's in love with me."

"Love!"

"He thinks he is. He probably is."

"Love! Goodness me, now that's a complication I hadn't considered. Do you love him?"

Paul pulled a face. "Leave it out, Mr Lawrence. Do I look like a rear admiral?"

"I can't answer that, dear boy. I wouldn't know what to look for. I have often wondered how you tell."

"I think it's an earring in the left ear, or it might be the right."

"I shall look out for that."

"Or it might even be both ears."

"Forget the ears, Paul."

"He forced himself on me. Inside, you don't have a choice. You stick your arse in the air or you get beaten senseless and your arse goes in the air anyway."

"That's terrible but that's all right then. Now I know that, you can stay until Christmas, Boxing Day I mean. No longer and, only if you make yourself useful in the shop."

His face softened in gratitude. "I won't be no trouble. Honest. I'll teach you to play chess. I'll do the cooking. I'll look after the shop. I'll get us a Christmas tree with lights."

Mr Lawrence shook his head in wonder. Today's youth! Who'd have them with their erratic enthusiasm and marvellous ambitions?

"Chess. I'll settle for chess."

"I'm a master at that, innI? The old Reti, the old King's Indian. Sound as a bell, that, that is. You saved me a lot of worry."

"Worry?"

"I was thinking about the turkey in the squat. They keep turning the electric off, see?"

"Well, I hope my electric is back on by then."

"No sweat, Mr Lawrence. I've got this mate…"

"No, Paul. NO. I'll use the Yellow Pages."

"Right."

"But what about this rampaging lover?"

"Come again?"

"The bastard?"

"Yeah. He could be a problem."

"You'll have to break it gently."

"Yeah."

"That his affections are not returned. It's a sad business when love is not returned."

"Sad, yeah, that's it."

A nurse walked through, stern and alarming. She paused at the end of Paul's bed and glared at the two of them. Mr Lawrence busied himself with the grapes, slipped one in his mouth and stuck it in his cheek. The nurse shook her head and went on her way. Mr Lawrence watched her go. There was something about women and uniforms. There always had been, he supposed, ever since Boudicca had been riveted into her breastplates.

By the time Mr Lawrence left the hospital the Sally Annes had changed their tune. They had moved on to While Shepherds Watched but the women, striding about flat-footed, were thrusting their *War Cries* and collection boxes with even more aggression. To get back to the bus stop and to avoid the women Mr Lawrence was forced into a detour around the block.

Lunchtime the following day there was bad news to come in The British. Rasher had given the road outside a crimson glow. The tarmac had been washed in claret.

Bad news like that was enough to turn a man to drink but the woman was coming later so that would have to wait.

Rasher was a casualty of the night.

It happened last night, shortly after Mr Lawrence had left.

Behind the bar, between the ranks of down-turned bottles riding on their 25ml measures—seventy proof rotors—the packets of tearaway peanuts waited to be plucked from their card. Beneath the nuts was a photograph of a naked lady and every time a packet was pulled a little more of her was exposed, a ready-salted nutritional striptease. So far on view there was one perfectly formed breast with a sixpenny nipple and three-quarters of a thigh. Next to the nuts was a calendar used to note the up-and-coming darts tournaments and December's photograph was of a bullfight in Spain. The nuts and the calendar hung directly opposite Rasher's usual position at the bar. And when Mr Lawrence left him the night before, there he was studying the girl, perhaps remembering his wife, then blinking at the bullfight, and then he gave his minders the slip and went bullfighting on the main road. And the bull got him.

His minders were now in mourning.

The bull, a silver 306 turbo-charged diesel Peugeot, driven by a social worker, had hit him and dragged him fifty yards along the steel railings.

Albert was a late arrival that lunchtime. He arrived only moments before Mr Lawrence. His stoop was more apparent, his shoulders rounder. He'd spent a large part of the night searching the road for the gold that had flown from Rasher's broken body. Albert was a prospector. He'd found a finger, he told them, but it was the little finger, the only one of Rasher's fingers that didn't sparkle. Sod's law, really.

"We'll have to tighten security," the colonel said seriously. "They got to him. She got to him. Lured him on to the rocks, or rather, into the road. Beware of the women's sweet song."

Mr Lawrence interrupted. "She left him."

"Exactly!" The colonel refused to see the point. "She left him knowing that he would be destroyed. My God, how I hate women. They never fight a single battle face-to-face, bayonet-to-bayonet. They come at you in the night, in the dark, in the back. Listen to an old soldier. Stay away from them. Just like the wops, really. Women and wops have a lot in common." To a young woman in a hugging black dress behind the bar he shouted, "You there, you with the Polish accent, another drink if you please." And while she poured it he kept his eyes open for the possibility of poison. He turned as Mr Lawrence put on his hat. "Are you off, then? Is it that time already?"

"Yes, it is. I have an early sitting."

"The woman?"

Paul must have told him.

"Yes."

"Good grief! You be careful. Take care. Can't stand any more casualties at the moment. Not until we get some reinforcements. Watch your back."

"I'll try to."

He left them to their mourning.

Two customers were waiting for his return. Three if you counted the woman. She stood aside while a young couple chose a painting: ducks flying from a pond surrounded by trees in grand seasonal decay. Even as he wrapped it and wrote their card number on the back of their cheque he cringed at the thought of it hanging anywhere outside a garden shed.

"Ducks!" he said to her once the brass bell had announced their exit. "My best seller. Ducks, and then tigers and horses and dogs and, of course, Oriental women with breasts bared. I ask myself what it is about ducks that make the masses want them flying up their living-room walls? They ruin hundreds of quite reasonable landscapes. But there you are. Ducks sell."

He led her into the studio.

"What is it about you today?"

She settled into her pose.

He wagged a finger. "There's something different. Let me guess. You're standing straight. There's a spring to your step. There's a glow to your skin. What's happened? You're messing about with my values."

"What is your favourite colour?"

He shook an irritable head and said sharply, "That's got nothing to do with it," and then, after a pause, he relented and all but whispered, "Yellow." He nodded. "Yes, yellow is good. That's the colour of the future."

"I'm sorry. Gosh, you're always so grumpy. Perhaps it's not me at all. Perhaps your temper has changed, your eyes clouded with red. They do look red."

"Perhaps. Maybe. But if that were the case then things would be darker, not lighter."

"You've had a bad day?"

"All days are bad. This one is worse."

"So it's true that the artist suffers."

"A sense of humour too, along with the spring. That's something else I hadn't bargained for."

"I want to change my pose. Is that all right by you?"

She slipped that in and took him by surprise. Knife and palette suspended, he stood rooted while his colour darkened.

"Will it mean starting over?" Her eyebrows raised over laughing eyes. Was she teasing him, by golly?

Her shrug was a little caress. "If we can change our arrangements so that you're paid by the session, or something like that, it shouldn't much matter. And I do so want you to catch me…just right."

Eventually, a small tremble spread up from his knees and he seemed to come alive again. He said, "Christmas is coming. There won't be much to wrap."

"There is always Easter," she said and gave him a broad smile. She sat on the sofa and leant back, lifting her legs so that her dress fell away to reveal an expanse of thigh. "Something like this," she said. Her thighs were slim and tanned, brushed with the colour of her copper-brown dress. Her skin radiated the heat from two glasses of Cadet. He was down to his last bottle of Merlot-Malbec and kept it back for later, for when he was alone again and could brood over the session.

She said, "I wonder what happened to Helen?"

"Mrs Harrison?"

"Yes, Mrs Helen Harrison."

Twice the sitting was interrupted by customers in the shop. Paul's absence was a nuisance—most inconsiderate of him—and slightly puzzling. He should have been home by now. Mrs Puzey arrived with her family and cleaning equipment and during the next hour while flying dust was cornered and lemon polish stung the air, he hid in the studio and continued with the painting. The woman had gone and left a curious hole.

The painting was coming along. The blocking was complete, the key, the composition, and the shape was pleasing; the sweep of the hip, the depth of one smooth thigh as it curved in against the other, drew the eye to the shadow caused by her dress.

The noise had ceased. The old bell had rung out a beautiful silence broken only by the sounds of tapping on the studio door. The door eased open and Laura glided in. Laura, she glided everywhere. A black streak of cover-girl potential hugged by a tight black skirt. A wide shiny belt bridged her skirt and a loose crimson top. No naked midriff for Laura. Not a hint of that firm, flat landscape with its glittering *omphalos*. Not that he had any reason to believe that she wore a belly-button ring but he could fantasize as well as anyone. More to the point, Laura was fashion conscious and mutilation was the fashion.

There were none of the flatlands of the Chinese delta about Laura, no paddy fields by gosh, more the lush hills of West Africa, he would say, or some bursting volcano in the Philippines. Somewhere jolly warm, anyway.

Her glossy lips widened into a tropical smile. There was a breathless honesty in Luscious Laura, the black vixen of The British, unusual in women, for there was no threat. No threat at all.

"Mr Lawrence," she said.

"What is it, Laura?"

"The phone went. You didn't hear it."

"My hearing isn't what it was. Who was it?"

"Paul, it was. He's gone now."

"Ah, Paul."

"He phoned from the hospital. They're keeping him in an extra night for observation and there's nothing to worry about. He didn't want you to worry."

"Thank you, Laura. I'll try not to."

With a flourish she closed the door behind her. The air, still stirred by her breathless words, was touched with Wrigley's Spearmint.

Having got used to the idea of Paul's return a slight disappointment drew in with the evening. Even the short walk to The British seemed stale. There was little sense of anticipation. He knew that the feeling would change. A few drinks would change it. In the pet shop window a hamster was going nowhere as it raced a plastic wheel. A bit like the customers in The British.

In The British Rasher's absence hung heavily. In the early evening the barmaids were even more indifferent as they contemplated their evening shift and the majority of the punters were on their way home, a swift half of courage to get them there. These were not serious drinkers. These people had families and were simply keen on a slight delay, a little pause in the perfunctory day before their perfunctory evening, the slack-shouldered clock-watchers, the would-be trainspotters who were merely passing through.

He was early. The familiar faces had yet to arrive.

The malevolent day was drawing to its close and alcohol, that treacherous friend of the lonely, would speed it on its way.

"Good riddance!" he said and the barmaid in a tight black dress blinked and looked over the bar at him as though he was mad. She was quite right, of course.

Beneath red-flocked wallpaper with its nicotine-stained edges they'd begun with 6 and 7, moved to 23 and 26 and finished with lychee and fresh mango. Two bottles of Wan-King, the house white, proved slightly more satisfying than its promise.

Laura came back from the loo. He noticed the dilation of her pupils and her sudden elation.

Laura giggled, wasted. The Wan-King was lethal; drink enough and you'd go blind, so they said, that's why the Chinese squinted, but that was probably an old Chinese wives' tale. She let him into a secret. "Paul asked me to look after you. He thought you would be lonely. That's why I made an exception. I normally keep to my regulars. I owe him one for the tele and video he got me. The DVD is coming, on a promise. He's so grateful that you put him up and for the grapes that he wanted to give you something in return so I agreed to perform a little trick for you, later. I have a whole box of them, Mr Lawrence. A whole box of tricks."

He lifted an overblown eyebrow. Leaving the tricks aside he knew a thing or two about boxes. Get to his age and, if the memory was up to it and that had a lot to do with diet—plenty of mackerel and walnuts and Heinz Tomato Ketchup—most men could remember the odd performance when they might have excelled. Even so, he was rather crestfallen and stuck out his lower lip. Eventually he said, "So it wasn't a coincidence then, our meeting in The British?"

"Mr Lawrence," she giggled like a teenager contemplating her first blow job. "Grown-ups don't believe in coincidence, do they? Come on. Swallow these and lighten up. You're much too dark."

Still downhearted Mr Lawrence said, "And what are these?"

"A bit of Adam, to use an old-fashioned term, that's all. Down them with your wine."

"All of them?"

"Go on, be an old devil."

"Well, perhaps this once, and only because it's been such a dreadful day. I'm not a druggie, you know? I'm not one of your long-haired surfers from Newquay."

"Come on, Mr Lawrence, take me home. Let me tuck you in and blow out your candle."

"I have electricity. It's back on, no thanks to my lodger."

"Yes, he told me about that."

"How about a cup of coffee and a brandy and we'll leave it like that?"

"As you like. It's all paid for anyway."

"Where does Paul get his money?"

"Who knows? Why do some birds hop and some birds walk? Why do some birds come and some birds can't? Who knows? But I have enjoyed talking to you. Maybe, one day, you could teach me to paint. I would love that. There is something about watching an artist work, you know, painting, that's really like, a turn on. I don't know. Understand?"

Perplexity pulled down his hairline. He said, "No. Not a word of it. It sounds like balderdash. But it doesn't matter. One day, Laura, I will teach you to paint. But you have too much living to do first."

As though she hadn't heard him she continued, "It's like, creating. That's it. Going after perfection. You should paint me, Mr Lawrence for I'm as close to perfection as you can get."

"I know that, Laura. My goodness, I can see that. But you're the wrong colour. Only the members of the Caucasian race can be perfect— pale white-skinned people. People like me. God made us in his own image and he was white, wasn't he? Sunday school teachers don't tell lies. Whiter than white with flowing blond curls and a perfectly trimmed beard. And his only forgotten—begotten—son, was even whiter, even after forty days in the wilderness. And no matter how I look at you, and in what light, you're not white and you certainly don't have a beard."

"Oh, Mr Lawrence, you've been looking in the wrong place."

He chuckled. "I've no answer to that."

"You might have later, if you play your cards right."

"That's the problem. I've never been a card player."

"Well, there you are then. They say unlucky at cards lucky in love."

He was pleasantly drunk and so was Luscious Laura. Her eyes were black and intense.

"I have another confession to make," she said coyly. The pretence made her even more delicious.

"What was your first? Remind me?"

"Paul, for goodness sake. That we didn't meet by accident."

"Oh yes, all these confessions. I feel like a priest."

"Those pills, they wasn't all disco biscuits. It was Paul's idea. He said you'd need them."

"What have I been fed, exactly?"

She blew out her cheeks and eventually admitted, "Two were adams, and they'll get you all loved-up, but the other two were Viagra, Mr Lawrence, and they'll keep you up all night."

"I'll probably have a heart attack. I can feel something throbbing even as we talk. You've deceived me, Laura, and I should be angry but I'm not."

Everything was outrageously funny: the total on the bill presented by a puzzled waiter, the look on a flattened duck's face in the window and the sign hanging on the huge brick Pentecostal walls opposite, the one frequented by Mrs Puzey and her tribe, which read CHRISTIANS, SING OUT WITH EXULTATION.

Even the sting of the night air could not dent their gaiety and it came as a surprise when suddenly he said, "I hate Christmas." But the twinkle in his eye gave him away. "It reminds me most of chocolates in bright sparkling wrappers and the orange and strawberry creams that are always left in the tin?"

"I like strawberry creams," she said.

"Yes," he said. "I thought you might."

Between the brandy and the coffee was the colour of her skin. Colours seemed deeper, all of a sudden. She wasn't going to go; she made him lock the shop door and turn out the shop lights and then she peeled off her green pants.

"Buttons! Mr Lawrence you've got buttons!"

"I'm an old-fashioned man, Laura. No till, no TV, no computer, no wireless and definitely no zips!"

"What's a wireless?"

She fiddled with his buttons then said, "Oh, Mr Lawrence, look at me now, I'm playing the mouth-organ. I'm following my old man into the music industry."

"But he disappeared, Laura. I hope you don't disappear."

"Like the missing women, you mean?"

"Exactly, but my goodness, you're right. I can hear the music. I'm finding it quite stirring, even patriotic in a strange sort of way. A bit like going into battle, I suppose."

After a while she stood up and licked her lips and he noticed that her pubic hair was different; to begin with there was more of it, with isolated tufts floating upward toward her navel, tiny tropical islands on a sea of rich Robot City tea. It all looked silky soft but felt quite coarse. The skin around her tight stomach had lost some of it's pigment: a harsh stiff-haired brush would do it; burnt sienna over West Indian sepia.

He was, nevertheless, looking into a black hole. And that was dangerous. Back in 1979 when Margaret Thatcher was in power and the USSR invaded Afghanistan, Disney had lost a fortune looking into a black hole but their special effects weren't nearly as good as these. But as Einstein had calculated, some time back, there was no escaping it. So Mr Lawrence didn't try. Not really.

"I can't. I can't," he said, not really trying.

"Yes, you can. You can. There, didn't I tell you you could?"

She was a furnace, a slippery furnace. And he was sweating. All at once sounds seemed louder. He could hear the rustle of her hair, a little moaning from her lips, the slip-slap of things farther south.

"Let it come," she said with burning breath. "It doesn't matter. Feel my stomach against yours," she whispered against his ear and he felt it turn wet. The sensation wasn't altogether pleasant. Water found its way into his ears very easily. For that reason he never went swimming or put his head under in the bath. Luscious Laura went on, "Feel my thighs against yours. Feel my perfect breasts with their perfect nipples brushing your chest. Tell me if you can, that all this isn't worth twentyfive quid!" And then quickly, like someone selling insurance, she added breathlessly, "No hidden extras. VAT—vagina, arse and tits—included in the price, and there's ten percent off for pensioners."

He laughed out loud.

"What is it? Is it something I said?"

She settled back against his arms, the hint of spearmint and wild flowers quite agreeable.

But the spit in his ear was still giving him trouble.

He said, nevertheless, "You know, Laura, without speaking of looks, you are very beautiful."

"Yes, I do know that, Mr Lawrence."

She snuggled closer and closed her eyes, safe. Her breath was soft and warm.

He fell asleep thinking that he ought to kick her out before he did. When you are older courtships should be longer. It takes time getting used to waking next to a nightmare: open mouth slobbering and spitting, zoo noises rattling, breath corrupted by life. Younger things smell younger and taste fresher. Older people should get out before falling asleep. It saves the younger people unnecessary brain damage in the morning.

And yet, and yet, it was too late now, for he snored a satisfied snore.

His erection woke him for it was so unusual. Pounding. Detached. Sweat poured from him and collected on his chest, a salty pool, another Dead Sea. He felt utterly wrecked. The sex tonic was taking its toll.

There is always a price to pay, old timers would tell you, and they knew a thing or two. If it happened again—and you never knew for even this chance came out of the blue—he would stick to walnuts and red peppers and what was it? Ah yes, Heinz baked beans with sausages in tomato sauce. An old-fashioned tin that needed a tin-opener; razor sharp lids that could slice off a finger and often did.

Life is so…grey, without the red.

He heard his own voice. "My goodness, what's happening?"

The dark vixen leant across him. "It's all right. You had a dream. You shouted out. Golly gosh, Mr Lawrence, what horror world do you sleep in?"

"I'm all right. Just a dream, as you said. I disturbed you. I'm sorry."

"Don't worry. It's only four. Only half way through my shift. Shame to waste it."

She was still glued with him and her, more of him, than her.

"Did you hear it, in the night?"

"Hear what?"

"It sounded like a baby crying."

"It was probably a cat. They sound just like babies, in the night."

Her breasts brushed over him, her nipples traced cool ticklish paths across his chest, through the pool. Her hand pulled him gently against her curls and she whispered, "We can try something else if you like. I can turn over if you like and you can try it that way or, if you like, I can eat you."

"Gosh, a second coming, and some say I am not a religious man. But that's the trouble with Chinese food," he said, making time while he made up his mind. "You want to eat again so soon afterwards."

He gave in to her first suggestion, that dark taboo. Perhaps because it housed that tighter place and tightness was the thing. And pain, of course, for there it lay. That fine flame-throwing moment, that swift stab of bliss, for just an instant, too short an instant, and then it was gone and then, only indulgence mattered.

But it wasn't easy, even with Luscious Laura, whose stumps had been shattered by a thousand googlies. But the pills she'd fed him had produced a wicked leg-break, and she squealed quite loudly, loudly enough for him to worry about the neighbours on the growing Richmond Park council estate.

His concern for the neighbours ended abruptly as an explosion of light from a large torch held them in its silver beam. Behind it the dark outline of a huge man was just visible. The stocking on his head rounded his shape even more. As the giant figure approached Laura yelped and dived beneath the sheets. But she could still hear his voice, filled with muffled accent. It might have come all the way from Leeds, or some other God-forsaken place.

"Where is he? The two-timing bitch!"

The sheet was ripped away leaving them cowering, quite defenceless. The heavy torch rose above them and the crazy beam zigzagged across the room before at last settling on Laura, first on her quivering breasts and then on her quivering curls. A giant hand reached down to part her legs and the beam focused its full intensity on her sticky wicket.

"It's a girl!" The muffled voice was full of surprise.

The torchlight went out. They heard heavy footsteps on the stairs, then someone falling and cursing and then movements in the shop below and moments later the brass bell ringing out the slamming of the shop door.

"Blimeeey!" Laura sighed her relief. "Who was that? Did you know him?"

Beside her, Mr Lawrence breathed his own relief. "No, I didn't."

They crept down the stairs to the shop. The blinking neon opposite, red and green, threw the shadows of the ballerinas in the window on to the far wall. They danced. The paintings gathered the light and the painted faces glinted grotesquely. Their bodies glowed red and then green and the green picked up the muscle tone and deepened the hollows.

"How did he get in? I saw you lock the door."

"These thieves of the night crawl through the crack beneath the door. Even the trusted brass bell let me down tonight. We need garlic, lots of it. It won't keep out the burglars but we can throw it at the cats!"

He threw the bolt on the door and turned back into the shop. She'd perched herself on the counter. Her legs dangled. The volcanic light poured in, framing her in its glow.

"Everything's so red and fiery down here," she whispered. "Just like hell."

"It is hell, my dear. You can smell the sulphur, hear the clank of chains…" He pointed to the faces in the paintings and then up to the overhead tackle. "See!"

The red turned to green and she became a corpse and her slick became a rotten streak of pus. He shivered at the unholy sight that, of course, was holey too, and he held his breath, waiting for the light to turn again and fill her veins with blood. As the red took hold she smiled at him, wistfully. "Come on, Sir Lancelot, you've frightened him off, whoever he was. Bring your helmet and, if you think you need it, your shield, and let's go back to bed."

The grey December light crawled in with the dawn, adding its gloomy touch to the bedroom. The windows were frostbitten even though the central heating had banged throughout the night. The bedroom was warm and stuffy. In her sleep she had thrown off the bed covers and lay naked, face down. Her breathing was gentle, her sleep untroubled by the creeping light.

He wondered whether he'd snored and checked his chin for froth. His hand remained dry and for a while he lay there pleased with himself.

She looked paler, mixed with buff-yellow. From the hollow of her back the curve of her behind was breathtaking. There could be no finer single line. Stroking it seemed natural. His stalk was still alive, stabbing at the air, made immortal by nocturnal witchery and a handful of pills. He wondered how many men had been inspired by such delight, how many had been led to disaster while drunk on such abandon. He was, nevertheless, aware that the circadian clock was ticking. He was feeling jet-lagged from his ride with Laura, or it might have been the pills, or the unlikely excitement of the night. Whatever it was, with the exception of his dong that was out of control, he was beginning to flag. Even the bedroom door opening made no difference to that.

Paul's face appeared, bright and early, his happiness reaching through the specks of dust held in the heavy air.

"I'm home, Mr Lawrence. Let out early for good behaviour. Gosh, Mr Lawrence, you should be proud of that! A Kodak moment, without a doubt."

The spell faded slowly, leaving Mr Lawrence befuddled. He tried to smile politely but it wasn't easy. One of his hands rested on Laura's behind, the other was full of his enthusiasm for it.

Paul looked from right to left then settled on the bed again.

Mr Lawrence said, "How in God's name do you people get in? I bolted the door!"

Paul winked. It was obviously a trade secret.

Chapter 12

The day before Paul discovered he had not much in common with Michael Faraday or Georg Ohm, DC Anian Stanford stood in Jack Wooderson's office in Hinckley Police Station.

"Why me, Guv? I'm part of the team."

The inspector liked the Guv bit. It tickled him. He also liked the fact that Anian Stanford was standing before him looking faintly manhandled and fragile. He enjoyed the moment, stretching it out. He flicked a speck of white from his uniform. It might have been dandruff, but his face was flaking too. The dark blue threw up everything that was wrong.

"I'm sure we'll manage, Anian," he said, not even trying to conceal his delight.

She looked over his desk piled with paper. Muddled, disorganized, it mirrored the man. She sat down without invitation and smoothed her skirt over her knees. A defensive move. The thought annoyed her. She said, "That's not what I meant."

Wooderson wanted a cigarette and thought about a walk to the garage. He said, "There's someone out there who doesn't like women, that's all I know. You must have heard."

She nodded. Of course she'd heard. Half the world had heard by now. One woman had a breast cut off and another needed fifty stitches to keep hers on.

"And then there's the bomb. They're stretched, calling in all the spare. We'll give it till Monday. If nothing breaks by then I'm afraid you'll have to go. It's out of my hands. DI Cole is due in this afternoon. I'll confirm it with him."

She coloured up, reddish-brown, hardwood, hard as hell.

Wooderson loved it. It stirred a memory. But that was wrong. The thought was always with him, day and night. Her bony thighs wrapped around him, her groin pressing against him and her hair, flashing along her parting, black as coal and charged with static. It was a gutless sensation. Like bereavement but worse. Time didn't make it easier. Not when he had to see her every day and listen to her conversation with the others, particularly Butler with whom she had formed some kind of attachment.

"Look," he said. "Believe it or not, I don't want to lose you."

"Why don't I believe you?"

"Anyway, even if you do go and, there's still what, three days? If anything breaks here you'll be back. I'll bell you personally. I've still got your number somewhere."

He'd said it for a response, nothing more. Control could get her day or night. It went with the job. You couldn't get away from the job. She said sharply, "Does your wife know you've still got it?"

Wooderson grimaced. The mention of his wife dulled the memory. "Get out of here. Go and iron something. Maybe that chip between your shoulder blades."

She glared across the desk.

The coldness between them, the result of fall-out, the radiation of bodies that had got too close, felt like the curious chill of too much sun. Looking at him now, nicotine stained, ruffled, even a faint trace of dandruff on the blue, she wondered what she'd ever seen in him. Even his aftershave hung around like a cheap cigarette. He looked like a civil servant or a banker who knew there was nothing else till retirement. That sort of acceptance dragged on the face as well as the soul. And the booze he drank the night before and, from the bottle in his desk during the day, came at you from every pore and every breath. Before long, she knew, he'd be history.

But right now, that wasn't soon enough.

She left him looking gloomily out of the first floor window. The city that he could see was dripping under a belt of cloud, the colour of a body on a PM slab, once the blood had been hosed away.

DC Anian Stanford was convinced that Inspector Jack Wooderson was a loser, a man who'd climbed one rung too many. Sooner rather than later he would be found out. Unfortunately, she found out too late.

In a vindictive sort of way, the way in which lovers part, she looked forward to his downfall.

Her origins lay in the subcontinent, but they were long gone. Thought of occasionally, particularly now that Asians were winning Booker prizes and making inroads into films and TV, but it was more out of sadness than anger. She never wanted to wear a sari, for Christ sakes, but she never knew where she belonged. She called herself British and, that's what her passport said, but the British—the English in particular—never accepted that and never would. She was born in England and raised in England but that didn't mean a thing to the English, whoever they were. But whoever they were they identified with one another and foreign looks and language and ways were not included. They were islanders, removed from the rest of the world. As far as they were concerned she was from over there, somewhere, and owned a corner shop or a takeaway. And the sooner she got back the better they'd like it.

She had never known her parents. Just hours old she'd been found outside a Catholic orphanage. Anian had been written on the cardboard box. For all the nuns knew, the box might have carried exotic fruit from Asia. Anian might have been the name of a prickly pear.

At a year old she'd been adopted from Our Blessed Lady's Home by the Stanfords, an English, Catholic, working class family that had a ready made sister for her. Lisa Stanford was two years older and white but in those days blacks and browns could go to whites and no one had a problem. Fucked-up adoption agencies and left-leaning social workers had still to have their day.

When she walked from the small office she found three uniforms and a detective sergeant waiting. There were a dozen more uniforms at Hinckley but they were out, on the streets or pulling nights. The four men turned toward her, asking the question. They all knew about her affair with Wooderson.

"I might be seconded to HQ," she said in a downbeat voice that came at you full of London Town.

DS Sam Butler tut-tutted the idea. He was the only man on the team she trusted. She could talk to him and know that it would go no further. With him there was no innuendo, no eye contact that went on too long and meant something else, no flirting whatsoever. Talking to him was like talking to family. Safe and easy. And predictable. Once Cole had gone and dinner had finished the booze had made conversation easy. The baby had cried and she'd seen him as a father. Some men, not many, were made for the job. Sam Butler was one of them. She'd wondered fleetingly, what sort of father Cole would have made. Not very good, very absent, was her guess. She'd held the baby. Lucy. Arms and legs and big eyes that had stayed blue and a little smile that was wind that kicked you in the middle.

"When?"

Butler's question dragged her back. "Monday, unless we can come up with something new. Oh, Sam, we've got to. This is a real shit."

"Don't worry. We've got a few days yet. I'll think of something."

The DS gave her his best smile of encouragement but it wasn't convincing.

She lowered her voice, "Jack's being an absolute arsehole."

"Expected nothing less, did you?" Butler resisted an impulse to mention office affairs and shrugged. "Men of his age, and mine come to think of it, we tend to panic when we know it's all gone by and there's fuck all in front."

She threw him a grin. It came from nowhere and changed her mood and his. Still smiling she said, "How can you say that with Lucy and all?" She turned toward the door. "Think of something, Sam. Quickly."

"I will, but in the office you shouldn't be so familiar—you'll get people talking and they do enough of that already. You should try sergeant or DS Butler or even skipper. I'm easy."

She turned back. "You've always been easy Sam." She stuck out her tongue. It was pink, girlish, and caught Butler right where it hurt.

The door swung shut.

Hinckley nick was quiet; it was that time of the morning, the uncivilized hour, the time when milkmen filching double rounds started out. The few patrolling coppers were parked up in their favourite corners, taking turns to close their eyes. A PC on the front desk yawned and stretched. It was close to the end of his shift and he was winding down, as he had been for the last two hours. The desk phone rang. He listened for a few moments then pressed hold. Or at least he meant to. Instead, he cut the line.

"It's Missing Persons, Sarge, about a message sent this afternoon."

Sergeant Mills groaned. He'd been hoping for a quiet end to the shift, now paperwork loomed large. He said, "Missing Persons? At this hour? Are they taking the piss, or what? Who filed it?"

"Came from next door. Sam Butler."

"Well?"

"Well what, Sarge?"

"Well, what do they say?"

"Oh, yes." He examined the note he'd scribbled on his pad. "They've made a link with these missing women and two more out of area. The other two are pregnant."

The Sergeant shook his head. "Pregnant? Are you sure it's for us? Sounds like a wrong number to me. I'll tell you what we'll do. We'll leave a note on DS fucking Butler's desk asking him to get back to… Did you get a name?"

The kozzer drew a quick breath.

"It's always a good idea to get a name, son, particularly if you're going to ring them back. Stick with me. You'll learn something every day."

Margaret Domey was based at Sheerham and known in the office as the psychologist from hell. When all five-four and slightly swollen belly of her breezed into the nick the duty sergeant pretended to be doing something else. She wore a grey two-piece, low heels, and thin lips. She wasn't unattractive and with her slightly fuller figure a lot of the kozzers took more notice than usual.

As she made her way to Cole's office uniforms stood aside and in the IR the conversation died and male defences went up along with the eyebrows.

"Margaret."

"Rick."

"Are you back?"

"Tomorrow. Heard a rumour about Geoff Maynard. Tell me it's not true?"

"It's true, but it has nothing to do with your absence. I'll show you."

Cole led her back into the incident room. The team pretended to be hard at it, paperwork, screens, not looking up. She took in the action boards and skimmed through the crime reports before shaking a bemused head. "Interesting. What does Geoff say?"

"Nothing yet. We'll see."

"But he is coming?"

Cole shrugged.

"He'll come. Sex and violence, it's irresistible. Of course he'll come."

In Cole's office again and with the door closed she said, "I did think he was in the past. It was a comforting thought."

He smiled easily, "I know what you mean."

She said tightly, "He got too close last time. I'll make sure it doesn't happen again."

"A lot of us feel the same way but the second attack sealed it. You should take a closer look."

"Tomorrow. I'll have a look tomorrow. They're letting me back for a couple of hours a day."

"Sam's been on. He'd like you to spend some time at Hinckley. The missing women."

"That old chestnut. For goodness sake, he's got—"

Cole cut her short. "He's got an idea or two. I think you'll be able to help him and—"

"And Sam needs all the help he can get. Tell me something new?"

Cole smiled. A couple of weeks with her head down the pan hadn't softened her at all.

"How are you, Margaret?"

She narrowed her eyes. "You want it in one?"

"Go for it."

"Pregnancy is shit. Don't let anyone ever tell you any different."

"Sounds good to me."

Her eyes narrowed further. "I know why I like you, Cole. It's your sense of humour." She smiled. Her lips filled out and for just a moment she looked just right. "I'll see you tomorrow. Right now I'm going to make the most of today. I'm going to spend some money which is every woman's favourite pastime. I've got my eye on a very old chestnut cooking pot."

Cole remembered that she had an interest in antiques. He guessed her home was cluttered with old things and that there would be little room for a child.

"You know the shop, down the road from the Indian? The Gallery?"

"I know it. Never been in, of course."

"Of course. But that's where I'm going now. I want the chestnut pan. But I want the feel-good factor too. I want to spend."

Cole laughed. Maybe he liked her, after all.

There was another man on the way whose feelings toward her had never been made clear. And she was frightened of him because he knew too much. He was the only man in the world who had ever made her feel inadequate. More than that even, for she had been quite happy with the subservient role. And now, with Geoff Maynard's return more than just a possibility, her feelings were edged in apprehension. There was the challenge, certainly, but with that came the possibility of failure. And failure, for Margaret Domey, was not an option.

It was some time later when the phone rang and Margaret Domey featured again.

"Ricky?"

"Yes."

"John Domey."

"Hello, John. How are you?"

"Good. Listen, old boy, you haven't seen my wife, have you? She mentioned she was popping in."

"Yes. This morning. Is there a problem?"

"No, not at all. It crossed my mind she'd got involved in something over there and forgotten the time. You know how she is? Once she gets involved with work everything else goes by the board."

Cole waited for more.

"We had an appointment at the hospital, that's all."

"Nothing serious, is it, John?"

"No, no, no. A touch of blood pressure, a scan, nothing serious. But I expected her back. She's probably gone directly there, forgot that I was going to go with her. You know what she's like."

"Of course. She stayed a few minutes. She was going off to buy… Hang on, it will come back to me."

"A nineteenth-century cooking pot."

"That's it."

"She's had her eye on it for some time. There's a place on the dining-room wall that's been earmarked."

A silence came between them. Something cold caressed Cole's back. He said, "John, get back to me, will you, when she shows up? I'd like to know that she's OK."

"Will do. Absolutely."

Cole hung up, considered the call for a few moments then glanced at the paperwork in front of him. He sighed. This wasn't police work. It was something, but it wasn't police work.

Mid-afternoon Butler found the note from night shift and made the call.

When Anian arrived just after five he called her to his desk, showed her the note and said formally, "They went missing in Mill Hill four years ago—Melanie Brown and Sophie Whillis. I'm going to go with Cole on this. We'll concentrate on the pregnancies. You check the index, I'll check Catchem and Mill Hill."

Catchem controlled the national database on sex crimes and killings of girls and young women.

He went on, "And that painting in Ticker's living room…"

"It was porn."

"Art, girl, art. But obviously Helen Harrison spent a long time with the artist, right? Just a thought."

Anian hesitated then said quickly, "Actually, Sam, I've already paid him a visit. He's painting my picture."

Butler frowned. "Go on?"

"I said I was a friend of Mrs Harrison, saw the painting and wanted something well... Not like that."

"You didn't flash your warrant card?"

"No. Should I have done?" She fell in and reddened.

"You should have told me. We're supposed to be a team, Anian."

"I know, I know. It was such a long shot. You're not angry?"

"No, surprised. It's done now. What's he like?"

"He's an old man, sixty or thereabouts and old-fashioned, weird but harmless. I've got a couple more sessions booked. If nothing else comes of it I've got a painting. He's really very good."

Butler nodded. "OK, see how you go. But keep me informed." His voice didn't betray him but apprehension edged into his thoughts.

They worked through the evening towards the last bell. Eventually Butler called a halt. His mood had lifted. He said, "Come on girl, I'll buy you a drink. Just in case you do get transferred you better know where the watering hole is."

She checked the office clock. "You seen the time?"

"I know this little place that's open all night."

Chapter 13

The White Horse was thick with smoke and the smell of smoke and booze. Dog-ends spilled from ashtrays and glasses stuck to sticky tables.

It was a British boozer.

A smoker's bar.

It was a place that, like many that coppers frequented, hadn't needed an extension to its licensing hours because they had never been observed anyway.

It was, therefore, an hour after the last bell had closed the doors and pulled the curtains on the dim lights. The place was busy with stale kozzers on the back-end of their shift doing what kozzers did best and that meant that the jovial old owner with his proud belly hanging over his leather belt and his sour-faced, thin-haired wife were full-time pulling pints and jerking shorts. There were a few others in the bar beside the policemen, good-as-gold regulars who made no noise when they left and wouldn't even cough if they thought it might cause offence, and that was good enough.

Big Billy Fisher owned the White Horse and ran it with his wife Doreen and their scrawny daughter Diane. Diane was in her early forties, had been around the block a few times and was looking decidedly rough around the edges. Rumour had it that back in eighty-five she had serviced a van load of coppers on the way north to the miner's picket lines and since then she'd been treated like royalty. Even now they called her princess. At the last count she had used up four husbands and been divorced three times. Her last husband had gone AWOL and was last heard of chasing youngsters in Thailand.

Chas Walker, leather jacket and gold earring glinting in the light from above Big Billy's bar, pursued that important meaning to life that women found so difficult to understand and said soberly, "Christmas ale, right! Four pints, right, and my fucking head nearly fell off!"

David Carter was enthusiastic. "I'll have some of that, then."

Peter Ward glanced at his watch for he had not long been married and said with more reticence than would otherwise have been the case, "That sounds like a cracking good idea."

Chas Walker, ex-army, REME, went on, "You need it strong to put up with the job nowadays. In our squad we've got two fucking dyslexics that take twenty minutes to read a caution and a Muslim who stops chasing villains to get his prayer-mat out."

Their conversation took an unlikely turn as they saw a tall rangy man carrying his drink toward Cole's table.

Walker frowned. Company and Cole didn't go together. Not for a while.

Martin James nodded as memory put a name to the face and he put them right. "That's Geoff Maynard," he said soberly. "A dangerous bastard."

"Him and Cole together," Walker mused for he had heard the stories. "Should be interesting."

Martin James nodded and, as his eyes dulled, he said seriously, "Maybe, as long as you don't get caught in the flak. And there's always plenty of that." He was remembering back to another case when rules were written for someone else.

Geoff Maynard found Rick Cole at a table at the back, partly secluded from the bar and the woodentops by a couple of thick timber stanchions treated to make them look ancient. They'd even got some dummy woodworm holes drilled in. It was a barrier of Cole's choosing.

Geoff Maynard said, "What are you going to do when they ban smoking in public places?"

"They wouldn't dare, would they?"

"You never know with these clowns."

"God save us from the meddlers and their junk-free lifestyles. The graveyards are full of them, smokeless, vegetarian, composting like the rest of us."

Maynard smiled. "You take the average family and they haven't got a clue about what goes on, not the things we see. We see things that no one should see; we hear things that no one should hear. Tell me how police officers hold on to their sanity?"

"Do they?"

"You're right. They don't. That's why they never make real friends. That's why their marriages seldom work. No one can live with them, except nurses, maybe, who see the results."

Maynard eased into a chair opposite and placed his drink on the table.

"Hello Geoff."

"Rick."

"You're not a police officer."

"True. But I can't get away from it. People like you keep calling me back."

Cole nodded. "You're paid a lot more than we are."

"Agreed."

"And you make more on top of that writing your True Crime books. And most of that's bollocks."

"They make less than you think. And come to think of it there are a few coppers around who get off on the same bend."

"Their books are bollocks too."

Maynard threw him a harmless smile. "So what have we got? More of the same? Fantasies, the fat dogs will tell you, can do no harm. Well, you go tell them that fantasy is where the sex crime starts. Fantasy is the fuse. The explosion comes when the fuse is used up."

"So tell me something new? That was in one of your books too."

"I didn't know you read my books."

"Only one of them. Couldn't get on with the first person. He did it all by himself."

Maynard smiled again. "That's not true. I turned you into a celebrity, photograph and all." He reached out and tapped Cole's glass. "Anyway, the coppers on the Jill Dando case were banned from drinking alcohol for the duration."

Cole lifted his glass and said, "I could get the wrong man without a drink. It would be that easy." He lost two fingers and returned his glass to the table. "The idiots who come up with ideas like that are about as useful as a special."

"I'm not arguing," Maynard said and made a suitable noise. "But do I detect a fractured and disconnected discourse within the Met? God forbid!"

Cole grinned and said, "What can we do? Our commissioner is so far up Tony Blair's arse his favourite line is he's having a Blair on Blair. We've got *Vote Labour* stickers on police cars and we've lost over one hundred detectives from the Murder Squad to boost neighbourhood policing. And that's apart from the shambles at Stockwell. Forget Condon who just about destroyed CID, this guy has destroyed the reputation of the entire force. Protecting the public has become a national joke. At least Stevens was on our side, fighting our pitch, not bowing down to the human rights and politically correct lunatics who run this government. You can't run a police force when the government is on the side of the criminal. Welcome back."

Maynard's glance skirted the scythes and other farming implements hanging from the walls, faintly sinister reminders of a cold-blooded time. There was something about the swish of the scythe, maybe because of its association with Death, that sent a shiver down his spine.

The place hadn't changed. They had, the detective and the therapist, but the surroundings were fixed in the past.

Maynard's sleepless eyes came to rest on Cole. They were warm but held a trace of mischief. "So what is Ian Blair up to?"

"He's blaming everyone else, as usual."

"Menezes?"

"That's part of it but that had more to do with the people who took out David Kelly than SO19."

Maynard nodded. "That makes sense. It explains a lot, and why the commissioner's take made less than sense."

"It doesn't do SO19 any favours though, having to cover for those incompetent bastards." Through the smoke of his JPS Cole threw him a smile. They knew each other too well. He said, "Where are you staying?"

"Just got in. The gear's in the boot. I was hoping your spare room was still spare."

"I think you've still got the key."

"Guessed it might come in handy."

It had been years but it felt like yesterday. They'd worked a nasty case and it had bonded them. Old soldiers knew about camaraderie and the shared experience. That's why sixty-five years on the few that were left were still going back to Dunkirk.

"So!" Maynard said. "What's happening in the real coppering world? You've got yourself a serial slasher?"

"A bit premature for a serial, but maybe. A bomb builder too."

"Let's talk about the slasher. It's more my line. Have you got anything at all?"

"Not that counts. You've seen the front pages and you can imagine our senior policemen knee-jerking like a bunch of geriatric rockers. Nothing changes. The arseholes remain in charge."

Maynard's smile was cut short as Sam Butler arrived carrying a tray of drinks. Standing next to him, rock solid on two-inch heels, was the slim figure of Anian Stanford. Her dark eyes were smarting.

"Hello Geoff." Butler met Maynard's friendly smile. "Heard you were in town. Same old story, is it? Women in trouble."

"It seems that way."

"We're not interrupting, are we?"

Maynard half-emptied his seat. "Not at all. Join the party."

Sam Butler glanced sideways at the DC. "This is Anian." His glance must have caught Cole for Maynard picked up on it. Nothing obvious, just a slight flicker of the eyes.

She slid into a chair and lifted her glass of red wine and only then looked at Cole. "Guv," she murmured.

Cole's nod of acknowledgement only served to increase Maynard's curiosity.

Butler said, "I promised Anian that I'd show her the local, just in case she's moved over here."

Maynard asked, "So what's happening at Hinckley?"

"We've got some missing women."

"But unfortunately," Cole cut in. "They haven't got a case!"

Out of earshot the Sheerham kozzers stole glances at Cole's table while Chas Walker filled them in. "She nearly killed Jack Wooderson over at Hinckley. He had to call it a day. He was going home smelling like a chicken Madras every night and his old girl was getting suspicious."

Peter Ward said, "She'll do me."

"You've got no chance, son," Walker said seriously. "Anyway, apart from Jack Wooderson even the fucking tide wouldn't take her out!"

Some of the uniforms propping the bar overheard and edged forward for more.

From the back DC Martin James put in, "It's all the Kama, isn't it? The bow and arrows, the bowstring of bees."

Vacant looks required an explanation.

"Saw the video. *Kama Sutra*. Watched it with the missus. She wasn't all that. Standing on her head with a banana up her arse didn't appeal. She said we could try it again if we get double glazing. Funny, though, it wasn't Pakis in that. Still, I'd give her one…" James nodded toward Anian.

Chas Walker looked surprised.

"Well, wouldn't you?"

The DC looked from James to Ward and back again. He said, "You two are supposed to be married and pillars of the community. But no, I wouldn't. Apart from the colour, she's too skinny."

"She'd be perfect for the part of Rosalind."

Ward's ears picked up. "*As You Like It*," he said and looked pleased with himself. "The daughter's reading it for the GCSE."

"Yes, mine too. Forcing me to play half the parts. Surprised at how much cross-dressing old Shakespeare got up to. Quite a party they had in those days. Gwyneth Paltrow's tits…"

Walker wagged a finger. "Now you're making sense."

"She was in that other thing, where they cut her head off."

"*Tale of Two Cities*?" Ward suggested.

"No! What the hell was it? *Seven*. That's the one. A cracker."

"I liked *Cracker*."

"Fuck *Cracker*," Chas Walker said. "Concentrate on Gwyneth. I don't know about you, but I'd fuck her without the head!"

"But she's very slim too, Chas, Just like Anian."

Two shots over the limit, Butler gave the DC a ride back to Hinckley where she shared a flat with two nurses who worked at the Royal Free. Their shifts were all over the place, worse even than Anian's, so life was noise free. There was always someone sleeping or trying to. In the car she said, "Tell me about him?"

Butler knew immediately that she was referring to Cole. "He's a DI at Sheerham."

"I know that much."

"What then?"

"Tell me."

"His wife left him some years ago. Went off with an American. Blamed the job, as you do. He was involved in a couple of high profile cases that... Well, they were pretty bloody nasty. He spent too much time on them and not enough on her. You know the score. Christ, Anian, you're in the job."

"What else?" She sounded tired, as if talking was keeping her awake.

"Nothing else."

"I heard some rumours, a certain policewoman."

Butler nodded and checked the mirror. The roads were quiet, washed with lonely electric. The silent shop displays blazed the Christmas message of false hope

"I heard them too." Gossip had never come easily to Sam Butler.

"Well?"

"I don't know. They might have got a bit too close, but they saw sense, backed off. She's married, happily I believe, moved back to Ipswich. End of story."

"No, no, you're not getting off there. Was it an affair?"

"I wouldn't put it like that. A daydream, maybe, a mental lapse, a day off. That's it, a day off. That's how I'd put it. Everyone's allowed a day off, just once. It's all forgotten now. It was a long time ago."

Under cover of darkness Anian Stanford nodded thoughtfully and smiled.

Chapter 14

The phone became part of Cole's dream.

"Guv, you better get over here."

DS Peter Ward's voice was vaguely familiar. "What's happened?"

"John Domey's been on. Margaret hasn't been home all night. He's panicking. Rang the hospitals..."

"Give me half an hour. You better let the super know."

"He's already here, with the chief, and he's not a happy chappy."

"Go on?"

"Nasty TA in the High Road. Fatality outside The British. Pedestrian was hit and dragged fifty yards. Took most of the night to pick up the pieces."

A TA wasn't going to bring out the super, never mind Chief Superintendent Marsh, so it had to be more than that and Margaret Domey was odds-on.

Cole hung up and checked his clock. Six. He'd had three hours sleep. Self-inflicted, he knew, but the thought made things worse. On his way to the shower he banged on his guest's door and heard a groan. In the mirror he faced his red eyes. Something had to give, the job, his liver, something... It felt like he'd taken a heavy boot in the side. He turned the shower to hot, until it hurt and took away the pain. It sobered him up, like it always did, as though the water was purifying. It washed away the corruption.

He was in the kitchen when Maynard appeared. Coffee was making noises and bursting bubbles. The therapist looked even worse than he did.

Maynard pulled a can of Diet Coke from the fridge. "Why the air raid siren? Tell me it's the end of the world, at least?"

"Remember Margaret?"

"Margaret Thatcher's twin sister? I'll never forget her."

"Remember Sam's missing women, all but one pregnant?"

"It's coming back. Last night remains a little hazy."

"Margaret Domey is pregnant and last night she didn't come home."

Maynard nodded and said quietly, "A sobering thought."

Cole went on, "And she didn't do a runner. That's out of the question. So go through the possibilities: she's ill, in hospital, she's fallen through a crack in the pavement or she's gone the way of these other women."

Maynard's features firmed up. "There's a shed load of possibilities— memory loss, disorientation, medication not taken, mental impairment, pre-natal depression and a whole bunch of psychological illnesses that aren't necessarily obvious. Panic for one. Panic can send you to any place and reason won't come into it. And then there's the game of hide-and-seek: come and find me—I need some attention. Maybe she just wants some time to herself. It's a bit early to speculate. But I do know what you mean. Most of it doesn't fit the Margaret we know."

"Let's go and find her. I've had enough of this shit. Someone's throwing bombs around, girls getting cut to bits, missing women. It's time to take off the gloves."

"Like the old days then?"

Cole levelled his gaze and nodded and in that moment the psychologist was glad that he was on Cole's side.

Detective Superintendent Baxter's features were set in concrete and carried the same shade of grey. He'd spent forty minutes on the top floor concentrating on the thin lips of Chief Superintendent Marsh as he weighed in with the gravity of the situation. Marsh's deputy, Assistant Chief Superintendent Bob Deighton, involved in cost-effective management, stood at the window, watching the crisp dawn break and wringing his hands at the sound of overtime. But he agreed with the chief that Margaret Domey was to be given top priority. She was, after all, part of the firm.

On his way to the office Baxter collected a coffee, left some of it in the corridor and, at the door of the incident room and with a sideways nod of the head, summoned Cole.

Settled behind his desk Baxter said, "You can tell the others that she wasn't the most popular girl on site but Margaret is one of ours. She's as good as on the job. Christmas has been cancelled. I know you're busy but you've got to keep a close eye on Hinckley. Jack Wooderson..." He shook a downbeat head then more abrasively said, "And Sam isn't going to win any inspirational awards, is he?"

Cole knew what he meant but it wasn't going to be easy. Coppers treated interference the same as anyone else.

Baxter went on, "We've got a dilemma here. No crime. Not even the suspicion of one. But we all know Margaret. She's not going to take a hike. I'll talk to John Domey and make sure everything's OK. But you get Sam to pull his finger out and make sure that Jack knows the top floor's looking over his shoulder. I want everything buttoned up, watertight. No one coming back to say we missed something."

"I've got Geoff Maynard here."

Baxter had forgotten. His hesitation betrayed him. He nodded and said, "Let him loose. That's what he's here for. Let's see what he comes up with. Officially, the assaults still take priority. Unofficially, one of our own is missing."

Cole paused at the door. "Jack isn't going to like it."

Baxter stressed, "Frankly, I won't lose any sleep about hurting Jack Wooderson's feelings. Go and find Margaret. Whatever it takes. What you do best. Right? Just, be careful. In this day and age a loose cannon is not appreciated. This is a one-off, a rare gift, and it didn't come from me. I want this little woman found, and quickly."

"Yes, Sir."

"And Rick, one other thing. You should have followed up John Domey's call yesterday. That wasn't good."

Baxter stared through Cole's vacant space, for a moment lost in thought. The day of the free-wheeler from C8 (The Flying Squad, Heavy Mob or Sweeney) and later C1 (Drug Squad) was long gone. Now it was about teamwork and conformity. Coppers like Cole had always been the villain's biggest threat because they didn't work by the book and they didn't conform and that was the very thing that made them unpredictable and dangerous. In giving Cole a free hand the superintendent hoped he had made the right decision. He wasn't convinced.

After introducing Maynard to the team Cole turned to the therapist and said, "This is PC Donna Fitzgerald and she's going to look after you."

Donna flashed Cole a thoughtful look. It landed in a sensitive place and had him checking out her engagement ring. It was still there.

She said, "We're still looking for Jason. The uniforms are looking in all the likely places."

Cole nodded and left them to it.

Although he would have preferred talking to Sam Butler direct he decided on protocol and called Jack Wooderson.

"Rick?"

"Hello, Jack."

"What's the problem?"

"Problem is right. I've decided not to transfer Anian."

A moment's hesitation, an antagonism that carried along the line, then, "What's happened?"

"Margaret Domey's gone missing, and she's pregnant."

"I heard. Is her pregnancy significant? Complications?"

"You didn't know the others were pregnant?"

"The other women? Sam might have mentioned one of them was. I didn't make the connection."

Cole's pause went on too long, a silent condemnation. Eventually he said, "Three out of the four, I believe. He should have mentioned it."

"Too fucking right."

"You better get your act together. The chief is making threatening noises."

Another hesitation. This time it was the thought of Chief Superintendent Marsh that did it. Eventually Wooderson said, "I'm on it. I appreciate the call."

Cole struggled with the next one. "I might have been the last person to have talked to Margaret. She was in my office yesterday morning.

You better get Sam over here. The super is talking to John, her husband. He might have something to add."

"Right. I'll get things moving." Cole replaced the handset and unconsciously reached for a JPS. Down the dead line Jack Wooderson put a call out for DS Sam Butler and before realizing what he'd done, he lit a Benson's.

An hour later Sam Butler walked into Cole's office. Without a doubt Jack Wooderson had carved a strip out of him and told him that Cole was the source.

"Sam, let's not waste time. Jack's spoken to you, that much is obvious. Margaret called in yesterday morning. It was nothing more than a social call. From here she was going to buy a cooking pan in the High Road. The Gallery. Know it?"

Butler nodded.

"As far as I know that's the last we've seen of her. Check out the Gallery. Let's establish whether she ever got there."

"Right."

At the door Butler hesitated.

Cole picked up on it and said, "I got you over here to explain why I had to bring Jack into the frame. I had no choice. The top floor is about to cave in on us."

DS Butler took it in, shrugged weakly, and left the office.

In Superintendent Tony Baxter's office John Domey was in tears. He was a slim fragile man. Baxter wondered how on earth he put up with Margaret.

"I know it's difficult," Baxter said. "But I've got to ask you this. Are you and Margaret OK, with the baby coming? What I'm trying to ask and making a complete arse of it is whether there are any problems I should know about?"

Sleepless eyes blinked up in surprise and met the super's gaze. "Everything is fine, Tony. But something terrible has happened. I know it."

Baxter knew the feeling, the utter helplessness, the cold fingers that tightened around the chest until you could barely breathe. He moved around the desk and placed a hand on John Domey's shoulder. It was the best he could do.

"You've got to help us find her. Let's start with her appointment at the hospital. Who was she going to see?"

It was lunchtime when DS Sam Butler called at the Gallery but the door was locked and a small sign read "closed". He used a heavy knocker but nothing that he could see through the shop window moved. Two hundred yards up the road in The British the owner of the Gallery was learning about Rasher's unfortunate accident. Two hours later a DC called at the shop on Butler's behalf but the door was locked. At that time the owner was bent over a canvas in the studio at the back, concentrating on a woman's devious eyes, and didn't hear the knocker. Much later still, DS Butler tried again but this time the owner was entertaining a luscious young lady in the Hong Kong House. Disappointed at not getting the chance to see Anian's portrait, Butler decided to leave it until the morning.

The following morning Cole walked into Hinckley nick and sensed the excitement. DS Butler and DC Stanford, flanked by Inspector Wooderson and a couple of PCs, were concentrating on a screen where an indexer's fingers were just a blur on the keyboard. Wooderson saw Cole and mouthed a silent 'yes'.

"What is it?"

Sam Butler kept his eyes glued to the screen as he said quietly, "This is it, Guv. Christmas!"

It didn't feel like Christmas. Cole had been up most of the night with another broken body. The Sheerham psycho had increased his count to three.

Anian Stanford looked up to meet Cole's fleeting acknowledgment and smiled nervously.

Butler went on, "The owner of the Gallery, one Mr John Lawrence, also known as The Underground Slasher. Did eight of a fifteen. Released on parole in eighty-four."

Cole's eyes narrowed in disbelief. Why the hell hadn't Sheerham picked it up? This previous would have made him a prime suspect for the assaults, certainly top of the list to be TIED. Coppers didn't believe in coincidence.

Wooderson put in, "I remember him. Went after pregnant women on the underground. Used a knife on their bellies. Slash and run was his trademark."

Anian asked, "Murder?"

Butler glanced up from the screen. "No, look, GBH, attempted murder."

Wooderson went on, "There were headlines in the papers. He killed the unborn child, two I seem to remember, so it should have been murder."

"A psycho?"

"Are you joking? Personality defect, what else?"

"OK," Cole calmed the situation. "Let's have him in. Get a warrant and get a team into the shop. Sam, get hold of the original crime sheets. Let's wrap this up quickly."

Butler cut in sheepishly, "There's something you should know, Guv."

Cole said, "Go on?"

"Anian's already made contact. We saw a painting at Ticker's place and she followed it up."

Incredulity touched Cole's eyes before they turned very cold. He looked from Butler to Anian and back again. Eventually he said, "The Gallery?"

Butler nodded.

Jack Wooderson's mouth dropped open, then anger tightened his lips.

Cole turned to the DC. "And?"

Anian felt the heat on her face and hoped it didn't show. She said anxiously, "It was just a feeling, Guv, nothing more than that. He's painting my picture. Just like he painted Helen Harrison."

Butler coughed.

She threw him a leave-it-out look.

Butler explained, "The painting of Helen Harrison was pretty revealing."

Cole shook away a fleeting image of Helen Harrison and said, "Does he know you're on the job?"

Anian shook her head.

"What's he like?"

She sighed relief and answered, "A bit old-fashioned, a bit of a gentleman. He'd open a door for a lady."

Wooderson muttered, "And slash her in the belly as she came through. Why didn't I know about this?"

Anian said defensively, "It was off my own back, Guv."

Wooderson responded quickly. "Then how did DS Butler know about it? Don't pull the wool, Anian, you're not good enough and, what's more, you're in deep enough already. And it's bat, off my own bat, not fucking back!"

Butler cut in, "We didn't make the connection, Guv."

Wooderson shook his head and brushed ash from his jacket sleeve. His anger was not without reason. The chief would never countenance the role that DC Stanford was playing. Ever since the Wimbledon Common set-up and the judge's ruling, senior coppers had been having nightmares about entrapment and even now they were unsure where they stood.

Cole defused the situation and said to Anian, "Well, it seems like your hunch was right but you should have shared it. Going forward you'll have no further contact. Cancel any future appointments. Tell him you've changed your mind."

"Yes Sir."

"And since you've made contact you stay out of the way. Let's not compromise the situation further." He turned to Wooderson and said stiffly, "Jack, I didn't hear any of this. Did you?"

"No, I didn't. And I don't want to hear any more." He addressed Butler direct. "You've put us all on the line. You better hope the chief doesn't get wind of it."

Anian insisted, "It was a personal contract, Guv, taken out before he was in the frame."

Wooderson made a suitable noise.

Cole wasn't convinced either, not by a long shot. DS Butler and DC Stanford had been playing a dangerous game. The DS should have kept

Wooderson informed and he should have mentioned it to Cole when he was asked to follow up the chestnut cooking pot.

DS Butler was looking a little wary. He knew pretty well what was on Cole's mind.

Cole wrapped it up. "OK, let's get on with it."

Anian glanced up again. Cole hoped the others didn't notice the speculation in her eye.

In that moment, when other things became incidental, they heard a distant explosion. The report came on, rushing at them, rattling the windows. Alarm bells sounded, tyres screeched and the lights flickered.

An indexer jumped and fell off her chair. Butler ducked. DC Stanford and DI Cole didn't move, still locked together by an unanswered question.

And Jack Wooderson said, "Fucking kids. I blame the single mothers!"

Chapter 15

In a police station nothing moves faster than rumour, not even a copper on his way to a free drink. Sheerham was like any other nick in that regard and was leaking more than Thames Water. Most coppers had a direct line to their mates on the local—it meant pocket money or, at least, a top-up at the favoured boozer. Even small change helped when the credit cards were maxed.

The top brass were in panic-stricken mode, hiding in their offices—sex and violence, one of their own missing—and even thinking about the headlines had Chief Superintendent Marsh reaching for the glyceryl trinitrate and he didn't even have a heart condition—not unless a cold heart counted.

There had been another slasher incident. More blues and twos, more blue and white police tape fluttering around yet another scene of crime. This time it had been in an underpass. Another girl had been attacked, just like the others. They'd established that she wasn't a tom and that gangland wasn't involved. And they were getting reports coming in that a woman might have been the assailant.

"CCTV from the hospital reception shows no sign of Margaret but our Mr John Lawrence walked through just after three."

Detective Superintendent Baxter tapped his pen on a bunch of papers on his desk. He watched Cole close the office door and said, "He followed her there from the shop?"

"We don't believe in coincidence, do we?"

"Good God, Rick, things are never this easy, are they?"

"We'll see."

"What about these two cold files from Mill Hill, Melanie Brown and Sophie Whillis?"

"It sounds like the same MO. They simply disappeared four years ago. They're certainly within shopping distance to have visited the High Road so maybe..."

Baxter nodded. "What about Lawrence?"

"Forensics are at the shop now." Cole glanced at his watch. "We should get a prelim in the next hour or so."

"And Lawrence himself?"

"They're letting him sweat, waiting for the report. That never does any harm."

"Who's his brief?"

"Doesn't want one. Told Sam that he would conduct his own defence."

Baxter made a suitable noise. "A joker, then. Will you conduct the interview?"

"No. Let Sam have it."

"Don't let Jack muddy the water."

"Sam's confident that it's just the loose ends."

Baxter looked up. "Unfortunately we've heard that before. So, what have we got, the slasher, the missing women? Is Lawrence in the frame for both? There's a whisper a woman is involved in the latest."

"The rumour came from the Square. One of the locals got hold of it and passed it on to LBC. At this rate it'll be on the news at six." The DI paused before changing track. "I think we can leave Barry with the kids. If they blow up another shed so be it."

"I've got no issues with that. The explosion... I spilt my coffee. It's a bloody liberty. When we get the little buggers there won't be a damned thing to do."

Cole managed to suppress a smile. He said, "They'll have to start insuring their allotment sheds. Some of it was found two hundred yards away."

"So what about this slasher? A woman?"

"I'm waiting for Geoff. I'd like to hear what he thinks."

By the time Cole had finished with the new attack Maynard had been in bed. Obviously the therapist couldn't handle two late nights on the trot, never mind the boozy wind-down. Come the dawn Cole had left for Hinckley before his guest had surfaced.

Baxter agreed. "So would I. Make Barry aware that my door is open. I want a twice-daily update from him."

They heard voices coming from the outer office. Through the glass they saw Maynard and PC Fitzgerald talking to the team.

"Talk of the devil," Baxter murmured.

Cole moved to the door and waved Maynard inside.

Maynard took a seat without invitation.

"You remember Detective Superintendent Baxter?"

"Of course." Maynard hid his surprise. The super had gained weight. A stone a year and that meant two and most of it around the middle. "How are you, Mr Baxter?"

Baxter weighed up the therapist, searching for something, he didn't know what. Carefully he removed his spectacles for a quick once-over with the yellow buffer. "I'm fine Geoff. Are you?"

"Good," Maynard responded. "It's good to be back."

Cole cut in, wanting to get on. "You saw Elizabeth Rayner?"

The psychologist nodded.

"And?"

"And nothing Rick. This wasn't personal. You've got a psychopath on your hands. He's struck three times in less than a week and there's more to come."

"He?"

"I heard the rumour. And Elizabeth Rayner has come up with something else. Remember the distinctive aftershave she recognized— well it wasn't. It was Amarige, a Givenchy perfume."

Cole nodded. "You OK with Donna?"

"You should talk to her," Maynard suggested. "She's got a couple of points that might interest you."

The DI shot him a thoughtful look. He said, "What's your plan now?"

"I'll see the other victims and try to find a connection, if there is one. Can you spare Donna?"

Now Cole knew it was personal. He nodded slowly.

Maynard smiled, enjoying himself.

Cole said, "We'll meet up later. If you can stand the pace, that is."

Maynard nodded and offered the detective a withering smile. Cole hadn't mentioned where but he knew exactly where he meant. So did the super and he wasn't impressed.

Once the door had closed behind them and while Baxter considered the situation he unwrapped silver paper and started on a thick sandwich: mature farmhouse cheddar all the way from Somerset and beef tomato from the Canaries. A feast, and what was more, Cole and Maynard on the job again. It was like old times.

On the way through the IR Chas Walker stopped them. "Guv," he addressed Cole. "Rodney Grant has come up with the goods. We've got Jason in IV one. But he's calling himself Brian Lara now, even though he's white and blond."

"Right," Cole said. "I want you to look into this rumour about a woman being involved. Find the hack responsible and sit on him till you get an answer. Make him understand that 'no comment' is not an option. Make him understand that he lives in a police state."

If he was joking it didn't show and Walker said, "Right, Guv, I can do that."

Cole turned to Donna. "You and Peter look after Brian. He'll know the score. We want to know about everything that goes down in the Square."

Chas Walker cut in. "We're waiting for the duty social worker. He's no more than fourteen. More like twelve."

Cole said sharply, "You still here?"

Walker persisted, "An appropriate adult, Guv. Never mind Social Services we'll be starting a civil war with PPU."

"PPU! FPU! CPU! They're in the wrong job anyway."

"We're bending the rules, Guv?"

"Bend some more."

Donna started toward the door. Peter Ward followed. And Maynard, without invitation, followed him.

Brian, for want of a better name, was pale, smooth and blond, with long eyelashes and a slim figure, and Walker had been right, he looked no more than twelve or thirteen. He had big innocent eyes that were as innocent as hell and a look that could lead you, if that was your bend, to hell. There was a redness around his nose and eyes and he sniffed the symptoms of a common cold.

Right away they knew it wouldn't be easy.

He was streetwise, as familiar with the police and police procedure as was his punter, Rodney Grant. He'd wait for the duty social worker, get an overnight accommodation and then leg it. He'd done it a dozen times before. No big deal. When it came to kids the police were helpless, strapped by so many rules it made it impossible. The system helped them back on to the streets. Secure accommodation, even when it was available, was a joke. Social Services were in the same boat as the police. At the end of the day it came down to funding, or lack of it, and the years of restraints or, more to the point, indifference, to the street kids and a society in free fall, would take years to redress. New Labour tried, like old Labour did, but they would botch it just like before because their people were simply not good enough.

Donna placed a Coke on the table.

"Thanks," he said and pulled the ring. He took a gulp as if it were life or death.

Donna said, "Brian, we need your help."

He wiped his mouth on the sleeve of his grubby sweatshirt.

"Remember the guy with the tattoo? The snake wrapped around the dagger?"

He sniffed, "So what?"

"He's a regular. You should. You turned a little trick in the supermarket car park, remember?"

He shrugged and slouched farther into the chair.

"He picked you up in the Square, your usual pitch outside the fitness club."

He remained blank.

"Can you remember what time it was? Or what day?"

Another shrug of his bony shoulders, then, "Eight, nine maybe."

"What about the day?"

He shook his head.

"Was it last week?"

"Maybe."

"What day?"

"Think it was the weekend."

"Can you think of something you did before, or after, that might help you remember exactly?"

Nothing.

"We're looking for someone who might have been acting suspiciously, watching the members of the fitness club as they came and went. Did you notice anyone at all?"

"Can't think. Might have done. It is the place."

"Try to remember, Brian. Someone hanging around?"

He shook his head again and swallowed some more Coke. He placed the can on the table and said, "Just the usual, the girls, you know?"

"The girls? The prostitutes?"

"It's the place."

"Do you know them?"

He pulled a face and shrugged again.

"Would you recognize them?"

"Maybe."

Maynard couldn't resist it. He broke in. "Brian, it doesn't suit you. Jason's better. Your real name would be better still. How long have you been huffing, Jay?"

The lad shot him a frown. "It ain't Jay. It's Brian."

"OK, my mistake, but you're still taking it up the nose as well as up the arse, aren't you?"

For a moment Donna was stunned. She gave Maynard a dark back-off look.

Peter Ward turned in his seat, uncertainty in his eyes, checking that the tape was off.

This was going pear-shaped.

Not at all perturbed Maynard went on, "You heard about these women who've been attacked?"

The lad's eyes narrowed suspiciously.

"One of these women was a member of the fitness club. We think that the person who attacked her followed her from the club. That person has probably been hanging around for some time, waiting for a likely customer. Get the picture? It's your patch. You know what goes on down there. Women are getting hurt, big time. The next one might be someone you know and care about. This bastard is cutting them to bits. Before long, a woman is going to get killed. It's only luck that it hasn't happened already." He threw up his hands to emphasize the point. "Maybe you can help us, maybe not. If you can give us some faces, anyone, then maybe we can stop it happening. That's why we need your help. This isn't about you. You go your own way, if that's what you want. Do a bunk like you've done before. Go and get mashed again. Why should we care? Think about it. If you stay with Social overnight you'll still be rattling for a huff by the time you can leg it."

The youngster's mouth dropped open.

Maynard said, "Talk to me, Brian. Don't worry about them."

Keeping his eyes on Brian he threw a little nod toward the police officers.

"What about my punter?"

"He's a nobody, right? You don't owe him a thing. Men like that should be put out with the rubbish. Wouldn't know which bin to use though. It wouldn't be glass or plastic, would it? Probably dog shit."

The lad grinned.

"What about these other girls? Can you help me out?" Maynard made it personal. 'Me' left the others out of it.

"I know them all, and so do your lot. Go ask Sergeant Wilson. He knows them." He frowned and raised a finger. "But there was one I hadn't seen before and the others didn't like it."

Maynard smiled. "Now that's the one I'm interested in."

"She was different."

"How come?"

"Classy, if you know what I mean. Sort of. My mates even fancied her. It was like, she wasn't, you know, playing the game. I don't know. It didn't look right. Maybe in a hotel. Not on the streets. I hadn't seen her before."

"Could you point her out?"

"Maybe. She was different."

"But you'd recognize her again?"

"Maybe."

"What about men? Did you see any men?"

"Only punters. Nothing special."

"Did she go off with any?"

"Not that I saw. I could ask around."

"We can't ask you to do that. If we did we'd all be in trouble. But you could point out this woman for me. There's got to be the price of a burger in it, right?"

He looked at Donna for confirmation. She shrugged and nodded.

And Brian, or Jason, said, "OK."

In the corridor something rather nasty was heading toward Sergeant Mike Wilson, eating up the distance between them. The duty social worker, incandescent, was firing threats loud enough for him to hear. 'Juvenile', 'presence' and 'appropriate adult' were just some of the words he snatched from the vibrating air. He thought on his feet. Fuck that, he thought and, without losing momentum, as though he'd remembered something urgent and hadn't noticed her frantic bid for his attention, performed a sudden about-turn and hurried toward the exit to the car park and garages.

For the copper, like the married man, the garage, like the garden shed, was a refuge, perhaps not consecrated, but as holy as any church.

As Rodney Grant was led out of the building, released from police custody, he saw the social worker's angry face and said to the uniform beside him, "Blacks, mate, all the same. And black dykes, fucking nightmare time! We should send them back to Wolverhampton or wherever the fuck they come from."

The kozzer agreed.

The six o'clock news had just begun when Jack Wooderson caught up with Butler in Hinckley's tiny canteen. The headlines were depressing, as grey as the December sky. The flickering lights in the shop windows had not done the trick. People did not believe the government's feel-good rhetoric. Plastic stayed in their pockets. And the shopkeepers were nervous. The street traders selling cheap wrapping paper, ten for a quid, were on a roll.

"Prelims in," Wooderson said. "Nothing. The garden hasn't been touched this century and the cellar's clean. They've found cobwebs down there that are older than the missing women. Dig up the floor and the only things you'll find are prehistoric. Their words, not mine. All the walls are solid, crumbling but solid. They've sent some samples to the lab, but don't expect a return. If we want excavation we'll need the chief's OK. But it will be a waste of time."

DS Butler groaned. They'd been counting on the shop, certain that evidence would be found.

"So what have we got?" The inspector asked, then answered his own question. "He's got form, fancies himself with a knife and was once known as the Underground Slasher. We can place two of the women in his shop. Truth be known, in just about every shop in the High Road. That's it. It's not half enough. Fact is, Sam, you're sitting on fuck all."

Butler didn't need telling. "Let's see what he's got to say."

Wooderson glanced at the television and saw that it was after six. He said, "You'll have to manage. I have a meeting."

Butler wondered what boozer the inspector used. He hadn't seen him in the locals.

As he made his way to Hinckley's only interview room, Sam Butler picked up on DC Stanford's questioning expression and paused by her desk. "The shop's as clean as... It's clean."

"What were you going to say?"

"A whistle."

"Why didn't you?"

"It sounds old-fashioned."

"Sam, you are old-fashioned."

Anian had seen the shop and the studio behind with its little kitchenette, but she was surprised that the cellar hadn't produced a return.

"They're bringing him up now. Stay out of the way."

She didn't need reminding.

He turned to a DC sitting in front of a screen. The indexers called it a day at five. No commitment. They weren't in the job. "Rob, you're with me."

DC Robert Foster jumped to his feet, eager to have a go at the Underground Slasher, and followed DS Butler into the corridor.

John Lawrence sat at the table relaxed and concentrating on his polished brogues. He looked up as the two detectives walked in. They sat down and went through the preliminaries. DC Foster busied himself with the machine while Butler arranged some papers on the table. Butler gave the recorder their names, time and date and then: "Mr Lawrence."

"Good afternoon, Mr Butler. Or is it evening yet? One does lose track of time in here."

"You know why you're here?"

"Indeed. The other officer, what was he called? The custody officer, he explained."

Carefully, Butler spread four photographs on the desk.

"I'm showing Mr Lawrence the photographs of Margaret Domey, Helen Harrison, Linda Brookes and Jenny Fielding. Do you recognize these women?"

He was holding back the photograph of Imelda Cooke. She was the odd one out, on two counts. She wasn't pregnant and she had two children.

Lawrence leant forward to examine the photographs. He took his time, concentrating on each in turn. Eventually he said, "Yes, I think so. I painted Mrs Harrison's portrait, and this one called into the shop on Friday. The others I'm not sure about. Their photographs, these photographs, are stuck to every shop window in the High Road. Mine included. But they may well have been in the shop." His voice was calm and slightly seductive. It put you to sleep, almost, just like his eyes, unless you had a question, and knew he was guilty as hell.

Butler tapped Margaret Domey's coloured image, an enlargement of her PIT. "Did Mrs Domey purchase anything?"

"She was interested in an antique cooking pot, but it was out of her price range. She wanted to haggle. I explained that my shop was not a souk in the middle of Tunisia and she left. Fortunately, that was the last I saw of her."

"Did you notice anything about her?"

"I noticed everything about her. You'll have to be more specific."

"Was she agitated or upset in any way?"

"Agitated? That's a curious word. After her wrangling and when she left without the cooking pot she was. Does that have a bearing?"

"What about when she arrived?"

"Ah, I see. You didn't say that. But no, I don't think so. On the other hand, with a woman like that it is difficult to gauge a mood. I imagine that to most people she would appear to be agitated all of the time."

"What time was that?"

"Well, I'm not sure really. Before lunch, certainly."

"How long was she in the shop?"

"Ten minutes, no more. I was serving another customer so she had to wait. She was rather impatient. No, even more than that, I'd say. She wasn't happy about being kept waiting. I thought she was an abrasive woman. I remember thinking that. I took an instant dislike to her."

"Do you have the name of this other customer?"

"Afraid not. Cash sale, I think. A print. Ducks flying from water. Ducks are a best seller." He shook a sad head. "While other men dream of Doris Day, I dream of shooting ducks."

Butler shook his head. Doris Day? Was she still alive? Were the men who fancied her still alive? He asked, "Did anyone see Mrs Domey leave your shop?"

"I've no idea. The pavement outside is always busy, particularly at this time of year. Someone must have seen her. Maybe we can appeal for witnesses. On the television." His eyes widened at the thought and he added, "Or maybe one of your CCTV cameras picked her up. With the number of times we're caught on CCTV—what is it, two hundred times a day?—it is surprising that anyone could go missing. It is astonishing, really, that with all the controls the government puts in, all the checks and the listening and the spying—gosh, they even spy on our dustbins—it is surprising that a crime can still be committed."

Butler tried to ignore him. "What else did you notice?"

Lawrence offered a sly little smile. "That she was pregnant, you mean?"

Butler said stonily, "I didn't think it was that noticeable."

"Didn't you? You have to know what to look for, of course, and it's more than just the rounded belly. The skin takes on a radiance. The eyes take on a secret sparkle as though no one else is suppose to know. It is a woman thing, a thrill that we can only guess at. One needs to play around with colour and oil to bring out the lustre. Do you have children Mr Butler?"

"Yes."

"Are you expecting more?"

Butler shook his head and smiled coldly. "Let's talk about Mrs Harrison."

"Fine. I'd like that. I liked Mrs Harrison."

"When was the last time you saw her?"

"She came in to pick up the painting about a week after the last sitting. The paint needs time to dry. Do you know anything about art?"

"No."

"I insist on a week, more if possible. But Mrs Harrison could be very persuasive. Did you know her?"

"No."

"She was a very beautiful woman. Stunning, I'd say. Not that I'm anything of a judge. The date of her last sitting will be in one of my diaries. I have two. They're kept in the shop under the counter. Perhaps one of your officers can collect them, unless, that is, you have already confiscated them as evidence. It was about a month ago, no more than that. But time is an oddity. A day is a week and a week is a day. But it was about a week after her last sitting."

"And has she been back since?"

"Mrs Domey hasn't. I don't think I'll see her again."

"Mrs Harrison?"

"Oh, Mrs Harrison. I haven't seen her. I've taken on an assistant. He might have seen her."

"Paul Knight."

"Yes, that's his name. He might have seen her. He has an eye for the girls. Particularly the pretty ones."

"Paul has a little form, as well, doesn't he?"

"Indeed he does. He will tell you it was a miscarriage of justice, that it was down to corrupt policemen. I had no truck with that. I told him that our policemen were the best. That in Britain we simply don't have corrupt policemen. I don't think he believed me."

Butler looked for the sneer but if it was there he missed it. He turned to his notes. "You were released on parole in 1984."

"That's true. I had to attend a clinic. It will be in your records. It seems a long time ago. My goodness, it is a long time ago."

"Things have a way of coming round."

"I think I know what you're suggesting, Mr Butler. But you're quite wrong. I did have a problem. I was diagnosed schizophrenic but in those days that covered a multitude of sins."

"It's the legal loophole, isn't it?"

"I see, the Hare Test, the accepted scientific proof of a psychopathic personality disorder and that only people with treatable disorders can be kept in hospital? For fifteen years I've been running my shop. I spend my time either there or in The British. You can find me in The British most lunchtimes and evenings and, if I'm not there, I'll be at the shop. Everyone will tell you. That is my routine and it hasn't changed in all that time. I was ill and I attacked those women on the underground. But now everything is fine and I'm no more a danger to the general public than you are."

Butler's smile was forced. He said, "That's good, but unfortunately we have some missing women and the thing they have in common is that they're all pregnant."

"All of them? I didn't know that. Goodness me. That is a coincidence. But the women, before, they never went missing. I always left them on the underground platforms. I agree that they weren't in, you know, tiptop condition, but I always left them there. They were never…missing. But I do get your point and I suppose that is why I am here. I suppose your computer has thrown me up, as they do. I don't understand them, myself, but perhaps that's an age thing. They sound absolutely marvellous."

"The missing women visited your shop."

"Did the computer throw that up too?"

"Forget the computer."

"I'd like to but, unfortunately, they won't allow us that luxury. They put us on to a spreadsheet, they give us credit or they don't, and what is more, when you speak to them on the phone, they speak in Indian accents. But, yes, you're right, two of the women did visit my shop."

"I think you've got them somewhere. Not on your premises, but somewhere else."

"Do you really think so? I hope you're not going to fit me up like those other policemen did to young Paul."

"Let's come back to Mrs Domey."

"Do we have to?"

"Did you discuss anything else?"

"Beside the cooking pot?"

"Her being pregnant?"

"We didn't discuss that at all. It never came up. I worked that out—that she was pregnant—all by myself. But there was one thing I remember. She mentioned that it was very dark and that it was difficult to see the details on the paintings and on the cooking pot. My lights had blown a fuse you see? I had a problem with my electrics."

"What else?"

"Nothing else."

"She didn't mention where she was going after she left the shop?"

"I wasn't with her when she left the shop so how could she tell me anything? I had things to do. Shops don't run themselves, you know."

"When she was there, in the shop, did she mention where she was going?"

"No, she didn't, and I didn't ask. Like I said, it wasn't a friendly conversation. More like the opposite, I'd say."

"And once she'd left, what did you do?"

"I took a deep breath, a sigh of relief."

"And after that?"

"Like I said, there was work to do in the shop, and then I went to The British for lunch."

"What about the afternoon?"

"The afternoon?"

"You visited the hospital."

"I did. By golly, you have been thorough. I wish all policemen were like you then we'd all sleep safer."

"Why did you visit the hospital, Mr Lawrence?"

I went to visit a patient. It's not something I often do but on this occasion I made an exception. I took him some grapes."

"The patient's name?"

"I can't imagine what bearing this has…"

"Bear with me."

"It was my lodger. He had an accident while playing with electricity."

"Paul Knight."

"One and the same."

"How did you get to the hospital? Did Mrs Domey give you a lift?"

"Mrs Domey? How could she have known I was going to the hospital? Was she going there? Gosh, that is an amazing coincidence. For your information I took a number 34 bus. It was a single-decker. I was rather disappointed. I like double-deckers. I have always found it rather satisfying to look down on the masses. It gives you an idea of how the police see things."

Butler collected together the photographs. "I'm not going to charge you at the moment, Mr Lawrence, but I will be seeing you again."

"Does that mean I can go? Will I get a lift back to the shop. I do so enjoy being taken for a ride. Do you?"

"He's as mad as a fucking hatter," Butler said down the line. He was angry with himself. He had let Lawrence get to him.

Cole answered, "Bailed?"

"Could have kept him overnight but what's the point? He isn't going anywhere. He's enjoying himself too much."

"What was he doing at the hospital?"

"A total blank. He went to visit his lodger, Paul Knight. Unfortunately it all panned out."

"Is he the one, Sam?"

"I've never been so certain of anything."

"That's good enough for me. What now?"

"We'll continue to dig. I want to know about everything since his release. I've asked for a search of the warehouses and garages at the back of his gaff even though I'll guarantee they'll be as clean as the shop. All we'll find over there are smackheads and their cooking equipment."

"The plods are going to love you."

"One way or another we'll get him." Butler's sigh carried down the line. He said, "Unfortunately we still haven't got a crime. You said it yourself. If it wasn't for Margaret we wouldn't have got the warrant to search the shop. And we certainly haven't got enough to take it to pieces. Not that it matters. The prelims suggest it's hopeless. They had the dogs in there. Apparently, in the cellar they got so excited they were performing back flips. It turned out to be decomposing rats and a couple of dead cats."

Cole didn't need telling. He had already heard.

"I was thinking about surveillance."

Cole's pause went on too long.

"Guv?"

"Yes, sorry. I'll get back to you on that. It'll be down to the super. Don't count on it."

Butler frowned into the phone. That wasn't like Cole at all. He was up to something. Surveillance would bugger his pitch. He knew the DI from old.

"OK, Sam. Fuck knows what I'll tell the super. I promised him a result."

The DS sighed again. He said, "I'll see you in the morning," then hung up.

Rick Cole toyed with the handset for a moment. The DS had been right. He did have an idea. He left the building and drove to a public telephone. His mobile was out of the question. You couldn't be too careful lately. The Yard was spending twenty million a year investigating its own. CIB3 was now the biggest single-purpose investigative unit in the Met. Add that to CIB2 and you could see why there were so few coppers on the street. What was more, since the Investigatory Procedures Act 2000 police officers were regularly bugged, more to discover whether they were racist or sexist rather than bent.

"It's me."

Ticker Harrison responded, "Yeah, recognize those London tones anywhere. You got something for me?"

"The art shop in the High Road, guy named Lawrence."

"I've heard of him. He painted Helen. Got it hanging in the sitting room. Good painter. Caught her just right."

"I think he knows something. More than he's telling us."

"Leave it to me, my son."

"Let me know."

"Fucking right."

Cole sat in the car for some minutes, filling it with JPS smoke. Now it was a matter of waiting. If the old man did know something then Ticker would get it out of him. One way or the other.

Chapter 16

The phone went.

"'Ello Boss. It's me. He's on his own now. The shop's been full all morning. Some sort of pensioner's convention, I'd say. Art lovers. Mind you, there were a couple of tasty little tarts, maybe models. Maybe I should take up the painting. Anyway, then he went to get his hair cut, then he went to the boozer for lunch and that went on a bit..."

"Yeah, yeah, all right. I didn't want his fucking life story."

Ticker hung up.

The villain Ticker Harrison had known for some time that if you wanted something doing well then you had to do it yourself, that accountability was something of the past. He blamed the politicians for trashing the old-fashioned values, loyalty in particular, and it came down to them letting in the foreigners so that national identity was lost. For fuck's sake, there were places in England where you'd be hard-pressed to find an Englishman.

Ticker Harrison sighed and said reflectively, "Maybe I should take up politics."

"I don't see any point, Boss. You already make up the rules around here. We got our own laws and, come to think of it, taxes too. Some people might call it protection, but it's the same, ain't it? No different. And they get more for their money from us than they do from that fucking Brown cunt. He ain't fucking human, Boss."

"He comes from fucking Scotland, that's why. But since when have you paid any fucking taxes?"

"It's the principle, Boss, the fucking principle."

"But I'd take up fucking politics, Breath, to get some accountability back into life, not because of the fucking taxes."

"I don't see where you're coming from, Boss."

"I told you I wanted her found. I didn't give a fuck what it cost or how many people got hurt. Take out half of Sheerham if you had to, I said, but find my fucking wife. I am fucking suffering here. I can't sleep, I can't eat and, sooner or later, maybe sooner, some fucker is going to get fucking hurt. You hearing me now? Is that fucking clear enough? You remember me telling you that?"

Breathless Billy's expression was shaped by painful haemorrhoids; a permanent grimace, even when he smiled, and that wasn't often. He said in a voice cut by emphysema and chastisement in equal measure, "Right, Boss. I think I get the message. I've got faces on the street. I've got faces in every fucking…you know, wherever they can fucking get, and we'll find her. But it takes time. And we got other things going on. This business is getting in the way of…business. What shall I do about the kids? You know what's going on in there. I'm telling you, Boss, Gilly will pull out and we'll be fucked. I've got major problems here. And you won't thank me for them! In case you hadn't realized, Boss, Christmas is coming and we said we'd have the place cleared by Christmas."

"Kids! Squatters! How can I think about kids when my wife is missing? It's all right for you, you ain't got a fucking wife. You don't know what I'm going through. Look!" Ticker pointed toward the painting of Helen. "Let's have some fucking priorities around here, eh? You're trying to change the subject. I ask you to do one simple thing, find Helen, and nothing. It's left to me to come up with something."

Breathless Billy checked out the painting and shook a sad head. What had Helen been thinking of to pose like that? And what was Ticker thinking of putting it on public display? For fuck's sake. It wasn't on.

Ticker noticed his right-hand man's uneasiness and relented. "I'm sorry, Breathless, but this shit is getting to me. I never realized how much I'd miss her. Christ, I feel like someone's gutted me. Look, take a couple of guys and throw some weight about in Avenue Road. Let them know we're serious."

Breathless Billy nodded. "OK, Boss, I'll do that. But what you said there, before, you heard something?"

Ticker said slyly, "Maybe, maybe I have. It's more than you lot have. You and me, we're going to have a look around an art gallery. You in to art? Picasso, Raphael, Flaubert? Flaubert said that one must sense the artist everywhere, but never see him."

"Fuck me, Boss, I didn't know that. I thought Flaubert was a writer. You know, that Bovary tart. Just shows you, doesn't it? Never see him, eh? That is interesting. They probably hide behind the fucking screen, the easel, when they're fucking, you know, doing the business, with the paint."

"Well, do you like the paintings?"

Breathless pulled a face. "I can take it, you know? The Tate. Never been there, mind. Fucking don't, do you? Fuck that. Walking around with a stiff neck. Pay to get in. Half the cunts don't make fucking sense. I can't see it. Painting half black, half white, call it black and white and bung a fifty grand tag on it. And the women in the pictures. Fattest fucking tarts I've ever seen. And they're floating, right? In fucking heaven or some place, with fucking angels. Little fat fucking kids with wings that wouldn't hold up a fart-filled balloon, right? I'm telling you, Boss, these artist people have got their brushes up their own arseholes. Sooner have a dead fish stuck on the wall."

"That's art!" Ticker pointed to the painting of Helen.

"Yeah, it's something. That's for sure. This ain't a criticism, Boss, no fucking way, but no way would I have my missus on show like that. Not so's anyone else would get to see it anyway. I mean, that's real. Any closer and you'd be giving it a tongue job. With respect, that is."

"I ain't got a problem with that. Helen didn't either. If you've got a problem then it's your fucking problem."

"Right. I was just saying—"

"No! No you weren't."

"Boss, it's a fucking turn-on. Do you want other geezers walking out of here with a fucking cruise missile sticking out in front of them? That's the question. If it was me, I'd want to keep it all to myself. For fuck's sake, I mean, the cunt's either made a smudge or that's the clit hanging from here to Southend."

"You always were a selfish cunt, Breath. You probably got Scottish ancestors like that fucker Brown." Ticker grinned. "Only kidding. Even you ain't that tight! Come on, let's go and look at some other paintings."

"I'm with you, Boss. Always have been, you know that. But I hope it's scenery, like trees or wild animals, tigers or ducks. Ducks is good. I ain't into all these acres of skin. Puts a shiver up my arse. Brings back memories of when I didn't have to pay for it."

"We all pay for it, Breath, one way or the other. We all fucking pay."

"Ain't that the fucking truth?"

Breathless Billy looked at the painting of red bricks and said, "See what I mean, Boss? That's a bunch of fucking building bricks, right, and the bastard's put a grand tab on it. Now what the fuck is the world coming to?"

The heavy old-fashioned blade of the guillotine came down and left Lawrence's index finger on the table. The three men stared at it for some moments. It moved. Some little nerve ends were left alive, or an elastic tendon flicked back. Breathless Billy let go of the handle of the guillotine and said, "Fuck that!"

But Ticker Harrison had moved his gaze to Lawrence's face. The old bastard had felt no pain, he was sure of it. He was simply staring impassively at his finger.

Ticker said, "If you don't talk to me, sunshine, then you're going to end up with no fingers at all. That ain't actually going to improve your painting, is it? Now I'm a fucking art lover and I hate to do this, but one way or the other, you're going to fucking talk to me."

"If we could negotiate."

"Negotiate? Where the fuck are you coming from? Negotiate? You ain't actually holding a very good hand at the moment."

Breathless chuckled. "That's good, Boss. That's fucking funny."

"Breath, that wasn't a fucking joke."

"It sounded like a joke. It was funny enough to be a joke."

"The cunt wants to negotiate. He thinks I'm a fucking Arab or something. Al fucking Fayed. He's losing his fucking fingers and he wants to negotiate. What sort of fucking world are we living in? Forget the fucking finger. Take off his fucking arm!"

Lawrence said calmly, "I was merely going to say that I'm bleeding rather badly. If I could have some tissue to stem the blood, then I'll be quite willing to tell you whatever you want to know. It was never a secret anyway. You didn't have to do this."

Ticker seemed upset. "You should have fucking said."

"You never gave me a chance."

"Breath, for Christ's sake find some fucking tissues."

"Got one here, Boss, in my pocket somewhere. But it's been used."

So Ticker Harrison discovered that his wife had a lover and was enjoying a romantic liaison in Spain—winter sun, Thompson, something like that—and she was going to phone Lawrence once she returned home, but that was still some days away. He had, during their sessions, become her confidant.

In the car Ticker Harrison kept shaking his head. He was stunned. Uncertainty had been nudged aside by anger. For the first time since Helen had gone missing, he was in charge again. Now he was working on how to pay her back for causing him such grief. He'd take her lover apart, no doubt about that, and to teach her a lesson he'd probably make her watch. What he was going to do to her he hadn't quite decided but one thing was certain, Helen Harrison wasn't going to enjoy it.

"You OK, Boss?" Breathless asked. He was still shaken by the old guy's detachment. There had been no scream or shout or cry. No reaction that you usually got. Fact was, Breathless Billy had noticed a smile on Lawrence's face as his finger came off. Now that was fucking scary.

"I'm fine, Breathless. I need to get my head around it, though. I can't understand how a fucking woman could leave me, that's all."

"I can understand that."

"What the fuck's that suppose to mean?"

"I didn't mean…the fucking women leaving you. I meant I could understand how you feel about it."

"They call that empathy."

"Do they? Fuck me. What's that mean exactly, Boss?"

"It means that you're a soft bastard."

Breathless Billy pulled a downcast face.

Ticker went on, "Some time alone. A little bit of space is what I need. Going to play the old Matt Monro records. Maybe some Dean Martin. My old man used to know him, you know? When he was on the buses."

"I never knew Dean Martin was on the buses."

"No, Matt Monro was on the buses. Dean Martin was with Jerry Lewis."

"Right, I remember the movies now. Great fucking movies they were. Black and white. Can't remember the titles though but, Dean, he was all right."

"*Little Old Wine Drinker Me*, remember that?"

"Do I."

"One of my favourites."

"And *Rio Bravo*, remember that, Boss?"

"Fucking remember it! When I was a kid I knew every fucking word. John T Chance. Angie fucking Dickinson, and she was a good looking tart in those days."

"Were you a John Wayne fan, Boss?"

"Yeah, still am, but don't spread it around."

"I won't say nothing."

Ticker nodded. "Now, like I said, I need some space to get my head around this shite, so I'm going to leave Avenue Road to you. Get some people together and get over there. I think we've had enough fucking blood for one day, don't you? So just give them a scare, right?"

"I get it. I know where you're coming from. I'll do that. Not a fucking problem. You can leave it to me. And Boss, I know this has hit you hard, I know that. For fuck's sake, I want you to know that if you need someone to talk to, like, fucking, a fucking shoulder to cry on or something, I'm always here for you."

"I know that, Breath, and I'm fucking grateful. Maybe you should have been a fucking social worker. But right now I want to sit in my bathroom. Is that all right with you?"

The big guy nodded and reached for a tissue to blow his nose, then remembered he'd left it changing colour on what was left of the old guy's finger, which wasn't very much.

Chapter 17

The Gallery had been filled with police officers, some of them in white overalls and calling themselves SOCOs. They carried the tools of their trade—ground-penetrating radar handsets, Hoovers and copies of the town planner's drawings. There were also a couple of springer spaniels straining on leashes. Paul heard some of their handler's conversation but it didn't make much sense to him. They were talking about how these dogs were different to your average police sniffer dog, how they could detect the scent of human remains through concrete. They were going on about something called NPIA and scientific training techniques and then, later, that the dogs couldn't work in the stink in the cellar and that they had got over-excited by the decomposing cats and rats. One of them suggested that they bring in the local authorities, that there must be a law against dead cats in a cellar. That was just before they sent out for some breathing apparatus.

To Paul the coppers looked more like dentists than policemen and unsettled him even more.

The search was completed long before Mr Lawrence arrived home. Paul was waiting for him by the stairs. Still spook-eyed and trembling it was clear he needed the gentle touch. He blurted, "What was it, Mr Lawrence?"

"A mistake, dear boy. They were on about missing women and stolen property."

Paul's eyes grew even wider, ready to pop. Mr Lawrence's explanation had not done the trick and he pointed an idiot's finger up the empty stairs. "They went in to my room."

"Is your gear stolen?"

"Well…"

"My goodness. Well, obviously they weren't interested in it. I think it was more likely artwork that they were after."

"Like the ballerinas?"

"Did they take them?" Mr Lawrence turned to check but there they were, still dancing. "Did they take anything at all? Did you make sure they signed for whatever they took?"

"Just your books. That's all they took, apart from little plastic bags of things they picked up with tweezers and things. And they used Hoovers too, small Hoovers. They used them in every corner and on every surface and on some clothes. There were kozzers everywhere, upstairs, my room as well. They even unscrewed our bathroom cabinet. Why would they do that? And they took the cistern to pieces. They spent ages in the cellar, with their tape measures. And in the studio. They looked at everything, even the floorboards. They looked behind all the pictures. I thought they'd never go. It was humiliating, Mr Lawrence."

"Yes, I'm sure it was. They think we've got a hidden stash of artwork. Someone's put them up to it, no doubt. Probably someone from The British. Probably Albert. There is something odd about Albert. I know he's Jewish, but there is something else beside."

"I'm worried, Mr Lawrence. Kozzers worry me even when I ain't done nothing. And I've always done something."

"No need to be. They have nothing to go on. Nothing at all. From now on, we have to be a bit careful, that's all."

"I've tidied up a bit, especially in the studio. And I've put up some more tape around the cellar door. The smell was coming through something awful."

"But the studio is out of bounds, Paul."

"I know you said that but…"

"Yes, the circumstances. Given the circumstances, just this once."

"They left a mess. All your boxes were on the floor."

"The Clingfilm?"

"Yes, your boxes of Clingfilm."

"I use it to wrap the paintings. It keeps the damp away."

"I guessed that. I guessed that's what you used it for."

The subject was good enough: an island of trees giving the illusion of a suspended mass, an object and its reflection bathed in light.

During the last week or so Mrs Unsworth had made experimental dabs, changing this key and that value and yet was still puzzled by its lack of depth. Mrs Unsworth was seventy, fragile, her tiny frame warped by arthritis. A widow, she had been coming to class for four years, making use of her enforced independence.

"I've told you before that you can't have the paint too thin where the light is weak. You've been skimping again. I know that paint's expensive but better to use a smaller canvas and get it right."

"Oh, I know, I know. I blame my husband, God bless his soul, but I've become so used to frugality. He used to boil the carrot tops, you know, you know? To put it another way, Mr Lawrence, he was a tight bastard. Right up to the day he died. It caused his death, you know, you know? We were in Sainsbury's, the meat section, when he saw the cost of lamb chops and died on the spot. Caused quite a commotion, I'll say. He went just like that. He saw the price per kilo and hadn't got a clue what that was, then slowly he converted it to English money, pounds, and then slowly shook his head in wonder and then, very slowly, he dropped to his knees. For a moment I thought he was praying but then, he slipped sideways and went all the way. I remember it so well, you know, you know? So very well. I just stood there watching. I couldn't move. His leg shot out and hung in the air for a moment, kicking, waving. Waving goodbye, maybe. And that was it, you know, you know? His final wave to me. Gone. After thirty-five years. Gone. Over a lamb chop. And you know, you know what the funny thing is? He was a liver and bacon man. Liver, bacon, mash and fried onions with thick lumpy gravy. He never even liked lamb!" She shook her white-haired head. "It's always amazed me, though, when I see the news, the farmers on the news, when they say they have to kill off their lambs because they're not worth the money.

You tell me if you can, if the farmers are getting pennies, you know, you know? Then who is getting rich, eh? Eh?" And with that, with a slender arthritic finger, she poked him forcefully in the arm.

Rubbing his arm, he said, "I wish I had an answer. Someone is, and that's for sure. Maybe the wholesalers, perhaps the owners of the abattoirs, or the hauliers or perhaps, more likely, those villains who own the supermarkets. Whoever they are, I'm sure their religion is not Church of England. I'm sure that pork scratchings are not on their menu. But, nevertheless, you have used that excuse before."

"Oh I know, I know. But time flies when you get to our age. Not that you're as old as me. But doesn't it just? How many days in your life can you actually remember? How many weeks? How many months? Such a waste, I think. And you know, you know, you never think about the waste of time until you're running out of it."

"You're so right, Mrs Unsworth."

"You can call me Dolly, Mr Lawrence. I think we've known each other long enough to end the formality. I was beautiful once and once you would have wanted to paint me."

"I have told you this before Mrs Unsworth—Dolly—my preference is for landscapes."

"I know. I know you have, I remember, but you know, you know, on a young woman's body, Mr Lawrence, are the most wonderful landscapes that you will ever find. And I'll tell you something else, for if you look closely so that you see beneath the weather-beaten surface, you'll find those same landscapes on an old girl too."

In the class there were six others beside Mrs Unsworth.

Mr Lawrence coughed for their attention. It was not an easy thing to hold. With the older members it tended to wander. And with the youngsters it was never there in the first place. But for the moment the group turned as one. "Now, because it's our last meeting before the festive break I've arranged a little something special. This morning we'll be concentrating on the figure. I suppose we could call it still life. At least, that is what I am hoping. We have a model."

This caused some excitement and they hurriedly unpacked their trappings.

The class was made up of five women and two men. Mrs Unsworth and the men were retired. Two of the others were forty-something spinsters and although they had something to smile about—not being married—they obviously didn't know it. The other two were in their mid-twenties. They were twins, both married, both with two children. Their husbands were builders, their children in nursery school and they had decided to branch out with a hobby. They had chosen the wrong hobby. They had neither the aptitude nor any real interest. Not that it mattered to Mr Lawrence for the club was just a pastime, an irrelevance, nothing more than a little diversion.

Hiding under the stairs and peering into the studio through a tiny crack in the wall he'd discovered and made bigger when running in the electric cable, Paul saw the legs first. Long tapered white legs bare of tights or nylons, and covered in tiny blond hairs, unusual to find nowadays with all the waxing and shaving and God knows what, but tricky. Two sets of them. Legs first and then the naked navels and then the faces of the twins. Paul had his priorities in order. Unless the legs were interesting he rarely bothered with the rest. But these were interesting. And the rest was interesting too. It wasn't long before he heard their names. Sandra and Susan.

Nice old-fashioned names.

Four long legs covered in tiny fair hairs that went all the way up to two very short black skirts.

It was funny how black was the predominant colour of women's clothes nowadays. It hadn't been like that when he went in. It was funny what you noticed when you came out. He noticed other things as well. That more women were wearing trousers, and these thongy things that they showed you whenever they bent down. But come back to the trousers. You rarely saw a skirt or a dress nowadays, not unless it was on a slapper, and that was a shame. But Sandra and Susan weren't slappers and they were wearing skirts, black skirts, short black skirts. And that was bloody excellent.

Both faces were tanned but Susan's was tanned and freckled. Their green eyes were bright reference books of information. Their lips, quite full and painted red, told him even more. They told him, for instance, that they were married.

He listened in on their quiet and yet quite intense conversation.

Sandra, more so than Susan, was restless, rather bored with motherhood and her narrow existence. And she was upset at being pregnant again. She didn't know what was best, but she would probably have the baby. Mainly because she couldn't afford the cost in Oxford Circus and she didn't fancy going to the NHS.

Paul shook his head. Funny old world, when you thought about it, that a life could be decided that way.

Sandra smoothed her skirt over her belly and held in her smooth, almost flat abdomen. "It doesn't show yet, does it?"

And Susan said, "I wouldn't have guessed."

But someone else had. And he smiled a wicked smile and spread his hands until the blood raced to his fingertips.

"Paul!" he heard Mr Lawrence call him. "Are you ready?"

Paul had been around so the thought of taking off his clothes for the class was of no consequence. Even with the bruises that taking on electricity had left he was proud of his body. In fact the idea excited him. It was another life experience. And his thoughts of the twins excited him even more. It was this excitement that caused concern, at first, and had the women in the class, particularly the twins, in fits of giggles. Even Mrs Unsworth was curious and she exaggerated his excitement on her sketch. The men, Mr Morgan in particular, who was retired and treasurer of the club, were hugely embarrassed and, with their large hairy ears and hairy noses blazing, they left early.

Paul had the devil's face on him; his grin was utterly irresistible and he was in his element. Mrs Unsworth was covered in charcoal and Mr Lawrence thought he had made a mistake but was enjoying himself immensely.

Afterwards Paul had only half-dressed when Mr Lawrence found him.

"It's time for us to talk. I can't have lunatics breaking in here and threatening me with light-sabres. Or threatening the company I might keep, either, even if you did lay it on."

"I know that. Grief! Do you think I don't know that? It's been worrying me silly. That's beside the kozzers. And seeing them gave me quite a fright. What to do about it? That's the problem. Perhaps I ought to make myself scarce."

"For a day or two. That's not a bad idea. I'm glad it was your idea. Either that, or we tell the police about him."

Paul froze. "No, no, no. I couldn't handle the police again so soon. I'd go to pieces. The man is dangerous, you're right. The kozzers will give him a name and then he'll be back. The kozzers are like that. And when he comes back..." He puzzled then nodded. "You're right. I'll make myself invisible for a couple of days, sleep at the chess club, or the squat. He might get fed up by then. Innit? Know what I mean?"

"While you're away you can make yourself useful."

"What's that?"

"There's a woman. I'll give you her address. I want to know more about her, for artistic—aesthetic—reasons, you understand? Nothing more than that."

"Nod, nod, know exactly what you mean." Paul smiled a knowing smile, his previous thoughts quite forgotten. "The woman you're painting?"

"Yes, that's the one. I'd like to know what she does, where she goes, who she sees."

His eyes lit up. "No bother. Right up my street. I'll make notes, just like for real. It'll be like, knowing your subject, adding depth to the expression, right? Innit?"

Mr Lawrence raised an eyebrow. Such an observation coming from Paul was quite astonishing. For a moment he felt giddy. He said, "Come and look at the painting."

"In the studio?"

"I'll make another exception."

Under the studio light Mr Lawrence drew back the cover.

"That's pretty good. You've got her just right. You could actually reach out and run your hand under the dress."

"Don't! It's still wet."

"Only kidding, Mr Lawrence. She looks as if she might be wet." He crept closer to examine it, hands behind his back, leaning forward just like an expert. "I'd like to stay and look at it some more, but I better be off. Wouldn't want to get caught by that bastard with my trousers down."

Mr Lawrence nodded and caught the twinkle in Paul's eye.

Between the restaurants and The British was an old-fashioned barbershop with a real barber who knew nothing about hairdressing. He was an ex-navy man and if you wanted to hang around long enough he would tell you about the ports he sailed into and the girls he had away.

Not long ago the barber had lost all respect when he tried to turn his establishment into a unisex affair. He reckoned without the colonel, The British man of action. Having to wait while the women were pampered, being on edge because they were there at all, was just too much, and he organized a boycott. The barber saw the error of his ways, particularly when he was ostracized in the pub and eventually he banned women from his shop and for good measure, making good sense and making amends for his shortcomings, he refused to serve men with earrings. His profits went up and he was happier. He was allowed back into The British, not totally forgiven, that would take time, but the regulars would at least pass the time of day.

"Fuck the women," he told the colonel.

"Exactly," the man of action, the action man, agreed. "Exactly. Dangerous as hell, they are, and there's a lot of them about. Dangerous as a cornered kraut."

So then, once a month, on the way to lunch, it was short back and sides. While the finishing touches were applied with a razor the barber said, "Someone's been looking for Paul."

Mr Lawrence tried not to show interest.

"A big chappy," he went on. "A gorilla, hirsute, but not on his head. That was bald. Didn't want a haircut, thank God. I didn't know what to say, whether to point it out, that he was bald. I mean, just think, if he hadn't realized. As it happened he just wanted Paul but I wasn't to know that. If I'd had a dodgy ticker I could have been in trouble, just seeing him in my shop. There should be a law against big bald bastards walking around in public. Maybe the National Health Service should provide a service, a warning like they do about cholesterol or smoking when you're pregnant, or maybe they should pay for someone to run five yards in front carrying a sign saying: Big Bald Bastard On The Way."

He shot hair lotion into Mr Lawrence's eyes and ears and brushed loose hair down his neck. Then he showed him the back of his head.

"That it?"

"That's it."

They trod hair to the till.

"Paul came in here, when was it? Earlier, I don't know. You lose track of time cutting hair. He wanted some hair. First time anyone has come in wanting hair. Wanted black hair, no grey, no brown, no speckled, just black. I didn't bother asking him what he wanted it for. You give up sometimes, don't you? The world's full of victims." The barber sighed. "Hair restorer? Comb? Rubbers?"

"At my age?"

"You can fantasize."

He pointed to the stack of magazines where finger smudges blurred the glossy images. "If you want to hang around for an hour May is good and August quite passable."

Mr Lawrence hesitated and raised a critical eyebrow.

The barber remembered the recent past and said, "Women! You're right. And so is the colonel." At the door he switched open to closed and took his coat from the hook. "Lunch? I'll walk with you."

"There should be a law against drunken barbers."

"You're right. Mind you, having said that, blood-letting was an important role at one stage. Think of Sweeney Todd. That's what the red and white pole signifies. Not much call for it nowadays, though. There's enough blood-letting on the street. It's put barbers out of business." He turned off the fourteen-inch colour portable. "Paul got that for me on the cheap. Bloody good lad, he is. Wouldn't want him to come to any harm."

On the cold platform the colonel was in good voice. He had an answer to the yob culture. "What you should do," he told everyone in all seriousness. "Is bring back the birch. It's laughable, really, all these so-called experts talking about absent fathers. What total bollocks. What about the soldiers fighting wars for years on end? Our kids didn't turn out to be hooligans. If they had, by God, they'd have got a bayonet up the arse."

He had a small audience of half-pint drinkers who were only half-convinced of his seriousness so they only half-humoured him. Some of these half-pint drinkers were strays, they had strayed in from the High Road looking for a little respite. They had not met the colonel before and were beginning to hope they would never meet him again.

"One other thing, before you go, and let this be a word of warning from an old soldier. Be careful of apples. The Eighth Army didn't fight its way through North Africa to let these damned immigrants from Europe pick our apples. Monty would turn in his grave."

The bargirls ignored him for they had heard it all before, and went about their business bending here and there. That's why Roger kept the bottles on the lower shelves when the top shelves were free. Roger wasn't stupid.

The British was musty, filled with the fumes of wood smoke and old wood and stale beer and the beef curry that was special for lunch. A tiny tributary had broken away from the pool on the bar surface and headed at snail's pace towards the edge. Sid the Nerve leant against the bar and the other customers watched the beer edge towards his back. Albert finished his beer and licked his moustache and concentrated on the stream.

Roger leant back, arms folded, eyes narrowed over his fixed smile. Eventually Nervous Sid said, "Shit!" and, with a shaking hand, tried to wipe his back.

The barber emptied his glass of bitter and said, "You know, Roger, you're the only boozer in town that hasn't bothered with Christmas decorations. Just an observation, that's all."

The owner remained silent for some time while his face ran through a series of pulls, then he said through gritted teeth, "Well, you can fuck off to one of the others then!"

"I don't like Christmas decorations," the barber said quickly as he waved his empty glass at a bargirl. "Reminds me of Christmas."

Roger said, "I'm thinking of renaming The British. Calling it The English instead."

"Why do that?"

"To make a point that we're not European, we're not British, we're English and proud of it. Saint George is the bollocks. Fuck Saint Patrick and Saint…the other fuckers. I don't want my kid to grow up a European, not knowing what a pint was. In this boozer the English pound is sacrosanct. None of that Euro shit. We've got more in common with the Russians than we have with the French or the Germans."

"The Boche! The Frogs! Here, here! Fought them for a thousand years so why should we be friends now?" The colonel fingered his medals with knackered fingers that had once caressed the cold trigger of a red-hot sten. My God, how he had enjoyed killing jerry and, after a few gin and tonics, the Nips. Not that he was ever in the Far Eastern theatre, apart from in his dreams. But age and booze had a habit of mixing dreams with reality.

It was the colonel's turn and Roger turned on him. "You're an old soldier, we all know that, for Queen and Country, a Desert Rat. Bet you've still got your Jerboa shoulder flashes hidden away some place."

"Maybe I have. What of it? I was proud to belong to the Seventh. But the Queen?" She had always presented the serviceman with a dilemma. Think of the kraut connection. Not an easy thing to think about.

Roger said, "Although they are banned from this bar we've got enough queens around here. We don't need another."

They all looked at the faces in the room to make sure there had been no infiltration and noticed that one or two of the more dodgy customers were slipping quietly to the back.

Roger went on, "I don't give a monkey's fuck about the Queen or her fucked-up family but I suppose we should feel sorry for them. It must be a bind to be born knowing that you'd never have to do a day's graft in your life."

The colonel seemed embarrassed and looked from left to right and made a conscious effort to force his rigid shoulders—without the flashes—to stand at ease.

Roger was on a roll and continued, "And I want the Muslims to know they're unwelcome."

"They already do," Albert said.

Nervous Sid's face cracked into a dark question mark. He said, "Don't get it."

Roger explained, "Think about it. The Muslims in this country call themselves British, right? Well, if they're British then I'm a fucking Chinaman. Also, in one hit, I can lose the Scottish, the Irish and the Welsh. Now that isn't bad."

Albert looked relieved and said, "I'm English."

"No you're not," Roger said. "You're a shonk. And when I change the name you're banned along with everyone else. Never trust a shonk, mate. Turn your back on the fuckers and you're likely to end up crucified."

The colonel said, "Jew boys caused us a lot of trouble in Palestine. Fifty years later they're still causing it."

"They're causing it in Westminster too."

Albert looked saddened and his head began to shake, "An unfortunate appearance I have, a larger nose than most, but a Jew that does not make me."

Roger said, "Maybe not, but I'll guarantee what you haven't got in your trousers does. Listen son, the English hate being lied to. That's why we don't like the Americans. We've seen your eyes when Sid brings in one of his rings. They light up like a couple of Roman candles. We can see them in the dark. Don't come it with us. You might just as well try and hide a Scouse accent. You're more Jewish than George Bush."

Albert shook a flustered head. "George Bush isn't Jewish."

"Isn't he? Isn't he? Well, the way he hates the Arabs he fucking well should be. But there's something else about you, I've noticed, that marks you out as a child of Israel—apart from your bowing down to the golden calf, that is—you never smile. One day you'll try it and your fucking face will fall off."

Someone muttered—it might have been the man who looked like a double-glazing salesman but more likely it was Mr Lawrence, "It sounds like a load of old *Cretan* Bull to me," but the others didn't get it. They might have done had they been Greek.

Roger picked up a sign and began pinning it to the wall. It read: No bad language or drug taking will be tolerated. No children under 25. No trainers. No football shirts with the exception of Everton. White South Africans welcome.

The last bit excited the colonel and it showed in his eyes but surprisingly it didn't bring any colour to his cheeks. He was tired and he knew it. It wasn't just age that had crept up on him, but life itself. Or rather, it was this new age that had crept up, where values—old-fashioned values—had been worn away. He wondered whether winning the war had been worth it, particularly since Blair had come to power. The gradual intrusion of faceless bureaucrats into his and everyone's life had been as imperceptible as it had been inexorable. It had been a '*death of a thousand cuts*'. He was a slave in his own country. It would have been easier had the Nazi storm troopers kicked in his door for then he would have known the enemy. What Tony Blair and his cronies had done was nothing less than treason. How he wished to have those men in the sights of his old Lee-Enfield. The Somme, wasn't it? He had been there, hadn't he? It was all so damned hazy now, like Iwo Jima and My Lai. But how satisfying it would be to put a .303 into Blair's grinning gob.

It was yet another dawn of disillusionment and dishonour, yet another cockcrow of contempt and another turning, in cold forgotten graves, for glorious forefathers.

He grimaced.

Christ! One of those storm troopers had shot him.

His mouth opened wide and left his false teeth hovering. Poligrip had not done the trick.

The stab of pain was deep.

He finished his drink, carefully placed his glass in the pool on the bar and sagged gently to his knees. His bony misshapen fingers felt for his medals and then clutched at his chest. He said, "Would someone be kind enough to send for an ambulance?" and then he keeled over on to his grey face.

Roger said, "If you're going to use the phone make sure you leave the money."

Nervous Sid said, "999 is fucking free."

"Is it? Is it? Make sure Gordon Brown doesn't hear about that!"

Albert grunted, "The beer it must be."

A bargirl dropped her filthy tea towel and burst into tears. Mr Lawrence doubted her sincerity for, as the late colonel had often said, women are good actors and can turn on emotion at the drop of a hat. Even so, it was a fair turn, and he watched her wailing and sniffing back her false tears. Eventually she gained enough composure to sob, "It wasn't the beer. He was drinking gin and tonic. Maybe he didn't exercise enough!"

And that had a few people, including the half-pint drinkers, raising their various eyebrows. A heart attack was one thing, but the thought of exercise was quite another.

Out of all that is bad comes an occasional good: lunch was extended. By the time the ambulance arrived, and the stretcher with its bearers, the colonel's medals had disappeared but Albert looked smugly satisfied, his chin beneath the fall of limp grey hair jutted higher and his eyes, black beads, concentrated on something on the ceiling. In each was the spark of a Roman candle.

It had been Albert who had leant over the colonel in what appeared to be an attempt at the kiss of life. He had pulled back at the last moment feeling faint at being so close to the ground, a sensation that tall men often experience.

He arrived back at the shop in a frivolous mood. He took off his hat and aimed at the hat stand and missed and his chortle could be heard on the pavement outside. He had all but skipped to the counter before he stopped abruptly and turned back to the window. There, with their backs to him, stood two splendid dummies, life-size and life-like: Father Christmas and a female assistant. Santa Claus carried a white sack overflowing with brightly wrapped presents and his assistant wore a red cape, some kind of red bodice, black suspender belt and nylon stockings.

For a moment Mr Lawrence was open-mouthed.

They stood either side of the ballerinas. Artificial snow frosted the window and covered the floor where they stood. The cold ivory-coloured skin of the mannequins glowed red as did the snow, caught in the soft glow of red window lights that blinked on and off. He wondered whether Santa's assistant went out in her underwear, and whether she'd feel the cold, or whether M&S or Robot City were searching for a missing mannequin complete with matching set.

Paul had crept back, as he had crept to the barber-shop, chancing that his suitor was elsewhere.

During the afternoon Mr Lawrence had an accident with the guillotine, although it wasn't entirely his fault. Had it been his left hand it would have been worse. Holding a paintbrush would have been difficult for he was left-handed, as most first-rate artists were. It took him an hour to stem the bleeding and, even then, a little blood seeped through the bandages.

The remainder of the shortened afternoon was spent in unpacking a crate of oriental oils. It wasn't easy one-handed.

Curiously, in the chest of fifty there were half a dozen that caught his eye. By a different artist, signed Dyson, they were good. Landscapes in a darker, subtle key; wild clouds and gentle hills, wind blown and heathery, with just a post in the foreground, or a single spindly tree. But the composition was excellent and the detail finely observed.

He put the six aside, leaving the mystery for another time, for time had flown and it was opening time. But there was something more than that tonight and Mr Lawrence was quite excited. He'd invited Laura to the theatre. They were meeting in The British.

Laura said, "What on earth have you done?"

"A little accident in the shop. Nothing much."

"Such a big bandage for nothing much."

"Does it really show?"

"The red does, Mr Lawrence. If you keep your hand bent down, then it won't show so much."

"Yes, I'll do that."

"How awful about the colonel," Laura said but she didn't seem too upset. She was dressed in a very short navy-blue pleated skirt that drew the eyes of the men in the room away from the bargirls, a white T-shirt with Michael Winner's face on the front and a denim jacket. Unusually for Laura there was plenty of navel on show, surprisingly flat navel at that, for Luscious Laura was a shapely girl. Her hair was tied back skullcap tight and a hint of make-up lightened her skin.

She pointed to Michael Winner's red face whose ears flapped Charles-like on her breasts. "It's the only thing I've got with a theatre connection," she said. "What do you think?"

"I think he's a film director, or was. Now he writes about the restaurants he's visited and he stars in silly advertisements. I've not seen his films."

Roger overheard, couldn't help himself, and cut in, "Best thing about him was the bird he used to live with. But she left him. Can't think of her name. But tasty. Although, having said that, one could argue that *I'll Never Forget What's 'Isname* was his best film. In fact it was just short of a great film."

The barber said, "I suppose one could, if one wanted to argue. Frankly, whether you like that or *Death Wish*, he is now a has-been. He hasn't done a thing for years."

Sid the Nerve showed up and put in, "At least he's a has-been. We—we're a bunch of hasn't-beens."

"Mr Lawrence isn't a hasn't-been," Laura said. "He's a painter."

Roger glanced at Mr Lawrence. "So is Bill Richards up the road who paints the double-yellow lines on the road outside. But we're getting away from the point. *Death Wish* was a good film. I'm a great believer in old-fashioned retribution. There's nothing finer than revenge served on an empty stomach. It should be a basic human right. Leave forgiveness to the sacrament of Penance—for you heathens, that's the confession. In that respect the Arabs have got it right."

Mr Lawrence looked a treat in his best clothes. Apart from the bandage. It tended to draw the eye.

Roger asked, "What happened to you?"

"A little accident with the guillotine. Nothing to worry about."

"I'm not worried, mate. Just curious."

In the corner Rasher's minders looked glum with nothing to do, their half-empty pints looked flat, their cigarettes in the ashtray had burned away leaving lengths of wasted ash.

Mr Lawrence glanced at his watch and said to Laura, "It's time to go."

And Luscious Laura put her arm through his and sashayed to the door letting all and sundry know that she was going up in the world. The art world. The theatre. She was on her way. So there.

They joined a chattering crowd passing beneath the life-size cut-out greeting from Anthea Palmer into the theatre's optimistic foyer where the smell of fresh paint still lingered.

Mr Lawrence hadn't been to the theatre since the 1971 revival of *Showboat*, and it was an altogether new experience for Laura. Once they'd settled in the darkened auditorium and the curtain went up she sat transfixed, as though not believing her own eyes.

The people next to them glanced at the bandage and eased slightly away.

After the show-stopping hits '*We Need More Female Gynaecologists*' and '*This isn't what Nye Bevan had in Mind*', about an hour into the show, the routine which led to the intermission took place.

Anthea Palmer looked radiant in her underwear and high heels, just as she'd done in a thousand newspaper photographs, snapped on the beach in tiny bikini briefs, topless if possible and, if not, then a shot of her behind. Behinds were definitely the thing, nowadays. She had a passable voice too. She sang the song, the song from the show that seemed to be heading for the Christmas number-one slot. It was played non-stop on the radio.

Laura had been singing it as they made their way up the Carrington's majestic steps.

Oh, Mr Lawrence, I think I love you
Oh, Mr Lawrence, I think you care...
Oh, Mr Lawrence, I think I love you
Oh, Mr Lawrence, we're almost there...

The act finished and people moved to the various bars but Mr Lawrence remained rooted to his seat. Laura shook him.

"What?"

"It's half-time, Mr Lawrence. It's time for a burger and a beverage."

"My goodness, my dear. I was totally carried away."

"They were singing about you, Mr Lawrence. Wasn't it good? It's the best thing I've ever seen. All that cross-dressing. Just as well Paul didn't come. It might have put ideas in his head."

"Indeed," Mr Lawrence said. "And he's got enough of those already."

What they didn't know as they sat enjoying the show, was that Paul was in the audience too. Up in the gods, two rows from the back, he sat utterly mesmerized, not knowing what time or day it was. He found the idea of men in women's clothing more than just a little exciting.

There was an easiness about the paid for evening. A candle flickered from an old bottle, the neck of which was gobbed with wax. Over her crisp fried-prawn jhuri she told him that she was saving her money to go to America and that her mother had found out about her 'sideline' and had gone 'ape', threatening her with all kinds of harm, including kicking her out of the house. None of it seemed to bother her for her soft looks seldom hardened. That is not to say that her looks were anything other than luscious but they maintained a gentle, yielding—even compassionate—quality which all men, everywhere, found utterly captivating. She was quite perfect, an Eve among Adams, at home and at ease in this Indian Eden.

"You should be like me. Then you wouldn't worry so much. You wouldn't have all those worry lines on your face."

He laughed at her suggestion. "As the bard would have told you, my dear, in words that are not as good as these: youth, like a poor man's plonk, has an end-date and to try for an extension is one of the most ludicrous things that men and women, can do. It makes for a pretty pathetic show. And as for me, I was born with these grooves."

"What about the white hair?"

"You're getting personal."

"That is part of my job. And I do know Shakespeare. He was the guy who said a good wine needs no bush. Maybe that if you drink too much you can't get it on. See? I'm not just a pretty face."

Behind her the pastel colours of the wall mural flickered in the candlelight. Disapproval and censure flowed from the obscured forms of Brahma and Vishnu and Shiva. No redemption—*moksha*—for him. He would have to come back and do it all again. That was a thought. She began on her shahi beagun and wiped a fleck of sweet coconut from her painted lips.

"Do you believe in God, Mr Lawrence?"

"My goodness. That's an odd question."

"I know, but even so..."

"It's a difficult one, my dear, and it's a question that's crossed my mind once or twice, particularly during those times when the socialists have been in power."

She frowned.

He went on, "But of course I believe. It's just that I call him something else."

"What's that?"

182

"George."

She pulled a face.

"Don't worry, my dear. So long as the Creationists keep taking the medication we'll be all right."

"Well, I believe."

"Good for you. Well done."

"Everyone's gotta have a dream."

"That's true."

"I've seen you about for years, before my mum started cleaning your shop. I often saw you in The British. You looked lonely. You were with the others but you weren't. Does that make sense?"

"You're very intuitive."

"Yes, you're right."

"But it wasn't loneliness, my dear. It was sadness. When you get to my age you realize it's too late to start again and then, looking at a girl like you, you feel a pang, perhaps of hunger but more likely of missed chances, of wasted time. I wasn't to know then that you would come along and brighten the day and lighten the night."

"But you've already made your mark, Mr Lawrence, your paintings for a start. In any case, you're not old, you're not as old as you act."

"It's nice of you to say so but I've always thought of myself as a friendly old fellow. Shall we go or would you like a sweet?"

"A sweet? Don't be so tight, you old thing. Can't I have a pudding?"

So, tucking into chilli ice cream and mango, she continued, "Oh, Mr Lawrence, friendly is not a word I'd give to you. In fact, I think you like people thinking you are unfriendly. Grumpy, that's it. It's your street cred. But you're not really like that. I've sussed you out. You're just a big softie, I know. Look at the way you've taken Paul in, and look at the way you help all the wannabe painters. See, I'm a psycho thingamabob. Let's get back and you can lie on the sofa and I'll show you a thing or two."

"Well, if you insist, two might be nice, just so long as you don't poke me in the eye—both eyes—like last time."

"Sit there," she told him. He still wore his hat. She dropped her jacket to the floor, poured some drinks and slopped one in his good hand. On his bad hand blood was once again seeping through the bandages. She stepped out of her pants and moved to the stack. She put on the CD from the show that she had insisted he buy from a hastily arranged table in the foyer and sang along.

"Oh, Mr Lawrence I think I love you…"

Then, perhaps with the brass ballerinas in mind, she performed a delightful pirouette.

"Isn't it marvellous, Mr Lawrence? I could be on the stage."

"I imagine you could. Yes, and from what I've seen of your dancing—in The British—you would make a perfect hoofer."

"Pardon?"

"Hoofer, my dear, with an F."

"Oh, one of those." Her voice was not convincing.

"If not a dancer then a player and I could help you. You could use me as a prop or, come to think of it, abuse me as a prop as well."

She punched his arm and he raised an eyebrow and, beneath it, his eye twinkled.

"You're joking, Mr Lawrence. You're taking advantage of an innocent young girl."

"Am I? Am I indeed? I'm not sure who is taking advantage around here and just who is so innocent. I suppose that's always the problem, isn't it? Who is guilty and who is innocent? And yet, the clues are all around."

Straddling him, she tugged at his buttons. He flinched and smudged her with blood. She raised her hands to his shoulders and lowered herself.

Sinking upwards, he watched his twenty-five quid's worth find a slow rhythm and shook his head in wonder.

He said, "Don't stop."

"I'm not going to, Mr Lawrence."

"Singing, I mean."

"Oh, is that all?" Her smile was infectious. "Oh, Mr Lawrence I think I love you…"

The shop and the flat above were filled with shadows and night noises. Headlights on the High Road slid past sending the shadow of the hook skidding across the walls. They brought the ballerinas to life and sent their shadows dancing across the wooden floors. They stretched the shadows of the mannequins and sent them chasing after the ballerinas. They caught an occasional passer-by and sent yet more shapes to join the ball. The wind sighed across the roof slates, the old water pipes clanked and the steel chain rattled and above it all, someone snored.

In the stuffy bedroom Laura lay awake listening to the night music and considering her future. Her heart was beating faster than normal. She had been entertained and wined and dined and put into a bed with clean sheets and it hadn't cost her a penny. Perhaps it was the grand theatre and the show and the mixing with theatre-goers who paid five pounds for their programmes that had led to her excitement but she felt a strange sense that things were on the move, something to change her life was on its way. She curled up closer to the soundly sleeping, bubble-blowing Mr Lawrence and wondered whether he, the artist, the celebrity, would figure in her intoxicating dawn.

Chapter 18

Paul had time on his hands so he took care of Mr Lawrence's little errand. He caught a bus to the Ridgeway and found the house he wanted, more of a cottage, really, with a large square of nipped grass surrounded by a waist-high fence. It was neat and moss free. You just knew the owners spent a lot of time fussing around with Black & Decker. It was a street where the houses had drives and extensions, and boys and girls delivered broadsheets instead of tabloids and always on time. There were fewer satellite dishes. Paul noticed things like that. And here kids used playing fields with real goalposts instead of concrete and shop fronts. And dogs? They were smaller. And mostly white. Funny, that in the more affluent areas the size of dogs and TV screens went down. Funny that, innit? And sad in a way, cos it meant that kids from the rich homes didn't have big TVs to watch. And that meant they'd probably end up with glasses, short-sighted or squinting, or something. Yeah.

He spent a couple of hours there, hanging around the street, watching the comings and goings. Eventually an old couple emerged from the cottage and the old man shouted over the fence.

"You there! Yes, you! We've got our eye on you. Clear off or we'll call the police. Understand?"

Tory voters!

Fuck that.

Paul cleared off.

It didn't take much savvy to reason that Mr Lawrence had given him the wrong address. The old man had got it wrong. They say age messes with the memory and they were right. There was certainly no girl living there. No beautiful Indian girl with dark eyes and black hair and legs that went all the way to… Yeah, right! And those two old Tory voters weren't her parents. No sir. NO SIR! No way.

By the time he got back to the High Road dusk was falling and the street lights turned on Saturday night. Christmas illuminations gave the road a party feel, added a little excitement and cheer, like three lemons on a slot machine. Like a cold smile from a bargirl that meant no chance sunshine, no chance at all.

Shops stayed open late and a choir sang Christmas songs while a dozen Santas collected money in fat Toby jugs. He looked in the shop windows for the Christmas message, the birth of Christ, goodwill to all men, but couldn't find it between the spend, spend, spend and the banks of computers and widescreen TVs tied in Christmas ribbon. For a while, like, twenty minutes or so, he stood in front of a window and a TV, and watched in Cinerama—you'd need an extension on the house to get it in—a million people on the move. Africa was a vast graveyard, still uncivilized and uncaring, and while he watched the dark leather-skinned children cry while their mothers gazed out of helpless eyes and the shadows of vultures slid across the cooking battleground, a choir sang, '*Oh come, all ye faithful, joyful and triumphant…*'

And suddenly, in front of that wide living screen, Paul knew that the whole business of religion, was crap.

He heard, '*All things bright and beautiful.*'

He ran down the High Road, trying to outrun the voice. But it caught him up and mixed up the harvest festival with Christmas.

> *He gave us eyes to see them*
> *He gave us leprosy*
> *He made the highest mountains*
> *To fall on you and me…*

See? See? See what I mean? Stop! Stop right now!

And Paul stopped. And passers-by looked at the strange young man who was sweating and steaming while a heavy frost fell around him and turned the litterbins white.

Christmas, goose fat, a penny for the old man's hat. Kick his head in more like. Steal his pension. Take that!

It was right, wasn't it, that in a lawless society those with would soon be without? It was right that at Christmas the bosses and toffs should get their comeuppance, that they should be forced to sleep in a stable... in Africa. Yeah.

And then it was Saturday night for real.
The scene was set, the third act, and Paul was in heaven. It was his first time in the theatre, and it moved him to tears. He cried out loud and the people beside him were, for a while, amused. The barber had given him the ticket in exchange for a TV set. It was a complimentary given to the barber when he agreed to hang a poster in his window. The barber wasn't an Anthea Palmer fan. He liked Sophia Loren. He'd been keen on her ever since he'd seen *Boy on a Dolphin* in 1957. He remembered the year well, he told Paul. The EEC was formed. Macmillan was Prime Minister. Sputnik took off. But the highlight was Sophia's tits poking out of a see-through vest. Nipples the size of half-crown pieces, the colour of a good claret. Technicolor. Remember Technicolor? It was going to change your life. Right? Paul wondered what a half-crown piece was.

The stage was a hospital ward and Anthea Palmer had arrived with her best friend.

Anthea sang:

> *I'm looking for the gynaecology department.*

And as she looked around for assistance, her best friend sang:

She's looking for the gynaecology department
She needs a professional point of view
A little sperm has found its way
And decided it wants to stay
And now she needs advice on what to do.

A male consultant passed by:

What have we here? Internal examination?
Cervical smear, dear? Contraceptive fitting?
Sit you on the end of a rubber glove, shall we?
Routine check-up, is it? High chair, stirrups
and a...speculum!

Paul experienced an urge to kill the consultant. His eyes narrowed to slits and a muscle in his temple began to pop.

Anthea Palmer, lonely and beautiful and drawing yet more tears from Paul, moved to one side of the stage and sang:

We want more female gynaecologists
Who understand our feelings and our fears
Why should we have this humiliation
Each time we need an examination?

Anthea sounded innocent and fragile; he just knew that in real life she wore white underwear. He saw the girl on TV, in front of the map of the British Isles, pointing at clouds spitting three huge teardrops.

And so Paul, Paul Knight, weeping, fell in love with Anthea Palmer, ex-weather girl, the blond-bobbed goddess of countless travel shows and tabloid front pages, and he couldn't get over her. His eyes were still red when he arrived at Avenue Road, the dangerous place of run-down terraced houses. But Paul had no option. Mr Lawrence had been right.

He had to disappear for a little while and keep well out of the way of his ex-cell mate. He couldn't think of a better place to disappear than Avenue Road. People had been disappearing there for years.

The area was in the process of being demolished to make way for a new development. Huge diggers and concrete crushers stood idle; giant stick insects reaching out of the red-tinted darkness. In the morning they'd come to life, noisy and threatening, belching plumes of black smoke, flattening the earth. And then, in time, there'd be another Robot City, where robots shopped.

Half the road was already levelled but numbers four to twelve and three to eleven remained largely intact, two rows of five houses facing each other across a rutted road in the midst of devastation, piles of brick and jagged-edged concrete and twisted girders, like a war zone, like one of the scenes from… Where was it?

Over there. One of those places where all the troublemakers came from. Paul was more interested in the place in Africa where the civil war was killing millions, the war our politicians weren't interested in. No oil, no aerospace deal. No interest.

Four to twelve, as with three to eleven, surrounded by great mounds of rubble, had broken windows, some of them boarded, and front doors sealed by the shadowy authorities. When the wind was wrong it whistled through the windows and filled the rooms with an icy blast. Once, Paul remembered, he'd woken up with frost on his blanket. But it was that or the Big Issue and some newspapers in a shop doorway. And praying that the guy sleeping next to you wasn't from Glasgow or, worse, Edinburgh.

Paul knew his way about, like most of them did. You took a shower in the local leisure centres when no one was looking, you visited the charity shops before they opened and went through the black sacks that were left piled in the entrances.

Paul knew his way into the even-numbered row. There were various windows the occupiers used as bolt-holes and one of the back doors had been broken open. The local kids called the place the Warren because holes had been knocked through walls so that there were internal passageways to all five houses. There were a dozen or more people living in the row. No one was quite sure how many because people would come and go. Some would stay for a night or two, particularly when the weather was bad, and it hadn't been good lately, and others had been there for months. The last house in the row, number 12, even though it was serviced by three passageways, one down and two up, was occupied by a single person and was out of bounds to all the others. That was just about the only rule. You didn't go into number 12.

An old-timer lived there. Rumour had it that he had South African connections but he didn't have a South African accent, more like Huddersfield, Paul would tell you, for there were some odd people from Huddersfield. There was also a rumour that he was an ex-Druid who still, on occasion, wore his old robes and made his way to Stonehenge every summer solstice. Truth told, they didn't know much about him. But they did know that his favourite time of year was November the fifth and the weeks leading up to it. He'd spend those weeks visiting the Paki shops, Londis and places like that, looking at the fireworks. He loved the fireworks, the big bastards in particular, those that cost a hundred quid a time and sent, like, a hundred bangers into the air that fanned out with colour and shook the earth. There was something about shaking the earth that he liked.

He liked to cook. But he wasn't very good at it. Not if the smell was anything to go by. Clouds of wicked steam that made your eyes water would pour through the passageways from number 12 and when that happened, which was often, then the occupants of number 10 moved down to 8, 6 and 4. It was inconvenient but no one complained. No way. The old-timer was in charge. That was never an issue. They called him Powder Pete.

Someone told Paul—he couldn't remember who—that Powder Pete had once worked in a paint spraying place, spraying metalwork and turning the silver-grey into black and blue, and that's how he got his name. But it was only hearsay.

Powder Pete was a bit special. That's why they respected his privacy. The authorities would turn off the water and he'd have it back on in minutes. They'd cut the electricity and gas but that made no difference either. He'd just go out in the night and an hour later the lights would be back on. He looked after them and, for that, they were grateful. People would pay him a little rent. Not much. Nothing if they were sick and couldn't go robbing or dealing. One thing Powder Pete didn't like was the kids on the game. Not the kids, just the game and the adults who played it. He said that he was trying to give the kids back their childhood and the game took that away. He didn't stop them. That wasn't his way. But he'd try and talk them out of it. In a subtle way so it didn't sound like preaching. Robbing was safer, he'd say. And dealing, that was the thing. That was the present and the future. Dope was the biggest growth industry going. Along with computers. Another thing he didn't like was the youngsters taking the drugs. Drugs are for selling, he'd say. But he understood that some of them were well hooked by the time they got to him, so the least he could do was make sure their gear wasn't spiked.

Take Ruth, for instance. A lot of men had. She was eleven years old and she'd been on the game for over a year. She was quite philosophical for her age. Her father and her uncles had been having a go since she was six. If she returned home it would carry on so she might just as well make some dosh out of it. And there was a lot of dosh out there. Paul had asked her about her mother. Apparently, her mother simply didn't believe her. Called her a wicked liar. Said she was trying to come between her and dad. Said she was making excuses for wetting the bed and bunking off school. Powder Pete got hold of a rubber sheet to cover her mattress and until it was sorted he changed her blanket every day without saying a thing. And he boiled her underwear to get shot of the stains. Got it clean as new. And he never said a thing to any of the others. As far as he was concerned it was their little secret, not important at all, not even worth talking about. It was Ruth who told Paul. And for a while back there, the sadness of it all got to him and he forgot all about the people in Africa, a lot of them Ruth's age.

For a while he thought of Ruth and nothing else and the way Powder Pete looked after her, bedwetting and all. Paul snivelled, "When you hear something like that it makes you realize what a wonderful world it is. That black guy was right. What a wonderful world."

Powder Pete looked after the kids that society didn't want, the kids that had fallen through the net. He was fighting a battle against everyone and everything to give them a future. He was up there with the good guys like…like Prince Charles, David Bowie, people like that.

One night, when Paul cuddled up to Ruth—no sex or anything—he explained to her that Pete, in a sense, was the social worker for the children of the night. The children that no one else cared about. He didn't give them rules, save the one, don't go into the end house, and he let them do their own thing, run wild, make a noise, make a mess, eat what they wanted, when they wanted. Play their music really loud. It was the best sort of home you could have. Outside a real one. With a mom and dad who loved you. And not the way your dad loved you.

At the time Paul hadn't known about her bedwetting. Not until the morning.

She had a beautiful little face and a smile, with crooked teeth, that was contagious. It made you want to hug her. But she died. Just like that. Like the best people did. Like…like Frank Sinatra and Prince Charles. Just like that. Before he went inside the last time. Pneumonia, or something. Powder Pete dropped her off at the hospital. He'd found her sweating and all his remedies made no difference. So he took her to the hospital but it was too late. She died two days later aged eleven and a quarter. And apart from the few months she'd spent at Powder Pete's, she'd never had a childhood.

Powder Pete blamed himself. You could see it in his wild eyes. Even now, over a year later, you could see it. He should have realized how serious it was, that it wasn't just a heavy cold, and so on. The sadness had pulled down a veil, like, and the colour, even the red rage in his eyes, was dulled.

Enough to make you cry. And when Paul heard it that's what he did and Powder Pete had to console him. "Pull yourself together, Paul. When life's had enough of you, it doesn't care whether you're innocent or not, young or old, see? Life's a bastard judge that'll sentence you to death at the drop of a hat. Just like that. No point in making long-term plans, Paul Knight, because life's got a cruel sense of humour. You gotta be rich for God to love you."

Some said, and Paul believed them, that Powder Pete never really got over it. That her death had galvanized him into more drastic measures. Cooking, perhaps, because that started in earnest after she'd died. Maybe concentrating on the recipes took his mind off the guilt. He still took flowers to a little nameplate by a white rose in a garden of remembrance. His were the only flowers. Probably cos the guy in charge didn't like flowers in that part of the cemetery. They were allowed on the graves, but not on the nameplates. Cremation, obviously, was second best. Stupid, really. That's why Powder Pete broke the guy's nose and promised him something worse. That's why the guy didn't mind the flowers anymore. He probably knew that when Powder Pete made a promise he kept it.

One other thing that stood Powder Pete from the rest of mankind, the kids had noticed, was that whenever he went out and, that was mostly at night, he wore a waistcoat of steel tubing. A dozen tubes about nine inches long, fastened together around his waist. The kids accepted them as part of Powder Pete. A new fashion, maybe. Beneath his black jacket, of course, once he'd buttoned it up, you wouldn't know the difference. Apart from the lumps.

A girl named Jenny had taken Ruth's mattress. She was older, fifteen maybe, and streetwise. And she had a foul mouth. But she was like, seven months pregnant, so she wasn't all that. Maybe it was all talk. Maybe she wasn't so streetwise after all. Her hair was all over the place, brown streaked with blond with mousy roots, in need of a wash. Bit of a stale smell. Smoke. Once she started to swell she started to roll her own, for the baby's sake, she said. Increased the weed and cut back on the tobacco. She was going to be one of those conscientious mothers, one of those green friends of the earth. Pity there weren't more like her, really, then the world would be a better place. She'd got a tattoo on her arm. Barbed wire, like, all the way round. Maybe that said something about her life. Maybe she was, like, being kept in, or out.

"Feel that," she said.

Paul hesitated. "No, I don't think so."

She showed him her belly, and a little ring in her bursting navel, and a trace of dark-brown hair until she pulled up her pants.

"Go on."

Tentatively, Paul reached out.

"See," she said.

"Fuck!"

"Yeah."

"Fucking right."

"See? Told you."

He felt some more, the ends of his fingers slipped under elastic.

She said, "That's far enough."

"Right. Just checking." He withdrew his hand. "Amazing that is, though. Makes you think, dunnit?"

He found Brian Lara in the shadows, tube of fuel in one hand, in the other a paper funnel to help with the huff.

"All right, Jay?"

"It's Brian Lara now."

"Fair enough, but you ain't black."

"You can have a black white man, if you want, if you ain't prejudice. I mean, no one's white, are they? They're red, they're pink, they're lightly cooked or they're well cooked. No one's white, except the Irish."

"Fair enough. How's it going, Bry?"

"Dick, dick, dick, dosh, dosh, dosh. You know?"

"Yeah. Waiting for Powder Pete, see?"

"Yeah. Powder Pete's OK."

"He knows everything, about the universe and important stuff. The scientists should talk to him then they wouldn't waste their time with telescopes and writing on blackboards. Powder Pete reckons it's all crap. He says you can't have something inside of nothing so that proves it goes on forever. The universe, everything. And that means it never started. That's it then, innit? No God."

"Who cares? Why bother? Waste of time thinking. It don't stop the sore throat, does it?"

"Good point. No point."

"Dick dosh, innit? Nothing else matters. Never did."

"Yeah. That stuff's probably done your throat."

"Gotta be done, though."

"Yeah, suppose."

"Tick tock, tick tock, dick dosh, dick dosh."

"Yeah, it's a living innit? I heard you was with the kozzers."

"Yeah, was."

"Fuck that."

"Yeah, that's what I thought."

"What they want?"

"About the girls getting knifed innit?"

"They thought you…? Where do they get off nowadays? No wonder the streets ain't safe no more."

"No, not me. Fucking hell. Thought I might have seen something, that's all."

"Oh, that's all right then. Did you?"

"Might of done. That's the point. You see people, don't you? But you don't. People is people. They're meaningless ain't they? When you think about it. A whole fucking person, but we don't give a fuck. I've been sitting here thinking about that."

"I've been thinking about the people in Africa."

"That's what I'm saying, innit? That's the point. Faces is faces. Can't remember. Thinking about the dosh. Don't see nothing else, do you? Gotta get through today. Dick, dick, dosh, dosh. Scratchcard later, maybe. Fuck tomorrow. All the faces innit? Don't give a fuck, see?"

"Absolutely. See that. Right. But, you helping them?"

"Sort of. Not grassing."

"I didn't mean that. Fuck that."

"The geezer they're looking for, right? Who might be a woman. They reckon he's going to kill somebody. Maybe next time. They think, maybe, one of the toms might have seen him. Like. So they want me to finger the toms. Bit silly cos they've only gotta go down the road and they finger themselves and they know them all anyway. That fucking sergeant geezer, you know the one, big geezer, he's always sniffing around the toms. But there's this one I saw, they're interested in her."

"Fuck that."

"That's what I thought."

"Yeah. No way."

"Then this other geezer, bright bastard, not a kozzer..."

They both laughed.

"He says, like, he'll give me his word that he ain't interested in anything other than the geezer who's doing it."

"You said it might be a woman?"

"Yeah, that's what he said."

"Did you believe him, about the other?"

"Yeah. Can't believe I did. You don't believe no one, do you? But I did. I got a feeling, just a feeling, you know? He'll be back. With dosh. Dick, dick, know what I mean?"

"Fucking hell!"

"Yeah. That's what I thought."

In the corner, in the flicker of candle, something stirred. Two girls, sharing a mattress. Paul caught their faces, didn't know them, put them around thirteen but who could tell nowadays?

"Keep the noise down," one said. "We're trying to sleep."

Maybe not thirteen, after all. Too confident. Maybe fourteen. Apologetically he whispered, "Yeah, sorry. Talking, see? Innit?"

They disappeared again beneath a dirty quilt. Between them, on top of the quilt, lay a black cat, disturbed by the girl's movement, its tail flicking like something from hell.

"Look what I got here," Jason or Brian said. He opened up a strong Robot City carrier. "Bats."

"Bloody hell, how many you got?"

"Six. Worth, maybe, forty each."

"Tennis."

"No."

"Squash, then?"

"No, no."

"Badminton."

"Yeah, that's it. And I got these trainers, bag full. Mostly Reebok, see? Need to offload them. What do you think? Will they sell in the shop?"

"The Gallery? Maybe. I could try."

"Half-half, right?"

"Sounds all right."

"Done, then. Take them with you. Get nicked around here as soon as I close my eyes. Can't trust no one, can you?"

"No. You're right."

It was much later when Powder Pete found him. Paul had been dozing, woke to find Powder Pete standing over him. It wasn't a pretty sight. Powder Pete was wide-boned and covered in clothes to go out in. They made him wider, more threatening. And lumpy.

He said, "Thought you'd got a job?" The bones in his face were prominent. And his skin, pale, stretched over the bones.

"That's right. Just gotta make myself scarce for a day or two."

"So how's it going? You learning to paint?"

"Yeah. Gotta learn about the classics first. That's the thing, see?"

"You're an arsehole, Paul Knight, you know that? The only thing you're ever going to paint is numbers, and even that'd turn out shite. The only thing you're good at is robbing, and you should stick to what you're good at. You got a gift, a divine gift, and you should use it. TVs and DVDs and computers. The future, the bollocks. Not junk. Playstations, Internet, Kings Cross, E-something. Mail. Shit hot. Right?"

"Right?"

"And car batteries. I need lots of car batteries."

"You in to cars now then, Powder Pete?"

"No, not cars, sulphuric acid, Paul. I need it to clean things up."

"What things, Powder Pete?"

"Things. The world. The planet. I've decided to become a one-man cleaning company. But never you mind about that and tell me what you're doing now."

"Staying out of sight for a while, see?"

"Staying out of sight is good. It's good for the soul. But this isn't the place to do it. Had visitors earlier, some of Ticker Harrison's mob. Started throwing their weight around. We gotta move out, find another place and build a stockade, a barrier against the so-called civilized world."

"Yeah, wouldn't want to mess with them. No way. How long you got?"

"Ten days, they said."

Paul shook a resigned head.

"But that's not the point. I told you last time, this place is for the youngsters. No one over eighteen."

"I know that. I know you told me. I thought you'd make an exception, just for a day or two."

"Over eighteens are over the road. It's the rule. My rule. The only one that counts."

"I do know that. But like, I fit in here, don't I?"

Powder Pete smiled. "Yes you do. I've noticed that. You've never grown up, Paul. Something went wrong with you and I don't know what. You're a rogue and a rascal and an impossible dreamer but most of all, you're innocent, you're one of the meek and, if you live, Paul Knight and, I have my doubts, then you'll inherit the earth. And that's why, before, I've made you an exception. But you're a grown man and these children are vulnerable and, no matter what your problems, I shouldn't put them at risk. They gotta come first."

"I'd never touch them, Pete, Sir, never! I'd take care of them, and I'd cuddle them if they needed it. And that's all it would ever be. If they cry out in the night I'd hold them till they settled. That's all. I'd fight for them, just like you!"

"I believe you, Paul Knight. Many wouldn't. But I do. You said it well and you can stay for a couple of days or so. And right now, you can come with me. I've had a tip-off, a word from the underworld. One of Ticker Harrison's villains that came to threaten us gave me the word. Even villains hate the nonces. There's a couple of children in trouble, and that should be everybody's business but it isn't. So it's down to us. We're all that they've got. So let's go. We won't be in time but we can pick up the pieces."

"I'm with you, Powder Pete."

Paul quickened his pace and ran to catch up.

Chapter 19

As they led the children through the silent backstreets bells chimed out midnight, the apogee of darkness, the time when cold-blooded things began to stir. Frost fell like snow. The children shivered. Teeth chattered. Their trainers smacked the cold pavements. The tiny hairs on the girl's legs stood out, caught in unearthly light. The same light that sparkled in the boy's frightened eyes. Paul tightened his grip on the children's sweaty hands. The wind whipped into their faces. It drew out their tears and snatched them away.

Voices, even their breathing, sounded deeper.

"You ever noticed, Paul, you take an 'o' out of good, you got God, you take the 'd' out of devil, you got evil? There's a mystery to life, more than we know."

"You're right, Powder Pete, I see that."

The pavements were bare. They seemed wider. The slabs glistened. They seemed harder.

The children clung on knowing instinctively that these strange men, the old man and his apprentice, were their salvation.

"Warm milk," the older man said suddenly, and left them wide-eyed and wondering.

They'd travelled a dozen streets, maybe ten minutes, when they heard the explosion, a huge ear-splitting thump that shook the ground and rattled the windows in the dark properties butting the pavement they trod. Then came the sound of breaking glass. Along the street a few lights went on and a couple of people came out to scan the rooftops.

Beyond the terraced rows a curl of smoke spiralled on the wind and a few stars blinked out.

Then came the urgent sounds of distant fire-engines and police cars.

"Bloody hell, Powder Pete, that was more than a sparkler, that was more than a Chinese cracker. I reckon you've taken out half the street."

"No, just the one house." Powder Pete's voice was calm and dependable. "They won't do it again, will they? Hope they find tranquillity for that's the sea that their bollocks are swimming in. That's what I call justice. Nothing else will do. Their names will never be on the sex offender's register, and they'll never come out of prison to do it again. And that is good."

They held the children's hands and led them back to the squat in Avenue Road, that huge run-down nursery for the children of the night.

Powder Pete told them, "Now's not the time to talk. It's a hot bath for you both to get rid of the filth, then hot milk and bed. In the morning we can talk." He turned to Paul and added, "Wake one of the older girls, the one who's pregnant will do. She can help this young lady to clean up. And she'll know if a hospital's called for."

Paul nodded thoughtfully. Powder Pete wasn't taking any chances. Not any more.

The boy said abruptly, "We ain't going back home. No way."

Powder Pete answered sternly. "Did I say that? Did I? That's up to you and your sister."

"It's me dad. He's not our real dad. But he does things."

The girl nodded in agreement. She was all of nine. The boy was older by a couple of years.

Paul said, "So you got her out of it, did you?"

"Had to. No choice."

"What about your mum?"

He struggled. "She don't know."

"She should know."

The boy shook his head and a tear squeezed from his eye.

"Those two geezers back there, they meet you at the station?"

"Said they knew a place we could stay."

Powder Pete cut in, "Now's not the time. We'll sort it in the morning. But you're too young to be on the streets. This is a dangerous place."

"So's my bedroom at home," the girl said suddenly, surprising them.

In the early hours the Warren was still and damp. Only the occasional flickering night-light, tiny candles in silver containers supplied by Powder Pete, shone through the darkness. Nightmares woke the kids and in the darkness they tasted the fear of abandonment. Those that were streetwise slept through it, barely disturbed. They had learned the hard way how to shut out the unforgiving world.

Powder Pete listened to their cries and sometimes he'd throw on his old dressing gown and fight with his slippers and he'd make his way through the tunnels to the source of distress. There, he'd stroke a sweaty brow and whisper. "It's all right, all right. You're safe. And I'll look after you."

The dark things that crawled in the night were outside and they couldn't get in.

"You're safe here," he'd whisper. "I won't let anyone hurt you. Go back to sleep."

The crying became a whimper and then a snatch of breath and then, moments later, soothed by his certainty, the deeper sigh of sleep.

Powder Pete was the guardian, the protector, the trustee. The bollocks, really.

The difference between hard men and the rest of mankind is not subtle. Hard men are willing to do things that others are not. They'd use a knife or a gun or a broken bottle without compunction, without a single thought to the consequences and without pity. The difference lay in a tiny gene, or the lack of it, that created a conscience, that moral sense that made cowardice a virtue. Paul's suitor was a hard man.

Suitor is probably the wrong word, for he is a man who pursues a woman. But Paul was becoming more feminine by the day.

Hard men can find things and other people easily, because people talk to them. It might have been the kids, or perhaps the trail started in The British, but someone talked, and the big hirsute—bald—unsavoury type turned up, just as Paul was turning in.

"Oh, it's you."

"You don't seem pleased to see me."

Paul tried to hang back from the beer-breath but it was impossible.

"I heard you'd become a painter of pictures."

"Yeah, something."

"Maybe you could paint me."

The words came slowly, strangled in the throat, fighting phlegm and swollen glands.

The lights were out. Only a distant candle gave Paul the outline and it was even bigger than he remembered.

"I've been looking for you. All this time I've been thinking of nothing else." His voice dropped a notch. "After you got out, I didn't know what to do."

"I, I, I thought of you too."

"That's good."

Paul felt his balls being stroked, then he felt them being crushed. He gasped out loud.

"I heard you been fucking hiding from me!"

"No, no, that's wrong." His voice rose a couple of octaves. "It was the kozzers."

"You was supposed to be waiting for me."

"I was waiting, honest, but they was all over the place. You must have seen them."

"I been fucking celebrity and I ain't waiting no longer."

"There's children in here."

"They're asleep, or they should be. This time of night."

Paul had no choice and it went like it always had. Surprisingly, to begin with, and it always happened even though he knew what was coming, it gave him an erection, but that folded when the beating started.

There was no doubt about it, if this affair continued, then Paul would be beaten to death.

"I'm sorry, Paul, this is difficult, but I can't have the children put at risk."

"I understand. I agree with you. It's my problem."

"I'd help you. But you're an adult, old enough to help yourself. Sort it out and you're welcome back. That man is a lunatic. Can't take the chance. Not on my account, but for the kids. Responsibilities, see? If it wasn't for the kids I'd help you out. But he's dangerous and I got to weigh the odds. And they don't come down on your side."

"I understand, Powder Pete. Really I do. I'll go."

"You could go over the road, with the dossers, but sooner or later you've got to sort it. He'll be back."

"I know that. I know that. It's decisions, innit?"

"Decisions, right. They're the things you got to make when you're an adult. And you'll know when you're an adult when you realize there might not be an answer. Where will you go?"

"Back to the shop."

"He'll find you there."

"Yeah. Mr Lawrence will help me."

"He's the painter?"

"Yeah."

"He's an old man. What can he do?"

"He's a thinker, Powder Pete. He'll think of something. I heard, somewhere, that brains is better than prawns."

"That's bollocks. Fear is the key, Paul Knight, the fear of death, that inventor of heaven and hell and all the gods there ever were. When people know that you have no fear then they will fear you."

"So I'll make myself scarce, then."

"Yes. I've got to let you go, Paul. I want to help you but, if I get hurt…bad… And time's against me. Gotta find a new place, a safe place. The villains, Ticker's men, are coming back and this time they'll mean business."

"You don't need to say nothing, Powder Pete. Just help me out, will you? I'm hurting a bit. Just a bit."

"You're bleeding."

"Yeah, a bit. It ain't much, is it?"

"You ought to get to the hospital, boy. Something might be busted, inside. But they'll ask questions. It didn't happen here, right?"

"Don't you worry about me, Powder Pete. You got enough to worry about with the kids. I'll make out. Always did, right? You take care of the kids. I'll be back... Terminator, innit?"

Powder Pete helped him through the window and passed out the bags containing the badminton rackets and trainers. He shook a sad head. Paul Knight was one of life's losers, a non-starter in the race of the nobbled. Had he been a dozen years younger then Powder Pete would have taken an interest, taken care of him, but lines had to be drawn. Aid agencies across the world drew them and one man could only do so much.

It was a shame, but there was nothing he could do but watch him go, damaged goods leaking on to the gutted road.

A dawn cry broke the silence, the cry of another day, and Powder Pete turned from the window and the forlorn figure of Paul Knight, a hunched silhouette against the shine of the city, clambering over the top of the world, the piles of rubble and the silent diggers. He moved towards the sound of tears and found their source curled up beneath a stained duvet.

He stroked a head of damp hair and said gently, "Don't be frightened. I'll take care of you. My name is Powder Pete."

Chapter 20

Two days earlier, the day before Brian Lara had met Paul Knight in Avenue Road, PC Donna Fitzgerald spent the morning with Geoff Maynard. She considered that Cole and Maynard made an unlikely alliance. Cole was direct, intense and dangerous on a number of levels—even the villains recognized it. He was good-looking too with a physique that would make a cheap suit look good. She couldn't imagine him involved in household chores or relaxing in front of the TV. But just the thought of him quickened her pulse. She was in trouble and she knew it.

Maynard, on the other hand, was relaxed and informal and the casual clothes he wore—she hadn't yet seen him out of jeans—were well-worn, even scruffy. She could easily imagine him at her old school, teaching one of those dusty subjects she'd chosen to ignore. But there lay the paradox. For someone who took in every word and clung to every gesture no matter how slight or inconsequential, he was simply too laid-back, and although he never challenged—as a copper might have done—she just knew that it was all noted and filed for later use. It was this undercurrent that left her uncomfortable and slightly on edge.

She was, however, fascinated by the way he worked and following him around, armed with a street map and retracing the victim's footsteps from, in the case of Elizabeth Rayner, the leisure centre to her likely destination, she found herself shaking her head on more than one occasion.

"Lose yourself in the surroundings," he had said. "Ask yourself the questions: why here, why now, was he waiting, or following, where from, was an exit considered, if not, why not…"

She hadn't really appreciated what he was getting at until they reached the spot where Elizabeth was attacked. The only clue that an incident had taken place was a poster, under the heading of 'Serious Assault', appealing for witnesses and information. There, he had offered two options—were they looking for a stalker or an opportunist? The stalker would know the route and lie in wait. He would have made his plans, followed her home on a number of occasions and got to know her routine. He would then have chosen the safest place to carry out his attack. Having already found a number of more likely places farther along Elizabeth's intended path, she knew without Maynard spelling it out that they were looking for the opportunist and that the assaults on Elizabeth at least, had not been planned. Equally, given the location of the attack and assuming that Elizabeth was followed, for if not then the attacker might have been hanging around for some time waiting for a likely victim and would not have taken the chance of being recognized, then the attacker must have come from the same direction, the leisure centre and the Square.

And after the assault which way did the assailant leave the SOC?

She nodded her understanding. She was beginning to understand his reasoning and caught his glance as she worked it out. He was willing her to get there, just like her old teacher.

"That way would be unknown territory," she confirmed. "So unless he knew the area he'd go back the way he came. He must already have made sure there was no one behind him—the attack only took seconds—so he knows that way is clear."

Maynard said nothing but she knew she'd got it right. They approached the High Road. He didn't need to ask the question that she was already working on—which way now?

To the crowd, she proposed. In a crowd people remain anonymous. He's heading back to the Square!

Wouldn't he hang around to see the ambulance and the police? Some get off on that?

No, he couldn't take the chance someone would approach from the other direction.

Maynard said, "So, we've got the time to within seconds and we know which way he came and which way he went. Any camera along the way would have photographed not only Elizabeth once, but the attacker twice within a few minutes, front and back image."

They walked on and checked every shop and business, searching for a camera that might have picked up the passers-by. They checked the higher buildings for any CCTVs that covered the street itself. They were some two hundred yards from the SOC, just a short distance from the Square itself, when they found what they were looking for.

"You're sure it's a him we're after? Could it be a double act with the woman acting as a lure, maybe, or even a lookout? Maybe she was fingering the victims and giving him directions on the phone—Fred and Rose West, Brady and Myra Hindley?"

Maynard pulled a face. It wasn't dismissal, exactly, but it was clear he wasn't happy with the idea of two people being involved. "You check the film," he said. "You're looking for a man—or a woman—wearing or carrying a dark jacket and, if it's a man, then you might look for a woman on his heels. I'm going to concentrate on Brian's woman."

"What is it about this woman?"

"She turned up at the right time and she never went off with a punter."

"She's probably a hack working undercover for the Guardian."

"A pro with prose? That's a thought." Maynard smiled. "Whoever she is I'd like to meet her."

Maynard walked away toward the Square and left Donna staring thoughtfully after him.

Later, Brian said, "You ain't a normal copper, are you?" He sat in the front of Maynard's car. He felt a lot more at ease without the others. It was never easy with coppers up close. They were only interested in one thing, a result. And they didn't care how they got it.

"I'm not a policeman at all. I'm a psychologist. Does it show?"

"Some things aren't hidden. Blue eyes is blue eyes."

"My eyes aren't blue."

"I know. They're brown. And they're all over me. They have been since you walked into the room."

"Maybe you're tired or maybe you're on something but you're way off the mark."

"Think so?"

"Yes."

"Please yourself."

"OK, I've no problem with that. What you think is your own business. Let's concentrate on finding this woman."

"The toms?"

"Just the one in particular."

"She ain't here."

"You haven't looked."

"I'm certain, Mister. She was different. She stood out. You'll see, when we find her."

"OK, we'll wait. Meanwhile you could tell me a bit about yourself."

"Yeah, like I would."

"Fair enough."

"What about?"

"How you ended up on the streets? We could start there."

"How you do end up anywhere, you tell me? Did you end up doing what you wanted to do?"

"No, I was going to raise pigs. My mother holds a little place in Lincolnshire and she breeds pigs. It's a small place and the smell is a bit dodgy, particularly on a hot day. But that's what I had in mind. So what about you?"

Brian shrugged. He glanced up into Maynard's eyes. "Been there, done it."

"Pigs?"

"Sort of."

They both laughed then Maynard said, "You were hurt?"

"Some of them like to hurt you, you know that."

"Well, it wasn't serious or you wouldn't be here."

"Two weeks in bed, couldn't eat, pissing blood."

Maynard nodded. "What about your parents?"

"Foster parents, kids home, foster parents, kids home, dick dock, dick dock, right? People don't adopt boys, not boys like me, see? They want girls, good-looking girls, right?" He glanced at Maynard again. The light caught his long eyelashes, drew you to his dark eyes. He gave the psychologist a tricky little smile.

Maynard reached to the key. "Think you're clever?"

The lad shrugged his bony shoulders. He said, "Where we going?"

"To the supermarket."

"What's there?"

"The car park, more toms, more rent boys. More people who are hurting. Your kind of place."

"Suit yourself."

"I always do."

The youngster threw him a strange glance.

They drove in silence.

Some of them like to hurt you.

Maynard knew all about it. Some of them were tuned into violence; it was part of the routine; an attempt at self-annihilation.

The High Road slid by full of Christmas shoppers, bulging bags, silly Santa-hats and rolls of see-through festive paper—fifteen for a quid. People weren't feeling good and even the street dealers were feeling it. The holes in the wall were sucking in plastic and fake Calvin Klein was snatched up by punters who fancied a tenner instead of thirty.

Maynard parked up. Five minutes went by before the lad said, "So?"

"Just watch."

"We could be here for hours."

"Got anything better to do?"

"Anything's better than this."

"We'll give it half an hour. If nothing happens we'll call it a day."

"What makes you think she'll be here?"

Maynard admitted wryly, "Just like you, I'm guessing."

Brian shook his head. The rebuke had claimed his tongue.

"Jason was pointing out the faces but not the one we wanted. He's streetwise and bright but he'll never grow old."

Sympathy was beyond Cole and he struggled. "You can only offer to help. Nothing more. You don't interfere in the animal kingdom, do you? You'd fuck up the food chain."

"You're a cold-hearted bastard sometimes."

"You're right. It goes with the job and my name isn't Canute. No point in fighting something you can't beat."

"He never believed he could stop the tide. He was making a point to the Bosham locals that there are some things a man can't do—even if he is king."

"Exactly. That's the point. There are too many Sidney Cookes and Lennie Smiths out there and too many kids who won't listen for us to make a difference. All we can do is take one body at a time and go after the bastard who did it—taking into account, of course, at all times, the bastard's human rights!" He made a suitable noise. Street boys and girls were easy prey and the city was full of predators. That was the reality. He shook the thought away and asked, "So what have we got, Geoff?"

"I talked to Mike Wilson and he agrees with what Brian and some of the girls are saying. The girls gave it to the Gazette by the way, and it was just speculation, perhaps jealousy. They run a closed shop. A blonde, short spiky hair wearing a black jacket, slim, good-looking and classy. She's been around for a few days. Didn't speak, remained aloof. Although she had plenty of offers no one saw her get into a car or go off with a punter. They figure she might be pricing herself out of the market. A high-class tom on the way down. It's worrying me. The woman I've been looking for is not well-built in the stocky sense. A woman of the size Brian described would find it difficult to manhandle even another woman."

"Motive?"

212

"Difficult one. Not control or humiliation. Something sexual, I'm guessing. Whoever it is, is obviously getting some kind of pay-back. The concentration on the breasts has got to mean something—jealousy or loathing."

"A woman with small breasts?"

"I doubt it. Haven't you heard of silicon?"

Cole pulled a face. "You said this isn't about control. Does she hate other women?"

"Hate is tricky. That's generally associated with revenge or indoctrination. She's getting off on something bigger than the attack itself. When we find her, it will be so obvious we'll kick ourselves for missing it."

"Choice of victims?"

"Attractive women under thirty. Beyond that, nothing. If it's random it leaves us with two categories—the opportunist or the stalker." He recalled covering the same ground with Donna and wondered how she'd got on with the CCTV. "For the victim it's a lottery and any women who fits the bill is potential prey. Whether she happens to take the wrong road at the wrong time or is stalked is beside the point. It matters to us because it reshapes the profile. The stalker is patient and calculating. The opportunist hunts; he's restless and hungry and more likely to make a mistake."

"A lesbian?"

"No reason to think so. A serial assailant, woman to woman, is not common."

"Once before you said find me the motive and I'll find you the killer."

"Nothing's changed. And if not already then before long we'll be looking for a killer. The level of violence will only increase. But it's the motive that's difficult. If we rule out inadequacy and jealousy, two of the same, then we can consider concealment by imitation, that apart from the real target the others are just camouflage. Given that scenario the real victim knows her assailant. I'm a long way from buying into that but it's important we're not sidetracked by grouping them together."

"What about our Underground Slasher? We know he's got a cast-iron alibi but he might have spoken to someone. You know what we think about coincidence."

"John Lawrence put someone up to it? Not a chance. I studied Lawrence and covered everything from saviour delusion to pseudocyesis—the delusion of being pregnant. There was a case of a woman who stole a baby from a neighbour's womb. She used a knife to break in."

"The saviour delusion?"

"Too late. It'll have to be another time."

Anian Stanford came out of the crowd of kozzers and said abruptly, "Can I join you, or is this private?"

Cole was caught off guard. He managed, "Anian."

She flashed him a nervous smile, placed a glass of red wine on the table, hooked her bag on the chair arm and slithered into the seat. She looked from Maynard to Cole. The pause became an awkward silence before she said, "Maybe this was bad idea."

Maynard jumped in and smiled warmly, "We were talking business, work from work, and you're very welcome."

She looked at Cole and said, "Don't let me stop you."

As he met her gaze through a trail of smoke Cole gave nothing away. He said flatly, "Sam said the interview was a disaster?"

"Sam was right. I wasn't there, obviously, but I heard every word."

Maynard put in, "During your session with Lawrence what did you discuss?"

She flashed the therapist an uncomfortable glance. Even before their first encounter she had heard about him. Who hadn't? People who made a living reading between the lines were always unsettling. Apprehension dried her mouth and she took another sip of wine. She held on to the glass and said, "I made out I was a neighbour—a friend—of Helen Harrison, had seen the painting he did for her and wanted one of me. I told him it would make an ideal present for my husband."

"I didn't know you were married."

"I'm not. Is it important?"

Maynard shrugged. "Maybe not, but most people can tell. And John Lawrence knows more about psychology than most psychologists. Don't let him fool you. He's as dangerous as they come. There's only one place for people like him and it's not on the streets."

Cole cut in. "I assume he was given the all clear?"

Maynard smiled. It was a psychologist's joke. He said, "You really don't want to go there. A personality disorder is just about the most imprecise term in the medical dictionary. It covers everything from the obsessive-compulsive to the narcissistic to the paranoid to the schizoid. You can control it, if you're lucky, but you can never cure it. As someone once said about X-rays, there's no such thing as a safe dose of radiation. The same goes with the personality disorder." He turned back to Anian. "Have you been involved in undercover work before?"

She shook her head.

Cole said sharply, "And as far as we're concerned she's not doing it again."

Maynard nodded. He'd hit a nerve. He said, "The fine line between eliciting an admission and entrapment."

"I know the difference," she said evasively. "Inspector Wooderson has already pointed it out. It's done with now so it doesn't matter."

Cole ground out his cigarette. "Let's have some background, Geoff. The original sheets leave a lot of holes."

Maynard paused for a moment while the past flooded back and once again he was looking for links to that mysterious agent that tipped a man toward insanity. He said, "An only child. Until national service his father was a local-authority driver who spent most of his time down the bookies or in the local. When he was posted away John and his mother were left sharing a council-house in South London with another, equally impoverished family. But his mother was the driving force whether his father was there or not and they formed an intense attachment. His father was posted to Cyprus and eventually they joined him there. In the military school in Nicosia Lawrence proved to be an average student, and the only thing that stood him out was his unwillingness or inability to make friends. Classmates and teachers that we traced all mentioned that he was shy and very much a loner." Maynard smiled and for a moment came back from the past. "It's become something of a cliché, hasn't it? Find me the loner and I'll show you next year's problem."

215

He nodded and continued, "He went through his school life without a girlfriend. A-level results earned him a university place. But let's go back to Cyprus. He was eight when his brother arrived. Massive complications during the pregnancy resulted in his mother coming back to the UK where she was hospitalized for some months. Even after the birth mother and baby were in and out of hospital and this is the first indication we have that the relationship between Lawrence and his mother was under pressure. With children, perceived rejection is even stronger than jealousy. In Lawrence's case I'm pretty certain that this perceived rejection lit the fuse. Despite two major operations to correct a congenital heart condition, his brother died at the age of two. His mother never got over it. Alcohol, liver disease, premature death at thirty-nine. John was nineteen."

Maynard looked from Anian to Cole, waiting for a response. It was too equivocal for Cole. He shook his head and murmured, "What else?"

"Nothing else. The trauma's never left."

Anian's eyes narrowed in concentration. "I don't buy it. You don't go attacking people because of childhood rejection."

"Some people do. There's not enough weight given to rejection at a certain age. Think of the crimes of passion in the adult world. The suicides. There is nothing more devastating than rejection."

Cole lit another JPS and through smoke asked, "What became of his father?"

Maynard nodded. "Good question. He left the forces on compassionate grounds, obviously, and a couple of years after Lawrence's mother died he married again. This was in the mid-sixties when Lawrence was at university. After that they met only a handful of times. His father, complete with new family, emigrated to Australia. He came back for the trial and there were a couple of photographs taken outside the Bailey but that was about it."

Cole said, "Earlier you mentioned the saviour delusion. What were you getting at?"

"We were discussing motives. I was convinced there was a religious connection."

"Knifing women?"

"Pregnant women. I was thinking about the massacre of the innocents, one of Herod's moments of infanticide—and there were many. But that was to do with the death of male children and when Lawrence carried out his attacks he couldn't have known the sex of the unborn child. Even if he had the medical records back in seventy-six sexing was not the general rule. Even then, he was clever enough to have made the distinction."

Cole said, "So, you've changed your mind?"

"I still think there's a religious connection."

"So, religion. What else?"

"Sex, obviously, and its result, pregnancy, and then the slaughter."

Cole said, "But against the child, not the woman?"

"That's where I was going. But it was a long time ago." He turned to Anian. "If you meet him again, don't mention you're pregnant."

"I'm not."

"Don't mention it anyway."

She laughed. Then realized Maynard was serious.

Cole said pointedly, "She's not going to meet him again, Geoff."

Maynard watched them, fascinated by the strange chemistry of attracting opposites.

Cole continued, "She's going to stay right out of the way."

Maynard smiled as though he knew something that Cole did not. "Of course she is," he murmured. "It was just speculation." He glanced again at Anian and in that fleeting exchange, her tell-tale eyes betrayed her.

Geoff Maynard hoped that he was mistaken and that she had indeed called a halt to the sittings, for he knew without a doubt that she wouldn't stand a chance with Mr John Lawrence.

Chapter 21

Before he slept Cole thought about the woman. He wondered whether there was any truth in the rumour that she had kept Jack Wooderson busy for a few months. Perhaps it was the ambiguity that he found so unsettling, the element of uncertainty, that she could be frivolous and irresponsible and yet, a moment later, quite cold and relentless. Somewhere there, lay the appeal.

In the next room where the windows and curtains were fully opened, where the lights from the traffic came in with the chilled air and skirted over the flower-patterned wallpaper—a reminder that Cole had once been married—Geoff Maynard was thinking about another woman.

If indeed it was a woman.

She's new in town, he thought, she had to be, and yet her knowledge of the area indicated otherwise. But people didn't recognize her and, what was more, she had no fear of confrontation with the competition. So if she was local could it mean…

Maynard's frown became almost painful.

…that she was dressed as the tom no one recognized!

Belle de Jour?

In this case the shrinking violet dressed up like a temptress? Able to go so far but no further and then, out of frustration, attacking the person she actually wanted to be.

Could this be something as simple or as complex as genophobia?

Maynard tried to shake the thought from his head.

Start again. People don't start this way. They start in little ways and while they are learning they leave behind a little form. The learning curve. Antisocial behaviour, shoplifting, minor infringements that carried nothing more than a warning. So where did she come from? Where was she staying? The answer lay in the Square, on that kerb of crawlers.

Maynard found sleep difficult at the best of times, but during a case it was almost impossible. He worried it until it was done. That was why after HOPE he had given it up and gone back to therapy. Interaction was where it mattered, where you could rebuild a shattered life. The people who shattered the lives came at you like waves on a spring tide and like Cole had said earlier, he wasn't King Canute. You could get one or two but there would always be more stacking up behind. They rolled in, wave after wave, bringing with them acts of depravity and wickedness that the civvies—the good citizens of this green and pleasant land—could not even imagine.

We see things that no one should see. We hear things that no one should hear.

Coming back was personal, nothing to do with Cole or Baxter or the closure of HOPE, his old department. If Cole knew why he had come back he would have laughed out loud. Everyone had secrets. Didn't they just? This wasn't about the challenge. This was about self-harm.

The dawn stole in from an overcast sky and set the day. Sam Butler was well aware that time was running out. What had seemed like crucial breakthroughs were simply not delivering and a sense of panic gnawed at his gut. He said, "They've held on to it since seventy-six?"

Anian shrugged and bony shoulders ridged her thin shirt. "It was high profile. And they still use it at Hendon. It was quoted verbatim in one of those true-crime books called…"

He was standing over her. A button was undone and he caught sight of some blue bra. Without looking away he said, *"The Underground Slasher."*

"Absolutely. Guess who wrote it?"

"Wouldn't be a guy named Maynard, would it?"

Anian threw him a flirty smile. She bent slightly forward—he was sure it was unintentional—and showed him some more of the vale.

"I read it," Sam Butler said, trying to pull back a memory, but the view was in the way and it wouldn't come. He shook his head—the vale of tears was right, he thought—and went on, "Crime does pay."

"It paid even more than that. It was serialized in the Sundays." She pressed play and the voice of John Lawrence came through. Not as resonant but unmistakable.

"I was a gentle child and so quiet that people would say I wasn't there when in fact I was. It got me into trouble on more than one occasion when my parents would ask how I had behaved at a particular function only to be told I wasn't there. I was very shy and you would always find me in a corner, hiding. It was only later that it came to me I didn't have to hide, that in fact, no one noticed me anyway.

"My father was in the army. We were posted to Cyprus. It was well before the country was partitioned but even then Makarios was causing trouble. He was a dangerous man. We lived in Nicosia in a white villa next to a dried-up riverbed. I remember we used to find a lot of dead cats in Nicosia. Wherever you went you came across dead cats and that was strange. The point? Yes, the point is that this is the riverbed where I used to catch lizards. Some of them were up to a foot long. Before that, when I was even younger, I used to make Plasticine models of chickens complete with their lungs and hearts and gizzards and, once I'd made them I would slit them open to extract their innards. It fascinated me. Even though I'd put them there and knew exactly what I'd find, it was still a moment of huge excitement. I never knew why. Now, a little older, I had the lizards. Using drawing pins, I crucified them on little crosses I knocked together. I'd put three of them on a little mound of sand. It wasn't a green hill but probably closer to the truth. Have you been to Jerusalem? There's not much green. And there wasn't in Nicosia either. But there were lots of red anemones. I remember them well. But they didn't last long. Just three days at Easter time and then, they died. Perhaps that is why they have become associated with Jesus and the resurrection. I used drawing-pins at first, until I got some tiny little tacks that would go through their hands and feet. They were better. More realistic. More like nails. You had to bang them in, like the Romans did. Hands? Do lizards have hands? Well, they did for me. If you slice off their tails before you put them on the cross they look quite human. They sort of moved, like Jesus might have done. You know? In agony. Or ecstasy. And they bled. But their blood was fatty, watered down. Not rich red, like ours."

Anian recalled Maynard's account of Lawrence's early life, the birth of his brother, his mother's hospitalization and his rejection. What was it the psychologist had said? It lit the fuse?

The tape continued. "After a while, about a month or so, that got boring, so I used to slit them open with a razor-blade. I'd sit for hours, watching the pale blood dry in the hot sun. When I stood up I'd get quite dizzy. A kind of religious experience. Point is, when I slit open one belly, a big white egg fell out. I say white. It was mostly white, but there was pus and green strands on it. Not much blood. But after that, I went after the females. At first you couldn't tell the difference until you slit them open. But after a while I learned. It wasn't only the swollen belly but the skin as well. Even the eyes seemed different. They hung there, on their crosses, with their mouths wide open and their little round eyes glazed over, but they didn't cry out. They made no noise at all. But finding an egg, watching it fall out while they were still wriggling, that was special. After that I started cutting open the eggs, finding the little brown tadpoles inside. Even in the burning sun some of them lived for more than a few seconds.

"Tell me, if you can, what more than that can a schoolboy want?"

Another voice came in, male, gentle. "You've told us about your parents. They forced you to go to church. Did that annoy you?"

Lawrence laughed. "Of course we were forced to go to church. People in the fifties still believed in God. I collected the Sunday-school cards like everyone else. Moses and David and Jesus, dished out by a fat woman in flip-flops who had her eyes on the padre."

"Did you have any friends in Cyprus? Did they cut the lizards as well?"

"Friends?" Lawrence's chuckle went on for some moments. The velvety tones of his voice sent a shiver down Anian's back. She could barely believe she was listening to the man she knew as Mr Lawrence, the man whose knife and brush had so perfectly captured her image.

The stranger's voice came back. "You never thought that killing the lizards was wrong?"

"Wrong? It didn't come in to it. At school we were dissecting mice and frogs."

Anian pressed stop and the room fell strangely silent. Police officers—a couple of them old-timers waiting for their pensions, who had seen and heard a few things in their time—shuffled in their seats and exchanged uncomfortable glances. They were repelled, mostly, by the matter-of-fact quality of Lawrence's voice but also by its—almost—patronizing tone.

Breaking the silence Sam Butler said softly, "One sick bastard. He's killing these women, or he's got them bottled up someplace. I don't know how or where, but it's him. We know it's him."

One of the PCs said, "What about having the lodger in, Sarge?"

"Paul Knight? A waste of time. Let's be kind and say that he is mentally challenged. He won't give us any more than he did at the shop and that's nothing. Lawrence is careful. He isn't going to confide in Paul Knight."

"That's a no then, Sarge?"

Butler went on, "Guy's have come back with zilch, so he's not up to his old tricks, at least not on the underground. So let's try it from another angle."

Guy's Hospital kept a comprehensive pathology database on wounds to the person. There had been no unsolved attacks on pregnant women.

"He meets them in the shop, through his art classes or, as customers. Worse case scenario, he's killing them. Best, he's holding them prisoner. We'll leave the why for the psychologists. Either way, it means there's another place where he does his business. How does he get there? As far as we know he doesn't have transport. How does he get the women there? Does he arrange to meet them, or does he take them? Are they forced to go along?"

One of the PCs cut in, "There's another possibility."

"Go on?"

222

"If he is involved then he might be helping them to get away from… domestic violence, unhappy marriages. Maybe he's a self-appointed marriage guidance counsellor."

"If Margaret Domey wasn't in the frame I'd say you had a point. But she wasn't running anywhere."

The PC persisted. "Can we be sure of that? Who knows what goes on in private? How many times have friends and family surprised us? My brother was divorced. I hadn't got a clue until it was, basically, all over. I thought they were happy as… you know?"

For a moment Butler thought about his own marriage and his wife's affair, but time dulled the pain, turned it to something else.

"We'll keep it in mind, Joe, but for the moment we'll assume the worst."

In another office a phone was ringing. Eventually someone answered.

DC Stanford suggested, "Maybe the women are driving him."

"Forced?"

"Not necessarily. But does it matter if he's getting to where he wants to go?"

"Fair point."

"No it's not," the plod interrupted again. "Linda Brookes didn't drive."

Anian Stanford turned on him. "OK, so they might have caught a fucking bus."

The copper shrugged. "Anian, it was just a suggestion. It wasn't to win fucking Mastermind."

She backed off and threw him a quick apologetic smile.

Butler put an end to it. "So he might be meeting them in this other place. Let's widen the net. Use some initiative. Get your sources to ask around. He's a regular at The British. Does he drink anywhere else? He must have a warehouse or a lockup someplace. I know we've been here before but let's try it again. We must have missed it. Get back to the friendly bank manager. Go through the statements again, line by line."

The plod said, "What about surveillance?"

Butler hesitated. Cole had been quite clear. He said, "I'm still waiting for the green light on that. Let's not jump the gun." He turned to DC Robert Foster. "Rob, check out the Mill Hill connection again. Go over the witness statements and get back to family and friends of Melanie Brown and Sophie Whillis. Somewhere there's a link to the Gallery. Stay with it until you find it."

The DC pulled a face. He'd already drawn a blank and he knew that going over the same ground would draw another.

Anian pulled her jacket from her chair and reached for her handbag. She smiled sweetly at Butler. "Tell me what you decide in the morning. I'm on an early night. A bath, a long one, then the theatre."

Butler nodded. Even though she'd mentioned it a dozen times he'd completely forgotten. "Bikini Line," he acknowledged. "Anthea Palmer. I used to like her on the weather."

"You and half the male population."

"One minute she's standing in front of the British Isles telling us it's going to rain tomorrow, the next she's cart-wheeling over everything in sight. She was on the front page this week or, at least, her knickers were. They snapped her getting into a car. A diabolical liberty, really. Maybe there should be a law against it. Invasion of private parts. Trespass by lens."

"Schoolboys enjoyed the picture. I doubt that many men did."

Butler pulled a face. "You know nothing about men, then, Anian."

"What paper was it in? The Sun? The Mirror?"

"I don't read crap." Butler smiled. "The Sunday Sport!"

She smiled back and said, "It's rare that a girl will show you her knickers unless she wants you to see them. And that includes photographers."

His glance was a double take. She had surprised him.

A uniform poked his head around the door. "Sarge," he addressed Butler. "Just had CB3 on. They've found Helen Harrison's car. Two roads up from the Gallery."

Anian hesitated.

Butler said, "Get out of here. Go and enjoy yourself."

She flashed him another sweet smile and let the door swing shut behind her.

The phone went. Cole said, "Cole."

"It's me."

"Right."

"Read between the lines."

"Right."

"You were right. He spilled the lot. Helen's got herself a lover. My fucking wife has run off with another geezer. Can you believe that? Even I don't believe that. She's shagging Jesus fucking Christ and she runs off with John the fucking Baptist. That fucker's going to lose his fucking head. She's carrying my fucking baby for fuck's sake. She's in the fucking Costas, can you believe that? Soaking up the sun? I can't believe that. Treated this Lawrence cunt as some kind of confidant. They got real fucking close during the painting sessions. It ain't surprising, though, not really, considering the pose. They say love is blind, don't they? Know what I mean? It takes a brain dead, lungless fucker like Breathless to point it out. I should of seen it, Rick. I mean, for fuck's sake, she had one leg on each arm of the fucking sofa. Anyway, she's still in contact. Going to ring him when she gets back. He'll let me know. Then I'll be paying her a fucking visit."

"Does he have an address?"

"Spain, but Spain's a fucking big place. I mean, I take her on a fucking boat to that other place. What was it again?"

"Greece."

"Right. I take her there in a luxury boat and she settles for paella and fucking chips."

"When Lawrence gives you the nod, you let me know."

"I'll think about that one."

"Think about this. Is Lawrence OK?"

"Yeah, I'd say, given the circumstances. Unfortunately he had an accident with his painting hand. Got a finger caught up in a guillotine. He uses it to cut the prints to size. Told him it was fucking dangerous, without a guard, but did he listen? He should be reported to Health and fucking Safety!"

"OK, take care of yourself."

"Too fucking right. I owe you one now." His emphasis was on the you. "Isn't that a treat?"

Cole hung up. For a moment he wondered how much of the call was incriminating. All of it, he imagined. But it was too late to worry, so he set it aside.

But Helen Harrison running off to Spain? Not a chance. Helen Harrison was dead and John Lawrence had got her tucked up some place, getting off on whatever he got off on. But it was coming to a head.

It wasn't often that Anian Stanford went out with her housemates. Getting their shifts to coincide was almost impossible but somehow, through luck and feminine wiles, they had managed it. The Royal Free nurses had come by a box at the Carrington Theatre. A consultant from Nigeria was making an impression on the youngest of them and Anian guessed it wouldn't be long before they'd be advertising an empty room. But for the moment they made hay.

In the bath she drank some wine—why did it always seem so wickedly indulgent?—and getting ready she drank some more and perhaps that was why, as they settled in their box seats, she was less than discreet.

She said, "Five rows in, three from the centre aisle, see him? Next to the black girl."

As Anian held back, the other girls eased forward.

"Mr John bloody Lawrence. He's got those women somewhere."

"Oh my God! The missing women?" The youngest of them, the consultant's target, spoke with that feigned enthusiasm at which all young nurses—perhaps young women in general—were adept.

Anian nodded. "He's got a poster in his shop window. Maybe a couple of freebie tickets came with it."

"Like us then," the nurse giggled. "But the girl—the black girl— must be thirty or forty years younger."

"She's a tom, works out of The British. A tart with a heart. She even gives discounts to pensioners."

"Oh my God," the nurse said then, more seriously, "Why take a prostitute to the theatre? If you're paying for it you should be on the job."

Anian laughed out loud. "I don't know. You tell me about men and what they've got to prove?"

The nurse leant forward for another look. "What's he got on his hand? It looks like a glove puppet."

Anian took another peep. "It is a glove puppet. It's got red lips."

The nurse shrugged and shook her head. "This is not normal behaviour."

Anian searched for Chief Superintendent Marsh but couldn't find him. Had she glanced at the other boxes she would have seen him sitting comfortably next to the Mayor. Gilly Brown had gold hanging from his neck. And at the back of the theatre, in the deep shadows, Assistant Chief Superintendent Deighton and his wife were finding their seats along with the councillors.

The nurse beside her touched her arm and pointed to the stage. The curtain was going up.

The curtain went up to reveal a street scene and a gang of youngsters, dancing to the right or left and pushing the passers-by aside. They shouted abuse across the steaming road. One of them daubed paint on a brick wall: Kill the Bill. And the gang began to sing:

> *There were a few skirmishes last night*
> *but nothing much*
> *Just a few friendly little fights*
> *but nothing much*
> *We gave the residents a fright*
> *but nothing much...*

The passers-by joined in. First the Politician as he introduced the others:

> *He's a criminologist and she's a sociologist*
> *And I'm a politician, vote for me.*
> *He's a police-inspector and she's a*

social worker
And I'm a politician, vote for me.
I'm into crime prevention, stop the windows
being broken
And I'm a politician, vote for me.

And with that slimy offering the politician flashed white teeth and produced a red, white and blue banner which read: Vote for me!

And the gang sang: *We're the pill-popping,*
heavy-drinking, glue-sniffing
gang from hell.
The gang's all here, born out of fear,
you see...

Passer-by: *Alienated youth, violence on TV, poverty,*
bad-housing, boredom and page three...

Politician: *And I'm a politician, vote for me...*

Street Cleaner: *I'm a street cleaner and I hose away the blood*

Council Worker: *I'm a council worker and I make the windows*
good

Vicar: *I'm the local vicar and I'm mis-under-stood*

Politician: *And I'm a politician, vote for me.*

And the gang sang: *We're the pill-popping,*
heavy-drinking, glue-sniffing
gang from hell.

The stage was a frenzy of movement and colour. The first half-dozen rows were all but hidden by smoke. Anian Stanford didn't really notice. She was watching Lawrence, trying to make out his features in the dimmed lighting and wondering if the girl hugging his arm was aware of the danger she was in.

Geoff Maynard was still out and the house was strangely silent. He'd mentioned earlier that Donna had come back with a nil return on the CCTV images and Cole guessed he was in the Square again, checking out the faces.

In just a few days the psychologist's domesticity had left a mark; silly things, like the dishcloth left hanging to dry instead of squeezed and left on the drainer, the Teacher's safely tucked away in the cabinet instead of its usual place at the foot of Cole's armchair. Cole switched off the light and carried a glass to the bay window. The lawn, in its winter coat and orange wash, looked thick and spongy. The wind was up, sweeping through the volcanic light from the street lamps, rushing through the trees and beating the fluttering, flame-like winter shrubs into submission. He felt the familiar bite of the Teacher's and shivered, waiting for it to lift his mood. This was no life, annihilated every night, dealing with filth every day. No intermission. Another day, another meeting, another seeing, speaking, sleeping. Just going through the motions without a purpose, apart from one, waking up to do it all again.

A car rolled to a slow stop at the end of his drive. He recognized it and checked his watch. It had turned eleven. He watched her lock the car and start up his path. She was biting her lower lip, ready to turn and run, searching for a light in the house and frowning at the darkness. Maybe she'd already checked out the White Horse and drawn a blank. She wore a grey jacket and a short navy-blue skirt that fanned in the wind. A sudden gust gave him even more of her legs. Almost casually, she reached down and held on to the hemline. He turned on the porch light and opened the door as she was about to ring.

For a few moments they stood in silence.

She levelled her gaze.

229

With a slight tilt of the head he beckoned her inside.

She hesitated for a second more then stepped over the threshold. In the bedroom window the stars dissolved in the condensation. In the volcanic light the hard-edged trees rounded like candle wax under a flame.

"You take them off," she said as she plucked the elastic below her navel.

He did and, some time later, lay back nursing a semi-skimmed dick.

In the morning the night was just a blur. Teacher's, before and after, got in the way of clarity. He remembered the stars as they found their cruel brilliance again as the condensation wept away.

During the night there had been an explosion and it wasn't an allotment shed or children with reconstructed fireworks. It had brought down the roof of a house in a terraced row. An old exhausted run-down place that needed demolishing anyway. According to initial reports the cause was a gas leak. It happened, more than people knew. The Fire Brigade was out in force and uniforms were cordoning the area. Safety experts were examining the scene. Two men had died. Blown to bits and the bits burned beyond recognition. In time there would be neighbours and scraps of documentation and dental records and reconstruction and numerous items that would give them the background, but for the moment they were just casualties of the night, written off as accidental deaths. It meant paperwork and time they didn't have and, hopefully, an uncomplicated transfer to the coroner.

In the car, in the morning, as they passed what was left of the house and skirted the flapping police tape, DS Sam Butler said, "With a bit of luck forensics will have something for us on Helen Harrison's car. And we do need something." He paused, then: "Did you enjoy the show?"

If Anian heard it didn't register. She said, "I almost went round to Rick Cole's last night."

Sam Butler was staggered, speechless. All he could do was shake his head in disbelief and keep the car from veering.

"Did you hear me?"

Eventually he found his voice, but it still came out sounding like someone else. "I'm having trouble with it. Tell me again."

"It's true. I was a bit pissed after the show. Couldn't help it. Wanted to. Couldn't. Stupid, isn't it?"

"Why?"

He sensed her shrug.

"I don't know. Nothing makes sense anymore. He made it quite clear the other night that he's not interested. Maybe that was it. The challenge. The old behavioural protocol becomes activated, doesn't it? Pride, anger, you name it. In a negative way it's still intoxicating. I'm getting hurt here, but I can't help myself."

"Back off, for Christ sake. I thought you'd had your fill of office romances. Think about it."

She sighed. "You're right. But that's not me, is it? All my life I've jumped in head first and lived to regret it. I wish I hadn't told you."

He nodded reluctantly, unable to make sense of what he'd heard. He said, "So do I."

"You're angry?"

"Leave it alone, Anian. I was surprised, that's all."

After a moment he added, "For a while back there I forgot I was married with a little girl that's keeping me up all night. All right?"

"That's fine. I understand."

He shot her a glance. Her dark eyes were on the road. He wondered whether she did understand, that back there, for a moment, jealousy—pure, irrational, blood-rushing jealousy—had got the better of him.

He drove in uncomfortable silence for five minutes then pulled up in a wide, well-maintained street the other side of the park. No line of parked cars here, just clean pavements and drives to every door.

"St George's Way," Anian said quietly. "Imelda Cooke?"

"Right," Butler said and climbed out of the car.

She followed him up the drive toward a two-storey detached.

Joseph Cooke had reported his wife missing three months ago. He had given up his job in the city to take care of the children. When he opened the door and recognized the police officers, the expectation of the

231

bad news he'd been dreading drained his features and left a terrible stain in his eyes. He'd been living a nightmare existence, waiting for the call, waiting for the body to be found, somehow surviving in a dreadful limbo.

Butler had seen the look many times before—the certainty, the disbelief, the helplessness, the realization of all those nightmares, and he was quick to reassure him. "It's all right, Joe. There's been no development."

Relief flooded back. "Thank God for that. I thought…"

"I know. There should be a way of ringing you first to let you know that nothing's happened. I'm sorry. Are the kids at home?"

"No. They're staying with their nan. I get a break from time to time. Come on in."

They followed him into the hall.

"Can I get you something? Coffee?"

"No, no, thank you," Butler said. "Listen, Joe, this is a bit delicate," Joseph Cooke looked puzzled.

"You remember we asked you whether Imelda was pregnant, or not?"

"I remember. She wasn't."

"Well, we have a number of missing women in the area and, with the exception of Imelda, the others are pregnant. I don't know what it means, exactly. I don't know why we're here, exactly."

Joseph Cooke smiled sadly, "Clutching at straws?"

"Yes, that's it exactly."

Anian stood aside, watching the detective sergeant as he skirted the issue, and the man beside him whose life had been shattered.

Cooke offered, "You want to look at her things again? I've already done it a thousand times, but I don't mind. They're just as she left them. Nothing's been moved."

"Yes, Sir," Butler stammered. "That's what I really came for."

Cooke waved towards the stairs. "Help yourself. I'll be in the sitting room. Are you sure about the drink? I'm having one. And it's stronger than coffee."

"In that case, Sir, Scotch will do nicely. What about you Anian?"

"Nothing for me, thanks. It's a bit early."

Cooke glanced at his watch and nodded. "So it is," he said and left them to it.

As they climbed the stairs Anian asked, "What are we looking for, Sam?"

"Anything. Something we missed. A letter maybe, an appointment to a private clinic. If she kept it from him, it's hidden. Think about it."

"Kept the pregnancy from him?"

"Something like that."

Anian shook her head and murmured, "In that case I hope we don't find it."

They didn't. They went through the bedroom methodically but found nothing of interest. It was always difficult for coppers invading the privacy of innocent parties and they felt embarrassed going through the drawers, particularly those containing underclothes.

They hit the landing again, ready for the stairs, when a little tug of memory caught Butler between steps.

"What is it?"

"Just a thought. When Janet did her test, she left the box and instructions on top of the bathroom cabinet. We hadn't got Lucy at the time but maybe it was instinctive, you know, a place where the kids couldn't get to it, out of the way. Every time I had a shave I noticed it. The bloody thing became a fixture. You never throw away old pills and medicine bottles, do you? I've got some chilblain ointment I used the other day then noticed the use-by date was November ninety-four. Seemed to work though."

"Too much information, Sam. You're spoiling the image."

Together they moved into the bathroom, a green-tiled bathroom complete with avocado bidet and shower cubicle and double-door bathroom cabinet. And on top of the cabinet, where it had lain for over three months, disturbed only occasionally by a Maltese cleaner, hidden by familiarity and a pink plastic bottle of baby lotion, was a white oblong box.

The detectives shared a look of amazement.

"There's no kit here," Anian said. "Just the box."

"In this case an empty box is good enough," Butler said and shook his head in disbelief. "And it makes five out of five."

Chapter 22

In Paul's bedroom there were six TVs in two stacks of three and he was back watching them. He sat cross-legged on the end of his bed. Sky News and ITV and BBC covered the same story. Paul's eyes were wide, his mouth open, his attention held by the six screens. There was no sound. He had the sound turned down. The colours of east Africa slid across the cuts and bruises on his face. His ear was torn and his clothes were stained red in various places.

On the six screens a migration had begun. Women carried dead babies and babies that were dying. Men staggered on makeshift crutches. Children held their extended bellies. Flies crawled into eyes. Behind them a war continued. Ahead of them was another African border with trenches and mines and guns. The Dark Continent had never looked so cruel. There was no oil in this African country. It didn't even have a name that anyone could remember.

At the door Mr Lawrence coughed to attract his attention.

"Mr Lawrence," Paul said and a shudder worked through his body.

"What the devil's happened?"

"Oh, Mr Lawrence."

Paul's eyes filled with tears that refused to roll. His hands were clenched in front of him. A vein on his forehead throbbed. "Oh, Mr Lawrence, I've been hurt a bit."

"Come on, Paul, try to lie back."

"I would, but the pain in my side…"

"Lie on the other side."

"Both sides, Mr Lawrence."

With his good hand Mr Lawrence pulled a plug and the irritating screens blanked out.

"That's better. Can't do with all that flickering. What is it? A Tarzan film?" Mr Lawrence sighed. "Goodness me. You've been gone… How long? Two Days? And look at you. What on earth shall I do with you? Now try to relax and lie back."

Slowly, painfully, he eased back. Mr Lawrence undid the three remaining buttons on his shirt. Deep bruises patterned his left side. Around his kidneys the skin was red and swollen and his groin was caked in dried blood.

"You need a doctor, dear boy, the A and E or casualty. You need checking over. X-rays and a thermometer."

"No! No! No doctors. They'll call the police. They always do. I can't get away with walking into a lamppost, not this time."

"You're right. Being run over by a bus would be more like it."

Using his good hand Mr Lawrence cleaned him up with a sponge and a bowl of warm water turned pink. He dried him off and dabbed Germolene antiseptic cream onto the cuts and covered him with a single sheet. He had tried the ointment on the stub of his own finger but it hadn't stopped the bleeding.

"Thank you," Paul said before sleeping.

Like a baby.

Mr Lawrence watched him for a few moments. The boy really needed pyjamas but his wardrobe was full of baby things. His own clothes were in a heap on the floor. On the hangers tiny one-piece baby-growers in five bright colours were packed in. On the shelf above, two cellophane cartons of disposables were packed next to a selection of bottles and sterilization equipment.

Mr Lawrence went down to the shop, his head still shaking in puzzlement. He was not the worrying kind but he was worried and it showed in the deepening lines on his forehead. Somehow he had allowed other people to creep into his life and things were getting out of hand, spiralling out of his control, and something else was on its way.

She arrived with a small battered green suitcase that had travelled. She shrugged her luscious brown shoulders and raised her eyebrows and threw him a wicked smile from cherry-red lips.

"Me mum's kicked me out! She said she would and she did."

He sighed his resignation. "Well, we don't choose our parents. If we did the majority of us would have different parents."

"He's given me a week. I told him I needed time. Told him I was confused by the electric, see? Confused, innI? Told him."

"Why did he hit you?"

"He's like that. He likes that. He hits everything, even the wall when he's really angry. Even the screws were frightened of him."

"We'll go to the police. That's what they're there for. Protecting the innocent."

"You don't understand, Mr Lawrence. The filth won't help. They're not interested. It was probably them that told him where I was in the first place."

"You said he loved you?"

"I did. I know. I said that. You hurt the things you love. You know that. He was just trying to straighten me out."

"And are you straightened?"

"I don't feel straight. To tell the truth, I feel pretty well bent right now."

"I've seen you looking better, Paul, that's true. But that's not the word I would have chosen. So, you've got a week?"

"Yes. Then I've got to give him my answer."

"And if it's no?"

"He'll kill me. I think he'll kill me. And if you interfere he'll kill you too. It'll be a crime of passion. I think I'll have to take off for good. Disappear. Trouble is, he's good at finding things, people. He found me in the squat."

Laura's voice travelled up the stairs.

"Mr Lawrence—customers!"

A middle-aged couple admired a canvas. He was short and squat and sourly. His banker's eyes focused on the painting. His wife was heavier and taller. They wanted the painting but they wanted a discount too.

"Mallards," he muttered and nodded to confirm it.

"Indeed. Notice how the artist has used the same colouring of the ducks in flight on the rich foliage in the foreground."

The man wasn't really noticing the colouring and was instead concentrating on the bandage on Mr Lawrence's right hand. He said, "Yes, I had noticed that, but thank you."

He tugged at his nose. "Well, Hon?"

"It seems a little overpriced," Hon said. So did her dress, whatever she paid for it.

"Good paintings are an investment. If madam would like to see some less expensive works in the other room...? The untrained eye would not spot the difference..."

An eyebrow raised. "Quite," the squat man muttered as he reached for his cheque-book.

"Get the hang of it?" he said to Laura once they had gone, and then to Paul a few moments later: "Where were we? Oh yes, you're safe until Friday. Are we certain of that?"

Paul's nod was lopsided. The swelling on his neck was worse. He confirmed, "Friday."

"I'll give it some thought. Perhaps I can come up with an idea. Did you get anywhere with your little errand?"

"Come again?"

"The woman from the subcontinent?"

"The Paki? Oh yes. Went across to the Ridgeway, to the address, like you said. She don't live there, Mr Lawrence. You probably got the number wrong. An old couple lives there. Saw me hanging around and gave me what for. Probably thought I was a dodgy character. There's lots of them about. Right?"

Mr Lawrence nodded thoughtfully. "When you're up and about, maybe later, I want you to help me in the shop. Christmas is coming and we're getting busy."

"No sweat. You done me a favour. I'll do anything for you. No questions asked."

"How are you feeling now?"

"Better. Be up and about in no time." He paused then said sheepishly, "Look under the bed."

Under the bed he'd lined up four pairs of trainers and a pile of rackets. "Squash?"

"Badminton," Paul put him right. "Taking it up once the swelling goes down. Might play with those girls from the art class, see, cos one of them won't be playing for much longer, will she?"

"Really?"

"She's pregnant, Mr Lawrence. You can't run around if you're carrying, can you?"

"I suppose not."

"So I'll play with the other one." Paul winked.

Laura called up. "Mr Lawrence—customer!"

"More ducks," he muttered.

"Mr Lawrence…?"

Mr Lawrence paused at the door. "What is it, Paul?"

"What happened to your finger?"

Once the shop was closed he found Laura in the kitchen ironing a black skirt. She rocked from one foot to the other as she listened to her Walkman or pod thing or whatever they were called nowadays. It probably came with pictures. The cassette or whatever rode her right buttock, held by the white lace of her pants. Her free breasts swung in time over the ironing-board. The scene reminded Mr Lawrence of the nature programmes on the television, rows of chanting natives with swinging breasts against a jungle backdrop. Inside, in those days, you were allowed to watch the nature programmes between six and seven. Now of course, it was porn on your own portable in your own cell. Even so, he doubted that even then they'd get away with a bunch of white breasts swinging along to '*I Wanna Be Like You*' before the watershed. Discrimination, without a doubt.

"You can stay here for a few days. God knows where you'll sleep."

She said, "I'll put my bag in your room for now," and offered him a knowing little smile.

They left it like that.

"House rules!" he said when she carried her ironing through. He'd intended to tell her to cover up but after consideration decided against it. He didn't want her thinking he was old-fashioned.

She paused in her step and hugged the ironing against her chest.

"While you're here I must insist that you give up your moonlighting."

"Mr Lawrence, you're jealous."

"I can't have the Gallery involved in…in… It's not on."

"But what will I do for money?"

"You'll manage. Treat it like a holiday. A few days off."

"OK."

"Promise me, Laura."

"I promise that while I'm here I'll give up the tricks."

"Fine. You can help out in the shop, until Paul gets better."

"That reminds me."

"What's that?"

"I did two hours down there today. What's the hourly rate?"

Chapter 23

At the rear of the studio a door opened on to a small yard of black sterile earth where even the weeds would not take hold. To the right of the door stood a rotting wooden shed. Its roof had fallen on to a rust-swollen lawn-mower. A cracked concrete path led across the yard to a blistered gate where two grey wheelie bins stood—recycling with all its false benefits and its hidden extras for the council and its councillors had still to make its mark in Sheerham. The heavy gate hung off its hinges and scraped the concrete path. An arc of scraped-clean concrete indicated that it wouldn't fully open, but the opening was sufficient for the bin men—the waste disposal executives—to manoeuvre the bins through.

The gate opened as far as it would go on to a back road that ran behind the shops. It was an empty road save for the parked cars and an occasional lorry that would stop to make a delivery to the back of one of the row of shops or restaurants. At such times the narrow road was blocked to any other vehicle and for that reason most deliveries were made in the High Road. Across the road a line of silent offices stood in various states of disrepair. Most of the dark windows were cracked. At some stage, before Mr Lawrence's time, the road had been a place of industry but now the offices were mostly unused and, the few that did flicker with light were dark again soon after for it meant that smackheads had broken in and were cooking with candles. Next to the row of offices stood a row of garages with corrugated roofs covered in moss. There was only one shop front in the road, and that was farther along, opposite the rear of the barber's shop, and it sold dolls. Dolls and dolly paraphernalia: doll's houses and cots and clothes and dolls of all description. It was called the Doll's House.

In that forgotten road the shop window stood out, dressed in white lace. An old woman dressed in long dark clothes and woollen shawls owned the shop but she was rarely seen. And customers were few. With Christmas coming, the only concession in the unchanging window was a single gold star that hung from a white suspended ceiling. A mangy black cat lived in the window and curled up on the cots. Its tail flicked over the plastic and porcelain skins and the beady lifeless eyes. Perhaps it looked content because it thought it had smothered a baby.

Mr Lawrence didn't often use the road for it was a depressing place, a throwback to an older time when grey was the colour and soot rained from belching chimneys. He saw it when he closed the yard gate on the mornings the bins were emptied. Apart from Christmas week when they were touting for tips, the executives always left it open. Only occasionally, when the gangs of youths were particularly boisterous, would he use that way to The British.

He'd noticed the gangs earlier as they left trails of lager cans behind them. It was interesting, Mr Lawrence considered, that these hard men of the time could not stomach bitter. And perhaps that was the difference between men and men who needed to be in gangs.

The British was full of office workers on their Christmas night out getting in the way of the regulars. They were loud and noisy, making the most of their once-a-year excuse, expecting other people to join their revelry.

How he hated Christmas with its merrymakers in their cheap office suits and last year's skirts that were now two sizes too small. How he hated the youngsters with the futures they didn't deserve.

Smoke drifted in thin layers. Cigarette butts were crushed on the carpet. Lager dribbled from the bar.

On the bar was a collection box for Rasher and the colonel. People edged away from it. It was the only place, a yard either side, where you could get served without queuing two deep. About the collection boxes, Albert told them and he wasn't kidding, they were a reminder of what

Darwin might have pointed out, that charity held back the future. That keeping the weak and the beggars alive to spread their what have you with the strong, was messing with evolution. And although the regulars didn't much care for Albert they had to admit he had a point. The doctor or the double-glazing salesman was there.

He asked, "How are the voices?"

Albert and Sid the Nerve shuffled closer to listen. The barber's ears twitched.

"I'm afraid they're getting worse."

"That's not good."

"He's been watching the news, the famine in Africa."

"It could be worse."

"Could it?"

"It could be in a country we cared about."

"I see what you mean."

"But it's not good."

"Why is that?"

"Famine in any country isn't good, is it?"

"Well, there's China, I suppose, or India, or any one of the Arab countries. But I see what you mean. But Paul, is Paul mad?"

"Mad? Madness is a state of mind. We all go through periods of madness, when we're angry or in love or chasing money in a slot machine. Insanity is different. Only if we're mad all the time are we insane. But if we're insane we can be mad some of the time."

Sid frowned.

So did Albert as he nodded thoughtfully.

So did the barber. He pulled at his right ear, searching for loose hair.

"But it's getting worse. What can I expect?"

The man bunched his shoulders, as though it helped his concentration. "Does he dress up? Perhaps as a woman? Like, for instance, Norman Bates?"

Roger the manager heard the name and edged over.

"I haven't seen him in woman's clothes."

"Well, watch out for it."

"It's not something I'd fail to notice."

"You'd be surprised."

"Anything else?"

"Reminiscence."

"He's got a good memory. He knows lots of chess openings."

"Not memory, old boy. It's a medical term used to describe inhibition dispersion."

Sid the Nerve said, "Right. Nice One. I remember. It's the String Theory, right? Yeah. Wormholes. Know where you're coming from."

The salesman shook his head and continued, "Most of our actions are inhibited by negative thoughts—boredom, lack of motivation, understanding and so forth. In the normal person a short break, a rest period, from a given task will give renewed vigour. With the psychotic this isn't the case. Basically, he picks up from where he left off. The rest period has made no difference. The reason is that the psychotic needs a much longer rest period for his inhibitions to disappear. Slowness, therefore, is a definite sign."

Roger said, "So we're talking about politicians, Gordon Brown and Jack Straw in particular?"

"Anything else?"

"Extroverts, watch out for the slow extrovert."

"What can be done?"

"Pills. Lots of them. Euthanasia for the politicians."

The street door opened and a blast of air shot in, followed immediately by Mrs Puzey. She waded in with her considerable bulk and people were flattened against the bar. She waved a threatening umbrella.

"You led my little girl astray!"

The crowd at the far end of the bar turned to look.

Mr Lawrence swayed this way and that as a professional boxer might have done, keeping well away from the point. He stuttered, "I beg your pardon?"

"You! You! You evil man! My little girl was innocent until she met you!"

He tried to pacify her by throwing up his hands in his best gesture of geniality. Mr Lawrence knew all about body language, the language of management. Keep eye contact, keep your knees pointing toward the opposing genitals, lick your lips and leave your tongue hanging— that sort of thing. She saw the streaky bandage and was momentarily distracted. Albert ducked out of the way.

"Calm down, Mrs Puzey, for goodness sake. No one is leading your daughter anywhere."

"She lives in your house of sin. I know. Don't you try to tell me otherwise. All them filthy pictures on your walls. I can hardly bring myself to clean them. Oh, sweet Jesus, what am I to do? My little girl is at the mercy of this... this..."

Roger helped her out. "Pervert," he suggested.

Mrs Puzey said, "Exactly. Pervert!"

Roger's smile spread out and spread to the others. Within moments the hilarity reached the far corners.

Such bracing acerbities were too much for Mr Lawrence and in a weighty and determined voice which was most unlike his and had the others that knew him quite nonplussed, he said, "Listen to me, woman!"

The shock of his sudden stand had her backing off but she managed, "Don't you make none of them clever excuses to me."

"Mrs Puzey, Laura is staying at the shop for a while until she can sort herself out. I have laid down strict ground rules. She has to be in at a certain time, an early time, and she can have no one back at any time. She has given up all her other activities. What is more, she is serving in the shop and I am teaching her about art. She stands on the verge of a new career. For goodness sake, have her back. Come and get her things. I thought I was doing you all a favour. I'm certainly not putting up with this nonsense."

She seemed flustered now, at once concerned that she had reached the wrong conclusion and that it might jeopardize her cleaning contract.

"Did I say that, Mr Lawrence?" She turned to Albert. "Did I say I wanted her back?"

Albert, crouching almost, shook his head. Dandruff took off. The air was still unsettled by the waving umbrella. The layers of smoke spiralled this way and that.

She turned to Sid the Nerve. "And you?"

Nervous Sid said, "I didn't hear you say that."

"There you are, then. What's all this about? How could I know she was learning to paint the pictures? You didn't tell me that. I thought she was in them filthy pictures!"

"No. Good Lord, no. I wouldn't have her in the paintings, Mrs Puzey."

"And why not? Are you telling me my little girl isn't good enough to be in them pictures, just because she's black? Is that what you're telling me?" She turned to Albert again. "Did he say that? Did he?"

Albert beamed and nodded. "It sounded like it."

She turned back to Mr Lawrence and said, "I take you to Race Relations." She stormed to the door, muttering.

Mr Lawrence wiped perspiration from his forehead. Sid shook a large drink and some of it made his lips.

Roger said, "Bloody hell."

The salesman said, "Now, that is madness and not insanity. You see the difference?"

With no little endeavour Roger gained a little composure and addressed Mr Lawrence. "Mr Lawrence," he said. "You might think that on account that I have a couple of South African wines on my wine list, that this place resembles that place in South Africa where Michael Caine beat off the Zulus, but you would be mistaken. You might think that VCs are easily earned in here. But you would be mistaken. If I have any more trouble with the Zulus or anyone resembling a Zulu, then you are banned along with Liverpool supporters and the singing of *Ferry Across The Mersey*."

Mr Lawrence thought about an appeal but instead shook a defeated head.

The evening was ruined. Mr Lawrence had never been one for surprises. He left early and made his way along the High Road. Candles flickered in the restaurant windows. Shop-side of the restaurant was the alley, narrow and dark, a gap between the Chinese and the pet shop, where the Chinese skinned the cats. Laura was there, just a dozen paces from the road, and the road lights picked her up. Her skirt was up and her knickers were down and she was being given a geriatric seeing to. She leant against the weeping bricks and sighed in her client's hairy old ear. Ears got bigger with age yet never seemed to work so well. Her customer was a short man and she had to bend her knees. His walking stick angled against the crumbling wall beside her. Laura saw Mr Lawrence and smiled sweetly. Her customer was too busy to notice her shrug of indifference above his bald head. He thought he was in, but memory was a curious thing and, in all likelihood and with a flopping piston rod on a four-stroke cycle he was simply stirring the air between her legs.

The mannequin in his shop window was different. She looked a little shop-worn. Mr Lawrence put it down to the drinks in The British and the cold night air and the distracting images of Laura's luscious thighs that wouldn't go away.

Susan, the freckle-faced girl from the art class, looked worried when she walked into the shop shortly after it opened. It was drizzling and her fawn-coloured raincoat was freckled too. With her was a muscular man in jeans and dust-covered T-shirt. He looked like a builder. She looked worried and he looked angry.

"Mr Lawrence, you haven't seen Sandra, have you?"

"Not since the class, my dear. Why?"

"Sandra never came home."

"My goodness. Have you seen her, Paul?"

From behind the counter Paul shook his head.

The man in jeans said, "Come on, we're wasting time."

Susan explained, "This is Sandra's husband."

Mr Lawrence thought about shaking hands. Instead he shook his head and offered them a grave expression.

Sandra's husband said, "We'll have to report it to the police."

Paul grimaced. "The police?"

"Got to. She's pregnant, you know?"

Mr Lawrence put in, "No, I didn't know until Paul told me, yesterday."

All faces turned to Paul who shrugged, "She must have said."

"Bloody worry that is. I've had to take time off work. Don't get paid for it." The man shook his angry head. Leaning closer he took them into his confidence and asked, "What's the point in being married if you don't get your dinner cooked? Last night I ended up with Chinese—all that fucking salt. What do you think of that?"

"Not good. Between you and me I've been worried about the Chinese for some time. But what about Sandra? You've left it this long?" Mr Lawrence raised his eyebrows.

Sandra's husband stepped back from the perceived rebuke. "I thought she might have gone to her mum's."

"Does she often do that?"

"Only on Saturday afternoons when she takes the kids. I meet her there, after the racing. We all go for tea. Always have. Isn't that right, Sue?"

Susan nodded.

"It's not much," he said gloomily. "Always the same—ham and salad, and the bread's always stale."

Susan turned to the door and said, "C'mon, you're right. We're wasting time."

Mr Lawrence wondered whether women with freckles knew just how attractive they looked. He wondered whether they were all over her body and not just on the bits he could see. He hoped so. He asked, "The last time you saw her, was it at the studio?"

They turned back from the door. Susan's eyes filled up as she nodded. "I was meeting my husband. I left early, remember?"

"I do, yes. Now I remember. You didn't clean your brushes. I've told you about that before."

Once they had gone Paul sidled across, a sideways crab-like movement. He picked up a duster and began dab-dabbing. It wasn't necessary. Mrs Puzey and her gang left the shop spotless. His mind was clearly on other things.

"I'm worried. I don't mind telling you. Things seem to be ganging up on me."

"Nothing's as bad as it seems."

"But if Sandra's missing."

"That's not a problem. We've got a waiting list for the club."

He shook his head. "That's not what I meant. The police will be back, Mr Lawrence. The police! What about the gear, the gear?"

"Oh, don't worry about that. They won't be looking for stolen property. Not now. They'll be looking for Sandra. You don't have a problem."

"I do have a problem. Friday is coming."

"Oh yes, your gentleman friend."

"He's not so gentle."

"You're right. I can still see the fist marks from his last caress."

"And on Friday he's coming back."

"I told you before that I will think of something. Don't you worry about that either."

Paul nodded, more confident in the knowledge that Mr Lawrence had not forgotten him.

"Now go and make some tea, and take a cup into Laura. She came in very late last night."

Paul tut-tutted the idea. "That girl will get herself into trouble one of these days."

"I think she's on the pill."

"I didn't mean that, Mr Lawrence. I meant that she'll meet some nutter. A real...nutter!"

"No. She's very choosy. She doesn't sleep around. Or stand around either, come to that."

"I don't know. There's an awful lot of nutters out there."

"So long as they're not in here. That's all that really matters."

"By the way, Mr Lawrence, I heard the cats again last night and they were crying again, like before."

"Yes, something must have upset them."

While the kettle boiled, Paul went back to his room and carefully, so they wouldn't crease, he replaced the baby-growers on the hangars and placed them in the wardrobe. They'd been left in a pile on his floor.

Chapter 24

Cole dreamt of the past. He had arrived home late to find his wife with suitcases pulling on her arms. She was ready to go out. "I'm leaving you," she had said. He discovered later that she was leaving him for someone else and that his occupation was only a part of it.

Morning broke with winter sun slanting in through the slightly parted curtains. Donna Fitzgerald blinked awake and once again recognized the strange surroundings of Rick Cole's bedroom and said, "Oh shit!" She grabbed at the bedside cabinet for the time.

Breakfast TV led with a press conference given by Chief Superintendent Marsh. "Given the length of time she has been missing…" The headline was Margaret Domey, the missing psychologist.

They drank their coffee in silence. Maynard joined them in the kitchen but remained noncommittal. If he was surprised at finding that Donna had become a fixture it didn't show. He concentrated on the TV.

"…None of her belongings are missing, her bank accounts remain untouched and her mobile phone has not been used. The circumstances of her disappearance are suspicious and we are exploring the possibility that she has been a victim of crime."

A BBC reporter pushed out a microphone. "Is there any connection with the other missing women?"

As the chief noticed the face behind the question his thin lips tightened and left his contempt in no doubt. He said, "We are exploring that possibility."

In the hall, in the mirror, Donna added final touches to her makeup. She gave up and said, "Fuck it!"

Cole caught Maynard's glance and shrugged. "Me too," he said.

Back at the office something had broken. When Cole walked in with Donna and Maynard in tow he recognized immediately that there had been a development and the stern expressions indicated it wasn't a good one.

"Hinckley have lost another woman," someone said. "An art student. Any guesses where her classes were held?"

Geoff Maynard left them to it; he knew exactly how it would go. Baxter and Cole would be leaning on Hinckley and Wooderson in particular. In turn Wooderson would take it out on DS Butler. DS Butler would use his only option, gather his team and pay another visit to the Gallery where more statements would be taken—either there or at the station and, if common sense prevailed, that would be that. There would be no point at all in more white-suited experts with their radar guns and tape-measures poking around the Gallery. Evidence of the girl would be all over the shop, the studio and the pavement outside. She had been going to classes for months. Lawrence was laughing at them, enjoying himself immensely. He would be anticipating more interviews and another visit to the station. There might be more gained by denying him that satisfaction, perhaps even ignoring him completely. Rejection, as Maynard had said before, was a potent brew. He smiled at the thought.

DS Sam Butler led the way into the Gallery and while Laura went to find Mr Lawrence and Paul stood statue-like at the counter, he studied the large painting of the bricks and wondered how on earth it could justify the price. A DC beside him said, "Brick in the Wall, Pink Floyd."

Butler nodded. "An old rocker, then."

Disappointment marked the detective's face. "Heavy metal, actually."

Butler said, "Really."

Mr Lawrence appeared at the stairs with Laura behind. He made it a grand entrance but the coppers didn't notice. They noticed instead how short Laura's skirt was as she negotiated the remaining steps and their knees bent in Dock-Green fashion.

Mr Lawrence said to DS Butler, "I know you said you'd see me again, but I didn't expect it to be so soon. As much as I like to help the police, you are starting to get in the way of business. Customers don't come in when the police are here. People have a natural aversion to the police. And can you blame them? Something to do with them shooting innocent people, I imagine, and the uniforms. Think of the staff behind the counters of the big banks with their spotted skirts and croupier fingers. You see what I mean?"

Butler glanced at his hand. "You hurt yourself?"

"A little accident with the guillotine, nothing much."

"Well, it's starting to bleed again. You should get it seen to."

"My goodness, you're right."

"Did you talk to Sandra, Sir?"

"Of course I did, and more than once. Her palette was entirely wrong for the subject. To be honest, I think the twins should think about another pastime. Art is not for them. It never has been. They should be out enjoying themselves in clubs with loud music and class A drugs."

They used the studio to take their statements. Finally, Mr Lawrence said, "That's my blood on the table, by the way. Not Sandra's. To my knowledge Sandra never cut herself here. I'd like to make that quite clear. Perhaps you could write that down in one of your pocketbooks. Those little books that you people always refer to in court. The books that are filled with your little white lies."

"I think I can remember the notebooks that you're referring to, Sir." Butler threw him a tight smile. "But I'm not sure about your little white lies. In the notebooks that I have seen there has been nothing little or white about them."

"I like you, Mr Butler. You have a stripe or two. You're a professional. It's your average plod that I'm concerned about, and they're really not very good, are they?"

Butler smiled. "You worry about the coppers like me, Sir. Not the others."

Mr Lawrence nodded and smiled back. "In that case I shall look forward to seeing you again. It has always been a pleasure."

Superintendents Baxter and Billingham shared a car to Hinckley. Given their uneasy relationship it was a measure of the heat they were feeling from the top floor. There was nothing like a common enemy in the building of a united front.

Cole was already there. He had left early to give Wooderson the nod and provide a few precious minutes to tidy the office.

In the CID office and with Billingham at his side, Baxter addressed the small team. "You've narrowed the field. You've made up your minds and you've broken the first rule in good detective work and that is to keep an open mind."

Billingham nodded his agreement, his sharp eyes shifting from Wooderson to Butler and lingering on Anian Stanford who sat at her desk looking dark and uncomfortable.

"You've made this personal," Baxter went on. "Every woman on your list will have visited every shop in the High Road. They will have visited the supermarket every week, if not twice a week, since it was opened. So what makes Lawrence your prime suspect? What makes him so special? His previous? That was over thirty years ago. I've seen your reports. The guy lives between his shop and The British and he has done for years. He visits the barber once a month and the supermarket once a week."

Billingham couldn't help himself. "Consider the form for a moment. It never involved missing women. Yes, back in seventy-six he attacked them and, yes, they were pregnant, but as Lawrence has pointed out, he never hid his handiwork!"

This time it was Baxter who nodded. He said, "The investigation has been sidetracked and weakened. So, you've had your fun, you've had him in and you've taken his shop to pieces, you've searched the derelicts and garages and you've been through his bank accounts. Enough is enough. You're going to start again, from the beginning, and if you've got to use the idiot list then do so. Tick every field—Red

Cross, Centrepoint, Crisis, National Centre, Shelter, even the Big Issue, go back to friends and relatives, health and medical, places, events, bank accounts, the lot. Use the procedures. We know the last place the last two women were seen. We have approximate times that they arrived and left. Somewhere in the High Road CCTV must have picked them up. I want every face in every frame from every camera, including those from the shops and banks, checked and checked again. Pick up some tips from CSR or NCIC or even Missing People. Something, somewhere, will throw up an idea that might give you a lead. Do not even think about a tea break unless you take it on the job."

Although their faces hid it well, the members of the team knew that everything the super had mentioned had already been covered. They were still working through the CCTV images for Sandra, and that would take them another day at least, but they were on top of it. The prospect of starting over sank whatever enthusiasm they might have had and they didn't have much to start with.

Baxter turned to Butler. "What happened at the shop?"

Butler said sheepishly, "Nothing new, Sir. We've taken statements from Lawrence and his lodgers."

"The lodger who was in prison at the time some of these women went missing and the girl who's off her trolley?"

"Yes Sir." Butler stood his ground. Cole was impressed. The DS went on, "We need to see the husband again and her sister, and we're following up with the members of the art class."

Detective Superintendent Baxter nodded thoughtfully then said, "Right, follow that up and then start again." He glanced at Billingham. "Anything to add, John?"

"I've not seen anything from the hospital regarding Margaret's visit. Are we absolutely satisfied she never got there?"

Butler answered, "She didn't show, Sir. To be on the safe side we are double-checking the CCTV footage of both the reception area and the car parks."

Billingham said, "Another missing car? Do my people know about it? Are they actually looking for it?" He shook his head. "Sidetracked again, no doubt. Sam, get your bloody act together." He glanced at Wooderson. "Jack, I'm very disappointed."

"So am I, Sir," said Wooderson.

Billingham turned back to Baxter. "That covers it, I think."

"Good," Baxter nodded. "Right, twice daily updates to DI Cole who will personally brief us at nine and six."

Butler said, "I would like to put Lawrence under surveillance, Sir."

The senior policemen shared a glance then Baxter said, "Not necessary. He's not going anywhere. And that reminds me, Assistant Chief Superintendent Deighton wants to know who authorized those specialist shit-sniffers rather than the bog standard police sniffer dogs. Apparently they cost a fortune and someone is going to pay for it."

They all looked at Butler but he remained tight-lipped.

"Right," Baxter said. "You all know what's required. Let's get on with it."

The meeting was over.

In the corridor Cole said to DS Butler. "Don't take it personally, Sam. They're just making sure they're fireproof, that's all. They like the sound of their own voices. It's what senior coppers do."

He left the detective sergeant staring down at his own feet.

Geoff Maynard spent most of his day revisiting the SOCs; he needed to be there, away from the distractions of the office, absorbing every detail of the surroundings, the hunting grounds, searching for the slightest detail they might have missed, perhaps an indication of the assailant's state of mind, arousal, impulse, anything. The questions were endless but, like he'd told Donna, even an empty road could give up some answers.

The youngster's voice brought him back.

"That's her," Brian Lara said and pointed across the High Road toward a slim woman with spiky blond hair. She wore a short burgundy shift—any year's colour—and a black jacket. Not a lot for a freezing night. "That's the one. Classy, like I said."

"Classy," Maynard agreed.

They'd left the car twenty minutes earlier to mingle with the toms, the punters, the pissheads, and the passers-by who hadn't got a clue what was going on. It was close to closing so between the four pubs in the Square the drinkers hurried to get in their last orders.

A north-easterly scoured the road and sent plastic bags and front pages demanding the return of the plod scudding past. It lifted hemlines and drew tears from the eyes so that the light from shop windows seemed oddly scattered. Overhead the festive lights swung on their cables. Higher still the sky growled angrily and the ragged clouds were the colour of congealed blood.

The pavements were packed yet it was still a lonely place.

Maynard said, "Are you sure?"

"I'm sure. That's the one."

"That's it, then. You've done your bit." He stuffed a twenty in the lad's hand. "Burger, right? Just remember what I told you. You can walk away. You do have a choice."

The score lit up Brian Lara's eyes. "Right" he said.

He watched the big man cross the road then checked out the note again.

A youngster wearing a hood and oversized clothes appeared from the shadow of a doorway.

"All right, Jay?"

"It's Brian."

"Yeah, cool."

"What you wearing that for?"

"It's the thing, innit?"

"You look like a dickhead. It'll never catch on."

The youngster pulled a face and dropped the hood. He said, "What's happening?"

"Tick tock, dick dosh, dick, dick, dosh, dosh, you know?"

"Yeah."

"I fancy a burger, all of a sudden."

"Good idea. That'll do. Bit of huff later, yeah?"

Geoff Maynard tucked behind and kept a distance of some twenty yards. The last bell meant the pavements were full and he had to weave his way through the celebratory crush. One face looked like another. One street looked like another. Maynard was sober but in this bash of false festivity he seemed to be the only one.

He didn't know the streets and even in the crowd he felt suddenly exposed. He followed her into a less crowded area away from the shops and boozers and found himself in bedsit land and student territory.

Geoff Maynard was a psychologist, a hands-on mechanic who delved into the cold, unconscious machinery of the criminal mind. He knew what made them tick and slash and kill. He'd spent his days wallowing in their fantasies, his nights sharing their dreams. He knew the dangers and the warning signs.

She had stopped and was looking back at him. She smiled an acknowledgement, a promise of the world and everything in it.

Without making it obvious there was no turning he could make, nothing he could do but continue on towards her.

"Hello," she said, flashing some perfect teeth and a tricky smile that reminded him of something from the distant past.

Chapter 25

They met in the corridor late afternoon, soon after Cole had returned from Hinckley. Donna had spent two hours at the North Mid but it had proved a waste of time. There was nothing to add to her original reports.

She said, "If we do it again it will start to get serious, won't it? Three times makes it serious. It won't be an aberration, or a requirement, or a wartime thing, or fling. It will be something else and we'll be looking for excuses and all that shit."

He smiled.

She softened.

He smiled again and she gave up altogether.

"Ten?"

That would give her time to get home to change and back again. Not that changing usually mattered. She nodded. She knew the place.

Chas Walker was half-cut and the stanchions in the White Horse, the kozzer's boozer, weren't wide enough. His flushed face broke into a Christmas-Ale greeting as he looked from Cole to Donna and said "Guv".

"We're just leaving," Cole said and turned to Donna. "I'll run you home."

Donna smiled awkwardly, sharing it.

Chas Walker nodded, guessing it.

And yet Donna looked decidedly uncomfortable, perhaps even embarrassed by the proposal. Chas Walker was confused and decided that maybe the DI was not nailing the seconded PC after all.

Donna Fitzgerald finished her drink and got to her feet too quickly.

Over his slopping pint Chas Walker gave her a knowing look. Her look back told him that he was right the first time.

Then Cole's mobile went and ruined it and Donna's shoulders sagged.

Cole listened, asked a few questions then turned to the others.

"Geoff Maynard's been stabbed. He's in the North Mid. The plods are roping the scene, taking statements." He looked at Donna, saw the concern mixed with disappointment. "I've got to get over there. I'll drop you on the way."

Deflated she said, "I'll come."

He glanced at Chas Walker.

Walker lifted his hands. "I'm with you, Guv."

In A&E a uniform told them, "A Stanley knife or something like it, across the face, cut his ear in two then right across the cheek to his mouth." To elaborate he used his finger and traced a line on his own cheek.

Cole said, "Shit."

"Agreed. It was a woman. We've got a description. A blonde, two legs, good looking." He shook his head and added, "I've never seen so much claret. We got him here with about three minutes to spare. Didn't wait for an ambulance."

"What's happening now?"

"They've stopped the bleeding. Surgery later on. It's going to take some needlework, believe me."

"Did he say anything?"

"Ouch, or something like that. He's not saying anything else till the stitches are in. Conversation was not on his mind."

"What's your name?"

"Kershaw."

"You should be in plain clothes."

"CID?"

"No! Out of the fucking job, son. We've got enough comedians in CID as it is."

They hung around until he was wheeled into surgery then Cole dropped her back at the smart terraced home she shared with her fiancé. He was a buyer for a civil engineering company in Victoria.

"Thanks for coming to the hospital," he said. "Sorry it didn't work out."

"Shame."

"Maybe next time."

"Next time leave your phone at home. It's got to be the worst invention ever."

"Will you be all right? It's late."

She glanced at the quiet house. "By now he's got used to a copper's hours. He'd have hit the sack hours ago."

He nodded. "That's what I had in mind."

"Yeah, me too."

The door slammed between them. He checked the dash clock. It was after four. He watched her move to the front door, concentrated on her behind. She'd been right. The call had finished it, he hadn't. Not this time.

In these early hours with the silent streets all but empty, he was about fifteen minutes away from the White Horse. Or he could go home and grab something to eat, something from the freezer, something he could nuke.

No contest, not really. Nuked food was not like the real thing.

Morning was the colour of the concrete tunnel linings that Donna's fiancé bought. He felt like shit. He shaved with Gillette's three blades then, while the coffee dribbled from top to bottom of the Kenwood he checked with the hospital. Maynard was comfortable—their favourite word. They suggested he ring back after lunch.

Cole reached the office just as Detective Superintendent Baxter walked in. The Super was chewing on a king sized sausage roll, one hand under his chin to collect the crumbs. Through a full mouth he said, "Been talking to Billingham. His plods are interviewing witnesses. We should be over there. This woman, we've got a good description. When can you speak to Geoff?"

"Late afternoon. And we are over there. Chas Walker is leading the team. I've pulled everyone available."

"Good." He finished his roll, dusted the crumbs from his hands and trod them into the carpet. "What about Hinckley?"

"Nothing on the new girl. They're checking out the members of the art class and, as you instructed, they're starting over with the CCTV. That will keep them busy. I'm pulling in some spare from Tottenham to help out."

"Good. Keep on top of it, Rick. It's still our number one. But both our psychologists out of action? Makes you think, doesn't it?"

Geoff Maynard sat up in bed, tried a smile using the half of his face that wasn't bandaged and failed. He said awkwardly, "They tell me that in a few days you won't notice the difference. I was lucky."

"They're letting you out in the morning. I'll pick you up."

Maynard nodded.

"We've pulled some good witnesses. We'll nail her."

"I hope it's soon. She isn't going to stop. She's on a mission. I caught up with her, she turned, and that was it."

"It shouldn't have happened. You made a mistake. You should never get close enough to be taken with a knife. You wrote the fucking manual."

Cole turned and the white door swung shut and Maynard said to the empty room, "Yeah."

It didn't help to know that the DI was spot on.

Chapter 26

It had been a most satisfying day. The police had surprised him by not requesting his presence at the station again, he had sold six paintings and two Italian vases and the woman was still to come.

Once the police had left Mr Lawrence said, "So, it's official. Another missing woman."

Paul, still trembling, said, "I was so nervous. I'm sure they noticed."

"I doubt it."

"What are we going to do?"

"We could advertise, I suppose."

"For Sandra?"

"No, to fill her space. There is now a vacancy."

"Not that, Mr Lawrence. The plan. Friday! The plan?"

"Oh that. It's not been easy. They say that love is blind and that might be so, but it is also a primitive, dangerous emotion. It is a time when even your average man crosses the line."

"I know that. He is dangerous."

"In this case it is even worse. It has more to do with lust than love, I fear. And lust is a deadly sin that can lead to the breaking of at least half the Commandments in one go. What is more, this passion overrides reason. It cannot be reasonably discussed. So what we have to do…"

Paul edged closed.

"We have to shock him into reason."

Paul frowned. "That won't be easy."

"Difficult things seldom are."

Paul nodded but his expression remained blank.

"Fear, Paul, that's the thing."

"That's what Powder Pete said. But how are we going to do it?"

"Tell him to come here, to the shop."

"He'll suspect something."

"No, he won't. Tell him that you're going to run away with him, do a disappearing act just like Sandra. Tell him that you're going to have my money box away along with a few of the more valuable paintings. He'll understand that. Tell him to meet you here tonight. That sounds good. By all accounts it's going to be a dark night. Two o'clock."

"It doesn't sound good."

"I know. Clock is an ugly word. I think it's to do with the cl sound."

"I didn't mean that, Mr Lawrence. I didn't mean the way it sounded."

"Tell him. Tonight, or rather, two AM tomorrow morning."

Paul went off to Robot City carrying shopping bags and list and a whole head of thoughts. Mr Lawrence needed more shoe polish—nothing but Kiwi would do—and Clingfilm and teabags, the Queen Anne blend of Assam and Lapsang Souchon.

Winter light is an impostor; it deceives the eye with harsh contrast. At other times it sucks out colour and definition. The light in the studio is diffused, as close to summer light as you can get.

The woman arrived and said, "My God, what's happened?"

"A scratch, my dear, nothing more than a temperamental guillotine."

"So many police about," she said. "Three cars in the road and a dozen policemen. They're stopping people."

"A girl has gone missing."

"Oh," she mouthed as though it were a common thing.

He forgave her detachment for, after all, it was a common thing, and said, "Have you had a good day?"

She pulled an indifferent face.

"Oh dear."

"I'll get over it."

"Well, let's get started, shall we? I've opened a tricky little Beaujolais. It's a wine that is very much hit-and-miss. It needs a good year and, according to legend, virginal feet trampling the grape. And they're in short supply nowadays. The summers, you see. We've had a series of wet summers."

"I thought Helen preferred white wine."

"Did she? DID SHE? Mrs Harrison never complained. What about you?"

"I like red."

"It likes you."

For a while he worked in silence.

Her eyes flicked around the room, searching the shelves and dark places.

At length she said, "The girl in the shop…"

"Laura?"

"She works for you?"

"I wouldn't call it work, exactly. There must be a better word. Through bad luck, really, nothing more than a mother-daughter's menstrual cycle coinciding, she's found herself homeless. Homeless, just like Paul. I'm putting her up for a few days and just occasionally, when the mood takes her and, that isn't often, she helps out in the shop. In truth, she frightens off more customers than she attracts and those she attracts are not really interested in art."

"You seem to attract the waifs and strays."

"They're good kids, really. They just need a little help, a point in the right direction."

"Her skirts are very short."

"Yes, I've noticed that. But she does have nice legs."

"Has she modelled for you?"

"No. Landscapes are my thing. I mentioned it before. You must have forgotten."

"What is it about landscapes?"

"They're natural. You don't have to search for honesty."

"Is that important?"

"It is for an artist. But that's something you must answer for yourself."

Her eyes darkened at the veiled criticism.

"Are you a religious man, Mr Lawrence?"

He recalled Laura bringing up the same subject and wondered what it was about him that led people to it. He said, "That's a very personal question."

"Yes, but we have become personal."

"Have we?"

"You are painting me. What can be more personal than that?"

"Not too personal, I hope. But to answer your question, I'm not an American bible-belter. I don't believe the earth was created shortly before the American civil war or that Noah navigated the Mississippi."

"You read the Bible?"

"I have done but not lately. I always thought it needed a good editor. Far too much begetting for my liking. But, my goodness, I hope there is not a God and an afterlife. I wouldn't like to think that all the people who have gone before and all those who are coming after will know my business."

"I imagine they'll be too worried about their own business to worry about yours."

"Yes, you're right. I hadn't thought of that. But think of this: if the people who died can see how the people who live carry on, they must spend eternity regretting their own propriety or spend it horrified at what they see. Either way, it doesn't lend itself to a contented hereafter."

"The painting you did of Helen…?"

"Mrs Harrison."

"Yes."

"What about it?"

"I couldn't believe what I was seeing. Not Helen, in that pose. And she was pregnant. Did you know she was pregnant?"

"Yes. That was the urgency. Getting it finished before she started to… show. It was nonsense, really. I mean, how long did she think it would take?"

"I couldn't pose like that."

"Shyness is all about lacking self-confidence and it is only for the moment. If you see your doctor, for instance, you might die of embarrassment the first time, but afterwards it is of no consequence.

And in any case, Mrs Harrison was proud of her body. Self-confidence was never an issue. She was posing for herself, I think."

"How did it happen? Did she just say paint me like this?"

"Yes, she told me from the start what she wanted."

"You must have been shocked."

"It was an unusual request and I imagine photographers are used to it, but…shocked is not the word I'd use. My only concern was whether I could do it justice. You might not believe it but I have a reputation to consider."

"What do you suppose happened to her?"

"The police asked me that very question but in such matters I'm no expert. If it were just Mrs Harrison my guess would be that she'd gone off with the devil who'd led her to the club but now these other women have gone missing, it does make you wonder. Perhaps the police should get someone to retrace her steps. I think they call it a reconstruction, to jog the public memory. They can give out one of those special numbers for the public to call. That might do the trick. Of course, whoever took her place would have to dress in the same clothes. They could get an idea of what she looked like from the painting."

"She wasn't wearing many clothes in that."

"I admit the dress didn't cover much but you could still get an idea of the style and colour."

"They might have difficulty getting someone to dress quite like that and, the BBC might have a problem in filming it."

"The watershed. I understand that anything can go out after the nine o'clock news."

"The nine o'clock finished some time ago."

"Well, I never. No wonder the country has gone to the dogs."

A little later he said, "One more sitting will do it."

"Is that all?" There was anxiety in her voice.

Before she left, her mood still subdued, she said, "I'm sorry I've been a pain today. I'm afraid I have a lot in common with Helen. You see, this morning my test proved positive too!"

She was clutching at straws, watching his reaction or lack of it. But it was a good move. And devious too.

From Paul's spyhole in the cracked wall there was a flicker of movement. He was back from the shops, errands complete. He was crouching beneath the stairs again, spying, watching and listening to every word.

Chapter 27

They needed the mannequin's clothes.

Laura squealed, "Look! Mr Lawrence, he's stuck hair on the dummy. He's given her a hairy fanny!"

Mr Lawrence glanced down at the offending fleece. The barber's missing hair came to mind. Funny how, if you waited long enough, things fell into place.

Paul looked a treat, although at the moment, because of the hair, a little embarrassed. Laura had been to work with her make-up and turned him into the model in the window. His skin was lightened and his cheeks glowed with blusher, his blue-grey eyes defined by mascara and blue shadow and his lips were bright cherry-red. Full at the best of times they were now rather kissable. He wore the model's auburn wig of short bobbed hair. The striking thing was his body. In the matching set he was almost perfect. Only his chest let him down and that needed filling. Cotton wool would do the trick. But they needed that for Mr Lawrence's padding so they used tissues. He hobbled in and turned over his right high heel.

For Luscious Laura and Mr Lawrence, keeping a straight face was difficult.

Holding his sides and whimpering, Mr Lawrence suggested, "You'll be all right so long as you keep still."

"I've shaved his legs," Laura said enthusiastically. "What do you think?"

Mr Lawrence squeaked, "I think he's beautiful." And then he could hold it no longer. He coughed a dozen times to hide his laughter and that started a coughing fit.

"I don't feel very beautiful. I feel like a dickhead. This isn't going to work, Mr Lawrence."

It wasn't easy but Mr Lawrence managed to compose himself. He said, "Have faith, dear boy."

"I'm losing it quickly, Mr Lawrence, the faith. I'm going downhill fast, and dressed like this isn't helping."

"You look fine, Paul, just fine. Now stop worrying and try to concentrate."

"I'll try."

Laura turned to Mr Lawrence. "Right then, it's your turn now." She glanced at her watch. "And we're running out of time."

Laura was enjoying herself. In a sense, with them playing the parts, she'd become the director. Power was a powerful emotion. An aphrodisiac, some old cowboy had said, and he wasn't talking about pork scratchings.

In the window, blinking red then green, it was hot beneath the padded suit of Father Christmas, and sweat trickled across his chest like some fast little insect. The cotton wool beard was giving him trouble too and loose strands made his nose twitch. He needed to scratch at every nerve and yet he dared not move. Paul was rigid. Mr Lawrence could see him from the corner of his eye. He looked better in green. The ballerinas were dark shapes and yet they seemed more life-like than Paul. From her hiding place behind the counter came the sounds of Laura's heavy breathing.

"I can't ever remember being so close to Father Christmas," Paul said. "He never came to our house."

"Hush now."

They stood for fifteen minutes but it seemed like an hour. Adrenalin was rushing through them and leaving its bitter taste. Their bodies began to ache. Mr Lawrence's knees began to give. He was thinking that perhaps Paul had been right, after all, and this wasn't such a good idea. But it was too late. A grotesque shadow was at the window.

Even though Mr Lawrence had only seen him in the dark, he seemed bigger than before, six feet and more with an egg-shaped head on a bull-neck. His shoulders were huge and his thick arms were long, apelike. Here was the missing link, without a doubt.

The trusty brass bell didn't ring for it had been taped up. Instead, it clanked a single reluctant clank as the door opened. And another as the door closed. He was in. The feeling of danger was incredible. Mr Lawrence's head was bursting from the rush and pressure knots bulged across his brow. The shadow moved across the shop. Thudding footfalls left the air vibrating.

From her hiding place behind the counter, Laura, in her deepest voice, called, "Pesst! Pesst!"

"Paul, is that you?"

"Pesst! Pesst!"

"Stop fucking around. You're frightening me. You know I never liked the fucking dark."

His back was to them. A huge burning red back.

From the window Paul silently turned. And without a whisper Mr Lawrence turned also, and from his bag of Christmas gifts he produced a long heavy wrench. It was Chrome-plated and glinted green and then red and reflected their faces glistening like cooking meat.

Mr Lawrence made the first blow, on top of the huge head. Shaped like a puffin's beak the point of the wrench cracked a hole. Grunting like a pig the man half-turned and saw Paul's attack. He saw a woman in black suspenders leaping forward. Gangling arms and legs and a high heel that had turned over half-way toward him.

"Fuck me!" he said, too stunned to take evasive action.

He watched a serrated bread knife disappear into his side, just below the ribs. He grabbed out and held Paul by the throat. A terrifying growl filled the room. Mr Lawrence hit him again with the wrench and only then did he go over but he took Paul with him. The back of the man's head caved in under another blow and then, after a shudder that seemed to shake the room, he lay still.

Paul struggled from beneath him, shaken and bruised and covered in blood. Laura appeared from behind the counter.

"Golly," she said. "Golleeey!"

With no time to lose, Mr Lawrence directed, "Help me get him into the studio. Quickly."

"Is he dead?" she asked.

"Of course he's dead," Paul said nervously. "Half his brain is on the floor."

"It could have been a lobotomy. Mr Lawrence is an artist."

Mr Lawrence was surprised that Laura had ever heard of the word.

"Well then," Paul offered. "Look at the blood."

He had a point. There was an awful lot of it.

Laura said, "I thought you were going to frighten him."

Mr Lawrence answered, "I think we did that."

"But you've killed him. It's murder."

"It's self-preservation. There's a difference. The law allows us to use reasonable force nowadays, unless you're a farmer, that is, and there are two thugs trying to rob you."

It took the three of them to wrap the body in Clingfilm and drag it into the studio and even so, they still left a long red skid mark. Mr Lawrence said, "Help me to drag him down the cellar steps."

Laura said, "I didn't know you had a cellar."

"Not many people do."

"I did, Mr Lawrence," Paul said. "The kozzers spent an awful lot of time down there."

A curtain concealed the cellar door.

"It stinks," Paul uttered as the door opened to the dark dangerous steps where cobwebs hung in streamers. "The coppers mentioned the smell. They were right."

"It's the dead cats. When they're alive they get in through the pavement grating and find themselves trapped."

"They might have been the cats we heard crying...like babies."

"Yes, you might be right."

Laura stepped back in disgust. "It smells like dead bodies. I'm not going down there."

"We can manage. It's downhill. Grab his shoulders, Paul."

They negotiated the steep narrow flight of concrete steps that in parts were worn away and crumbling, down between the thick walls of brick that had never seen the light of day, through a decaying archway at the bottom to the black earth beyond.

"It does stink down here," Paul repeated.

"The damp has rotted everything. One day the foundations will give up and the whole of the Gallery will fall into this place. Hopefully I won't be here then. That's in the future and who knows about that? Come on, let's get the door closed and sealed before it pervades the shop."

"That's a neat word, Mr Lawrence, pervades. What does it mean?"

"Permeate."

"Oh, right, permeate. Hairstyles. Right?"

In the studio he told them, "While I finish in here clean up the shop and for God's sake hurry. Get rid of the blood, wash the knife and, Paul, get out of those ridiculous clothes. Quickly now, put the models back in the window before they're missed. Dawn will be breaking soon and the milkmen will be out."

They were just completing their tasks when Mr Lawrence carried the Santa outfit into the shop. Laura carried a bowl of pink water through to the sink and Paul was dressing the model in the window. He seemed to be enjoying himself. He needed reminding about the wig. Together, they dressed Father Christmas and finished in time to hear the faint rattle of the first milk floats.

"Come on, we need a few hours sleep. The shop might be a little late opening. I'll make an exception."

"I'm not sure I'll be able to sleep," Paul muttered. "I'm still shaking."

"Keep the light on. The demons don't like the light."

Laura seemed unconcerned. She handled it well. Or hid it. Women were like that. Devious. And being a creature of the night, working the night shift, she wasn't tired. While their eyes stung hers remained bright and alert.

She lay in his bed naked and cool. Later, with dawn creeping slowly, Paul crept in and climbed into bed on Luscious Laura's side. "You'll never guess, Mr Lawrence," he murmured.

"I bet I can."

"I couldn't sleep. I went down the cellar to check he was dead and…"

"What is it, Paul?"

"He's gone, Mr Lawrence. He's gone!"

"Don't worry yourself. Cuddle up. Under this sheet you're quite safe."

He cuddled up against Laura's behind. She must have liked it between the two of them for her breathing grew louder. Sex and violence; sex and violence; they went together like a…

Paul lay still and frowned.

…silence? Absence?

Paul's eyes became narrow slits.

…horse and cart. Yeah!

Laura fidgeted and Paul smiled, and moved again.

Laura whispered, "Oh, Mr Lawrence…"

But Mr Lawrence was sleeping like a baby who'd been fed a teaspoon full of brandy.

But Paul was awake and he was enjoying himself. And Laura responded and moved in time with Mr Lawrence's snores. And as she moved she whispered, "Oh, Mr Lawrence, I think I love you…"

But Mr Lawrence was out of it, somewhere else, somewhere where faint hearts couldn't follow, rattling like a rattler.

The man who looked like a doctor smiled wisely. "Mr Lawrence, isn't it?"

"I wonder if you could spare me a few minutes?"

"Sit down, you mean?"

"Yes. A few private moments."

"I hope it won't involve a prescription?"

"No, not at all."

"It's really not on. You could come to my office during office hours. Oh, why not? Come on then. Over there. Does that look private enough?"

"It's good of you."

"Yes, you're right. How is Paul?"

"It's Paul I wanted to talk to you about."

"Thought it might be. Well, fire away?"

"His room is filled with baby things. Dolls, rattles, clothes."

"What about the voice?"

"He's often difficult to understand."

"Gibberish?"

"Absolutely."

"Let me give you some background. You need to understand what you're dealing with. In this country about one person in one hundred..."

"One percent."

"Exactly. One percent of the population is subject to schizophrenia at some time in life. Loosely that means that in every street of about fifty houses or so someone there suffers from schizophrenia."

"Goodness me, that is surprising."

"Now you'll probably want to know exactly what it is. Well, no one knows. If they tell you they do, they're lying. That's the top and bottom of it. Opinion is divided. To the layperson it is madness, the lunatic with the split personality. Norman Bates, Jekyll and Hyde. The specialists are in two camps. Some see it as a biological illness and others believe that external factors alone are the cause. In other words no one is born with it. Most scientists believe in the biological condition and indeed, they have a powerful argument. Twins, parted at birth, both suffering from the same condition and so on. They, therefore, are in favour of neuroleptic drugs—thioridazine, pimoxide, orphenadrine, and these do have a calming influence. They certainly silence the voices. As a matter of interest, have you ever considered double glazing for your shop?"

"Not really."

"You should. You should give it some serious thought. Prices are bound to rise next year. And this year is nearly done. This government is hell-bent on putting everything up."

"Yes, you're right. The Dome, the London Eye..."

"The other school considers that these psychological disorders have their source in childhood, that the subject has adopted a behavioural pattern in order to shield himself against family madness. Now this is interesting. Part of the treatment is reparenting—the cathexis technique—

to take the patient back to the baby stage so that they can begin again. You see the connection? Babies, dolls? This treatment is controversial. Some would call it brainwashing, that it breeds dependence and doesn't get to the root cause which is biological. Both camps are locked in this bitter dispute. The patient, of course, when reason is lost to bitterness, is the loser. The truth, probably, almost certainly, lies somewhere between both camps, as truth often does: that it is biological, but that it is exacerbated by external influence. But there you are. There is nothing on earth more dangerous than the expert. If I were you I'd consider the new PVC lines. It saves an awful lot of time in painting and varnishing and all those uncivilized chores."

"What about the voices?"

"Ah, yes, the voices. They talk to you. Sometimes they call you names, and not your own name. You fear them. They are generally deep frightening voices, unless they are female. Not many are. They are unfriendly and threatening and you can't turn them off. Pain silences them. That's why a lot of patients hurt themselves. With knives and razor-blades and matches and, sometimes less obviously, with chicken vindaloo and jogging and visiting the gym. In older people the voices lead to acute persecution complex—paranoia."

"And the outlook?"

"Without help, things will only get worse. The voices, after all, represent one's own subconscious."

"They told him he was an electrician and he blew up my shop."

"Exactly."

"They told him he was a salesman and he sells a lot of ducks."

"Ducks?"

"Yes."

"Ducks, flying? Yes, that makes sense. Do you have many paintings of ducks in your gallery?"

"They do very well."

"They're obviously on his mind."

"They're on everyone's mind, or so it seems. They fly up walls over cheap and nasty gas fires."

"I wonder if he dabbles in acid."

"I could ask him."

"It would explain a lot."

"The police came. Talked to him. Apparently a girl he knew has gone missing."

"What was she like?"

"Average, slim. Her name is Sandra."

"No! No! I mean interests. Do they have anything in common?"

"Badminton."

"Shuttlecocks! Feathers! Ducks! Good grief man! Norman Bates stuffed birds. He was a taxidermist!"

"I see."

"You could recover your costs easily. Your heating bills would be cut in half..."

"I'll tell you what," Mr Lawrence said in all sincerity. "I would like you to come around and give me an estimate. You've talked me into it. And when you come perhaps we could discuss Paul a little more."

"Absolutely. Good idea." He rubbed his red hands together. Mr Lawrence noticed the red scaly patches of psoriasis.

"There is one thing..."

"Go on?" A slight look of concern wrinkled the brow.

"There's a roof light in the cellar. One of those old pavement lights, you know the sort of thing. You'd have to do something with that."

"My dear Mr Lawrence that will be no problem at all. We'll sort something out. Would you like a drink? Exactly how many windows and doors do you have in your shop?"

"Enough. A few. Enough to throw light on the subject. And then you can measure up the cellar window for me. That's always going to be the tricky one for you."

He stuck up a firm finger. "Don't you worry about that. When it comes to cellars I'm an expert."

Mr Lawrence smiled a wicked little smile.

Chapter 28

While Superintendent Billingham's blue machine ticked over at a rate that rarely accelerated even when a major incident broke the routine—uniforms, it seemed, came with a built-in pacemaker that was set at slow—Baxter's team faced the flak from hysterical headlines and increased interference from the top brass. More time was lost in explanation, reports and management meetings, and the resultant pressure was telling. It was not easy to make progress when you were constantly watching your back. Scoring points in a job where it was common knowledge that scapegoats were essential for progression resulted in isolationism and the value of teamwork so necessary to any investigation was lost. Negotiating a path between the wreckage of busted egos while getting the job done was par for a DI's course.

Stiff and weary coppers climbed from their cars and others took their places, vans rolled in and unloaded the dregs of society, sore-footed plods returned in pairs and others went out, crimes came in day and night, the villains never slept.

At Hinckley the depression was deep. Helen Harrison's car had produced a nil return and also, as expected but made all but irrelevant by HQ's visit, forensics confirmed that the swabbed, bagged, tweezer-collected and Hoover-sucked samples from the Gallery had produced nothing new. The team, bleary-eyed from viewing footage from the CCTVs covering the High Road and from the local shops and banks, concentrated once again on the specialized charities and other outfits that involved missing persons.

Not many of them believed that Lawrence was still in the frame and even DS Butler was having doubts. Only DC Anian Stanford remained convinced, but then, she knew him more than most and she had what the others did not—a woman's intuition.

The DC didn't need an A-level to work out what was wrong with Sam Butler. Apart from the dressing-down he'd received from Wooderson and the criticism from Detective Superintendent Baxter that had upset him even more, confiding in him about her feelings toward Rick Cole had been a big mistake. Even so his reaction had still come as a surprise. And it should not have done. She was old enough to know about men by now, and when it came to women they were all the same.

So much for his wife and kid, Janet and Lucy. So much for the doting dad!

Plato eat your heart out. You got it wrong again.

But what of Cole himself? Anian had picked up a rumour that he was more than friendly with a certain PC who'd been seconded to his team. She wondered if it was the PC who'd taken her own place. The way her luck was running it wouldn't surprise her at all.

She sat in her car thinking about it all, Cole included, aware that she was running out of time and options. The final session with Lawrence was on her. It was her last shot and she hadn't got a plan to take it forward.

What was it Geoff Maynard had said? Use the religious card? She shook her head. Religion wasn't going to excite Lawrence, not any more. Even if it had figured in his past he'd got it under control.

And that left the other option, every girl's secret weapon. And there was something inevitable about the way it had panned out, that sooner or later she had always intended using it. She felt quite dispassionate and focussed.

In the office she caught up with DS Butler.

"Sam, I have a confession to make."

He was still smarting and almost said, 'Another one', but that would have been too churlish and she didn't deserve it. Instead he tried a conciliatory smile that wasn't too convincing and ended up more like a grimace.

She made sure they were out of earshot and said hurriedly, "I went for another session with Lawrence. He's still painting me."

Butler sat down heavily. His face darkened as he waited for more and she worried that the others in the room would pick up on it.

"I couldn't give up," she insisted.

"You were told..." His voice sounded oddly broken.

"I know. And it's down to me."

"It was a formal instruction, Anian, and it wasn't mine. You'll lose your job here."

"I know."

"I'll have to report it."

"I know that too."

"For Christ sake, why?"

"Because we're that close and because we know he's guilty."

Butler swallowed air.

"The thing is, it's my last session with him tomorrow and things are coming to a head..."

"Wrong! It was going to be your last session."

"Sam..."

"Sam nothing. We're on the line here, right out on a limb. Do you think they'll believe I had no knowledge of all this? Everyone knows, or they think they do, how close we are. Partners, isn't that the word?"

"It's too late now. We can't stop now."

"Yes we can. And we will. You will!"

"Then I'll do it without you, Sam, and if it goes pear-shaped I'll deny you had any involvement."

"Like I said, you think they'll believe you?"

"You can't stop me. Not now."

"Don't call me Sam," he said without a smile, playing for time.

He was in a corner and he knew it. All he wanted was out. A result was no longer a priority. Survival and a pension came first.

He said, "I don't like it, Anian. We're way out of our depth."

"It's our last shot. If this fails we've got nothing, not a thing. Nothing will go wrong. He doesn't take chances. He's not going to tip

278

Rohypnol or anything else into the wine. Somehow he's got to get me out of there to wherever it is he takes them. Whatever happens it won't be in the shop. He's not going to carry me, is he?"

"He could use a threat, a knife—maybe we missed a firearm."

"Sam, nothing was missed. Sure he could use a knife, but he's not going to frogmarch me along the High Road and if he comes out back, you'll be there."

"Will I?" he said. "Someone should be out front. What if his lodgers help?"

"He won't involve them. John Lawrence is a loner. And who else would you get?"

He nodded reluctantly. "No one."

She threw him a tentative smile. "But you will help me?"

"You're not giving me a choice. I can't let you do it alone."

"That's what I'd hoped you'd say." She reached forward and touched his sleeve. "Don't worry."

"It's how I am. I'm never happy unless I have something to worry about."

"Well there you are then, I've made you happy at last."

In the corridor at Sheerham nick Cole caught a look from Donna that asked a question and he ushered her into his office.

"Guv?"

"Donna, you all right?"

"No."

"You're not letting it get to you?"

"Not the case, Guv. Other things. You've got to me. Being cut short last night shook me back to reality. I was dreaming. It wasn't real, was it?"

"It seemed real enough at the time."

She shook her head. "It was an emergency, Guv, that's all it was."

"I never misled you, Donna. It was you that knocked on my door."

"Wrong. You opened it before I knocked. But I'm glad I did. In another way I'm not. It's nothing to do with you. You never said anything except come to bed. I've got a fiancé who buys concrete tunnel linings and my favourite DVD is Titanic." She turned back to the door then paused. "I'd like to go back to uniform, Guv."

"Any reason in particular?"

"Maybe it was the phone going, maybe Geoff getting hurt. I don't know. Maybe we've been saved by the bell."

"About going back to uniform?"

She offered him a tricky little smile that reminded him where it had started, then said simply, "Status Quo. My favourite band." For just a moment she hesitated then said, "Gotta go," and with a swirl of skirt she went and the door closed behind her and with a curious certainty, he knew that was the end of it.

At his table in the White Horse, partitioned by the stanchions, Rick Cole sat alone. It was well after closing—three, four, who counted? And the room was swimming. He'd come out to hear some noise, any noise, and even Chas Walker's voice filtering in from the far end of the room was mildly satisfying.

He considered calling it a day, selling up, selling out, starting somewhere fresh. But he knew he wouldn't. It was just Teacher's talk. Come the winter's late dawn he'd be back on the job, poking the bad men where it hurt.

He thought about Donna Fitzgerald at home with her fiancé, and Anian Stanford in her single bed. He thought about his own bed and the wife who'd left it. Ex-wife, now, of course. He checked his watch. God knows why because he was thinking in years.

It had been a long time ago. Last he'd heard she was living in Sunshine on the California coast with her American husband, two kids and an outdoor swimming pool.

Now, where was it the San Andreas fault ran through? His smile was humourless as he nodded and emptied his glass.

He had blamed the job, and so had she. But that was crap. Staleness had grown into indifference and from there it was always going to be a matter of opportunity. And yet it had all started so well—his foot on the ladder in a job he loved, a quick promotion, the beat of London and a beautiful young wife. The future had never promised so much.

"I'm leaving you," she had said. "I never minded you being a policeman. I just didn't want the house turned into a police station!"

"Coppers aren't normal," she had said.

He'd had enough. He shook away the memories and levered himself out of the chair. He looked at the door—the exit to reality and a cold house—then at Big Billy's excellent daughter, Diane, who stood behind the bar. She smiled and headed his way and made a fuss of cleaning his ashtray. Heavy veins ran the length of her long skinny arms. Nicotine-stained fingers bridged by her old wedding rings worked furiously with a duster.

"Hello, Princess," he said.

"You off, Ricky? Can't you handle it no more?" The H in handle was left behind somewhere between the river and Hackney.

Rick Cole sighed and sat down again. While she hovered, looking down at him with a question in her eyes, he settled himself and lit a JPS. One for the road sounded good.

Chapter 29

It had all happened so quickly, too quickly for Paul—Sandra going missing, the police calling again and then in the dark they killed his ex-cell mate, his suitor, or did they? Dead men don't walk away. And there was no body in the cellar, nobody at all. But Mr Lawrence had it all in hand. "Don't worry," he kept telling him, so he didn't.

And then it was all about planning, the list of things he had to do. Mr Lawrence went over them, time and again, until it gave Paul a headache. And out of the headache came the other familiar voice.

From Boots he obtained some bits and pieces and then he spent an hour or two putting on his face. Lipstick and mascara and eye shadow and blusher—it was never-ending and quite an art, but the result was wonderful and, as he turned this way and that for the mirror, he experienced the most incredible rush, he could actually feel his heart pounding. It was like sniffing something very special, the feeling you got when you were doing something you shouldn't, nicking or something; a sexy, intoxicating feeling of danger. It was amazing what a bit of dollop could do. It wasn't a man's world after all. Men only thought they were in charge. He wondered whether other women knew about the power they possessed. Maybe they did. That would certainly answer a lot of questions. That was a thought.

The thought stayed with him and grew until, as he walked up the High Road—not forgetting, of course, the swing of his hips and newly acquired handbag—he was walking on air.

In The British Mr Lawrence was thinking about the gender-benders, the phthalates with their endocrine-disrupting chemicals that could be absorbed through the skin and were present in soaps and perfumes and deodorants and shampoos and just about everything that was made of plastic; even tablets from the doctors were coated in them. He nodded. Maybe they were the cause...

In The British the priest from The Church of our Blessed Virgin stood at the bar. He was in civvies. It was the first time the others had ever seen him in civvies. His face was flushed and he was clearly angry. They overheard him talking to the manager.

"Would you believe it? Could you believe it? Even I don't believe it. Give me a large scotch. Make it a treble."

"Ice?"

"Forget the rocks."

"Water?"

"I washed already."

Roger nodded and said, "Straight it is. So what is it you can't believe, Father? Surely not your belief in...?"

"No, no, no, not that at all, at all. What I'm having trouble coming to terms with is that anyone could rob their own priest. They broke into the church and stole my best frock. My frock! My working clothes, would you believe! A curse on them all."

Roger shook a sad head. "There's trouble all over," he said. "The late colonel was probably right in that it has to do with the ending of conscription. As a matter of interest and with the colonel in mind, perhaps you can help me on another point, a point that has been troubling me? Why was it that after the war the Vatican first hid and then helped so many Nazis to escape?"

The priest narrowed his eyes, then shook his head and said, "Make that two doubles, or whatever it is that four is called."

Paul stood in The British like a common slapper but no one recognized him. Except for Mr Lawrence.

Just goes to show. There isn't much difference. Just clothes and a smudge of eye shadow and lipstick. And some tissues down your chest. If only they knew, these geezers giving him the eye, wanting to give him something else. Bastards, mostly. If only these old men could see themselves, if only they knew how pathetic they looked as they strained for eye contact, conscious of every move they made in their alcoholic bubble, flexing their flabby muscles, hiding their blemishes, pulling in their heavy beer bellies.

We girls should sympathize, really, and feel sad for them. How awful it must be to be old while the heart cries out to be young. How awful it was to be old in today's rushing world. A world where there's no such thing as maturity, not in the mind, where men's thoughts are never seasoned or mellowed like a ripe cheese. Old wrinkled bodies with childish minds. Life's a joke, innit? Only thing is, the punchline ain't so funny.

A tart, innI? An A-listed long-legged slapper.

And half the bar fancied him. And the other half was jealous.

But the clothes...the clothes he wore, wonderful! The rich blue figure-hugging dress he'd nicked from Acadamy, the poxy air whistling up his legs, the soft lace moving against his...his... Check it out. He'd borrowed all that from...from...the model... Anthea. Right? And now he was excited just being alive. Just standing there. Being clocked by all the geezers. You wouldn't believe the feeling. You wouldn't believe it. It was like...exciting, being looked at like you were a celebrity or something. Madonna. Yeah.

Dressed like that, keeping in the shadows, it's like chess, see? A solid move. A Yaya defence. A defensive move. A modern defence. Take your time, build, wait for a weakness, strengthen your position, wait and see what the opponent's got in mind and then, go for it. Counterpunch. Crunch!

Together they walked back to the shop, the artist and his neophyte. Paul was getting used to the heels and had even fashioned something of a sashay. Being a tart, a crumpet, a...a...goddess, that's it, was a doddle, a piece of cake. You just had to learn to moan about everything and men in particular. There was nothing to it at all. He would have to work on the voice and the quick and easy put-downs but in time they would come.

"Timing, Paul," Mr Lawrence had told him. "Timing is important."

"Know what you mean. Keep the opposition. Like chess, see? Like the old Reti. Follow a plan. Endings. More important than anything else. They're even more important than the openings, Mr Lawrence."

"I'll take your word for that, young Paul, even though, in my experience, openings are pretty important. Off you go then. The woman from India is due at any moment."

"India? I thought she was a Paki."

"No difference, not really, just a border with a few thousand guns and the odd nuclear bomb."

"Will you finish the painting?"

"Yes. Just the final detail. It won't take long."

"The final moves, eh? The end game, like I said, Innit?"

As Paul went out the woman came in. She didn't recognize him, but then, why should she? Paul was Paula now, and dressed for the occasion.

Chapter 30

DS Sam Butler checked her handbag for a third time, making certain that the head of a tiny microphone was concealed beneath the flap.

"Where did you get it," she had asked.

"Don't ask questions, girl," he had answered.

He hid the quick cuffs and a small canister of CS spray beneath a flimsy headband she'd supplied. She had turned up half an hour earlier and he'd been freshly astonished at the sight of her in the loose flowing dress. Something in his chest fluttered. He tried to remain indifferent but he didn't fool her, not for a moment.

"Sam..."

He started the car and turned toward the High Road, supermarket end.

"Sam, I'm sorry."

"For what?"

"For not realizing you cared."

"Oh, that. That's in the past. Forget it." He fought an impulse to glance her way. Instead he laughed a false laugh and said, "Funny thing, even I didn't know till you told me about Ricky Cole. So much for self-awareness, eh? Somehow you'd just become a part of the future without me knowing. Took you for granted, that you'd be there. Must have crept up in the dark. I never thought I'd want any more from you than just the part of you sitting next to me in the car, or across from me in the office—company, friendship, something more than a colleague, but a colleague nonetheless. That's the wonder of it all. I'm in love with my wife and my daughter's just about the most precious thing I've ever had and yet…you tell me? What the fuck do I know about it? I've never been unfaithful and I never will be, leave that to all the others. But it doesn't stop me loving you. OK, now I've said it. I feel foolish as hell, but now you know. Nothing's to be done. It requires nothing. It's my problem, a bit like arthritis or the toothache."

"I never meant to be frivolous with you, Sam, or to give you the wrong idea."

"You didn't."

They met the High Road. He drove past the supermarket. The car park was full. People struggled with bulging trolleys full of Christmas crackers and fancy tins of sweets and a bottle of last-minute sherry for the old neighbour who might drop in. And the guys selling Christmas wrapping paper were running out of time—their voices were louder: twenty sheets for a quid.

"It's been a tough lesson, and I've learned it late. You might think you're in control but you never are. All it takes is a special person, a little smile, and all your planning can go out the window. Everything you hold dear becomes secondary and you'd put it all on the line. For a dream. You're a special person, Anian."

"Oh, Sam…"

On the left the lonely pet shop window slid by. In the distance the Carrington loomed. The pavements were packed. It was getting close.

"OK, so let's concentrate. We've been over it a dozen times, I know. This is a bad idea. We're supposed to be experienced coppers."

"Sam, it's now or never. We're in too deep to pull out now."

He grunted.

"It's my fault, I know. I got us into this but it's too late to give up. And really, we've got nothing to lose. If nothing happens no one will ever know."

His nod was reluctant. He wondered how on earth he had landed in such a position, blinded by a fantasy, a dream that in reality he would never have allowed to happen.

"Sam, don't say anything, but this is going all the way, understand? Whatever it takes. Don't you come blasting in unless I'm in big trouble."

He nodded and said, "Go easy on the wine."

"He's not going to drug me."

He made a left and then a sharp right into the dark run-down road behind the Gallery. The Doll's House slid by on the left, the old office buildings were in front. He pulled to a slow stop.

"This is it."

She turned to face him full on. She flicked him a little smile then she was opening the door, struggling out, leaning back in for her handbag.

"Be careful," he said. "I couldn't bear it if you got hurt."

"I'm not getting hurt, Sam."

Her eyes levelled on him for one more time, blinked, once, twice, and she murmured, "See you in a bit."

And then she was off.

He turned and watched her walk away the way they'd come, the brown dress picking up a breeze, hugging her thighs enough to make him shiver. She didn't look back. She turned left and, with a little skip, like a shooting star that was sudden and unexpected and excellent, she was gone.

Chapter 31

She breezed in and reminded him of the Indian subcontinent, colourful and exotic and enigmatic, full of riches and poverty, of strict morals and great wickedness, God's own country, no less. And as with the country she had come from nowhere and was suddenly a major player, just one of the billion people, give or take, all wanting a piece of the action. Paul passed her on his way out but if she recognized him it didn't show. Mr Lawrence locked the door behind her. "We won't be disturbed," he said.

"You've lost your assistants?"

"Paul is on an errand and Laura is asleep. She came in very late."

While he set up his trappings she flitted about the studio, glancing at the covers of huge books that contained prints by David Davis, Corot and Hobbema, peering through the grimy windows at the back of the shop, checking that the back door was unlocked, flicking through a pile of sketches that had been half-concealed by the wall curtain but not really looking at the sketches.

"Where does this lead?"

"The cellars. They housed the electricity meters until they were moved under the stairs. In Victorian times the coal was emptied through the pavement grating. The Victorian coal dust is still down there."

He moved into the kitchen and pulled a red from the cupboard next to the sink.

"I've saved this till last," he said, bringing out the crystal glasses. "Chianti. It's one of my favourites. It's dark and mysterious, like the Vatican itself. Indeed, just like you. If taste can have a past then this is it."

"I'm not mysterious."

"I'm talking about your looks."

Glass in hand, she reached the sofa and asked, "Ready?"

"Yes. Where shall we begin?"

"How about with Sandra? It's odd… It's odd, isn't it, that Sandra should run away like that?"

"You've been listening to the news?"

"Yes, the local news. Your art class was mentioned."

"People are always running away from something, sometimes themselves."

"But she had nothing to hide, according to her husband."

"What would he know? Husbands are the last people to know. We're all hiding something."

"I think you're wrong."

"We all have our secrets, my dear."

"Not all of us. With some of us what you see is what you get."

He pushed in a darker shade around her eyes so that the mystery deepened.

He said, "Do you think I'm hiding something?"

"I have no doubt."

"Anything in particular?"

"People talk…"

"Indeed they do, but most of what they say is rubbish. I suppose going deaf might have one consolation after all. You wouldn't have to listen to the rubbish that was spoken."

"I heard that you were in prison."

"A long time ago."

"What did you do?"

"I had a breakdown. It was a childhood thing that came home to roost. Or so the experts said. I hurt some people and they locked me up. I had what they call a personality disorder. It meant pills, lots of pills. I served my time and afterwards, became a voluntary patient for a while."

"Did it help?"

"No. There was not a couch to be seen. We sat around in groups listening to each other's problems. I decided I had enough of my own."

"And what now?"

"Now I am fine, just fine, if that's what you mean. A little more cantankerous as I get older, I suppose, and perhaps a little more impatient, but that is all. I think it was a part of growing up. Some people take to dressing oddly and others to visiting gyms and things. But now? To paint. To go on painting. The finished product is not the objective. It's the journey that counts. A lot of journeys are like that. Some of them go nowhere. They're the best kind, I've always thought, when you've time to enjoy the scenery without worrying about the destination. But the lease on this place runs out soon and, although I have an option, I have not yet made a decision."

"Where would you go?"

"Who knows?"

"But wouldn't that be like running away?"

"Ah, we've come full circle. All the way back to Sandra."

"It is odd that she should run away like that."

"Prenatal stress, perhaps."

"In the first few weeks? I doubt that."

"They interviewed her husband. He was on the television. Terribly upset, of course. I don't own a television but I saw it on Paul's. When it came on he got quite excited and called me in."

"I'm not surprised he's upset."

"Paul wasn't upset. He was excited."

"Not Paul. Sandra's husband. Did the police come here?"

"Of course. The art class was one of the last places she was seen."

"Not the last?"

"Obviously not. Someone else must have seen her, unless she fell down the pavement grating. Maybe I should check the cellar. They interviewed my lodger, Paul, but he couldn't help. Then they asked me lots of questions. They knew about my previous problems. The police make a big thing about previous. Understandable, I suppose. They keep files, you see. Most people inside have been inside before. And more than once at that."

"Gosh."

"Yes. But I couldn't help them either. She left. Simple as that. What more could I say? But I don't know if they believed me. But I do wonder whether her husband is the father. Could it be she's run off with the real father?"

"She would have told her sister. Sisters confide."

"Do they? I haven't got a sister so I wouldn't know about that."

"You have a brother?"

"No, but I don't suppose brothers confide either."

"So for the moment this was where she was last seen. In here? I'm surprised the TV cameras didn't come in here."

"Goodness me. That would have been something. I might have been on the TV. That would have excited Paul even more. Probably a good thing it didn't happen."

"There's still time."

"I have a feeling there isn't. But anyway, someone must have seen her leave. It's early days yet. One of these cameras they've put up to spy on us and keep us safe will have caught her. She'll turn up, a few pounds lighter, perhaps, but I'm sure she'll turn up."

"I don't know. With all that's going on today, women being attacked in the street, the other missing women, Helen included, it's all a bit of a coincidence."

"Maybe."

"The painting of Helen?"

"Mrs Harrison?"

"Yes, Mrs Helen Harrison. Did she just come right out with it? I'm pregnant, I want you to paint me? Did she throw off her clothes and say 'like this'? That doesn't seem like Helen at all."

"I seem to recall covering this ground with you before. It wasn't like that at all."

"What then? Tell me? If there's going to be a reconstruction I'll have to know?"

"But, my goodness, you don't look a bit like Mrs Harrison. You're the wrong colour for a start. She was a blonde and very pale."

"I'm sure you could manage. You have every colour in the universe in those tubes."

"You've seen the picture yourself. She was sitting more or less where you are. And she was thrilled with the idea, I have no doubt about that. I'm convinced it was a performance and she was loving every minute. I'll go further. I think she'd rehearsed it. It seems ludicrous I know, but there you are. I remember it well, the dress around her waist baring her breasts. That's how I would have chosen to paint her. Just like that."

"So she was braless when she arrived?"

"That's right, she was." He wagged a paintbrush. "But don't read anything into that. I had noticed before, when she came in to make the booking, that she often left off her..."

"Bra?"

"Right."

"Can you tell that I'm not wearing a bra?"

"I hadn't noticed. But today I've been concentrating on your face. But now you mention it I would have a problem because you are rather...slim, that's the word."

"Small is better. I have small breasts."

"Yes, that's it. Mrs Harrison was rather generous in that area."

"What then?"

"Then? Then she hitched up her dress and we got on with it."

"If I wanted you to paint me that way...?"

"I would think you were joking."

"And if I wasn't?"

"Then we would start again."

"What is it about the nude?"

"The experts will tell you it has to do with the timeless universal quality of art. To wrap a figure in clothes immediately dates the painting. You're restless, getting uncomfortable. Shall we take a break? I'm nearly through in any case. I'll pour us some more wine. That one is wearing off. I like the way it brings the colour to your face."

"I'm fine. More than one glass will go to my head. I'm not used to it at all. Do you think Paul could have something to do with Sandra's disappearance?"

"Could he be the father? I doubt it. I think he only saw her the once."

"And no one's seen her since?"

Mr Lawrence shrugged. "Someone must have done."

"Is it possible that Paul met Helen?"

"Mrs Harrison? It's possible. This is his hunting ground, after all, and she came here. Tell me what you're getting at?"

"OK," she said. "Let me play detective." A smile fluttered about her lips. She continued, "We have a number of missing women. None of them took their personal possessions."

"Didn't they? I didn't know that."

"It was in the paper, I think. Anyway, that means that they didn't run off. Some of the women were involved with you, one through your art class, another through the painting. They were married, one of them happily—"

"Who knows whether they were happy?"

"Granted."

"What else?"

"They were expecting. Did you use Sandra as a model?"

"For the class?"

"Personally."

"No, not for the class or personally."

"It's a fascinating idea."

"Yes, I can see that. And certainly I'll agree with you that I am a common factor."

"And their pregnancies, and the fact that they are local."

"Right, they have all that in common."

"Did Helen ever visit The British?"

"I never saw Mrs Harrison there. It's not really her kind of place."

"What about local restaurants? We know that Paul met Sandra. Maybe he met Helen too. Maybe, after finishing a session with you, Helen went for a drink or a meal in one of the local restaurants, and there she bumped into Paul."

"Let me stop you there. Mrs Harrison sharing a drink with young Paul Knight could not happen in a thousand years. Mrs Harrison would die sooner than acknowledge the existence of a youngster like Paul Knight. I'm not for one moment suggesting that she is choosy with her company, simply that, for her, the Paul Knights of the world don't exist. In any case, at the time of Mrs Harrison's disappearance, Paul was being entertained at Her Majesty's pleasure. Hold it just there!"

"Well, he is a bit odd."

"I mean keep still. I'm dealing with your eyes. They seem to have narrowed slightly."

"Sorry. I was getting carried away. I can't get Helen's disappearance out of my head. Perhaps it's an unhealthy interest. She was my friend."

"I hope she still is."

"Of course."

"I've noticed during this session that the hem of your dress has moved up a little. It is undoing my composition."

She moved one long leg against the other and said, "It must be the wine. I feel quite giddy. It's just that... I was just wondering about that reconstruction you mentioned. Whether it would jog a memory, something that you missed, something important."

"My goodness, I was wondering about that too."

Chapter 32

He had things to do, errands for Mr Lawrence. He had to stay in the shadows for in the light the filth were about looking for the missing girl, Sandra. And they were on to him. Paul was sure of that. If he were staying he would have to get shot of everything. Couldn't leave it in the room. They'd find it all and that would be that. End of story. Checkmate, mate! You could guarantee they'd make another search, find a hair from his ex-cell mate, or some blood between the floorboards. DNA, that's the word. Right? They'd find the DNA and that would be that, without passing go. They'd blame him for everything. Even Sandra. He'd be lucky to get out with a walking frame. Still, he wasn't hanging around for that to happen. No way. Time to retreat. Like Dunkirk. Like the old soldiers…like…like the colonel, but not to the same place. Legging it, innI?

It had been a funny sort of day. Special days always were—the days of weddings and funerals and court appearances where you're stood up in front of a beak. Colours seemed different, darker, and sounds seemed different, louder. It started early, he remembered, earlier than most, before the sun was up, before it was…light. It was still dark when Laura came in. Her eyes were sleepless and her legs were shaking and a little bandy and she looked altogether exhausted. That was the night shift for you, he supposed. It did you no good at all. Mr Lawrence made her some tea and forced her to drink it. He looked after her. She was asleep before her head hit the pillow. Only half-undressed. Or dressed. But they completed the undressing anyway, so she wouldn't… You know?

Strangle or something.

Mr Lawrence gave her bottom a little pat and Paul gave it a little stroke, little gestures of endearment, perhaps parting gestures, for their leave-taking was fast approaching.

But Paul had important things to do.

First he had to go to Boots. Mr Lawrence had spelt it out. He had to visit the booth and have his photograph taken. He spent some minutes admiring the image of the girl looking back at him. Then he had to take the strip of photographs along with a brown envelope that Mr Lawrence had given him across town to a small backstreet shop where a thin grey man named Arnold took the strip of photographs and the brown envelope and told him to wait. He waited for almost an hour before Arnold appeared again and gave him yet another envelope. He didn't look inside but he knew that the envelope contained two passports. He'd guessed that all by himself. Maybe they were going to Scotland or some other place where the law couldn't find them. He nodded. Mr Lawrence had it all in hand.

Arnold said, "Anything else I can do for you—firearms, bomb-making equipment, recipes? I've got a nice line in Iraqi headgear, only slightly smoke-damaged—call them seconds."

"No," Paul stuttered. "No, thank you."

He needed to get out of there. It was too heavy for him. He hit the pavement, still stuttering.

Then he was on the move again, back to the High Road where he knew his way around.

In the travel agency a woman wearing thick foundation whose hair was thinned and split by too many perms in the seventies gave him a funny look along with the tickets. He'd noticed that women of a certain age, like, maybe forty or fifty, looked at other women differently, threatening like. He'd noticed that. He got a bit flustered by the threat, said Paul instead of Paula, that sort of thing. Easy mistake. But he wouldn't make it again. Probably forgot to wiggle his behind as well. Such is life. And what was more, the tissue fell out of his left breast as he bent to sign. When that happened the woman behind the desk was immediately sympathetic and fingered a little pink ribbon she'd pinned to her cardigan. Amazing how, once the threat was no longer relevant, girls stick together. Men weren't like that. The glue that held men together was only temporary, just for the moment, made up of alcohol. It wasn't lasting. Men didn't have friends, as such, only opponents. They promised they would stay in touch because words were cheap, boozy words cheaper still, but they never did. At the end of the day men were destined to be alone even in a crowd. It was the nature of things, probably because they couldn't have babies. Yeah.

He made himself scarce for an hour or two, following Mr Lawrence's instructions. Timing, remember? Timing's important, Paul!

"It's Paula, Mr Lawrence. It's Paula now, innit?"

"Yes, you're right. I see it now. Silly of me not to have noticed."

After picking up the tickets he kept to the backstreets. The filth were in the High Road, in force, stopping people in the street and showing them pictures of Sandra. It was like the war, like the cold, cold war, like Moscow, like Berlin or something, that's it, hiding in dark doorways, running across streets, dodging traffic, in high heels, keeping your back to the wall. A dangerous game. An excellent game. You knew you were, like, alive. Like the old soldiers used to say—like the colonel used to say, when he was alive—there was nothing more exhilarating than a game of hide-and-seek. And the dress riding up all the time. Like a king pawn opening, he'd say. Like the bloody King's Gambit and, that was bloody dodgy.

Darkness crept in mid-afternoon, but that suited him. The old four o'clock was growing through the foundation. Another hour or two and he'd look like a Spanish housewife. Sod that for a living. He crept back to the shop. It was closed. The old man was in his studio and Laura was still sound asleep. He climbed under the stairs. Wanted a last look. Kneeling down in a tight dress proved a right game. He had to pull it to his waist. In the darkness the studio light flooded through the crack in the wall. He adjusted his eyes. He loved cracks.

The old geezer was still there, standing behind his easel like Vinny Gough. Dab-dabbing, mixing, squinting, a knife here, a brush there, the whole game. A serious bloody painter, Paul would say.

But hold on! Hold on just a minute! Forget the painting. Paul couldn't believe his eyes. Not the Indian! Not the Paki! That sort of thing was against their religion, or so he thought. Paul's mouth dropped open.

Bombay duck! Holy Fuck! It was like a brown liquorice allsort, brown and brown with a streak of black running through the middle. This was the Golden Gate, mate, the Grand Canyon, Niagara bloody Falls no less. This was cowboy country and he, Paul, wanted to mount up. Talk about excitement. Talk about *Basic Instinct*. Sharon Stone is on the phone. Hit the pause, Santa Claus. Christmas is coming and so is Paul Knight.

Even the voice was getting excited and he could hear the excited words. "Fuck! Fuck! Fuck!"

And she was giving him the come-on. Not much. Paul could see it all right. But the old man didn't seem to notice. Maybe the angle was wrong for him. But he noticed. Paul didn't miss a trick like that. And the dress was raised. No kidding. Paul's dress was raised. And the soft lace was tightening by the moment. The old lingerie was wonderful. No wonder the catalogues were full of it. Paul reached down. No option, really. Not really.

In the narrow road behind the shop the red glow from the High Road painted the sky above the rooftops. The sky groaned. It was going to unload, rain or, more likely, snow. It was certainly cold enough. The red light poured like lava down the sloping slates and curled around the thick clumps of crawling moss. It seemed to cling to everything as it edged down the walls to the narrow pavement.

The filth was there, waiting for him. Mr Lawrence had been right. You had to give it to the old guys. If they'd left it another day, another hour, it would have been too late. When Mr Lawrence told him, Paul didn't believe it at first. Just goes to show. Experience, all that. Paul crept up to the filth. He had the car window down and was listening to the radio. Paul could hear Mr Lawrence's voice, then the woman's. The woman from India. She was wired. Mr Lawrence was right about that too. Clever old geezer. Just goes to show. You couldn't dismiss the old geezers out of hand. That's why they won the war, he supposed. Paul could still learn a thing or two.

The hammer was in his handbag until he took it out. Just an ordinary hammer with a wooden shaft and steel head. The steel glinted red. The filth didn't know what hit him, just above the ear. Phut! A dull thud. Like the noise you got when you stuck a knife into a white leather sofa.

Paul looked about. The road was still empty. He turned off the filth's radio and straightened his breasts. On the way out of the narrow road, on the way to the station, he picked up the suitcase he'd left just inside the back gate. Now he was going. Trains and boats and planes. All that. Defensive play. Don't try and win a drawn game.

Life's like that: a game of chess—winning, losing, but mostly stalemate, innit? You only lost at the end of it. Like…at the…end of it.

He started down the steps of an underpass, taking care in his high heels. And that's when he noticed a woman following him. A blonde. A blond spiky-haired woman in a short burgundy shift with matching painted toenails—every year's colour.

Chapter 33

The first guest to arrive for the party had stayed till the end. It had been touch and go and his plans had been unexpectedly modified. It had meant a change in venue for the last dance. Auld Lang Syne had to be played away from the Square, somewhere else, on another crowded street where one pretty face was lost among others. His encounter with the big guy had probably been a mistake and still he wasn't sure who he was and why he had been following. He hadn't looked like a copper or, come to that, your average punter, but nowadays who could tell? Long gone were the days when you could go by looks alone. The police force, in particular, was more than likely employing dwarfs, Gypsies and—he smiled—even trannies to satisfy the PC brigade. And as for the punters—lords, MPs, film stars, judges, you name it. The world had gone mad.

Still, since being seen was no longer an issue, it meant he could look into the eyes and that was always special.

And so for this final frolic he had chosen his partner and he stared across the road at the young woman who was struggling with her suitcase, uneasy on sky-high heels. She moved along the pavement, her right arm and shoulder sagging under the weight of the case. At times, as she moved past the window displays, she was bathed in light. Her tight blue dress was a second skin. But she needed a coat. It was freezing. If she wasn't careful she would catch her death.

She was different to the rest and she reminded him of someone else, a face in an old photograph. But it was only the image that he remembered. He couldn't remember the person. No matter how hard he tried he couldn't bring back the touch or the soft breath. Oh, he fantasized of course, built a character around the picture. But he never knew her.

But who was this? This nudge to the past? She might have been a student. Or a tom. No difference from a distance. Not to look at. It was only closer you saw the hardness about the tom. But there was something uninhibited about the way this one moved—free and easy with an adventurous touch, the perfume of the campus—and he did love students. He appreciated intelligence even though he knew that most students didn't have any. But it didn't matter for these students with their dreams of better things handled the situation and their fear so much better than their elders—until they realized the inevitable—and then they could appreciate him for what he was: a predator, a jungle cat, a lover. His courtship was the pursuit itself, the hunt, the stalk, his phallus the red-hot blade. Swish, swish, said the blade. He loved the whimper when they saw their own skin parting to reveal the deep pink flesh—pink, before it turned to red.

He never knew them and that was part of the thrill, reading about them afterwards, the write-ups in the papers, the lives they'd lived and their indiscretions accompanying the photographs of them in bikinis taken on their last holidays on tropical beaches. The newspapers loved bikinis, and tits, if they could get them.

The screamers were the worst. You sorted them out quickly. Go for the neck to stop them screaming and you'd get covered in blood. No good at all. Just cut it short. Make them know. Take their tits away. It's mostly fat and no blood, no blood to splatter anyway. Do your business and get out of it.

The wetters were a nuisance. You could end up getting wet. They wet themselves at the sight of the knife, after he'd used it just once, before he used it again.

Then the talkers, trying to talk their way out of it even while their blood splashed down.

Then the kickers, the evening class karate and Kung Fu experts with their coloured belts. Pretty useless, that stuff, unless you knew the danger. And no one ever knew, until they felt the blade.

He watched her and he wondered what she'd be: screamer, wetter, talker, freezer? He watched her move toward the underpass, struggling with the case.

He ran across the road, dodging traffic and red lights, and entered the underpass from the other end. Dangerous places, underpasses, where the lighting isn't good. Lonely places, underpasses, where the helpless leave their blood.

As he went down the steps he heard the click-clicking of her shoes on the tiled floor. The tunnel was an amplifier. As he appeared she seemed to recognize him, just for an instant, but it was there, in her eyes. Perhaps she'd seen him before. Perhaps she'd clocked him on the pavements, while he was clocking her.

She was midway along the underpass as he drew level. He threw her a smile of acknowledgement but it met with no response. He'd got her wrong. This was no student. This was a hard bitch. There was a yard between them, no more than that, just a single step, a quick, sudden step.

He made his move.

She dropped the case, ready for it.

Swish, swish, said the blade, with the deftness of a surgeon's scalpel, into the breast. In, out, then swish again, right across the chest.

But she didn't struggle, or grimace, or scream. She just stood there smiling like some mental retard on the steps of the European Parliament. And from the neat cut in her figure-hugging rich-blue dress a thick wad of tissue bloomed like a white rose.

The first guest to arrive said, "Fuck!" And then he saw the hammer. A simple hammer with a long wooden shaft with a steel head smudged in red. He was transfixed, watched it move towards him, all the way to his head, wondering in that instant, where the red had come from.

Phut!

A dull thud.

And then darkness.

And then some vague light again, filtering in through a swirling mist.

He felt that warm sticky feeling, no pain, not yet. Just a burning sensation that grew steadily hotter. But he knew what had happened. He couldn't believe it. His eyes bulged in disbelief. The bitch had hit him, taken him by surprise and for a moment or two he'd been out of it. But now…now she was using his own knife on him. And she was talking, in two voices. One sounded like a woman. But the other very definitely did not.

In the whole of the city, out of everyone in the world he could have chosen, he'd come up with his own personal A-One fucking moon-worshipper.

"Try it on me, would you? Try it on Paula? Forgot my minder, did you? Bad move. Weak move. Not a book move."

And the first guest felt helpless as the woman pulled the black jacket from his shoulders.

He heard Paula say, "Niiice jacket."

And then the male voice came again, out of those same full red lips. "You keep it, sweetheart. Call it a trophy. Like a tiger skin or something. Like we've just bagged a tiger and skinned it, in…in Africa."

It was all so fucking disconcerting.

And the first guest watched the stain spread out in slow motion, still not believing. He watched the blade come down again and felt a slash across his cheek. There was something strangely intimate here. He felt his flesh opening, cleanly, quickly, deeply, but it felt just like a sting, like a burn. But there was blood everywhere.

"Try to hurt my Paula, eh? Eh? Bad mistake, innit?"

"Let's go. We haven't got time for this. Mr Lawrence will be waiting."

"Look away, girl. Won't be a mo'. Like Powder Pete said, see? Gotta make sure these bastards don't do it again. He looks after the kids, don't he? See? I'll look after the girls. No one else, is there?"

With each swish of the blade a soft and gentle sigh emerged from the first guest's lips. He lay there, oozing and spurting.

She was cutting the straps of his dress, the bitch, pulling the flimsy material down over his flat chest and laughing while she lifted the lace bra, A-cup, 34. He was helpless, his arms and legs jerking on the cold stone. One of his size 7 black sandals with its three-inch heel flew off and bounced from the curved tiled wall close to where an artist had expressed himself with PK loves JL.

Then she was lifting the hem of the shantung fabric, exposing the lace briefs that were the colour of his lipstick.

"What are you, anyway? That's not what you'd call your average snatch, no way. Here, Paula, look at this, will you?"

"Gosh, now that is a surprise!"

He felt the knife again, in and out of him, but now in dangerous places, liver, kidneys, stomach, struggling and rooting between ribs to get at his heart. He knew he was dying, filleted, a pig on a butcher's slab, flesh opened up, blood pumping, red fountains in the stagnant piss-filled air. But it was all so painless. Even the slash across his penis, and the feel of blood across his legs, left him strangely disconnected.

He wasn't screaming here. He was no screamer.

And he wasn't wetting. He was no wetter.

And the girl, if that's what she was and who the hell could tell nowadays, cleaned herself up with some of his shantung fabric and struggled into the black Paul Smith jacket and covered the tear in her dress where the bulging wad of white tissue showed signs of red. And then she simply gathered her case and continued on her way, as though the entire business had been a little interruption, of no consequence at all.

The first guest to arrive at the party had stayed to the end.

Wanna Party?
Wanna come?

He remembered the invitation and drew in a final breath of piss-filled air and smiled as the joke sank in.

Chapter 34

Everything was important but the subtlety lay in the detail. With a fine brush and a mix of raw umber, *terre verte*, Indian red and Chinese yellow—he did like Chinese yellow—he concentrated on her face.

"I think, perhaps, that the pregnancies are of greater significance."

"You mean the women ran off with the real fathers?"

"Probably. It's the obvious conclusion. How do you feel about that? At the end of our last session you said that you might be pregnant. I got the feeling that you weren't too happy about it. It's very personal. I shouldn't have asked."

"It's OK. I hadn't realized my misgivings were so transparent. You're very intuitive."

He smiled.

She shivered.

"So, you find yourself in the same position as the missing women. It's ironical, isn't it? It must have something to do with my shop, perhaps the air in here, or the paint. Maybe I should open a fertility clinic. That's a thought."

"It could only have something to do with your shop if all the women had been here."

"Yes, I see that. But who's to say they weren't? A lot of people come and go and my memory isn't what it was and it was never very good. At school I could never remember all those dates of the battles we had with the French and the names of rivers in Mauritania."

"So your memory needs a little jog?"

"Ah, the reconstruction."

"Since I'm pregnant it would be even closer to the truth."

"I suppose it would. But you have to remember that Mrs Harrison knew exactly what she wanted. She could be very direct and she came prepared. There was no dithering. She simply arrived and we got on with it. If there was ever a problem it was all mine."

"Did you have a problem?"

"Well, there was a sudden retreat, certainly. The easel became my Maginot Line."

"I believe that was breached."

"The Germans used the back door or, rather, a side door known as Belgium."

"What then?"

"We retreated from Dunkirk."

"You know what I mean."

"Well, then, I got on with the painting, what else?"

"So Helen was sitting here, where I am, and you finished the painting. Was that the last time you saw her?"

"My goodness no. A week or so later she came back to collect the finished product. It takes that long for the paint to dry. But she'd brought with her one of her minders to carry it so she didn't stop and we didn't really talk."

"And that was the last time you saw her?"

He leant over the easel as though paying particular attention to some finer detail and it seemed that his pause would go on forever.

She turned suddenly, so that she faced him side-on and rested her chin on the palm of her right hand. The hem of her dress tipped over the side of the sofa and skirted the floor and it left a triangle of yellow for him to see. When he eventually looked up he murmured, "Yellow, my favourite colour," and his eyes locked on to that uncomplicated yet tricky place—a paradox, on a par with a generous fairway on a golf course that opened the over-confident shoulders and led to disaster. Not that he ever played golf, God forbid. His gape went on and for her there was no respite and, even when she moved one leg provocatively against the other, there was no flicker of an eyelash. The pause was unnerving, interminable, until, with what seemed to take an immense effort, he dragged his gaze back to her face. "Yellow," he repeated. "You remembered." He nodded as if understanding came reluctantly and said, "But Mrs Harrison...she did come back again and this time she was alone." His eyes were drawn once more to the flimsy covering, the yellow peril. He went on, "She'd had an argument with her husband and she was angry but I never found out what it was about. There was a bruise on her chin but I didn't like to ask. You don't, do you? Not about things that go on between husbands and wives. Not unless you're working for Relate. Even though she'd already had a few tipples, I'd say, I fed her some wine and she talked freely but that never came up. So how she got the bruise and exactly what led her back here remains a mystery."

Her look was wide-eyed and quizzical. She asked, "How long did she stay?"

Without looking up and quite matter-of-factly he said, "A long, long time."

"Did she tell you where she was going?"

"Going, my dear? She wasn't going anywhere."

Her pulse raced. He couldn't fail to notice her sudden glow. The revelation had been so careless she wondered whether he was aware of making it. She snatched a deep steadying breath and said, "So what now, Mr Lawrence? Where do we go from here?"

His eyes flicked from her groin and once again focused on the painting. She should have felt some relief but didn't. A pause might draw him back and give him time to reflect on his indiscretion.

Still studying the canvas he said, "If you would let me see you in all your splendour then you can see Mrs Harrison in all of hers."

She had been waiting for the suggestion, certain that it would come, yet she could barely believe he had made it. It had to be a ploy. He was playing games again.

"You know where she is?"

"Of course."

"Where?"

"Not far."

"How far?"

"A short walk. I'll take you."

"But first you want me to take off my clothes."

Now he looked up and met her gaze. He said, "Yes."

"I thought your thing was landscapes."

"I'm thinking of a career change."

"What then?"

"Then a few finishing touches to the painting and then I'll take you to see Mrs Harrison."

"Helen first."

"I think not. I know what you women are like. An old friend of mine—an old soldier—told me. A few final touches and then I'll take you to see your friend. I'll leave you with her and then I can get on. So, what do you think? It's what you came for, after all."

"How do I know you'll keep your word?"

"You don't, but apart from the loss of a little dignity which I'm sure you'll manage, what else have you got to lose? Up to you, my dear. How much do you want to see Mrs Harrison again?"

In their intensity her eyes became very dark, almost hooded, and her thoughtful nod, when it came, was barely discernible. Had he not been waiting for it, he would have missed it altogether.

"I imagine you will require a little fortification. I know I do. I'll fetch us some more drinks then, shall I? I have this strange feeling that you have been right all along. My memory just needed a little jog."

Without looking back he shuffled into the kitchen. It took him longer than usual, as she guessed it might. He paused at the door. He looked odd, different, his eyes cast with that slow, esoteric quality she'd seen before on a smackhead. The wine made tiny waves against the sparkling crystal. It looked rich and potent.

"Chianti, in particular, must be taken at cellar temperature." His voice was strangely different too, slightly husky, his speech more measured and delayed. "It comes originally from Gaiole, Castellina and Radda. Don't be fobbed off with the re-drawn area that takes in just about the entire region of Tuscany."

Those sleeping eyes caught the crystal and flashed awake. He came on with deliberate steps. "As with all wine, my dear, you must go with the most expensive that you can afford. You might remember the fiasco with its straw jacket. They're often used as candleholders. The wine itself is irresistibly feminine, and mysterious—I mentioned that before."

She stood beside the sofa, her long hair cutting black trails over her breasts, her dress clinging to her thighs, her back reflected in a painting that leant against the wall behind her, birds flying from a pond.

Ducks, he thought. How wonderful.

He nodded, hugely satisfied, for he had begun to wonder whether events would turn out as he had planned. Where women were concerned, as the late colonel had often stated, nothing could be taken for granted. Logic, that key to the door—the dawn—of man, had been lost in the unfolding of woman and replaced by that curiosity, female intuition, that damned and satanic second sight that had led her to him. He handed her the wine. She returned his gaze with a steadiness he found endearing.

"We might as well finish it today."

"That sounds very final."

"All things come to an end and the painting is, save for a few final touches, all but finished."

"But we're not, are we?"

He retreated quickly to his Maginot.

She drank her wine in one. Her lips were left with the touch of sangiovese grape—*sanguis Jovis*—the blood of Jove. She reached down and placed the glass on the small table where her handbag lay, just out of reach from the sofa. Her breasts sagged slightly then firmed up again as she stood upright.

"So this is what it has come to."

He smiled sweetly.

She reached beneath her dress and bent again and her breasts sagged again and she stepped out, one foot then the other, and left the flimsy yellow underwear on the oak floor. She watched his eyes but they didn't flicker. But his lips moved and she was drawn to them.

"Everything is coming back," he said. "It is all so clear now."

She reached down to the hem of her dress and drew it over her thighs, over that tricky uncomplicated place, the Devil's Triangle, over her navel and jutting hips.

Navel and jutting? Naval and Jutland came to mind, the largest naval battle in history, the battle that no one won. Life's like that, he thought, with both sides, life and death, claiming victory.

He smiled. He couldn't help it. Everything, suddenly, was so maddeningly clear. The Devil's Triangle, also known as the Bermuda Triangle, seemed so delightfully befitting.

He shook away the thought and concentrated again on that glossy overgrown thatch, black as coal and burning bright, the burning bush, *hayah* on Mount Horeb, the downfall of so many men—a blue would do it, with burnt sienna or raw umber and in that way, the sheen, the rainbow of split coal, would have the heart leaping with spring lambs in the silence of a dewy meadow. What was it about the common crack, he wondered, that could send men wild, to murder, to suicide, to go head-to-head with antlers or knives and guns? What was it about the crazy slit, marked indelibly and incomprehensibly in the head and no longer requiring the stink of readiness or the animal clock, that slow turn to spring, that could send the blood—Chinese blood in particular—rushing to the rut.

It was beyond him and he shook away the questions but another came at him, out of nowhere, and he smiled again.

Was he a religious man?

What simpletons to ask such a question? And what a silly girl to think that the dance of veils—in her case just two—would be the answer.

And from the pond and through the dark bracken the ducks took off across her sleek behind.

And Mr Lawrence shook his head in wonder.

"On or off?" she said, tugging apprehensively at her dress.

He remembered their first meeting when she'd asked that very same question about her spectacles.

"Off, for now," he said, repeating his line too. It could all have been a rehearsal, he smiled, and now it was for real.

She dropped the dress and stepped out of it, all arms and legs. Her breasts were nothing more than small swells, no more than force two or three, with dark nipples that stuck out and reminded him of the pink rubbers on the end of school pencils that you could nibble and suck until your lips turned pink. He thought about his school in Nicosia and the first girl he'd ever played with. She was a Cypriot so didn't count and a couple of years younger, about five, maybe. While the sun blistered his bony shoulders and before covering it with huge rocks he carried from the dried up riverbed, he'd explored every inch of her limp body.

Even then he knew that rigor would not begin to set in for three hours or so.

But Cyprus, the birthplace of Aphrodite, that goddess of beauty, was where it started. Cyprus and its flora—the red anemone, the symbol of Christ, and the marigold, the flower of pain and death, Mary's gold. Mary the Sinless, the incorruptible, the ever-virgin whose perpetual virginity he would defend. Infidelity was not an option. Twin flowers, red and gold. In the beginning was the marigold, death, and at the end of it, the very end of it, the red anemone, the resurrection

For a few moments she stood motionless, staring at him out of hooded eyes as though expecting him to say something or even make a move, but then without taking her eyes from him, she took three long strides to the sofa and keeping her knees firmly clamped together, she sat down.

He selected a brush and nodded. "The finishing touches," he said.

An unexpected feeling of panic tightened her chest. Her risky position became all too apparent and even the knowledge of Sam Butler stationed outside did little to stem her sudden reluctance to continue. She said quickly, "You can't blank out the dress so easily. I don't want my picture ruined."

He tut-tutted. "I'm only concerned with your face. I want that uncertainty that your nakedness has brought about. I have seen defiance and provocation, even a challenge, but never before this hint of fear."

"I'm not frightened of you, Mr Lawrence."

"Not that. Not that at all. It's more to do with modesty and propriety."

He filled a fine brush with the colours of blush.

"I want to bring out that vulnerability a little more. I'll tell you what we'll do for, after all, at the core of your splendour is your pudenda."

"I don't think so. That's a little too far."

"Mrs Harrison went that far."

"I saw the painting. I don't need reminding. And I'm not Helen Harrison."

"But you do want to see her."

His suggestion brought a sudden rush of thoughts, jumbled and confused, and she felt quite disorientated. For an instant she considered the whole situation ludicrous and she laughed out loud.

Mr Lawrence shared the joke and smiled back.

Colours deepened in waves and she felt light-headed. She put it down to anxiety and the adrenalin she'd used up. She gulped a few deep breaths, trying to control her racing pulse.

She thought of Butler listening to it all and imagined his expression should he burst in. She laughed out loud again. The DS might have dreamt of her in such a position. For a moment she wanted him to walk in just so she could see the look on his face.

"Sam, you better get in here," she called out and Mr Lawrence's smile widened.

She felt the heat radiating from her body and the colour rising in her face, just as Mr Lawrence wanted, but she laughed again in the knowledge that it was out of elation rather than embarrassment. Mr Lawrence had got it wrong. She was leading him on, too far gone, invincible, and nothing else mattered. What was it he wanted? Giddy with euphoria and with the room starting to slant this way and that, she tried to bring back the notion of what she was doing and why she was there at all. Even as she frowned in concentration she knew there were things she had to do and defiance returned with a steely look.

Mr Lawrence smiled knowingly.

She lay back, without hesitation, and in that same moment drew her knees apart.

"It's such a mysterious place," he said. "A little Milky Way, a spreading supervulva."

"You shouldn't be looking, not really. I shall have to arrest you and take you in. I feel strange, like I'm swimming."

"Relax. Do what you want to do. It's the wine, you see, or rather, what is in the wine. I should market it."

"Oh, Mr Lawrence, my head is spinning and I'm out of control. Why haven't you seduced me, Mr Lawrence, like the others? Did you fuck the others, Mr Lawrence?"

"In my own way, my dear."

"Are you going to fuck me, Mr Lawrence?"

"In my own way, my dear."

He put aside his brush for the painting was complete and just right. Those questions in her dark eyes were answered by a subtle smile that left the faintest of dimples on her cheeks, an enigmatic expression— *alluring and aloof*—that hinted of triumph.

She watched him move from behind the easel and shuffle to the very edge of the studio. There, using a steel lever, he prised up a long floorboard. He moved again and pulled the hook and tackle along the rail until it hung directly over the narrow opening. He used the controls to drop the hook. The steel groaned and squealed as pulleys turned on their blocks and released the chain. As each clashing link fell over the wheel the chain extended with a clanking and screeching that reverberated through the room.

She sat quite immobile and watched a brick wall rise from the floor until it stood as tall and as wide as a door. Clumps of dusty black cobweb dropped from the crumbling edges and settled on the floorboards.

It was a monolith; she'd seen a film, she remembered, a boring film a distant boyfriend had raved about, a space film, and he'd told her it represented a building block of life. At the time she'd thought it was all bollocks and she'd got rid of him soon after, but now...now it all made sense.

He moved back to the sofa and extended his hands toward her. She reached up, childlike, and took them and he pulled her to her feet.

"I feel so shaky," she said and began to wobble. He slipped an arm around her waist and held her steady. Her skin beneath his cold hand felt smooth and warm. He stroked that infuriating hip, that ball-and-socket joint, and realized that he no longer found its prominence disagreeable. In fact, this tall skinny figure had grown on him.

"Let me show you," he said and guided her to the wall.

"The wall, Mr Lawrence. It's the wall in your picture...in the other room!"

She leant against him, a long streak of Indian amber. She was living in a distant place, a place called rapture. He could see it in her eyes, not that they were slipping for they were wide and fixed on the dusty bricks.

He caressed her slight breasts and tugged gently on the extended nipples.

"Oh, Mr Lawrence, what are you doing?"

"Indulge an old man, just this once."

He dropped his hand to her behind—that flawed wonderland that had given him so much grief in the painting—and traced between her buttocks until, finally, he cupped that seat of genesis and let his middle and ring fingers slip upward. Unconcerned, perhaps even unconscious of the source of this digital sensation, she began to gyrate and writhe and swell until she ended up on tiptoes.

"Oh, oh, Mr Lawrence," she said.

He pulled his hand away and her feet came down to earth.

"I think it's time to find Mrs Harrison."

"Shall I get dressed again?" she asked, surprising him. It wasn't simply the way she said it, which was lucid, but what she said as well. That she could put words together that made any kind of sense, was extraordinary.

"Not necessary," he said. "We would only have to take them off again."

With his hand gently resting on her right buttock, he directed her to the cellar door.

Chapter 35

Mr Lawrence pulled away the sealing tape then led the way down the dangerously dark and narrow stairway, reaching back to hold her hand as she placed one tentative foot after the other on to the crumbling steps.

"It's wet. The steps are cold and wet."

Again her words and observations surprised him. Should he come across a girl like this again he would need to stiffen his cocktails. You could never generalize with women; some were even more difficult than others.

They reached the ground safely and he threw a switch and forty watts from a bare dust-encrusted bulb threw its dim glow on the chamber. Save for a discarded mattress and the dark lumps of rotting rats and cats— some no more than stiff fur shells—it was an empty room. The walls were damp and decaying and clusters of black cobweb hung from the flaking edges. In parts the flooring had given up to black compacted earth. On the far side was the black hole that the wall of bricks had left and, as Mr Lawrence had observed once before, nothing could escape a black hole.

"Be careful now," he said as he led her into the narrow passage. "There's no lighting until we get to the end."

"It smells horrible," she said.

"I'll light some joss sticks."

"I like joss sticks," she said. Once again he caught hold of her as her legs gave way.

At the end of the passage he pushed open a solid door and threw another switch. The room was bright and reasonably clean. The brick walls on three sides were sealed and whitewashed and the floor, although lumpy, was covered with green linoleum. The other wall was screened from floor to ceiling by a heavy curtain patterned with threads of red and gold. Mounted on a steel tripod a spotlight threw its intense beam on to an examination couch that came complete with thick foam wear-resistant black vinyl top with an elevated platform that avoided finger accidents—or so the advertisement had promised. Next to the couch stood a gleaming portable trolley and a high stool.

She steadied herself on one of the twin fixtures at the bottom of the couch. "A bed," she managed.

"It is. Why don't you get on board and rest a while?"

She nodded enthusiastically and he helped her. For a moment her feet dangled, until he lifted her legs up over the side. She lay back.

"That's better, isn't it? You'll feel better now."

She nodded again but already he noticed that her eyes had lost their previous lustre. Already he could feel the heat radiating from the spotlight on to her skin as he lifted her legs into the stirrups.

"Many years ago this place belonged to the shop next door. It was owned by an old lady, Mrs Meacham, who sold wool and knitting-needles. But her shop was knocked down to make way for the new road up to the council estate. For some reason, perhaps the lack of funding or, more likely, contractors on the fiddle, they only filled in the one room. This was left completely as it was. If some of the bricks hadn't been dislodged during the building work I would never have discovered it."

From the trolley he produced a white apron that he tied around his middle.

"I mentioned before how small your breasts are." As though it meant nothing at all he leant over and stroked them again and gently pulled a nipple between thumb and forefinger. "If we let the pregnancy continue they would fill out and your nipples would get bigger too."

She struggled with the idea and her frown was exaggerated. She turned her face from the penetrating light and said, "I'm so tired."

"I know, but try to stay awake a little longer."

Her eyes were slipping now; nothing seemed to have a definite beginning or substance, everything was animated. Even his voice seemed distant.

"Gosh," she said. "That tickles."

"I thought it might. Maybe it will wake you up a bit."

He worked a shaving-brush around her groin.

"It's cold and wet, Mr Lawrence. What are you doing?"

"Nowadays, as I understand it, shaving has gone by the board. Maybe it's part of the NHS efficiency programme that we hear so little about. But I'm just an old-fashioned man. I believe today's term is the Brazilian. Perhaps it has something to do with the cutting down of the rainforests. Now, this will tickle again."

She felt the cold lather and the bristles of his worn brush and then the razor and the slight tug as hair was cut away.

"My goodness, you haven't been to your beauticians lately, have you? I suppose we could call this *Bikini Line*, should we require a title. Did you enjoy the show, by the way? I forgot to ask. I did notice you in your box in the Carrington."

"That feels funny."

"There we are, all finished now," he said as he used a towel to dry her. "Didn't want to get lost in the bush, as they say in Zululand and maybe even Mumbai."

Her eyes settled again and she smiled sweetly as he bent over and examined her vagina, inserting two fingers into her vaginal canal. He placed his bandaged hand on her abdomen and applied a little pressure while he searched for the position of her uterus. A little smear from the end of his bandage marked her stomach.

He fumbled around in his trolley for it was full of boxes and instruments—forceps, dilators, pessaries, speculums, suppositories and Aquagel lubricating jelly which he preferred—he did like to be up there on the cutting edge. He toyed with the adjustable speculums and tried to recall what he'd used on Margaret Domey—small, medium or large—but it wouldn't come back and he settled on small. Once, not long ago, they resembled a duck's bill but now they were more like adjustable spanners used by filthy plumbers to unblock drains.

As he opened her vagina her mouth dropped open more out of shock than discomfort and her frown turned to a grimace as he used the dilators on her cervix.

"Oh, oh, oh," she uttered and tried to sit up, failing even to rise to her elbows.

Without looking up he said, "It's true that women the world over are all alike, even women from the subcontinent and that's a surprise. Only the Orientals are different, so I'm told, by my barber, believe it or not—for everything about them is on the slant and that wouldn't do at all. As the old Duke of Edinburgh—Philippos the Greek—might say, it would be like putting a round peg into a slitty hole."

He replaced the gleaming instruments and wiped his hands. "And now," he said. "You wanted to see Mrs Harrison."

Mr Lawrence moved to the curtains and drew them apart, first one then the other, fussing with the rope fastenings that held them to the wall.

It was a scene out of hell and she laughed at it and Mr Lawrence saw the funny side too and joined in. He couldn't remember the last time he'd laughed out loud.

"There's Helen!" She pointed a shaky finger. "And there's Margaret. And there's Sandra too!"

"Interesting," he said. "I hadn't realized that you knew Sandra."

Into the small brick-walled enclosure the bodies had been tightly packed. Some of them lay in their sheath of film, some of them sat against the rough wall and some at the back, were wedged in so tightly they were almost standing. The bodies of two men lay at the front, fully clothed and left as if of no consequence, perhaps hastily dumped. Their faces beneath heads that were splintered and cracked apart, were caked in clotted blood yet still held odd quizzical expressions. Beyond them were the women and beneath their transparent wrappings they were naked. Through the glistening Clingfilm the features were grotesquely distorted and some were decomposed. Inside their envelopes they swam in bodily fluids and the sudden light seemed to stir the viscous yellow liquid so that threads of red and pink resembled nematode worms as they slowly curled this way and that, searching for the juice of a warm body. At the rear, some of the older bodies whose torsos were held above the slime had dried out and the skin and tissue on their faces had shrivelled and peeled so that eyes bulged and lips were pulled back. On others, rotting flesh had fallen away so that a cranium glinted here and a clavicle there. Some of them were covered in green mould and their wrappings were straining under the growth. The abdomens, from navel to crotch, had been sliced open and pulled apart and left gaping and viscera and mucus and fat and streaks of clotted blood had congealed and filled and tightened the transparent film.

"There you are. I told you you'd see her again."

She smiled happily and watched the light bounce from a scalpel in his hand. The light danced on the blade and held her attention. She watched it move closer until it hovered just a few inches above her pubis, more prominent now, still smarting from its recent attention.

She heard his voice. "I'm going through the walls of the abdomen into the uterus. You can watch. Sandra managed to watch the entire operation."

She felt the blade against her belly.

"It's cold," she said and giggled like a schoolgirl.

"Julius Caesar was born this way," he said.

In her drug-induced sleep Luscious Laura lay face down on the bed. She had barely moved. On tiptoes and with a gentle touch he pulled a sheet and tucked her in. She would sleep soundly through the night.

He carried his case down to the shop. Everything was in order now; the loose ends had been tied and everything was done.

Above the rooftops the sky haemorrhaged through the December darkness. Along the High Road Christmas decorations winked and rocked in the strong wind. Dishwashers and freezers were tied in Christmas ribbon. It was the age of the gadget, of starvation and obesity, of ignorance and information. It was the age of madness. For a moment he paused as the girl's image came back again—just as it had after their initial encounter—the amber princess, the colour of the gods. It stemmed from an old Arabic word—*ambergris*—perfumed oil secreted by the sperm whale.

He nodded thoughtfully. "Mmmm," he thought. Sperm counts had halved since his father's day and sperm whales faced extinction.

Helen's was a new face.

Helen, Mrs Harrison, smiled from the latest posters stuck to the bus shelters next to the pictures of Japanese fishermen harpooning the sperm whales.

In front of him, blocking his way, a drunk lurched.

"Penny for the guy, mister. A cup of tea?"

"Guy! Guy! You idiot, that was last month! Where do you people come from?" He came from Liverpool or Newcastle or somewhere else north where the accent was as painful as bloodstained piss.

Mr Lawrence swung his heavy case and the drunk went down, bleeding.

Chapter 36

Rick Cole woke suddenly with the image of Donna Fitzgerald superimposed over the darkness of his room. As he groped on his bedside table for the glass of Teacher's he'd taken to bed, the dream faded slowly. He leant back against the headboard and waited for the alcohol to kick in. He lit a JPS and brushed the odd spark from his chest.

His mobile went and he heard Sam Butler.

"Rick, thank Christ! I'm in trouble. I'm parked up at the back of the Gallery. Help me out."

"Talk to me, Sam. Sam?"

But Sam Butler had gone even though the line remained open.

Cole finished his drink in one and stubbed out his JPS. Anger hardened his features. He knew without being told that the job had been compromised. Now it was limitation time. And without any doubt at all it was going to take every trick he knew to keep them all in the clear.

He poured another drink and headed for the bathroom. A dozen things went through his head and they were all to do with Chief Superintendent Marsh. He'd had Cole in his sights for years and Sam Butler might have given him the ammunition.

He turned the shower to hot until it hurt and washed away his thoughts of Butler and Marsh. He emptied his glass and brought back instead those last illusive impressions of Donna Fitzgerald.

On the High Road traffic was thin. The Carrington slid by. He slowed by the shop, the Gallery, but it seemed as spent as the rest of the road with no movement in the windows and just the dummies looking out, Father Christmas and his assistant. But the assistant was naked. The Christmas lights blinked on the mannequin and Cole looked twice. He'd never known a shop-window mannequin to have hair before. Christ, how things changed. Forget the nipples that poked you in the eye, they were really going for reality nowadays. He wondered, fleetingly, whether it constituted an indecency charge. He made a right and then another and passed the only shop in the run-down street. The window was lit, but dimly, and the dolls in it were the colour of snow. Dark round eyes stared out of anaemic faces. A cat's quivering tail caught his eye as it curled around one of the heads.

Now there were offices on his left, abandoned, their windows boarded, doors chained and padlocked. And then he saw the shadow of Butler's car and pulled up before it. His headlights blazed on the windscreen.

"Jesus, Sam!"

DS Butler raised his hand and motioned toward the shop's blistered gate.

"What the hell happened?"

"Hit, through the window. Didn't see it coming."

"You need an ambulance."

"What I need is for you to get in there. It's been hours!"

"She's in there?"

Again Butler attempted to point toward the gate but his hand fell away. He was leaning forward, slumped against the wheel, his arm hanging loose and useless. The hole in his head was dark. A swelling had increased its depth. Blood seeped out, congealed in yellow fat. His mobile lay in the passenger seat. He was holding on, hoping for a reprieve. This business could end his career. He'd gone out on a limb, compromised the entire operation and placed his colleague in danger. Butler had his wife and baby on what was left of his mind, and somewhere at the back of it, maybe, in an area more damaged than the rest, was Anian Stanford.

"I'll make the call," the DS managed. "I just need a minute."

Cole nodded. Despair and panic clawed at his gut and as he pushed open the back gate he felt a cold sweat collect on his forehead. The gate scraped loudly on the concrete path. He crossed the small garden of bare dirt and reached the door, surprised to find it unlocked. He'd been ready to kick his way in.

Behind him, in the car in the street, DS Sam Butler passed out again.

The door opened on to a studio. The main lights were out but illumination squeezed through a small kitchenette at the far end. There were boxes of books and paintings on every available surface. There was a sofa and an easel holding a large canvas and a box of paints beside it. And in the tray was an oval palette with globules of paint arranged around the edge and in the centre a mix of flesh tones.

Cole looked at Anian and she looked back, life-like, with that familiar petulance in her eyes. But in her pose with one leg raised against the other and her dress riding her thighs she looked special.

Whatever else Lawrence was, he was an artist.

At the side of the room was modern art. Suspended over a hole left by a missing floorboard, secured by tackle and chain, was a wall of bricks, the size of a door. It took Cole's breath away and kicked him in the midriff.

For a moment he was bent double.

Then he saw the open door only partially concealed by the curtain and then he was falling down dangerously narrow steps, scuffing against the rough walls until he was standing on dirt.

It was only then he noticed the foul air, as if he'd walked into a cloud of stinking gas, and automatically he clamped a hand over his nose and mouth, forcing back the bile that all but blocked his throat. He careered through the room into the passage, knocking the single bulb as he went, sending shadows slithering from floor to festering ceiling. He'd come across the stink of putrescine before, many times, so even before he reached the end room he was already bracing himself. Even so, he was unprepared.

Helen Harrison was circled in the full intense beam of the spotlight.

For a ludicrous moment he wondered if she had been chosen for his benefit.

Rick Cole said, "Holy shit!"

And given the time of year he was probably right.

"This is well out of order!"

At his side, away from the beam and just another shadow among many, something stirred. And behind him, wrapped in a white sheet, negotiating the passage and still slowed by her drugged sleep, Laura approached. The room opened before her just moments after Cole had entered. She saw what Cole had seen and screamed.

It wasn't just an ordinary scream for, as with everything else about Luscious Laura, it was outstanding, and woke up a number of residents on the Richmond Park Estate.

Rick Cole turned and took her in and noticed that even in her crumpled style she had definite possibilities. He said, "I'm at a loose end, sweetheart. Play your cards right you could be the next Mrs Cole!"

Chapter 37

The double-glazing salesman might have said that there is a condition where a wound to the chest does not necessarily cause much bleeding, not on the outside. The bleeding takes place in a sac that the heart sits in and eventually it constricts the heart and stops it altogether. It is known in the trade as a pericardial tamponade.

Heathrow was busy with the last rush of Christmas and the security arrangements to combat the fundamentalists didn't help.

Paul's face appeared out of the crowd. A painted face, not unattractive, with cherry-red lips and pencilled eyes and sky-blue eye shadow and cheeks that blushed with the hint of rosehips. He recognized Mr Lawrence.

"Mr Lawrence," he shouted excitedly and people nearby turned to look.

"Hello Paul. Oops! Paula, I mean."

"Oh, Mr Lawrence."

"It's not Mr Lawrence now, Paula." And in his best Irish accent that wasn't very good, he added, "It's Father or, rather, Father Kerry from Kerry in County Kerry."

"I didn't know there was a Kerry in County Kerry."

"Did you not? Well, there you are then, you learn something every day. I bet you didn't even know that it was a girl's name, either? Now, tell me this if you will, is it the time to check in?"

Paul shook his head. "There's still half an hour before the check-in opens and I needed the loo," he explained. "Nerves. Never been on a plane before. I used the Ladies. Never used the Ladies before.

They smell different, sweeter, and there's no piss all over the floor."
His balance on the heels was more confident and as he walked his hips
swayed. But there was something else about him. He seemed in pain.
Mr Lawrence let it go. The beating he'd taken had been severe. Perhaps
he was still troubled by that. Perhaps that was it. Paul looked him up
and down. "Mr Lawrence, Father Kerry, you look wonderful. Give us
a twirl."

"Not here, for goodness sake."

"Only joking, Mr Lawrence."

"That's a nice jacket, Paula."

"I've had to clean it up, Mr Lawrence. There was dirt and...blood
on it. I've had to soak some bits. Does it show?"

"The policeman's blood? No, Paul, it's fine."

"It's a Paul Smith, Mr Lawrence, says so on the label. My name,
innit? And my size."

"I've heard of Paul Smith, but that was many years ago. My
goodness, thirty years ago, I'd say. But it looks expensive. Where did
you get it? No, don't tell me. I don't want to know."

"Get you, Mr Lawrence. That's one of your jokes, isn't it?"

"Have you got everything?"

Paul patted his bulging handbag then grimaced again. "Passports,
tickets, bottled water, everything. And some other things. Women's
things. You wouldn't believe the things that women keep in their
handbags. No wonder they're always so heavy. Maybe that's also why
they need so many."

"Well, dear girl, I'm not going to ask."

"Good thinking, Mr Lawrence—Father Kerry—you don't want to
know."

Paul's rich-blue dress was figure hugging and presented the outline
of underwear including suspenders. One or two men nearby offered him
admiring glances and a couple of coppers armed with machine-guns
and Glocks looked him up and down and thought they'd like to give
him one.

The coppers reminded Mr Lawrence of another copper. He asked,

"What about the policeman?"

"You were right, Mr Lawrence. Absolutely. He was parked just outside the gate. Listening to you both. You were right. They were on to me without a doubt. What about you? Did you finish the painting?"

"Yes. But tell me what happened?"

"He had the window down. I could hear you. Jesus, am I lucky." He paused and said regretfully, "But I made a mistake. A bad one."

"We all make mistakes. What was yours?"

"I didn't just knock him out, Mr Lawrence, like you said. The hammer went right in, right through the side of his head. I didn't mean it."

"Accidents happen."

"I'm so grateful to you, Mr Lawrence. If it wasn't for you, I'd be… I'd be check-mated."

"Good. Come on, brighten up. But do remember it's Father Kerry and not Mr Lawrence. We've got time to grab a cup of airport coffee. I've heard it isn't the best but we'll see. Have coffee. I don't want you drinking orange juice anymore."

"What's wrong with orange juice, Mr Lawrence?"

"Well, far be it from me to distress you for I know you're partial toward it, but according to the late colonel orange juice is full of something called E-numbers and they have a strange pull on a young girl's fancy."

"Getya, Mr Lawrence—Father Kerry. Bit like the pull of weed, you mean? Understand that. So, coffee it is, then. I'll have mine with lots of sugar and a Coke on the side." Paul paused in his step. "But I do have a problem."

Mr Lawrence hesitated. "Go on?"

"They won't let us take the water through so we'll have to drink that as well."

"You're right, it is a dilemma."

"And there's something else."

"I hope it's not as serious."

"It's the security check, Mr Lawrence—Father Kerry—the security check. We've got to take our jackets off at the security check and I've got a tear in my dress."

Mr Lawrence tut-tutted and continued on his way. "Don't worry, Paul-a, all of the men and some of the women in uniform, will be looking at your arse. Most people in uniform are obsessed by arses. The older you get the more apparent that will become. They won't notice a tiny tear like that."

And Mr Lawrence was right, as was usually the case. They didn't. All of the men and some of the women in uniform looked at her behind. And *her* behind was right. Paul no longer existed. She was Paula now. So to hell with him.

They moved unobtrusively forward in a queue toward the counter, a tall, slim, fairly attractive girl named Paula and her travelling companion, canonical dress in perfect order, cassock freshly pressed and heavy cross swinging gently across his chest.

"Milk or cream, Father?" An assistant asked from behind her steaming silver counter. "Ooooh, you've had an accident?"

Mr Lawrence said in Irish that was getting better for he was growing accustomed to squeezing the vowels, "You're very observant, my dear. Indeed I have, but it's nothing much, wouldn't you know, just a septic quick."

"Such a big bandage. Wouldn't a plaster have done?"

"It's turned nasty, as things often do." He sighed and was about to offer her his best shot at a condescending Church-of-England smile before remembering he was in Catholic garb and changed it to a boozer's stupid grin with a bit of perve thrown in. "I'm going to over-indulge, just this once. Cream please."

She served him, feigning that unlikely affection shown toward people who talk to God.

"Bless you, child," he said to her and, one-handed, picked up his tray.

The assistant turned to Paula at his side and her attitude hardened. In Paula the assistant saw a threat. Paula noticed and lifted her head defiantly as women do when confronted with their own kind. She remained cool and aloof and hopelessly, adorably self-assured. A couple of men in the queue behind instinctively glanced at her behind.

It was questionable who would be the first to the cellar. He hoped that it was Laura. But it might be the policeman. If Paula had been mistaken and he was still alive then he would come round and panic and then reach for the radio. Or he might be found in the car. That was unlikely for the road at the back of the shop was quiet. In the evening it was a parking place for wrecks and courting couples, usually one and the same.

But he hoped that Laura got there first.

It would be the making of her.

In the small hours she would stir, waking from her drugged sleep. She might check the time first and then move—stumble—to the window. The drug would take a little time to wear off. Her head would be heavy. Holding her heavy head she would make her way down the stairs and see the light coming from the kitchenette.

And once in the studio she would utter, "Crikeeey! Shiiit! There's a fucking wall growing out of the floorboards and…the cellar door is open!"

My goodness, Laura's scream would be heard three streets away.

But it would teach her an invaluable lesson, that shoes can tell you everything you need to know about the man.

From the tiny porthole the lights of ships or oil platforms winked their private message that life went on down there—and death, of course.

Paula was nervous, her body rigid, her head forced back and her slender hands gripping both armrests. She trembled, as the more attractive women often do. Only her eyes flicked from side to side. One of the stewardesses kept a discreet eye on her, and smiled sympathetically. Nowadays, quite rightly, they weren't called stewardesses. Now they were trolley dollies.

"Is it her first time, Father?"

"Like a virgin? Yes, it's her very first time, but don't worry, I'll take care of her."

The trolley dolly, in an excellent thigh-hugging blue skirt tightened her lips at his mention of the word virgin. She eyed the bandage. "Are you all right? That looks nasty."

"You wouldn't believe what happened," he said. "Caught my ring finger in the confessional. All but tore it off."

"You're right. I wouldn't believe it."

She went on her way, checking the other passengers, making sure that their belts were clipped and their luggage was tucked away, noting on the way, which passengers would buy her duty-free and which were tight-arsed.

"Are we up yet?" Paula asked nervously.

"Dear girl, we've been up five minutes. We're over the Channel, somewhere, heading off to the Continent where Neanderthal man still lives. In a few moments you will smell garlic and the fear of subjugation, both of which have led to thriving industries in the production of expensive perfume."

"Don't leave me."

"I'm not going to leave you, Paula. Goodness me, I'd need a parachute to leave you here. Or wings, maybe, and I'm no angel."

"Please don't leave me when we're there, either…"

"Of course not. We'll find this artist fellow first, this Chan or Chang who produced those wonderful paintings and we'll find out what he's got to offer and then… Who knows? Australia or Canada. Anywhere where people love fine art. There was nothing finer than Evonne Gollagong and Margaret Trudeau. I saw a photograph of Mrs Trudeau, once, long ago. It must be as faded as my memory by now. It was in the barber's shop while I was waiting for a haircut, in one of his magazines, a photograph of Canada's First Lady, no less, displaying a particularly dense landscape. I had often thought, after seeing that, that I should like to see more of the count…try. And their artistic development has come on a treat, perhaps because of that photograph, in both impressionism and expressionism. But Canada and certainly not the USA, let's be quite clear about that. South of the Great Lakes the idea of art is a double cheeseburger. But we'll need a few weeks in Hong Kong to sort things out. Obtain fresh papers. It's a crowded place, you know? They have a population explosion there. Too many babies being born. And, my goodness, we do know, don't we, that this world is no place for children?"

"Is it true what they say about Chinese women?"

"I've heard the rumours just like you, but honestly, I don't know.

But we will find out. There is one thing, though, Paula, and take careful note of this—write it down so you don't forget, on the back of your hand, if you like. It's the salt in their cooking. We must remember that no matter how much we enjoy sizzling king prawn Kung Po style and duck and bean sprouts Cantonese style and crispy won ton with sweet and sour and egg fried rice, we must watch out for the salt."

Paula flicked him another nervous smile. But the smile held too the look of a child who wasn't old enough to understand. There was, about it, the look of complete dependence. Mr Lawrence peered from the porthole just as they broke through a dense layer of cloud and the heavens stretched out before them, sparkling with riches, playgrounds for the freed souls.

But Paula didn't see the splendour; her eyes had closed and her head tilted lifelessly forward. The black jacket had fallen open and just below a neat tear across the breast of her blue dress, a patch of purple spread out and resembled an opening bloom of a perfect welted thistle.

That strange sac that no one had ever heard of, had filled up and overflowed, like the cup that had overflowed, and she was in her green pastures, as she raced toward the glorious dawn of another Christmas Eve.

And beamed across the universe from all those great dishes that could be seen from space, caught here and there by the mobile phone masts erected near junior schools to give the children brain tumours, perhaps catching up or even overtaking Paula's freed spirit, were the radio waves that carried the Christmas number one.

> Oh, Mr Lawrence, I think I love you
> Oh, Mr Lawrence, I think we're there…

Chapter 38

"He won't get far," DI Rick Cole said to Sam Butler.

Butler's wife and daughter were in the corridor and knowing how impatient Janet could be Cole was keeping it short. She was one woman he didn't want to upset.

Butler's eyes sparkled. "He's pretty bloody clever at keeping one step ahead."

"Every exit and entry point in the known world is bottled up. He'll surface."

Butler nodded glumly, too wise to know that entry and exit points, particularly in the UK, didn't mean a damn, then grimaced and instinctively touched the thick swathe of bandages around his head as if checking that they were still there. He asked, "What's Marsh doing?"

"He's doing what he always does. Hiding in his office and hoping it goes away. We've found the missing women and there'll be no more going missing, at least for a while. One way or another it's a result. And to Chief Superintendent Marsh that's all that counts. That doesn't mean you're in for a citation, Sam. It doesn't mean that I'm not going to kick the shit out of you when you get out of here. You were well out of order." Cole relented and shrugged. "If Marsh could have us without any flak, then he would. But he can't. Wooderson's on our side because he's got nowhere to run and Baxter's not going to say a word out of turn. The official line is that you were both on official business. Surveillance, recommended by me and approved by Baxter."

Relieved, Butler asked, "And Anian?"

"She's all right. She's going to be fine. She was pretty well out of it. The wonders of Rohypnol or GHB and whatever else he used. She can't remember much at all, which is probably a good thing. She's up and about already and a hangover from hell isn't stopping her."

"She's got some bottle, I'll give her that, but she's the luckiest girl in the world."

"She passed out so didn't see him leave. Geoff reckons that once Lawrence realized she wasn't pregnant that was the end of it. He never killed for killing's sake."

"Very considerate of him. But how could he tell?"

Cole shrugged again. "I think he knew all along. This was just an ego trip or to teach her a lesson."

"I'll go for the ego trip. He was taking the piss from the start. I can't imagine he'd waste much effort on a DC, a slip of a girl. This has all been a fucking joke and, somewhere, he's laughing out loud. At us, at me in particular."

"The final count was two men, unidentified, and eight women he'd operated on. Cause of death almost certainly blood loss or physiological shock."

"Why didn't the radar handsets find the cellar?"

"Good question and it's already been asked. There's a few red faces in Tech Support but apparently they don't penetrate areas they're not pointed at. The operating theatre was twenty feet away from the Gallery's own cellar accessed by a narrow corridor that was bricked up."

Butler nodded again and flinched again.

"Well, anyway, that's about it. There's someone in the corridor that wants to say hello."

"Janet?"

"And Lucy, of course."

Sam Butler smiled. He watched Cole move to the door then said, "Rick."

With the door half-open Cole hesitated and turned to face his old colleague. "Forget it, Sam."

Butler nodded.

"We need you back. There's been a whole bunch of shit come in."

"Like?"

"Like our slasher's had another go. Big time. This time she killed someone in the underpass. Cut him to bits. I say him, but he was dressed as a woman, a fucking cross-dresser would you believe. We're working on the theory that she got a bit pissed-off when she discovered it wasn't a woman and really went to town."

"What else?"

"The gas explosion."

"Go on?"

"It wasn't. Or rather, it was, but detonated with an explosive charge made of aspirin."

Butler whistled. "Jesus, that's a big step from allotment sheds. A double murder. What's happening to Sheerham? Cross-dressing, transvestites coming out the woodwork, bombings, slashers, murders. It's becoming a dangerous place to live."

"Yep. That's what comes from taking the plods off the street."

The DS grinned. "Have there been any results at all?"

"Yep."

"Well?"

"Remember the mannequin nicked from the supermarket? Found her. Took her back. The manager had to give her a bath to get rid of some unwanted hair."

Butler frowned, wanting more.

Cole smiled, not giving any.

And the white door with its square window swung shut.

Chapter 39

He'd been dying.

He'd given up without a fight.

He'd watched his blood spreading out and he just lay there, not caring one way or the other.

He needed help. He needed someone like himself to help him.

He was giving in too easily.

The midnight light caught the boy's face and turned it as smooth as ivory. His eyes had darkened and his eyelashes seemed incredibly long. His slim frame leant toward the window.

"I know you, don't I? Yeah, yeah. It's you. I thought you might be back, some day. One day. Like, you know, don't you? Dosh, dosh, dick, dick. Gotta be it. Can't hide it. Not really. But you don't hang around here, do you? Or didn't you know?" The voice was confident, older, and faintly taunting. This was his turf, after all, and there was someone in the shadows listening in. "What happened to your face?"

"Doesn't matter."

"Nice one. Bet it wasn't shaving. Well, shall I get in, or what? Dick, dick. Make up your mind?"

"You've got the wrong idea, just like before."

"Yeah, yeah. I know. Honest I do. Well, time's ticking. Time is dosh. Dosh, right? Dick dosh, dick dosh. No time to chat, right?"

The street was surprisingly busy. But maybe not that surprising. Revellers staggered from the boozers toward the clubs, green bottles swinging. It was party night and it had to last until New Year's Eve.

"Get in."

He pulled open the door, waved to the shadow who watched from a shop doorway then slid into the passenger seat. Closer, lost in the leather, he seemed even slimmer than before. The sweet scent of weed filled the car. Female leaf or maybe pollen. It was strong. It was on his hands and in his clothes.

The car pulled out into traffic and neon strip washed the windscreen. In the car the lights slid across their faces. The boy stirred nervously, his feet tapping the devil's dance, his laced fingers opening and closing. It was always a gamble. You could never tell. Psychos looked like the man next door. This one worked with the coppers but that didn't mean a thing. He knew this one, but you never knew, not really.

"Tick tock, dick dosh."

"What do they call you now? Has it changed?"

"Anything you like."

"You choose?"

"Noel then. I like Noel."

"Christmas?"

"Oasis. Noel Gallagher."

Maynard smiled into the darkness. Another strip blinked red as they passed a fried chicken takeaway. It flared on his stitches. He asked, "How old are you?" The red went out and left him in green from the dash.

"Thirteen if you like. Or sixteen. Or eighteen if it bothers you. I'm easy. I know a place. Supermarket car park is good, at the back. Empty at this time. Dick, dick. That's the place. The barrier's always up."

Maynard shook his head. He skirted Lover's Wood and pulled in at the back, beyond a line of shivering firs. The floor beneath was thick with needles and cones that crunched under the wheels. The car pushed through grass and bramble that swiped at the windows and sprang up behind them. He turned off the engine and they sat in the dark listening to the wind. The woods creaked and the grass brushed against the car. Patches of night sky freed itself from the rushing clouds and glistened enough to glow on the boy's delicate features.

Maynard said quietly, "It's almost Christmas Day."

The boy glanced at the dash clock. "Yeah, that's a thing, innit? I'm going to be your Christmas present."

Chapter 40

They had cleared out the Warren.

The kids had gone along with the weird bastard who looked out for them. When Ticker Harrison and his men arrived it was silent. There was no Christmas cheer and there were no glad tidings. There was no peace on earth and goodwill—and definitely no rest—for Ticker Harrison's merry men. They knew who paid the bills and for this year at least the herald-angels kept their hallelujahs in check. They broke open a door and marched in, ready to knock the shit out of anything that moved. But they'd gone.

Breathless Billy said, "Told you I had it all in hand, Boss. We didn't need to check, not on a night like this. For fuck sake, I can take care of a bunch of fucking...kids!"

"Yeah, you're right Breath, but the cunt that was with them, there was something about him I didn't like. He was a fucking nutter and you never know what's going on in a nutter's head."

Ticker had coped with the news of his wife's death better than anyone expected. There had been no mourning, not that they had seen. As far as Ticker was concerned, she'd had an affair with some fucker in Spain, more likely than not a greasy fucked-up paella type with a mouth from here to Barcelona. She'd had her affair, come back, gone to the shop, and that's where Lawrence had gutted her. Lawrence, that old fucker, had saved him the bother. He would have shaken his hand, the one with the missing finger. He had even taken down her picture from that place above the fireplace. Given it to a charity shop. They had sold it the same day to a man in brown shoes, for two pounds and fifty pence.

"But I do know where you're coming from, Breathless Billy. I've learned a few important lessons in the last few weeks. And one of them is you can't trust anyone. Fuck me, if you can't trust your own wife, who the fuck can you trust?"

"I know that, Boss. I know that. But women is different. You learn in fucking junior school that you can't trust them. Even then they're nicking your fags, ain't they? Think of that fucking, you know, what's her fucking name?"

"Eh?"

"Mata Hairy or something."

"Never heard of her."

"Then there was fucking Eve, right? Read between the lines and she shoved a fucking apple up her muffta."

"Since when have you read the fucking bible?"

Breathless Billy shook a sad head. "You can't fucking trust them. But men are different. Some of us. Some of us is trustworthy. Like your brother, maybe, or your fucking priest. Or, and this is the point, Boss, your fucking right-hand man. Namely me."

"Yeah, you're right, Breath. I'm sorry."

"You should be. I've always been here for you. You've never had to ask that question. I'm your fucking, you know…fucking… Right?"

Ticker Harrison nodded sadly. Breathless Billy, for all his faults, was his right-hand man and just lately he'd been taking him for granted. He heard the voice again, the breathless wheezing voice.

"Boss, what's this piece of fucking wire stretched across the room for? For fuck's sake, ankle high, you could trip over that fucker and do yourself some damage."

"Breathless, for fuck's sake, don't touch—"

Chapter 41

The moon was in its last quarter and the stars were as bright as he'd ever seen them. There were some dark clouds shouldering in from the east but for the moment they were unloading over Lover's Wood. It wouldn't be long before they reached the office. Cole turned from the window to face the silent incident room. The midnight oil had run out, the long unnecessary paperwork in duplicate and triplicate completed. Anian placed a coffee on his desk.

"You're going to have people talking."

"We're the only ones left, apart from the front desk. Sad people, aren't we?"

He tasted the bitter coffee and pulled a face then said, "You should be at Hinckley or on sick leave. I'm surprised the North Mid let you out so soon."

"Unless you're dying you're kicked out at Christmas, you know that Guv. I'm all right, honest. Even the counsellor agreed, said it was the best thing for me."

"For God's sake, Anian, you weren't keen to come here when you were needed and now we can't get rid of you."

"Hinckley's on holiday. There's a notice on the door saying that in an emergency contact the Sheerham desk."

"Is this an emergency?"

She held his gaze for an instant too long.

"You should be at home putting out mince pies and hanging up your stocking."

"I don't wear stockings. I thought you might have noticed."

His smile was unexpected and warm and his blue eyes caught the overhead and sparked.

"Well, this is an emergency, Guv. You can tell me to go if you like."

He said eventually, "I was just off to the boozer. I don't suppose you'd fancy a pint?"

She gave him a little cat's grin. "I was hoping you were going to say that. I don't want to be alone tonight. It's Christmas Eve and my flatmates have pulled duty."

"Nurses, who'd have them? Their shifts are even worse than ours."

"They drew straws and got New Year's Eve. It's always one or the other. Now Geoff's gone I was wondering if I could use your spare room, or even the sofa?"

His pause seemed to go on forever before he said, "It's probably not a good idea."

She nodded thoughtfully. "You're probably right."

"On the other hand, if you know how to cook a turkey…"

A sudden smile lit her face. "You've actually got a turkey?"

"Well, not at the moment, but there are people who will open a shop for me at any time day or night."

"You'd have to get the trimmings too. Brussels sprouts and Christmas pudding and pigs in blankets and crackers and…chestnut stuffing –"

He was about to respond with a Rick Cole line that was as good as you'd get on a dark December night when a case had been put to bed and a Teacher's beckoned with its promise of fool's gold, when a distant rumble had him turning back to the window. It took him a few moments to realize it was another bomb.

He shook his head and in almost a whisper said, "I wish I knew who was doing that."

"Kids," she responded. "You'd think they'd have something better to do on Christmas Eve, wouldn't you?"

He considered telling her about the house that had been demolished and the two accidental deaths that had been reclassified as murder but decided it could wait for another time. "Come on," he said instead. "Get your coat."

From outside came the sounds of shouts and car horns and distant sirens and, above them all, a lone drunken voice: "Happy Christmas everyone! Have yourselves a very happy Christmas!"

Deleted Scenes

Deleted Scene.

Saturday. Early. A time for nurses and milkmen and bakers and insomniacs when the rest of the world was asleep, when Friday night and no alarm clock in the morning had got the better of the rest, an ethereal time when silly thoughts took on immense profundity and last night's problems were less severe. For the plods the long night was drawing to its close. They'd dozed in their secret places, of course, but it wasn't the same.

First Year Probationer PC Simon Thomason had started his shift the previous evening, showing a presence to the local teenagers. He was twenty-two. He'd left college with A-levels, passed the interviews, the physical and psychometric tests, and joined the force in August, the month that produced the worst crime figures. The schools were shut for their summer holidays during August but the experts will tell you that this is just a coincidence. Other experts will tell you that the hot weather is to blame. Members of the general public, less expert in such matters, would wonder why the yob culture had not spread to the countries where the sun shone relentlessly. The experts would tell you that it had nothing to do with the fact that in those countries the prisons were such that even prison visitors did not want to visit.

PC Thomason faced a two-year probationary period, combining classroom studies in law and procedure with on-the-job training. He'd been at Sheerham a week but it seemed longer. It seemed like a lifetime. He worked under the guidance of an experienced officer, sometimes a sergeant, more often than not a PC father figure. But last night he'd been let loose for the serious crime was drawing all the manpower. So he'd been plodding, waiting for calls, showing some uniform. He'd dealt with someone's scratched car and moved on a bunch of kids using a shop window as goalposts. But for him the night had died young. Perhaps they had forgotten he was out there.

Dawn was fading in and he was looking forward to a healthy copper's breakfast of bacon, eggs, sausage, black pudding and fried bread, when the shout came through.

The operator said wearily, "A disturbance at Robot City, you should be close."

He responded, "Just round the corner."

"CB1 is on the way. There will be flashing lights and a loud siren. For your information, just in case you're a career copper, the lights and siren are known in the trade as blues and twos. Try not to miss them."

It was far too early for sarcasm and it flew unnoticed over Thomason's head.

First Year Probationer Simon Thomason arrived before CB1 and the supermarket manager, Mr David Solomon, collared him at the door.

"I've been waiting for you," the manager said, tapping his Disney watch and straightening his Mickey Mouse tie. He carried a walkie-talkie to let everyone know how important he was.

Flustered, the first year probationer said, "Sorry, I was round the corner."

"For what do we pay our rates? For law and order. If I were late the shop wouldn't open, then what? Pensioners would go hungry, women would have nothing to do, nowhere for them to bring their disgusting sticky-fingered children to leave their sticky fingerprints all over the stock. My stock!"

Mr Solomon tugged at Thomason's arm and all but manhandled him through the revolving door. Breathlessly he explained, "One of the models has gone missing."

The probationer narrowed his eyes and asked, "Is she pregnant?"

The manager paused and threw him a strange look then rushed ahead, a thin short streak of black flapping jacket and baggy pinstripe trousers.

Thomason hesitated and called after him, "We had better wait for my colleagues, Sir. They'll have some Missing Person's forms." His words fell on deaf ears or never caught up with them for Mr Solomon was getting more distant with every short quick step. He resembled a circus clown, as supermarket managers often did, in more ways than one. The probationer's walk quickened into a jog as he moved into the bowels of Robot City trying not to lose sight of the flashing black streak of retail management. On he went through the fruit-and-veg section where a sharp left took him into the bakery where whites and browns and wholemeals were stacked and then the delicatessen with its cheeses and cooked meats and then the fresh meat and fish counters where farmed salmon was always on offer and then the tins of goodness knows what from all corners of the world and then the Christmas sweets in fancy Christmas cartons and then, eventually, into the fashion hall, the women's fashion hall. It was here that Mr Solomon was waiting impatiently for him and where other members of staff in their green Robot City uniforms stood in small groups to watch, their expressions dark and serious.

This was obviously a serious business.

The probationer asked reluctantly, "Can we have the name of the missing…?"

"Name?"

"Yes Sir?"

The manager shook his head and pointed to an empty stand between the shelves of flimsy bras and pants.

Thomason made an O with his lips and left them open. Eventually he composed himself and uttered, "A model, a mannequin, a dummy. I see." He took out his notebook. "When did you notice its absence, Sir?"

"This morning. An hour ago."

"Is there another one that I can see, Sir?"

Solomon looked horrified. "Each one is unique. That is what this boutique is famous for. Individual styles that are affordable."

"And this one, the one that is missing, what did it look like? Was it a full figure like that?" He pointed to another dummy at the end of the row. "Or just the bust, like this?" His pointing finger moved to the bra counter.

"Full figure."

"Dressed, Sir?"

"Of course, in our new designer range for the sophisticated woman. We sell all sizes between 8 and 12. Make sure you note that in your report. We don't want anyone accusing us of not catering for the fuller figure."

"Underwear?"

"Yes." The manager wagged a thoughtful finger. "But wait a moment. I do have something to show you. In the stockroom. Came in last night. Something very similar. You will notice that these models share a likeness with Keira Knightley?"

"Yes, Sir. They are very thin."

"Not thin, perfect. Perfect for our new range of lingerie."

"Like a coat-hanger, you mean?"

The manager paused, then continued on to the stockroom. In a rush he opened a single door and ushered Thomason in. Before him lay cages of unwrapped goods and shelving that went on forever.

"This is the one," the manager said, halting before a partially dressed mannequin. "As near as damn it."

Beneath the model a soft-covered book had been left open on the shelf. The manager pulled a dismissive face. "What's this? *Atonement*? McEwan? Never heard of it, or him." He sighed. "I wish the staff wouldn't use the stockroom for their tea-breaks."

"I see what you mean. She is like Keira. Saw the film, just last week. She was in a football strip, poking through, gorgeous. What was it called?"

"*Pirates of the Caribbean*?"

"No, no, not that one." Thomason shook his head, trying to shake back the memory. It came out of nowhere. "*Bend it Like Beckham*, that's the one!"

"Didn't see it," Solomon confessed. "Football strip, you say? I'll get the DVD. By golly, thanks for that."

A woman in green poked her head around the door. "Sorry to disturb you, Mr Solomon, but we have a problem."

"Right," the manager snapped in his efficient mode. "Be right there." He turned to the probationer. "Make notes in your notebook. Be back in a mo'." He paused, for Miss Knightley had made all the difference and they were now a brotherhood, and added, perhaps in confidence, "It's probably the lottery. It causes more trouble than it's worth." Then he was gone and the door, a fire door that swung shut automatically, swung shut.

And First Year Probationer PC Simon Thomason was left alone in the stockroom with the mannequin that looked like Keira Knightley and, come to that, a dozen other stars that graced the silver screen.

He made a few notes, height, colouring, no obvious blemishes and so on and his closer inspection got closer still and, given the circumstances, to obtain a complete picture, he pulled aside her pants.

And that was when the door swung open and Mr Solomon, the manager, and the occupants of CB1, PCs Wendy Booth and Carrie Jones, stood framed in the doorway. The manager raised an ominous eyebrow, the brotherhood forgotten instantly, and together, as one, the PCs burst into uncontrollable laughter.

Shit street. There's one in every town.

As he walked through the police car park to the rear entrance no one seemed to notice him. The uniforms strolled to their cars without giving him a second glance. In the corridor much was the same, not a glance or a knowing look. Until, that is, Sergeant Mike Wilson stopped him. He looked after the probationers. His uniform was too big and flapped around his legs.

"Where are they?"

"What's that, Skipper?"

"The cigs, lad, the cigs?"

"The cigs?"

"Listen, lad, you're sent out on a Friday night for one reason only. You work the precincts and you collect the cigs from the little hooligans who hang around them. Confiscate the cigs. Share them out with the lads. A dozen packs or so should do it, depending on how full they are."

"No one told me."

"No one told you? You're going to be the bloody flavour of the month if we've got to start buying our own cigs. Have you never heard of initiative? It's what good coppers are made of."

The sergeant checked his watch. "Now, after your break, go out again and check the arcades. Some of the little bastards won't have gone to bed yet."

PC Thomason realized his mouth had dropped again. He closed it quickly and said, "Skipper, it's the end of my shift."

"Wrong. You got it wrong again. It would have been if you'd used your initiative. See?"

The PC nodded gloomily.

"Just remember," his sergeant went on. "The older kids have wised up so go for the eleven and twelve-year-olds. And boys, not girls. The girls give you too much lip and it can cause a scene. It's the hormones in the food."

"Right."

"Oh, and by the way, a word in your shell-like."

"Skipper?"

"Had a call from the manager of the supermarket. Didn't use your spray on the model, did you?"

Consternation shook Thomason's head. He stammered, "No, no!"

"That's good. We only use that on pensioners." Sergeant Wilson nodded. "No problem. I talked him out of making a complaint. Told him you were still learning the trade. Anyway, get out there and do your stuff. Remember, keep in mind that the enhancement of a charge is good for the figures, that abusive behaviour or drunk and disorderly can be written as resisting arrest and assault on a police officer. It's a simple spelling mistake. We call it poetic licence. In the job we're all fucking poets. Right?"

PC Thomason watched the flapping uniform move off down the corridor and was still thinking about CS spray as he pushed open the door to the canteen.

In the canteen everything seemed normal, as though nothing had happened, the other coppers hadn't heard about it. He caught sight of Wendy Booth and Carrie Jones in front of full English breakfasts and they barely acknowledged him.

First Year Probationer PC Simon Thomason breathed a tremendous sigh of relief as he joined the queue at the stainless steel counter. Behind him the first snigger began to spread and various faces reddened as laughter was held in. Lips trembled as they tightened and cheeks blew out until it all became too much. And then in the room of twenty or more uniforms the uncontrolled laughter cracked the faces and shook the uniforms beneath them.

PC Simon Thomason stood rooted to the spot, plastic tray in trembling hands, dying a death that awaited all first year probationers. It was a playground, a vast nation-wide playground, and it was playtime again.

Deleted Scene II

"I'm going to be your Christmas present."

Maynard reached forward and turned the key. "See, kid, you got it wrong again."

"What then?"

"Remember the pigs, my mother's place? Thought you might come up and meet her and spend Christmas Day with us, that's all. I'll drive you back on Boxing Day, if you like."

"What, like Christmas dinner? Turkey?"

"If you like."

"Real pigs?"

"You'd have to get used to the smell."

"That don't bother me."

"Well then?"

The wheels skidded on wet grass and bounced back to the road.

"Left or right? Left is where you came from." Maynard said. "Your call?"

The clouds had shouldered in again and rain pelted the windscreen. He turned on the wipers, for a moment blurring the patch of road caught in the headlights.

Jason or Brian or Noel said, "Can I feed the pigs?"

In the darkness Maynard smiled and turned right, north, away from the...city.

......

AUTHOR'S NOTE

Thanks to the usual cops and robbers for the insight (they know who they are) and to Dromey Car Sales, Maltby le Marsh, Alford, for the supply of Ticker Harrison's classic cars. Thanks also to Dr Yaya Egberongbe, Consultant in Paediatric Intensive Care, Kings College Hospital, for the advice on medical matters. Any errors are down to me. Thanks to Andrew Grant for the extracts from Bikini Line. Apologies to Shayne Ward for supplanting That's My Goal, the 2005 Christmas Number One.

Liberties have been taken with the weather conditions during the weeks leading to Christmas 2005. There was a cold spell from the 11th to the 15th and northerly winds brought hail and snow to Norfolk on the 17th. From the 21st until Christmas Eve it was mild and cloudy and the wintry showers did not reach London until the 27th.

REVIEWS
COPS AND OTHER ROBBERS (1998)

The same crime shelves that gave me Paul Johnston's books also gave me Cops and other Robbers by I. K. Watson. It's a nasty book about a nasty subject. A paedophile has killed one of his victims. Another child is missing.Can the police find him before this one too is murdered? This is a raw and nasty story and the writer pulls no punches. No details are omitted, no veil is drawn over the brutality. It is no secret that I like gory, gruesome books; but this one was a bit too much even for me.
- **Alan Robson (Coprolithicus)**

I picked this one up with apprehension—are we tired of police procedurals? Not if they have the energy and idiosyncratic detail that Watson specialises in. Even the now overexposed plot devices (including a hunt for a paedophile) are handled with a commanding freshness, and it's axiomatic that writers as talented as Watson can shuffle warmed-over ingredients to produce something rich and strange. Watson is also good at dealing with the disillusionment involved in the day to day life of a copper, and DI Rick Cole is a trenchant hero, even if his drinking is another one of those over-familiar touches. The plotting is bracingly original, and this deserves to do every bit as well as Watson's earlier books.
-Barry Forshaw (Crime Time)

This is not a very nice book. It's peopled by a cast of rank low-lifes and strungout cops and the villain of the piece is a killer paedophile. You can almost smell the sweat and stale nicotine in the police canteen, and the panic, fear and hopelessness on the mean streets you have to walk in Watson's new novel. There is a numbing mundaneness to the way the characters talk, reflecting the fact that the horrors they face, horrors that should turn their stomachs, don't any more. Much as you might want to find out exactly why DI Cole had to leave Scotland Yard for Sheerham, and what happens when the paedophile kidnaps DS Baxter's daughter, it won't be a pleasant journey. This isn't so much a work of noir fiction as grise fiction, bleak, soulless and so hardbitten it's got no nails left. Dark entertainment, if that's your fancy.
- **Publishing News**

Serial killers, drug dealers, prostitutes, cat burglars and corrupt coppers abound in this above-average La Plante-esque crime thriller about a detective inspector's daughter who goes missing—last seen getting into a car with a policeman.
- **Focus**

Another sensational novel from Watson. A furiously paced story line leads the reader from scene to scene whilst the in-depth knowledge of police procedures lends an air of realism to what at times is an almost frighteningly gruesome read. The reader is dragged from one horrific scene to the next torn between the compelling story and the need to escape from the darkest side of human nature. The cold descriptions add a new depth to the shocking scenes of child abuse and the reader has no difficulty empathising with the hardened policemen as they reel from shock at the sights they are forced to endure. An exceptional new novel from the country's leading crime writer marrying an almost gothic horror with an in depth guide to police procedures. This book is simply too good to miss.
- **Seamus Kelly, Amazon**

GRITTY, GRIMY, FURIOUSLY exciting police procedural in which the squad at Sheerham nick postpone their own sexual misdemeanours (adultery, occasional harassment) to pull out the stops which will identify and nail a paedophile whose crimes culminate in ritual murder. Action counter-pointed with violent doings of local drug lords. A deeply disenchanted (hence, realistic) view of our boys in blue who, despite their flaws ranging from graft to ultra-horniness get the job done, Unlikely to make you sleep more soundly, but well worth reading if you're lying there, awake and worrying.
- **Philip Oakes, Literary Review**

Det Insp Rick Cole has an exceptionally dirty case of paedophilia to solve when it starts to look as if victims are being picked up from school in a police car. The language and action are uncompromising. Only for strong stomachs.
- **Oxford Mail**

This twin-themed novel part police procedural hunt for child killer, part gangster turf war—is an uneasy mix in places, but gripping, and packed with gruesomely authentic detail.
- **Mike Ripley, Daily Telegraph**

REVIEWS
WOLVES AREN'T WHITE (1995)

"You're alive today because you do not interfere."

Not since Ted Lewis's Get Carter has there been such a tough, uncompromising novel about the realities of life in the British underworld.
- Peter Day

If you like your crime writing on the tough uncompromising side, then IK Watson is the man for you.

His second novel, Wolves Aren't White tells the story of tough guy villain Paddy Delaney, who is back in town. He likes to hurt people, especially men who make a pass at his little sister Julie. Not surprisingly, he gets the hump when Lennie Webb, singer with the Wolves Aren't White jazz band, gets fresh - but Julie wants Lennie, that's the trouble.

In fact, Lennie finds himself in trouble not only from Paddy, but from Julie's nasty habit of lighting matches in the middle of the night. Caught in a situation from which he can't escape, Lennie is forced to unravel a web of deception and murder that has made Julie's life a nightmare.
- Sandra Feekins (Burton Mail)

Hard boiled crime in the tradition of the late Ted Lewis.

REVIEWS
MANOR (1994)

The Smiths are London's leading crime barons, but Dave Smith's old man is close to death and the family empire, suffering from its past refusal to enter the drug trade, is under siege. The Liverpool mob is in town for a spot of whoring on an up-market Thames barge. The Scots contingent, led by Mad Mick McGovern, is getting out of hand, and the pushy Americans, who want some of the U.K. drug trade, include Tony Valenti, who once caught Dave servicing his centerfold wife and isn't about to forget it. The book, which recalls Barrie Keeffe's The Long Good Friday… Features several scenes of nasty brutality…
- **Publishers Weekly**

It was "like the marriage of two royal families" when Tom Smith's son wed Coddy Hughes's daughter, a union that joined two of England's most powerfulcrime dynasties. But even the best families fall out, and in his sleek first novel, Manor, I. K. Watson gives a cool account of the savage mob wars that erupt when business alliances are compromised by nasty domestic quarrels. Ten years after that royal wedding, Tom Smith is dying, Coddy Hughes is fading fast, and the younger generation may not be ruthless enough to turn back the barbarians. "The end of an era was drawing in," says Dave Smith, to whom his father's empire has fallen. "The men, the legends, were dying out." Without softening these hard men or adulterating the cruelty of their crimes, Mr. Watson has us rooting for the royal scum.
- **Marilyn Stasio (New York Times)**

I.K. Watson, a British writer, tells a great story in his debut novel, Manor, of the Smith family. They're the modern inheritors of the crime kingdom of the Krays and Richardsons who now find themselves under siege in this hard-boiled crime novel that I feel is destined to become a classic.
- **Gary Lovisi, The Hard Boiled Way**

A good, old-fashioned gangster story of revenge and factions warring over who controls what, where and for how much…
- **Liverpool Daily Post**